where passion goes beyond the dance

NOON

Katherine Warwick

Grove Creek Publishing

This is a work of ficiton. Names, characters, places and incidents are either a product of the author's imagination of are used fictitiously, and any resemblance ot actual persons, living or dead, business establishments, events or locales is entirely coincidental.

A Grove Creek Publishing Book / published by arrangement with the author

NOON
Printing History

Grove Creek Publishing edition / July 2007

All rights reserved.
Copyright © 2007 by Katherine Warwick

This book may not be reproduced in whole or part without permission. For information address: Grove Creek Publishing, 2 South Main St., Pleasant Grove, Ut. 84062

Cover artwork by Jennifer Johnson.
Book Design by Julia Lloyd.

ISBN: 1-933963-99-9

Printed in the United States of America

for my girls

where passion goes beyond the dance

NOON

Katherine Warwick

Grove Creek Publishing

Noon - Katherine Warwick

One

She was there again, to deafen her head with loud music, to drown in the company of men who would make her forget. It would be easy – so easy – to entice someone for her own purposes. For a moment she felt guilty. The moment passed and she pushed through the crowd to be closer to the dance floor.

She'd always had the need to move to the music. It compelled, enticed, and drove her like nothing else – with one exception. Like the rhythm of her heart, music lured her to the floor with pulsing sounds: tantalizing words of love and hope.

She watched as eyes watched. Some lingered, some searched, others darted. Behind them all, Nicole saw yearnings as different as the music. Each its own story, its own need for an ending – at least for the night.

Colored lights flashed over her face and she moved through the crowds, looking.

"Wanna dance?" Nicole Dubois didn't even look to see the face behind the voice. She just said yes. The face, the man, was inconsequential, and soon she was on the dance floor.

After she'd felt the music dive in and seize her, she looked at him. He was watching her – they always did. They would lose themselves and become hers. It was a power that she'd learned could be dangerous.

The power wasn't something she used purposefully; it came from whatever had caused her first steps to be a swivel of hip, rather than one foot followed by another.

"You're an amazing dancer," the man said, leering at her.

Nicole only smiled the smile she used when performing – empty yet dazzling.

"Are you professional or something?" he asked.

She continued dancing next to him. "Something."

This was paradise. Music so loud she could forget the pain. This was her world, the crowds cheering and clapping, expressing their awe and enthusiasm in shouts, and whistles of appreciation and envy. They loved her – at least for the moment. But she'd take that moment. Some wanted her; that she knew. Dancing had taught her she could go anywhere she wanted to go.

It was better than any high – except one.

Dance was the only way she had felt another's heartbeat, known another's soul, without giving the ultimate gift. She'd held on to that. There'd only been one man she wanted, only one she had ever wanted to give herself to.

The song ended.

Nicole smiled at the stranger, batted her eyes, and left him standing in glowing admiration as she moved off the dance floor. After watching her, admirers trailed her like the tail of a kite.

She continued through the pressing crowd toward the refreshment bar.

"You were something out there," the bartender said. He was eager and ready to please, and he lit up because she'd come straight to him. He patted the bar for her to sit, and she found an empty stool. Nicole saw how his eyes flitted behind her and she knew there were strangers eager and waiting for her.

"What can I get you?" he asked.

"A mineral water," she said, leaning toward him on her elbows.

The bartender slid her a chilled glass with a lime twisted on the rim and a smile on his face. "There you go."

Leisurely she sipped, allowing the gathering of men behind her to ripen.

Suddenly, chords rang hauntingly through the air and everybody slowed, quieted because of it. She knew the song. It was the kind of song that made you weep before the first verse had even been sung. Then the words – the melody – all of it, imprisoned your heart.

It had been their song once.

The piano rang out, the chords gained strength, the lyrics spoke the words of her soul. *Someday I'll find my way back to you.*

Nicole's heart was pulled down, the weight of the melody pierced deep. She wondered if she would ever be able to hear the music, let it move her, without thinking of the one man she could not forget.

"Another mineral water?" the bartender asked. Shaking her head, she put down her glass and pushed herself up, back towards the dance floor. She'd prove to herself that she could be there, hear that song – and dance without him.

Even as the impossibility of it whispered over the music, she scanned the crowd for someone, anyone she could take out there.

She approached an innocent bystander with her prettiest smile, as she'd been trained to. "Hi, I'm Nicole, would you like to dance?"

The man's eyes lit. "Sure."

On the dance floor, she pulled him close, the need to forget as great as the need to prove to herself that she could, but the song pounded in her ears, dove into her soul, as she swayed in the arms of the stranger. In her mind she felt the body and saw the face of only one man. Only one man moved like vapor and velvet.

She slid and dipped, feeling empty without him. Her body had spent years nestled next to his, his arm tucked around her back, holding her, chest to breast, face to face, sharing one breath. The need to flee from the floor rushed through her.

Closing her eyes, she willed herself to stay. She would wait until the pain in her heart passed. It wasn't getting any easier; time wasn't healing her as she hoped.

"Excuse me." She heard a voice and her eyes flashed.

For a moment she couldn't speak. She stared at his face in shock. This was the last place she would have expected to see him. He seemed to enjoy the fact that she was without words. It was in his eyes, sapphire blue flickering with pleasure.

"I need to cut in," he told the stranger and swiftly stepped between them. His gaze locked with hers as he slid one arm around her waist, taking her to a place where the light shone just for them.

He moved with such ease, Nicole glanced down at his feet only momentarily, knowing the gesture might offend him, before letting herself look into his face again.

Much had changed, though he still looked wonderfully the same. His dark hair was longer now, with teasing curls just at his collar. The blue of his eyes was so magnetic, so dark; she couldn't look away for the years her heart had missed. And that smile was just as she remembered, broad and glittering. The hot spark she felt inside forced her to gaze over his shoulder, unable to forget just how his lips had once felt against hers.

◎ 3 ◎

She'd missed his face – the strong lines that pulled tight when he was angry or possessive, that eased into a smile and made every bone in her body liquid with the beauty of it.

"You look good, Nic," he said after a moment.

"Breck." She ignored his compliment and said his name, even with the bitterness it left on her tongue. "Your upbringing once again overrides your sense of propriety."

"Which upbringing would that be?"

It would be the cruelest thing she could do, to say it. She knew it, and wondered whether she would feel the trembling in his hands like she used to. Because he'd hurt her, she felt she owed him the pain. "Your blood upbringing."

She recognized the familiar hateful glint of something old in the dark of his eyes and she looked away, shame pinching her heart. Ready for the next move, she only felt the slightest pressure from his fingers, twined with hers, before he turned them both.

"That was rude to interrupt us." She felt his grip shift and knew, even before he took another step, where he was taking her.

"Rude, but necessary." He twirled her away from him but his hand held on tight.

The floor was clearing around them now and he brought her in, smiling as if they were back in time, dancing as they had for so many years, for the judges' approval – for the prize.

"How do you know he wasn't my fiancé?"

His lips brushed her ear. "Because there's only one man for you."

He brought her against him with a demand that sent thrill racing up her spine. When he snapped her out, she remembered the many times he'd let go, letting her fall flat on her rump, and wondered if he would do that again. Squeezing his hand on the thrust, she made sure he couldn't, and she grinned, first at him, then at the watching crowd, until he whipped her back so fast, she almost lost her breath.

His body felt wonderfully familiar next to hers as he deliberately slowed them down and took them through the steps of the samba. It had been their dance; the fight, the passion – equally shared.

"Some things never change, do they Nic?" he asked as their heads came

Noon - Katherine Warwick

in close, cheeks barely brushing.

"If you're speaking of my well-deserved anger at you, then you're right."

"I'm speaking about the fire that always pulled us together."

She pushed against his chest. Nothing would bring her more pleasure than to leave him there on the dance floor. But he snagged her wrists, his fingers lacing with hers so fast, she had no option but to follow his lead. In one downward whip, he had her back pressed near the floor so that she was at his knees. Raising a brow, he grinned at her.

Bringing her up, he pulled her against him with a force she remembered well and always made her wince. That she knew he took pleasure from as well.

"What would our partnership be without your stubborn wit?" His face broke into that beautiful smile that could liquefy her. She jerked her head toward the crowd and didn't let it.

"There is no partnership," she told him. He whirled the two of them into a spin that rivaled a top. The move made her dizzy and weak and completely dependent on him; she knew he knew that, wanted that. If she'd had the will, she'd have pushed away, but she'd never learned to put pride over professionalism and the weakness kept her clinging to him for the sake of the dance.

His laugh was low and teasing in her ear as they spun round together. "We'll see about that."

When the song slowed, he slowed, as the last words sung softly into the thick air surrounding them. He eased back and looked at her. The applause was like fire, heated and cracking. The lyrics pointed, like an iron poker in the flame.

Someday I'll find my way back to you...

Only moments had passed not agonizingly long years, and Breck couldn't tear his eyes away. Her hair still glowed like sunbeams had cast their fingers through it. She wore it down and liquid to her shoulders, bare shoulders he so wanted to skim with his hands to ease the need he felt inside to touch her, not just dance with her. Red had always been her color, and the sparkling dress she wore now clung to every inch he'd dreamed of in the years he'd been gone.

She'd been shocked to see him; the pale gray of her eyes had deepened to midnight when their eyes met. That pleased him, and reminded him of all that he'd missed. Of all he intended to take back now.

From the first day Breck had seen her, he'd known that for him, there would only be Nicole. She'd seen the dregs of his past and held his hand as they danced through awkward teenage years. Together they'd forged a bond that dance alone had gifted to them. He'd known then hers would be the only soul that could truly understand his.

The glow of her now was too beautiful to bear. More than anything, Breck wished he could turn back time, but that was impossible. Her eyes blazed a warning he knew better than to ignore. He merely held her close, knowing he could, without her resisting, until the song ended.

When it did, they both faced the crowd, hands linked tight. Through the deepest valleys of his life, it had been that way.

Bodies filled in around them as the bass thumped and the lights flashed. Breck still had her hand and when she turned away, he brought her around. They were pressed together in the center of the dance floor – the heart.

"The spark's alive and well," he said over the music. Neither of them moved much, used to the simple sway of the other.

Nicole's gaze wandered the crowd. "No, Breck, it died when you left."

One thing Breck had learned from her was when she said or did one thing, often times it meant something else. She'd been a very good teacher. He had the battle scars to prove it.

He wrapped his arms around her. "What we had couldn't be extinguished by time."

"Don't be so cocky, Noon." It was the name she'd always used when she was angry with him. Hearing it now only pleased him, even as she placed her hands on his chest and pushed. "That was your biggest problem, once the world knew who you were."

"No. You were my biggest problem." He leaned to her then, covering her mouth with his.

Nicole could barely think. Her heart was beating faster than the music; too fast. Her breath vanished and everything about him threatened to consume her. In the deepest corners of her heart, a place he alone had had ownership of, she wished that she could take back time.

Needing air, needing space, she pushed against him and finally freed herself.

Without a word, she forced her way through the crowd to the door. Tears, hot and humiliating, burned her eyes as she shoved the door open and let the cool of the night sting her face. When the door paused just after her, she closed her eyes, hoping it was he that had followed her. Always, he'd followed her.

But her shoulders remained chilled and she found herself alone. Fighting the cold, she rubbed her arms and the tears fell. Nicole took in a deep breath and wiped her cheeks. She had vowed to hurt him, just like he'd hurt her. She'd promised herself that when this moment came, she would be strong, but her heart was threatening betrayal. She missed the heat, the spark, the electricity that had kept them joined, like two opposite forces that, when brought together, made their strength as one. One, that's what they'd been for years, since that awkward day when Reuben had pushed them both together and said, *"Dance."*

Twelve years earlier.

"Nicky, I want you to meet Breck," her mother said.

Lois gently nudged the tall, gangly nerd toward her. His head was bowed so his dark hair hung in his face. Nicole let out a curious sigh and stepped forward with her hand out, ready to shake properly. His sable curls and waves moved a little when he reached for her hand and they shook, but Nicole still couldn't see his eyes.

"You two know each other, right?" Lois Dubois asked.

"Yes, we know each other," Nicole let out a sigh. He was that skater that never said a word in any of the classes they shared in school. He was a loser. When he didn't say anything, didn't even look at her, she began to dance independently in front of the mirror. How she loved to see her body move, gracefully, elegantly. She'd spent her life perfecting movement. Now it would be smothered by this guy with the baggy clothes and hanging hair. No one would ever see her again.

"Breck's an excellent skater," her mother said. "I've been very impressed with his style and finesse."

"Ever danced before?" Nicole asked, sarcasm sharpening her tone.

"Nicky!"

Breck's head shook once and he lifted it just enough for Nicole to see he had dark eyes underneath and behind that hair. Brooding eyes, the color of which she couldn't see under brows that were slashes of dark.

"Reuben's a perfectionist, and so am I." Nicole turned and made sure her hips swiveled a punch of displeasure.

"Nicole can be stubborn," she heard her mother say. "Just ignore her."

Nicole whirled around, and she kept whirling, watching herself in the mirror. She loved to impress with how long she could twirl without stopping.

"She likes to show off, too," Lois whispered to Breck.

"This place just for her?" he asked, looking around.

"Of course." Nicole stopped. "Serious competitors need their own studios."

When Reuben came in, Nicole thought Breck looked like he'd seen a ghost. He was going to fall flat on that hair-hidden face of his. He knew it, she knew it, and now Reuben and her mother would know it.

"Hey, everybody." Reuben slipped a duffle bag off his shoulder. "You must be Breck." He was over with his hand out to shake. Breck looked at the extended hand, then at Reuben's skin color as if he'd never seen a black man before he timidly reached out. "Reuben LaBate."

"Breck...Noon."

"Breck Noon, let's see you two dance."

Nicole sighed. She couldn't believe her mother was serious about her dancing with this skate-park loser.

She followed Reuben to the center of the dance floor.

Breck didn't move.

"Come on," Reuben beckoned with a wave. "We won't bite."

Breck rolled over and stopped a few feet away from the two of them. Nicole folded her arms. "You can't wear those on the floor."

"Lose the rollerblades at the door, buddy," Reuben told him. "Lois will get you some dance shoes."

"We'll do that right away," Lois piped from the sideline.

Breck dropped to the floor and took off his shoes. His socks were sooty and stiff-looking with holes like Swiss cheese. Nicole grimaced. Didn't he care about how he looked? His patched, thread-bare jeans and beaten-up navy tee shirt looked like he shopped at a thrift store.

"Okay." Reuben waited for Breck to stand. He eyed them shoulder-to-shoulder. "How much do you know about dance, Breck?"

Breck's shoulders lifted, his head lowered.

"We're going to teach you all you need to know." Reuben nudged them together. Then he circled, his piercing green eyes scanning them from head to toe.

Nicole snuck glances at Breck. How could anyone expect her to dance with this guy? All she could see was visions of Nicole Dubois, rising star of the ballroom dance world, crashing downward.

After discreetly checking Breck out, she shot Reuben a glare, showing her disagreement. Maybe he'd have the sense to see that this was doomed to failure. Her mother, clearly, was blind.

Reuben made no effort to acknowledge her frustration; rather, he kept his keen eyes focused on the two of them. Nicole could see by the way he ran his palms over the smooth, chocolate-colored skin of his naked head that his mind was preoccupied with making this work.

She blew out a breath.

Reuben demonstrated the basic moves in cha-cha and Breck lumbered through the steps. Shifting feet, folding her arms, Nicole stood a few feet away sighing loudly to show her displeasure.

"And one two cha-cha-cha, two two cha-cha-cha. Three two cha-cha-cha...very good Breck – you've got the step down," Reuben yelled over the music. "Try to move your hips like I showed you. That's better. Like you're getting ready to lift over that half pipe and twist. And one two cha-cha-cha, come in at the center two, cha-cha-cha. Better, Breck."

As soon as the music stopped, the two of them stepped further away from each other, moving like cats in a cage.

There was no way this was going to work. Nicole stared hard at her mother, then at Reuben, sure they would get the message and all of this would be over. Then she could search for a real partner and leave this left-foot in the dust.

"Maybe this wasn't such a good idea." Breck's shoulders slumped.

Immediately, Reuben took both hands and pressed his shoulders upright. "Up. I'd say you did pretty well for a first timer." Reuben put a hand on Breck's shoulder. "You'll get it. She's been at this a lot longer than you have. Now, I want to see you two dance together."

Breck's eyes widened. His heart pounded against his ribs. He looked at Nicole, then at Reuben. With a tug of hands, Reuben brought them both together. "Okay, from the beginning."

Breck still couldn't move.

"She won't bite," Reuben told him with a chuckle. But the words didn't calm him any. She was Nicole Dubois, legend personified. There she stood, waiting – arms out – just for him. . Her eyes, so blue he'd never seen anything like them except the sky near sunset, were looking into his and his heart was a rocket racing up in that sky.

The moment seemed impossible, bizarre, and incredible at the same time.

Nicole let out another sigh and gestured for him to take her. His throat was so dry, he craved a drink. He stunk of sweat, and that only made him more embarrassed to touch her.

With a firm tug of his elbow, Reuben brought him face-to-face with her. "Good," Reuben said. "Now, put your left hand at her waist and extend your right hand. She'll put hers in yours. I just want to see how you fit together."

Fit – together? Should he be saying that with Mrs. Dubois sitting right over there? Breck glanced at the woman. She was, as always, wearing a smile. It reassured him just a little. If it were okay with her, he'd touch her daughter.

Nicole was close – closer than any girl had ever been to him. He felt her breath every now and then on his neck. Her hands were so warm and soft. She smelled like flowers and soap.

Reuben circled them, arms crossed, one poised by his mouth as his dark eyes scanned them. Breck stood like a statue under inspection until Reuben smiled and patted his shoulder. "Relax, buddy. Relax."

He tried, but she was right there, and her eyes were on him. He wondered if she saw his heart thumping under his tee shirt. He was sure she felt his sweaty palms.

"Okay." Reuben stopped circling. "At ease."

Noon - Katherine Warwick

In that instant Nicole broke free and wiped her hands on her clothing. "There's a little thing called baby powder. Get some for your hands."

* * *

For three weeks she'd had her feet abused by this lead-foot, and she wasn't about to take one more day of it. She was a competitive dancer, not some amateur trainer.

Her mother had been so vague about Breck's circumstances. All that her mother had said was that he was to be her new dance partner. That whatever needed to be done to bring him up to her level, was to be done. Why she'd insisted on Breck Noon, Nicole was still trying to figure out.

Her mother was always looking for the underdog, somebody to rescue. That's how they hired half of the help that tended their property. But this guy was a loser with a capitol L and everybody at their high school knew it. Just the way he skated around with his head down. She wasn't sure he'd even had a face until he'd walked into the studio three weeks ago.

In the meantime, the name she'd worked so hard to establish for herself in the dance community was at risk of being tarnished.

After yet another rehearsal, she stormed over to Reuben, waiting until Breck was across the studio gathering his things before she let it out. "I can't dance with him. Everything I worked for will be over – gone. No one will take me seriously ever again. I will not set foot on this floor with him one more day."

Reuben ran a hand over the smoothness of his shaved head, something Nicole had come to recognize that he did whenever he pondered.

"Why can't I dance with Trey?" Nicole asked, her gaze fixed on Breck. He was finished changing out of his black dance shoes and had slipped on his tennis shoes.

Nicole checked her reflection in the mirror. She looked moist and messy but she ignored it for now, her gaze wandering back to Breck.

"You know why you and Trey aren't paired." Reuben put the CDs down and reached for his sweatshirt.

"But Breck's—"

"He'll get it." Reuben cut her off as he slipped the sweatshirt over his head. "I'm amazed at how quickly he's picked up the steps in just three weeks. He has real potential." He glanced across the room, but Breck had vanished. "Where does he go after rehearsal?" Reuben slung his bag over his shoulder.

"How should I know?" They walked together toward the door, their feet echoing with the rhythmic steps of two dancers bound to the perfection of movement.

Nicole followed Reuben out the door into the night, her mind spinning, feeling trapped in something she had no control over. She certainly didn't care to know anything more about Breck.

Breathing deep, she took in the scent of nutty aspens and tall evergreens that sheltered her home and dotted the family estate.

"Does he live around here?" Reuben asked.

"I heard he lives down by the railroad tracks in that trailer park."

Out in the darkness of the Dubois property, there was no sight or sound of Breck now, and she and Reuben made their way from the studio to where Reuben parked his car.

"He skates everywhere – even at school." Nicole dug her sweater out of her dance bag and slipped it on. Reuben's gaze was fixed down the drive that led from the Dubois estate to the main road, now shrouded in blackness.

She laid a hand on his forearm. "I can't dance with him."

It was then Reuben finally looked at her and smiled. "You can dance with anybody." His hand covered hers. "See you tomorrow." Reuben whistled as he strolled to his car.

Nicole stood alone, listening to the chirp of crickets fluttering on the night air, as she watched Reuben's car disappear. Drawing her lower lip between her teeth she frowned, and let out a sigh.

Two

Breck skated in the darkness with speed and without fear, dodging on-coming cars with the finesse of an alley cat. The air was misty, visibility was bad, but it only added to the fact that he didn't care whether he made it home safely.

He wasn't safe at home.

He rolled up to the trailer park, jumped the railroad tracks just before the entrance, then slowed. His stomach knotted as he rounded McFarlaine's grungy blue trailer with its broken, white shutters.

He could see home, and he wished he were anywhere but there.

Home was a once white, now yellowed mobile trailer with windows whose panes had been scraped out from years of opening and closing. Graffiti was scratched on the wall facing the railroad tracks – odd shapes and designs, like foreign wallpaper, foul in its language. Breck's father had never removed it. Breck figured he liked it; his mouth was just as foul. Broken pots with petrified plants had been left where his mother had put them, when she'd been alive. A bike frame and a stray wheelbarrow rusted to orange sat resting against the trailer littered with trash blown from the trains that passed nightly.

Breck heard the TV droning inside. He protectively tucked his backpack under his arm before opening the door and sneaking in. Inside, the air was thick with cigarette smoke, and he didn't glance to see where his father was – he knew: in his La-Z-boy chair, plunked in front of the television, a beer in one hand, a Marlboro in the other. Whether or not he'd notice Breck depended on how many empty beer cans were discarded at the side of that chair.

Not being noticed was all that mattered to Breck. He kept his head low and ducked into the back of the trailer, to his bedroom and shut the door.

Then he sighed.

He waded through piles of clothes, paper, books, files, old photo albums and tools he shared the room with. It wasn't really his bedroom. It was the storage room he got to sleep in. His bed was a mattress in the middle of the floor that had no bedding, just an old army blanket with stains that he had no idea where they'd come from.

He fell onto the mattress, unzipped the backpack and took out the black dance shoes. Bringing them to his nose, he took in their leather scent on a deep breath. They were soft, matte leather and, pretty cool. What Reuben could do in dance was something he'd never seen before.

Breck hid the shoes back in his backpack, not willing to risk discovery. School was just a place to get rid of him for a few hours every day. His father didn't care if he breathed or suffocated when it came to grades, so he never touched the backpack, never asked if he had homework, books to read, assignments he needed help with.

Breck forced a laugh. It didn't hurt, the neglect – hadn't for a long time. He knew his father wouldn't help if he were taking his last breath.

Carefully he set the backpack aside. Grabbing his headphones and CD player, he put on some Linkin' Park and closed his eyes. He understood now that this was not music you could dance formally to. Reuben had shown him the difference. But he could still drown himself in it. It was good for that. And he still felt the need to drown.

The music he was learning to dance to was different. In fact, there were so many sounds and beats, he'd thought there was no way he would ever understand how the steps would go with any of it. But he was beginning to like the music. He was beginning to see that the steps in dance could be more than just moving to the music.

When Reuben danced, he couldn't take his eyes off of him. He was, at first, embarrassed and ashamed to watch a man that much. But he was captivated by the ease, beauty, and sheer joy that emanated from Reuben when the music played and his body moved. It looked, to Breck, as though the man was in another world. Any time Breck could escape to another world, he'd take it.

He'd tried inhalants of various sorts; there was plenty to inhale left lying around the trailer park. He'd been tempted to try cocaine but hadn't been able to find a connection, nor did he have the money for that trip. Now, he was thinking he might not try it. After seeing what dancing did to Reuben and Nicole – dancing was cheaper. Even though he doubted his life mattered much to anyone, deep inside, it mattered enough to him to be careful.

He was making money at least, and that had been one of the reasons he'd

Noon - Katherine Warwick

agreed to the arrangement with Mrs. Dubois. He tucked what money she gave him each week inside his dance shoes, inside the backpack. That he had secrets from his father was something he'd learned to live with, out of survival. They had secrets they shared, dark secrets Breck wished could be hidden with the ease of a backpack and zipper – secrets he would be free of once he had enough cash to be on his own.

He wondered if a family like the Dubois' had any secrets like that – any secrets at all. He doubted it. Money could buy safety from some secrets, because you could run and still survive. Without money, you were a prisoner in whatever life you'd been given.

And the Dubois' would have no reason to run. They had it all.

Nicole. She was a legend at Pleasant Grove High School. He'd never seen a girl move with such – he knew it now – grace. She looked like a princess, snuffing out lowly commoners as she walked around school surrounded by her pack of friends.

To her, he was lower than a commoner. He didn't even exist in the world of Princess Dubois with her copper Mercedes Benz, her fancy boots with stick heels and fancy purses. She'd never so much as granted him one of her famous glossy smiles – the kind where she flipped her head, sending that silky blonde hair shimmering like it was electrified.

Not until three weeks ago, when her mother had persuaded him that he had what it took to be a champion ballroom dance partner to her champion daughter.

Lois Dubois had been sitting in her car at the skate park, watching the boys skate. He'd noticed her and her fancy Mercedes in the parking lot. With no reason to be at home, he hung out until it got dark and everybody began to vacate the outdoor arena with its grinding rails, half-pipes and quarter-pipes. Then she got out, and came right toward him.

"May I speak with you a moment, young man?" she'd asked with her tone that was sweetened naturally, like oranges. He looked around, and finding himself alone with her, kept a safe distance.

"You're very good on those rollerblades," she began. "I've been watching you for the last few hours."

No one ever watched him skate, certainly not anyone who was so motherly. Her face glowed with something he hadn't seen before, and he didn't get a creepy vibe when she told him that she'd been watching.

Still, he kept his head down.

"My name is Lois Dubois, and I'm looking for someone excellent at what they do."

Excellent? Is that what she thought he skated like? He rolled around, keeping busy. If he was excellent, he'd keep practicing.

When she smiled, her eyes twinkled. "You're very agile and athletic, mister…"

"Breck."

"Mister Breck, I—"

"It's Breck Noon," he said a little louder.

She tilted her head. "Breck Noon."

It was getting dark, and he had to catch the bus. He started to get concerned that he'd run out of time. "Uh, I need to get going," he said.

"Can I give you a lift? We can talk on the way." She gestured to her car with a kind smile that comforted him deep inside.

"I take the bus." He dipped his head. The lady was nice and he knew she'd take it as an insult that he was choosing not to accept the ride.

"I understand. Would you be interested in learning competitive ballroom dance?"

His head jerked up, and he stopped skating. "Dancing?"

She nodded, grinning like she'd just given him the most valuable gift. "What do you think?"

Think? He was trying not to laugh. "You serious?"

Still with the gleam of bestowal, she waited. "I'll pay for your time and your lessons with my daughter."

"Daughter?"

"Yes, she needs of a new partner. She has her own coach and we have a studio in our home. Will you consider it Mr. Noon?"

Daughter, studio, private coach, money…it was then he got that quiver of warning. Nothing could be this good, not for Breck Noon anyway. "I don't know." He rolled back a few feet.

"Here's my phone number. Think it over and call me. I'd like you to

Noon - Katherine Warwick

come and meet her and her coach. Does that sound agreeable?"

He took the ivory business card with her name printed on it and looked at her again. That warm feeling returned when her eyes, light blue he noted, sparkled into a smile. She reached out and touched his arm. "I hope you'll call. It's a wonderful sport."

Sport.

He laughed now as he lay on the mattress. *Yeah, I guess you could call it a sport.* He had the sore legs and blistered feet from learning the steps and breaking in the shoes. Keeping Nicole happy was a test of endurance and will that was proving to be just as challenging as learning how to cha-cha-cha and not look at his feet.

Rolling onto his side, he felt hungry and wished he'd remembered to stash something in his backpack on the way home from the Dubois'.

Tonight he'd pay for his stupidity.

The chilly air seeping through the broken window had him reaching for the only blanket and pulling it up tight. The window had been fixed by his father's drunken hand one night, as he stuck a piece of ill-fitting plywood over it and hammered it in place. Through the years, Breck learned to live with the cold air that snuck in, the occasional stray rat or cat, and the wasps that hovered during the summers.

He'd even escaped through it once.

Tonight, the lull of a train approaching coddled his mind, along with the music Reuben had played over and over during rehearsal. He could smell the broken leaves littering the tracks as trains drove over them, sending them flying, scenting the air.

Smoke snuck under the bedroom door – his father's cigarette burning. Tired, he dismissed the fear he shouldered that one of those cigarettes would fall from his father's fingertips and spark a fire. He'd stopped caring, worrying about it. He'd get out if he could, and if he couldn't, he doubted anyone would care.

No one cared about the father and son living in the trailer that looked like a rusted storage shed. There'd be no more late night screams; no more sounds of unspeakable things that made neighbors slam their windows shut and turn their heads.

Sleep settled over him heavily. Mrs. Dubois might miss him. It was the most comforting thought he could think. Yes, Mrs. Dubois would miss him. There was something kind in her that, as he saw her face in his mind then, caused him to draw his legs up and squeeze his pillow.

Formaldehyde and ether hung thickly in the air, tickling Breck's gag reflex. He sat in biology with his hand poised over a blank piece of paper. The room was silent except for Mr. Ingersoll who stood droning and pointing to giant, pull-down graphs of the human body. An occasional sigh, sneeze and yawn muddled the lecture into a strangely dull experience.

Normally attentive in biology, the odors and sounds pricking curiosity, Breck was supposed to be taking notes, but all he could think about was getting the jive timing down right.

Absently, he began to sketch a boy twisting over a half pipe, his mind counting the kicks in the jive. After four months of being introduced to all of the dances that were a part of international and Latin ballroom, it was under his skin now; an itch that intensified with every new step learned, every combination polished. He didn't know when it crawled under there, wouldn't have believed it ever would have, but it was there. He thought about dance constantly. The moves, the steps, the music, and Reuben – his drive and enthusiasm.

Nicole.

It was Thursday. He'd ride home with her and Lois for their three-hour private lesson with Reuben. They were getting ready to perform in what would be his first competition, the Pleasant Grove Invitational, and already he felt a tickling in his stomach.

He made sure his socks were clean and he'd dabbed some of his father's aftershave on after his shower that morning.

Breck glanced up at the clock. Five more minutes until lunch. He'd head to that corner of the parking lot behind the garbage bins and go over the jive steps again until he could do them perfectly.

Shifting in the confining desk, he wanted to bolt from the classroom he was so ready to dance. He'd show her today. He'd keep up with her, leave her standing with that pouty mouth of hers gaping open.

Man, she was vain. He guessed it came from growing up in front of mirrors – and being beautiful. Glancing around, he wanted to make sure his thought hadn't betrayed him. Everybody thought Nicole was beautiful, but he could only admit to himself that he agreed.

He was still getting used to touching her, still getting used to seeing himself from every angle in those mirrors. It had been weird at first, watching himself move like that. Seeing the way they moved together – that had been really cool.

He shifted again, suddenly feeling warm.

Breck knew she'd gotten used to him now, after four months and hours of rehearsals. Used to him, but still just tolerating him.

The bell rang and startled him. He had only one thought now, to practice.

Nicole was standing by her locker, surrounded by girls and boys he recognized as being in the elite social group. He kept his head low as he passed, his fingers clutching his biology book until his knuckles turned white. He heard the group laugh and his heart dropped, heat flushed his neck and face. He wanted to think the laugh hadn't been aimed at him, but deep inside he figured it probably was.

No one knew him at Pleasant Grove High School. He was just another one of the nameless, faceless kids that came without notice and would leave without notice. It hadn't mattered up until recently. Now, he was starting to look at the posters decorating the walls for senior prom, games, pep rallies and other school activities with more interest. Maybe he'd start going to some stuff. He lived close enough that he could skate over. It would be another place to be other than home.

Once outside, he felt the thrill of freedom to practice. In his head he heard the music, and he let the tunes fill his blood. He'd sweat, even in the sneaking cold of October, so he pulled off his sweatshirt and tossed the garment aside.

Closing his eyes, he saw the studio, the floor, Reuben, and Nicole. The beat of the music in his head traveled through every fiber until his feet began to move. Stepping forward, sliding into a ball change, then the kicks, fast and sharp. A spin, two more ball-changes followed by more slides. Over and over he did the combinations until his heart took the thrill pumping through him, and shot it out in every direction of his body, leaving him gulping in air, wiping his face with the hem of his tee shirt – ready to do it again.

"Very good."

He whirled around to see the dance team coach standing behind him.

"I know most everybody who dances here at the school, but I've never seen you." She stepped closer, examining him with a grin on her face. Her blonde hair was slicked straight back, her blue eyes smiling.

His heart tripped into his throat. "Uh, I…" Gathering his sweatshirt and books, he was ready to split, but she took another step toward him.

"So who are you?" she asked.

"Breck Noon."

"Lola Verado." She extended her hand and they shook. "How come I've never seen you dance?"

He shrugged. "I just started."

"You're kidding, right? How long?"

"Four months or so."

Now she was circling him, shaking her head. "Where've you been hiding? Do you come out here every day during lunch?" With his head lowered, he nodded.

"I'm impressed." She stopped circling. "Would you be interested in joining the team? You know we win the formation championships every year. Really great group of kids. Ever seen us?"

He had, so he nodded again. But Nicole was on the team. What would Mrs. Dubois say? She'd hired him to be exclusively Nicole's partner.

"I have to check with somebody first," he said.

"Definitely check it out with your parents. It costs, but we have fundraisers and some heavy donations by parents and businesses that sponsor us."

"It's not that." He shifted feet. "I dance – I *work* for somebody, dancing with their daughter."

Lola tilted her head. "Who's that?"

He didn't want to say the wrong thing. Was he the only boy who got paid to dance with a girl? He had no idea, but since it sounded like it could get him in trouble, he thought for a few moments about the ramifications. The more people that knew, the higher the danger that his father would somehow find out, and then it would be over.

"Come on, you can tell me," Lola coaxed.

"I don't know."

"There are only a few people with the resources to pay someone for dance services like that. Is it Nicole Dubois by any chance?"

When he nodded, she smiled. "So you're the one I've been hearing about." She patted his shoulder. "Be honored, Breck Noon. You're headed for great things if you're dancing with the Dubois'."

He felt inadequate then, like all of his practicing meant nothing because he was seen only as Nicole Dubois' sidekick. He'd work harder, longer, and be better with or without Nicole, he decided.

After Lola Verado convinced him to transfer into her class, she left, and Breck stood alone behind the garbage bins, ready to practice again.

Three

When school was over, Breck headed out front to wait for Mrs. Dubois. The air was nippy and he didn't have a coat, never had, only the brown hoodie with the broken zipper, which he now brought more tightly around himself. Most of the kids had cleared out. A few loitered alone, waiting for rides, trying to stay warm.

Nicole was waiting too, but farther down the semi-circular drive – with Trey Woods.

Breck sat on the base of the brick marquee so he could inconspicuously watch them. Ripples of jealousy coursed through him as he watched her smile and light up under Trey's gaze. *Mister popularity*, he thought with a snip of envy.

They were touching each other. Little, innocent, playful stuff, Breck noted, but still, a touch is a touch. He'd never been touched that way.

He heard them laughing, and looked to see Trey lean down and try to kiss her but she ducked away. Then Trey dropped his backpack and took off after her. Breck knew it was just a game.

Turning, he'd not watch when Trey got her. Just thinking about it made him sweat a little, had his heart jumping. Girls both frightened and intrigued him. There hadn't been any in his life since his mother had died. He didn't count any of the painted and perfumed women his father occasionally had over.

When Nicole and Trey's laughter died it was too much for him not to look and see – to look and want.

Trey had her pinned against his red Audi Coupe and was lowering his lips towards hers. Again, she jerked her head out of reach, and when Breck saw her place her palms on Trey's chest as if to push him away, his feet wanted to bolt over and pull the guy off. But he didn't.

"Don't," Nicole shouted, squirming.

"Come on." Trey looked around at the empty parking lot, his eyes lighting on Breck. The two of them stared at each other. "Get lost, loser."

Breck dipped his head momentarily. But the burning at the back of his neck forced him to look up again.

Trey was still looking at him, still had Nicole pinned. "I said, get lost."

Breck shifted his gaze to Nicole whose eyes were wide with fear. In a moment of male bravery and hoping to impress her, he spoke. "Leave her alone."

Trey stood upright and when he did, Nicole slid out from underneath him. Trey strode over fast and Breck's heart raced. Lois' black Mercedes pulled into the pick-up area.

Breck gathered his things in time for Trey to stop right in his face. Nicole wasn't far off, but she kept her distance, heading toward the car – watching them with her bottom lip between her teeth. "Come on, Breck."

Trey glowered. "He's going home with you?"

Nicole nodded, and opened the car door. Trey's eyes narrowed at Breck. "Unbelievable. You keep your hands off her."

Breck leaned close. "She's my dance partner, I *get* to touch her."

"You're the one." Trey looked him up and down. "I don't need to have a reason to touch her."

"Maybe you'd better ask her first." Breck's body was tight as a fist. "It didn't look like she wanted it."

Trey shoved him. The move sent Nicole jogging over and got Mrs. Dubois out of her car.

Dropping his backpack, Breck charged Trey and would have started in with his fists had Nicole not stepped between them, her hands pressing them apart. "Stop it!"

Mrs. Dubois ran over to the three of them with her lips pinched, her eyes wide with concern. "Everything all right?"

Grabbing Breck by the sleeve, Nicole tugged him in the direction of the car. "Let's go."

"You boys getting along?" Lois asked. The kindness in her tone drained the anger from Breck. Without another word he picked up his backpack and headed to the car.

Breck got in the backseat of the car and shut the door, his nerves still coiled. Flushed, he kept his face toward the window. It didn't take but a snap for him to respond to any threat, and that was as humiliating as facing off Trey.

"What was that all about?" Lois asked.

Noon - Katherine Warwick

Breck and Nicole looked at each other but neither said a word.

Nicole stormed from the car straight to the house with a flustered Lois on her tail. "Go on ahead, Breck. Reuben's waiting for you," Lois said.

Obediently, Breck headed toward the studio. He was still in awe of the sheer beauty of the Dubois' estate. The mansion sat up on the lower benches of Pleasant Grove, apart – secluded.

The house itself was big and long, with six white pillars holding a balcony that ran the length of the second floor. Breck liked the red brick and white shutters, thought it looked like something out of the south, a plantation maybe, sitting on the hill regally surrounded by orchards. He didn't know what kind of trees were in the orchards, just that there were endless rows of them, bushy and colorful.

Of course he'd never been inside the house. Despite Lois' many invitations, he didn't feel worthy. Once, he snuck around the back after rehearsal to see the redwood deck that spanned the length of the back, and the kidney-shaped pool painted sapphire so it looked like nature had put it there.

Another night he took his time strolling down the driveway on his way home and had looked at the house, all lit up, and thought he saw Nicole in one of the windows. When he blinked, the light was off and he didn't know if he'd really seen her, or if his wishes were playing tricks on him.

He put his backpack over his shoulder and went into the studio. He found Reuben dancing and stopped just inside the door to watch.

Reuben moved like a vapor of smoke across the floor. There was no music, no sound. His body hovered with ease, dipped with swiftness, and shimmied with the beauty of an aspen in the changing breeze.

Reuben looked at him through the reflection of the mirror, spun to a stop and walked over with an electric grin. "Hey."

Breck was used to him now. The misgivings he'd felt that first day had vanished. He realized his father's scarring attitude toward black people wasn't true, at least where Reuben was concerned.

"Where is she?" Reuben asked.

"At the house." Breck set down his backpack, took off his sweatshirt and sat, ready to change shoes.

"Well." Reuben moved toward the center of the studio. "We'll work without her then."

Breck was anxious to show off his steps and he did, earning the praise he craved. He watched his reflection in the mirror. The steps and the styling were right on, and he smiled.

"Excellent. You've been working hard and it's paying off. You sure your daddy ain't black?"

Breck dipped his head to hide a grin. As the studio door swung open, he jerked the hair out of his eyes. Nicole came in, followed by her mother. Her step was fast and mean, and Breck stepped back, giving her as much space as he could.

"I'm sorry to keep you waiting." Lois joined Reuben and Breck.

"No problem." Reuben didn't even glance Nicole's way. Breck knew then this was not the first time the Princess had acted up.

Nicole went to the same spot she went to every day, dropped her bag, and put her dance shoes on with the grace of a flamingo shifting its feet. Without eye contact, Nicole came to Breck, chin held high. Lois cleared her throat before heading to a seat and settling in.

"Okay." Reuben ignored the iceberg Nicole was pushing his way. "Let's review for the competition. We'll start with samba."

Breck took one look at her and wasn't sure he should move, let alone dance with her. Taking her hands was tantamount to reaching out and taking two live electrical wires and he took another step back. Then he straightened, responding to her rigidity with his own frustration and at last reached out, taking her into the stance.

Reuben counted out the steps as Breck led them first to the right, then jerked her against him, their bodies pressing in close before both stepped to the side again. He'd never felt the need to communicate with the dance, but he did now. He would control her here, she would move to his demands and her anger would be abandoned to his will. Again Breck snapped her in then pressed her out, before turning her into a slow dip.

She tried to keep her eyes pinched and angry but with each tug and press, each jerk and dip, he challenged her, shocked her. He'd caught her by surprise with his skill. She thought this would be her dance, that he would be under her commands. Surprise shone on her face, and a thread of pleasure dangled deep inside him.

When they turned into the final position, he tightened his fingers, and brought her in close for a moment. Their chests heaved in unison. The smell of her body mixed with his. Her face was near, its sheen from the glow of wonder as much as hard work, and his blood went slippery in his veins.

Her eyes darted to his mouth, lighting that fuse dangling inside of him. "Let me go now," she demanded. He gladly did, and she dropped to the floor with a thud.

"Very good." Reuben clapped, extending a hand to Nicole and pulling her up. She was ready to complain, but Reuben talked first. "You did that well, Breck."

"Very well," Lois chimed from across the room. The smile had returned to her face and Breck couldn't help but grin.

Nicole locked her eyes on his in a heat that promised a scarring burn. Nose up, she skipped away with a teasing combination of freestyle. The move was something he couldn't do yet, in that he'd only learned specific steps within the confines of each dance, and he stood watching.

With an easy seduction, Nicole moved and wiggled, thrust and dipped, shook and shimmied.

Lois' shoes echoed purposefully across the floor. Her arm snapped out and stopped Nicole in the middle of one of her hip thrusts. "That's vulgar, and you're acting like a child."

Like a whip cracking, the reprimand shocked them all. Nicole shook her mother's arm off with a jerk, her eyes ignited. "I'm done for today."

Lois grabbed her again, her friendly eyes narrowed. "There are two-and-a-half more hours of rehearsal today, young lady. You have a competition this week."

"If I was dancing with Trey, we'd be done."

"If you aren't prepared, you may lose that place to Trey and Kit. Is that what you want?"

Biting her lower lip, Nicole frowned.

Noon - Katherine Warwick

Lois walked calmly toward Breck and placed her hands gently on his shoulders. "Everyone has heard the rumors that Nicole has a new partner. It's quite an exciting thing, to be starting anew, getting your names out there, and the new name on everyone's lips will be Nicole and Breck."

"Still, I'm done for tonight," Nicole said.

"You're not," Lois' voice hardened. "You will finish rehearsing or your father will be notified."

It was the first time Breck had heard mention of Mr. Dubois. All he knew about the man was that he was a renowned doctor who seemed to never be around. But when Mrs. Dubois dropped his name, Nicole's demeanor changed like a child struck.

There were no more words exchanged, Nicole simply crossed to Breck and Reuben. She stood close, ready and waiting, but there was distance in her eyes.

* * *

After rehearsal, Reuben met with Lois by the chairs. At first, Breck was concerned about his future. Maybe Nicole's unhappiness was because of him, and even though he was making headway, they were going to decide it wasn't worth the stress for her. Well acquainted with being cast aside for the convenience of others, Breck felt a familiar hollowing inside. What would he do without dance? He looked at his feet, his toes pressed up against the soft leather shoes. Cuban shoes, he knew now, for Latin dancing.

He slipped off the shoes and ran a hand fondly over them then looked at Nicole. She was standing in front of the mirror, smoothing her hair back, but their eyes met and hers pinched just enough to worry him. She jerked her head toward the door signaling that she wanted him outside.

After he put his shoes in his backpack, he cautiously walked over to where Lois sat with Reuben.

"Yes?" Lois asked.

Breck toed the floor in front of him. "I – Lola Verado wants me to dance with the team at school. I told her I'd have to ask you first, since I'm, well, you're, I'm—" Something about their arrangement bothered him when verbalized.

"It would be a great opportunity for you," Lois said.

"Yeah, you'd learn formation dance, which is good," Reuben added.

"However," Lois said, "Lola knows that I don't care for Nicole switching partners. She has danced with all the boys on the team, but none of them will go where we intend the two of you to go."

Breck looked up then, at both of them. How could they see something so clearly that he couldn't see at all? Their faith left him humble.

"Okay." He wanted to say thank you but was afraid the words would tear his throat on the way out. He turned and jogged to the door where Nicole stood, arms folded, eyes promising an unleashing.

He held the door open for her and she sashayed out. She was used to being followed, Breck could tell. Because his future with the Dubois' was intact, he stopped.

She turned around, fisting her hands on her hips. "We need to talk."

"Talk." He dropped his backpack like an anchor.

"Fine."

When he didn't move, Nicole conceded and stepped closer. "What happened today at school is none of your business," she whispered loudly. "And it isn't anyone else's."

Speaking out against Trey Woods had been a leap for Breck. Left speechless plenty of times by slaps from his old man, he'd never been verbally slapped by a girl. He wasn't very good at hiding his emotions either – they were always painfully plain on his face. It was something his father used against him, so he tried to hide behind long hair.

"Understand?" She was satisfied to have cut him down, he could tell by the sassy sway in her hips when she turned and started to walk away. It taunted him. He strode just as fast after her, but silently – as he'd learned to move across the dance floor. Everything about her bugged and enticed him at the same time and he shocked them both when he reached out and took hold of her arm.

"Hey. I was just trying to help."

"I don't need your help."

"Then why were you telling him no, and he was ignoring you?"

"Just because I was saying no, doesn't mean I meant it." It was then they both noticed he still had a grip on her arm. He let go. Her answer confused him. He'd seen her fear, her need to break free of Trey.

He took a step back, driven by disbelief and the need to distance himself from something he didn't understand. It was the way he protected himself. He retrieved his backpack and turned. Giving his back had been another way he'd protected himself, at least temporarily.

"Watch your step, Noon," Nicole called after him.

She watched until he disappeared into the darkness. The wind was picking up, and she looked into the grey sky. It smelled damp, even though the clouds still held like a pregnant woman. It was going to rain and he'd be out in it; she thought briefly and for a flash, almost yelled to him to wait—she'd give him a ride, but she stopped herself. Let him get wet.

Once inside, she was alone, and the house echoed with the reality of it. Rubbing her arms was a vain attempt to keep away a chill that went beyond the skin. It had nothing to do with the temperature.

It was eight forty-five, and her father still wasn't home.

She pulled some bread out of the breadbox and dropped it into the toaster. Her gaze wandered over the various family photos stuck with magnets on the refrigerator. It made her smile seeing her older brother, Brian, his wife Tami, and their two young girls grinning back at her. She'd see them for Halloween in a few weeks; they came over every year and went trick-or-treating in the neighborhood.

The toast popped up, and Nicole set it on the counter to butter it. She was going to a party for Halloween and still hadn't decided what she was going to wear. What would Breck be doing for Halloween? She wondered why she'd thought about it.

She was still angry that he'd seen her mother reprimand her. Secretly, she was glad he'd jumped to her aid that day. Trey liked her, that much she knew, but she was still just seventeen and figuring out things that puzzled her heart.

Toast in hand, she made her way upstairs.

Her bedroom always calmed her; the soft yellow hues soothing like the sun at morning. Ribbons and trophys hung here and there, their colors jewels in her crown of achievement. Of course most of them were due to her skills as an individual dancer. She had yet to win the awards she coveted with a partner.

She and Trey had barely scraped sixth in competition when they'd been partners.

Now, with Breck as her partner, those awards would be still farther off.

Biting into her toast, she tugged the picture of her and Trey off the corkboard hanging on the wall. It had been her choice to change partners, not Trey's. Both Reuben and her mother felt like Trey wasn't taking dance seriously enough to be partnered with her anymore. In her heart she knew it was for the best.

She and Trey had looked good together, she thought, dropping the photo into the trash basket aside her vanity table. But that wasn't enough. She wanted more. She wanted wins. So now Trey was dancing with Kit, and she had Breck.

Plunking into the chair, she turned her face back and forth in front of the mirror as she ate her toast. She'd graduate soon, and she couldn't wait. Each year promised more freedom. She could come and go as she pleased. Like tonight, she'd have left the studio and driven off to a friend's house.

She'd find out where Breck lived – go there.

The thought made her flush. He'd been someone different today at rehearsal, and she had been so taken aback by it, she'd been unable to do anything but hide awe behind anger.

Eyeing herself in the mirror, she vividly remembered the ease with which he'd done the samba. The strength in his arms, the hard lines of his body as it brushed hers. She was forced to admit that he was amazingly gifted. He'd improved to the point where she felt like she was dancing with a man, not a boy.

She'd been in the arms of boys for as long as she could remember. It had confused her when she was a child but she came to understand the feelings were her body's natural response to being close to the opposite sex.

There were boys she'd had crushes on, and plenty of boys liked her. That she knew as well as the flecks that colored her eyes to lavender when she wore the right shade. Trey liked her now, and it flattered her. He was the most sought after guy in school.

But she wasn't ready to do what Trey was pushing for and considered why, when being close to another body in dance could be as intimate as a kiss. She couldn't think of Trey and kissing him in the same thought.

A first kiss should be as exciting as the samba.

Noon - Katherine Warwick

Electricity started at her toes, the warm trickle both delicious and disconcerting. She thought of Breck, of how he'd held her in that last dip of the dance, his face so close she saw that his eyes really weren't black or brown. They were blue.

She forced herself away from the mirror, not liking what she saw. The pink in her cheeks embarrassed her.

To lose her thoughts of him, she scanned her shelf for a favorite book and chose a mystery. But the moment she settled into the softness of her bed, surrounded by things warm and cuddly, she found Breck's face in her mind again. She bit her lower lip, flushing, and replaced the mystery with one of her favorite love stories, *The Scarlet Pimpernel*.

Lois shut the backdoor and locked it, setting the alarm that would help her feel protected in her husband's absence. Just when she would hear Garren's car rattle up on its diesel engine, she didn't know. Nighttime meant many things to Lois – one was the uncertainty of her husband's return and the loneliness that dragged her along with it.

Tonight there was another uncertainty. Lois understood a mother's love could never change, except to grow. But children seemed to love from day to day, when it suited them. Kind of like cats, she thought, and began the ritual of turning off lights on the main floor.

She'd stopped leaving lights on for Garren's convenience years ago.

Climbing the stairs, she gripped the banister, rubbing her other hand over her forehead. Arguing with Nicole always drained her, but watching her dance was invigorating, and took her back to when she'd pursued her own career in ballet. She'd been just as gifted, just as driven, just as distracted and owned by the dance. It had looked so promising, her future, until she'd gotten injured. That had stolen it all away from her.

She'd make sure no one took Nicole's dream.

Lois paused outside Nicole's bedroom door, her knuckles poised to knock. Light shone underneath. Things looked so perfect now that Breck was her partner. Why did Nicole fight it?

◎ 31 ◎

A smile spread across Lois' lips. She'd forgotten a good many things because they caused her pain, but first loves could not easily be forgotten. It didn't bother her that Nicole was fighting something she probably wasn't even aware of. Nicole would be professional, work through it, even if there were conflicting feelings present.

But Lois felt motherly towards Breck. That opening inside of her, somewhere in the middle of her heart, pulled her to those that needed help, even when they didn't know they needed it. She'd felt the pull, hard this time, when she'd seen him skating at the skate park, his head held low and his shoulders slumped. She'd been drawn to the fluid ease with which he took the pipes and rails, with the way he kept himself apart – like a stray cat.

She'd gone there specifically to search for someone for Nicole to dance with. Kit's mother had bragged about how well her little boy was doing in ballroom because he rode the pipes on rollerblades and it had given Lois the idea to go to the skate park in an effort to recruit.

There were never enough boys in the dance community. Her offer was without flaws; to be paid to learn a skill that could enhance self-esteem, physical capabilities, teach social graces and round out a life in a way only perfecting and competing could do.

In the four months Breck had been coming over every day, she had carefully approached their friendship from a safe distance, sensing his deep hesitancy. Slowly, she had extended herself the only way she knew how – with her heart gaping his direction.

She hoped Nicole would do the same, in her own way.

Knocking softly, Lois waited.

"Come in," Nicole called.

Lois smiled when she entered. Nicole lay on her pink and yellow bedspread like a little girl, on her stomach, with a book propped in front of her face. "Everything all right?"

Nicole closed her book and nodded, turning onto her side.

"I'm sorry about today."

"Yeah."

"He's doing so well, isn't he?" Lois crossed to the bed and sat, settling in for a long chat.

Nicole shrugged. "I guess."

"He's really a very nice boy, don't you think?"

"He's okay, I guess."

"Lola asked him to join the team."

Nicole's eyes widened. "Really?" Then her expression flattened. "Oh, no."

"What?"

"Now everybody will know."

"It's going to happen sooner or later. The rumors are out there."

Nicole looked away. "I know."

Lois reached over and pressed a hand to her daughter's. "He'll fit in well with the kids. He has great potential. And he's very cute."

"In a stoner kind of way."

"In a very normal way." Lois's eyes twinkled. "You watch he'll knock the girls over like a ball in a bowling alley."

Nicole laughed. "Bowling alley? Mom, you see everybody through these glasses only you can wear."

"Try them on for a day." Lois ran a hand along Nicole's cheek and pushed away a stray hair.

Nicole burrowed more deeply into the pile of pillows on her bed. "He's bad for my image."

"What about what you can do for his?"

"Oh, please." Nicole pulled at a pillow underneath her and squeezed it tight to her chest as if doing so would relieve some of her frustration. "Is he another one of your charity cases?"

Lois' smile faded a little and her head lowered just enough to sock Nicole in the gut with guilt. She reached out and touched her mother's arm. "It's okay, Mom. If you want to take him on, I won't get in your way."

"You could help me."

Nicole let out a sigh, unwilling to let their eyes meet for commitment. "Maybe."

"Just be your sweet self."

That made Nicole laugh. "I can only be sweet to people I like."

"Don't be too hard on him; we don't know where he's been and what he's going through even now."

"What do you mean?"

"Something's amiss in his life, that's all I know."

A kernel of concern worked its way under Nicole's skin. But she saw her mother's brain at work, laying a plan, and that soothed her a little.

"Maybe he'll trust us someday," Lois said.

"I'm sure he trusts you."

Lois's eyes glistened, opening Nicole's heart. She laid her hand over her mother's and squeezed. "Mom."

"He needs to trust you." The crinkle in her mother's voice dove straight inside. She wanted to think it didn't matter if Breck trusted her, but knew from experience that, even in dance, partners needed trust, and that meant commitment.

They both heard the far off thud that had their eyes locking. It was Lois who got up then, straightening her wrinkled clothes first before running her hands along the sides of her hair." 'Night, honey."

After her mother shut the door, Nicole waited for the deep tone of her father's voice to put her to sleep. When there was only silence, it took her forever to drift away. Tonight, she would succumb willingly. It would be her last submission for the day.

Four

At eight a.m. Nicole had her hair in rollers and was sitting at her makeup table, pots of color laid out like an artist's palette in front of her. Breck still had not arrived and they were going to be leaving in forty minutes for the Pleasant Grove Invitational—their first competition as a pair. The first time the world of dance would see just who Nicole Dubois was dancing with, and most importantly, the start of establishing their name together as a competing couple.

I might as well be starting over. She slipped on the body stocking that would go underneath her elaborate dress. Her nerves hadn't jittered like this since her career began.

Pulling on her satin warm-up pants, she eyed the deep navy jacket that set her eyes a blaze of blue before she slipped it on. Each couple wore different, matching warm-up ensembles during competitions. Breck would look striking in the shade. It was one reason she'd chosen the color.

Holding her Latin dress out, she studied the garment. The sapphire dress glittered from neck to sleeve to hem with beads and rhinestones. Their coordinating costumes would be just the showstoppers she and Breck needed to make their first appearance memorable for the judges as well as other competitors.

She'd approved their costumes weeks ago. She hadn't involved Breck in the costuming decision, because he didn't know enough about such matters to make an educated opinion. It had irritated her mother when she'd left him out of the process, but Nicole had a reputation to uphold, a new name to establish, and she was not about to let some beginner partner in on something as crucial as costume design.

For that reason, along with the fact that she had an irresistible desire to see him in something tailored and attractive rather than the scruffy clothes he always wore, she couldn't wait to see him in costume.

Lois came through the door with Breck, her hands on his shoulders and a smile on her face. "He's here."

Nicole looked at him through the reflection of her mirror. His wild hair had been blown by the wind, and covered his eyes, baring only his broad, full mouth and the sharp lines of his jaw. A tremor slivered through her. Her mother had his matching shirt in her hands and moved him around to face her, holding the shirt underneath his chin.

"This will look very nice." She turned him with a pat to his back. "You can put it on in the bathroom."

Breck took the shirt, looked at the snaps that would attach at his crotch and his eyes popped. Lois laughed. "It stays in place that way."

He glanced at Nicole before heading off down the hall.

"Did he say why he was late?"

"He skated up," Lois kept her voice low. "I wonder if his parents even know he's competing." Lois looked down the hall, brows tight in concern, then back at Nicole.

A few moments later Breck stood behind Lois, wearing the deep blue shirt and black slacks. He looked, Nicole thought, as good as any of the professional dancers she had ever seen. Nicole blinked, and her heart began a slow, steady thump in her chest.

"Are these pants supposed to be this tight?" he asked, voice cracking.

Lois' eyes twinkled. "Yes. They fit just the way they're supposed to." She looked at his hair, all but covering his face. "Perhaps we should do something with your hair."

He froze, his eyes shot wide. Nicole hid a smile. "Like what?" he asked.

"The judges like to see animated expression, smiling – you know," Lois said. "Ever used gel?"

"Uh, no."

Nicole piped, "Maybe you could pull it back in a pony tail."

"You mean like a girl? No way."

Lois smiled, turned him around and winked at Nicole before she gently nudged him back into the bathroom. "Just get your hair wet and we'll see what we can do."

* * *

Nicole finished dressing and waited for Breck. She looked at her reflection; at her eyes made huge with garish false lashes, more colorful caked with shadow and glitter. Today everyone that mattered in her life would know who Breck Noon was. Her stomach wouldn't stop flipping.

She had to admit her opinion of him was slowly changing. The fact was he was the best dancer she'd danced with yet. That would make showing him off a deserved pleasure.

She couldn't wait to see Trey's face. And to see Kit's mouth drop because she had been the one to find a diamond in the dirt – that would be most satisfying.

Flinging her garment bag over her arm, she waited in the hall for Breck and her mother. She heard her mother talking in her calming voice.

"Look at you," Lois was saying. "Very, very nice."

When Breck appeared from around the bathroom door, Nicole's heart stopped. Gone were the wild curls that shrouded his face. His hair was straight back, slicked with heavy gel. For the first time, she saw drama in the sharp pitch of his forehead, beauty in the angles and lines of his jaw and cheekbones. His eyes looked like the sky, nearest to night. The fullness of his mouth was exposed, soft and magnetic, and she had to force her gaze away.

"Doesn't he look great?" Lois asked.

Nicole took a deep, fluttering breath. "We should go." She passed him quickly, before her heart could pound, handing him his navy jacket that matched hers. "Put on the jacket. Nobody can see your shirt – shock factor is everything."

Because the competition was held at the high school, and the school was only minutes from the Dubois', they pulled into the crowded parking lot before Breck had a chance to feel butterflies flock in his gut.

"Are your parents coming, Breck?" Lois asked as she parked the car.

Breck shook his head. He'd had to make up an excuse as it was, to be gone all of Saturday. Fortunately for him, his dad was spending a lot of time with the blonde lady that lived at the end of the trailer park. "There's only my Dad, and he's busy," he said.

"Oh." Lois opened the trunk of her car. "Well, would you carry the cooler in for me, please? It has our lunch in it."

"Sure, okay."

Noon - Katherine Warwick

It seemed that everyone they passed stared at them, and Breck felt the butterflies in his stomach grow wild. Nicole nodded, smiled, and said hello with the ease of a celebrity on the red carpet. He trailed behind her in silent awe.

"We paid for a floor table," Lois told him as they entered the auditorium. The room was electric. Bodies moved, some in dance, others simply in the thrill of reuniting with friends or in preparation to observe the competition. Sweat and perfume hung on the gradually thickening air. As dancers warmed up, so did the temperature of the gym.

"Everyone's staring," Nicole whispered. She lifted her head a little higher as she led Breck to a table with their name card on it.

Lois merely began to set things down, smiling and waving at a few chosen faces. "Let them stare."

"Yeah," Nicole added. "By the end of the day they'll be drooling."

Breck swallowed. "Drooling?"

"Let's go sign in." Lois gently touched his elbow. "Breck, you come with me, they'll give you the number to wear on the back of your shirt."

He swallowed again and pulled on the waist of his pants. He felt like he was naked. And he'd be out there dancing. The thought had him wanting to sit down, but he followed Lois.

A petite blonde with her eyes locked on him made her way over. All bounce and femininity, she looked him up and down before facing Nicole and Lois.

"So, is this the mystery man we've all been hearing about?" She extended her small hand to him with long nails painted bubble gum pink.

Nicole didn't bother hiding her lack of enthusiasm. "Breck, meet Kit."

Breck shook her hand. "Hi."

"Don't you go to PG?" Kit's lashes fluttered. Breck nodded. "I thought you looked familiar. You're hair is different though, right?"

Breck nodded again, his cheeks warming. Her hand still clutched his and the warmth in his cheeks was spreading everywhere, making him sweat.

"Breck just joined the dance team." Nicole came around Breck's side and hooked her arm in his, tugging his hand free of Kit's. "But he'll be dancing with me."

Kit tilted her head. "Obviously."

Breck noticed Trey coming up behind Kit. He had a scowl on his face, and Breck wondered if they might fight right there on the spot. But Trey only took Kit by the arm and smiled congenially.

"We should get back to our table." He looked at Nicole and one corner of his lip curled. Then he shot Breck an icy glare.

"They're perfect together," Nicole muttered, "the pair of snakes."

Lois settled herself, opening her program. "Just a few months ago he was *your* dance partner."

And he'd been all over her. It had been flattering and frightening at the same time. Nicole disguised the inconsistency of her mood by hiding behind obvious disdain for an opponent.

Breck turned to see Reuben coming across the floor and a wave of relief swept through him. Reuben made stops at most of the tables, then laced through the bleachers shaking hands and greeting people. He seemed to know everyone.

"Hey, guys." Reuben set his coat down then came in close for a huddle, pulling both Nicole and Breck in tight. His green eyes glittered. "Let's find a corner and warm up."

There were dancers everywhere, turning and kicking, twisting and stepping. Some of the faces were familiar to Breck. He recognized all of the steps, but couldn't identify serious competitors from those more novice, his eye too unskilled yet.

Reuben took them through a set of warm up stretches and then they worked out the trouble spot of their routine. Nicole was to kick her leg up in samba and Breck was supposed to catch it as she arched back before a quick turn out, making the move look effortless. He still looked like he was readying himself for a basketball being pitched across court at him.

When the announcer spoke, Breck's head went up and the sparklers in his stomach lit. He looked at Nicole. For a moment he heard nothing, saw nothing, but her. She was speaking to him with her eyes, bright like colorful lavender jewels. He was sure the secret message was meant only for him, but he wouldn't trust his heart.

She reached out her hand. "Ready?"

Five

Music blasted, shaking the walls of the building like the tremors of an earthquake. The auditorium hushed to whispers – a buzzing current of anticipation. The first couple was announced and the two competitors took off their jackets, tossing them into the arms of their coach who stood nearby. The line of waiting dancers collectively whispered at the sight of their bright costumes before the couple disappeared through the curtain and onto the dance floor.

Breck's arm pits were sticky, his palms were wet, and his heart was thumping to the cha-cha beat. Every breath he took sucked in the scent of sweat and Nicole's hairspray. He thought he might be sick: the sparklers in his stomach now threatened to ignite. It seemed to take hours rather than minutes for the preceding couples to be announced, and he agonized through the wait.

"Couple fifteen-twelve," the emcee finally called. Applause crackled even before they walked out onto the floor. He saw the flash of thrill in Nicole's eyes and led her, just as Reuben had instructed, onto the center of the floor.

Curiosity from the audience danced through the air in whispers. In the fringe of his vision Breck saw the bleachers filled with faces and bodies, Lois and Reuben at their table, but he focused on Nicole.

Drums chanted, cymbals sung and the familiarity of the smooth Latin beat helped Breck relax as he shifted into the steps of cha-cha. He heard Reuben's voice echoing in his mind, seven eight, cha-cha-cha and turn two cha-cha-cha. Energy shot and sparked between him and Nicole, and a perfect flow unfolded from his body to hers.

How had he gotten here? Breck Noon dancing with the most beautiful girl he'd ever seen, in front of hundreds of eyes. It was easy to be pleased, to smile. To feel something he would later come to know as confidence.

Applause roared and broke through some moments later, and he grinned at her when they'd finished their rotation. "We did great," he whispered.

"We did." The fire in her eyes spoke of victory.

With only a change of music, they went into their samba routine. Because confidence was fueled by the audience whistling and cheering, it was easy for Breck to lose his fears in the performance. Commanding Nicole's moves with the drive from his hands, they moved as one fluid draft across the floor, sweeping and taunting, bribing the audience with hot liquid movements, electricity jagging like lightening between them.

They finished as he pulled her up from the kick floating with ease into the spin out. He held tight to her hand and did a discreet bow, then twirled her out for her curtsey.

Applause splintered through the air like a thousand whips, and Breck led her off the dance floor and over to the side where couples that had already competed stood watching.

They waited there, gasping for air, trying to breathe discreetly. Bubbles and prickly nerves started to settle as Breck watched the other couples go through the same procedure. Some eased through their routines, while others looked stiff or made obvious mistakes.

Since he'd never competed for anything before, he had no idea what level of skill was required to place. He only knew what Reuben had demanded of them. That he'd worked hard, practiced long after he'd left Nicole at the studio, and had even found himself dreaming the steps in his sleep. Would that be enough for them to place?

The first heat ended and twenty couples were trimmed to sixteen. Breck rolled his shoulders and flexed his hands. "So, we're in," he said, his stomach easing with the news.

Nicole leaned over for a whisper. "We're doing great." The sweet spearmint on her breath sent a warm tingle down the side of his neck, but the way her eyes stayed with his, in a look that was pure joy, made his heart jump.

They took their places off deck and waited as the same process was repeated except the music was changed. There were four heats completed, each time the music was altered and the time between competitions shortened to weed out those pairs who got sloppy and tired, leaving only those who continued to perform with perfection until six couples remained.

Breck's stomach growled. He was glad the music was loud. Having not eaten that morning, when the meal break came, he devoured the sandwiches, chips and fruit Lois had packed.

"You're doing great out there," Reuben told them.

Breck sat back, fatigue creeping over him. "This is the last heat?"

Lois nodded. "Everyone's very impressed, Breck."

"They're more than impressed," Reuben's voice rolled on a low chuckle of pride. "They're speechless."

Breck looked around as casually as he could. The eyes watching him were warming up, and he was glad. He'd had something to prove.

Busily pasting stray hairs into place and smoothing her costume, Nicole had not said anything about their performances since the first heat. Breck wanted to talk about it but kept his mouth shut.

"Remember your form, really push for this last set," Reuben reminded.

"You're going to place." Lois confidently collected their lunch trash after they'd finished eating. "As far as I can see, Trey and Kit are your only threat."

Both Nicole and Breck looked over at the other couple. Trey sat legs splayed, arms lazily draped like the competition was no big deal. It probably wasn't, the guy was so good, Breck thought. Then Trey grinned, lifting his soda can in his direction with a taunting nod of head.

Breck wanted to be better, wished he'd danced longer and knew more. Time, he told himself, he'd pack in more and make up for the loss.

The pressure to succeed built and Breck's insides squeezed. When the announcer spoke and the final heat was open, they headed off stage to wait until their number was called.

He led Nicole onto the floor and the applause withered into thick silence.

The drum beat, mariachis played, and the music sent another streak of lightening through Breck's veins. He didn't need to think the steps anymore. He didn't have to try to smile. He just listened to the music, let it reach inside and take him. When Nicole smiled, the whole room dissolved into nothingness. All he heard was the music, and the only thing he saw was her. Each step and combination went beautifully, the timing like the inner workings of a clock.

It started at his toes, the thrilling vibration driven by the final applause, and for a few seconds they held their last stance. Faces close, hearts beating in unison, Breck felt the need to pull Nicole in and hug her, so overcome with joy, but he dismissed it, afraid she wouldn't approve. He took his bow. The grin he wore glittered as he spun her out for her grand curtsy.

After the final heat, the couples made their way to the screen where the overhead projector would display their scores. As third was placed, Nicole grabbed Breck's hand. It made his insides move a little, the way she held it close to her heaving breast.

When they didn't place third, his heart sunk. "Could we be out?" he whispered.

She shook her head, eyes fixed on the screen.

When their number went up next, she released his hand and merely clapped. The audience thundered with applause. He took pats on the back and gracious handshakes from other competitors. What he really wanted was to pick Nicole up and whirl her around, he was so elated. As instructed by Reuben should they place, Breck took Nicole's hand and led her to the awaiting judges who handed them their ribbons.

They had but seconds to enjoy their victory. The number one place went to Kit and Trey who glided to the center of the floor to receive their trophies. Breck remained next to Nicole, and watched her out the corner of his eye. There was a smile on her face but her eyes were glistening.

As the next competition began, the dancers cleared the floor. Accustomed to taking the lead on the dance floor, as he'd been instructed, Breck trailed after Nicole back to the table.

"You did awesome." Reuben slapped Breck's palm before bringing him in for a full-bodied hug. "They're talking about you, man."

"Yeah?"

"Yeah." Reuben brought Nicole against him, holding her tight for a few long moments. "Good job, Nic."

When Nicole eased back, Breck saw tears, and the thrill he'd carried popped like a balloon. She went to her mother's arms next, and stayed there.

Reuben pulled him around gently. "Don't worry about anything, Breck. You two did great, you really did."

"Why is she crying?" They'd worked hard, given everything they had, and they'd placed. He was happy – why wasn't she?

"Like I said," Reuben placed a hand on his shoulder. "You did great."

But the comment did little to help Breck's bruised, confused ego. He watched Nicole wipe her tears away like an Olympian who had just lost everything.

The next week they both stayed after school for dance team practice in the gym. Nicole chatted with the girls. Breck stood alone. The other male team members tossed a basketball back and forth, waiting for Lola Verado.

"Isn't that him?" In spite of her best effort, Nicole noticed that Tiffany couldn't keep her eyes off of Breck. In fact, all of the girls' curiosity had locked on Breck the moment he walked into the auditorium. She knew the buzz about Saturday's competition was the main current of the day's gossip at school, but above that, she heard the lusty whispers of conniving females.

Breck sat down on the first row of bleachers and set his backpack aside.

"So," Tiffany started, flipping a long, dark lock of hair over her shoulder, her brown eyes sparkling. "We know he can dance. What's he like?"

Annie was watching with interest as well, and Nicole recognized that eager look behind her friend's dainty, silver-rimmed glasses. "I heard he's in a polygamist family."

"What?" Nicole scoffed. "No way."

"I heard his dad's, like, some drug dealer or something," Tiffany piped.

Kit sashayed over, flipping sun-bleached hair behind her shoulders. Nicole thought she looked like an ice cream cone, with her vanilla waves and toasted cream teeshirt. "Well you should know, Nicole – he is your partner."

Nicole shrugged and broke into some simple steps. "He's kind of quiet about things." It was her fault she didn't know more about him. Pride blocked her curiosity. It didn't bear well on her character to look uninformed, shining a vain light on the perfect image she worked hard to display.

"So," Kit faced Nicole. "Aren't you going to congratulate me, Nicole? Or is the pill of loser too big and you're choking on it?"

"Congratulations." Nicole would be cordial but nothing more. She continued dancing independently with an eye on Breck.

"He's totally hot. Is he nice?" Tiffany's gaze remained glued to Breck. Kit followed the admiring stares and her lips tugged upward.

◎ 44 ◎

Noon - Katherine Warwick

That her friends were oogling over Breck was harder for Nicole to swallow than Kit's win. Possessiveness and jealousy was no stranger to her. What surprised her was that she felt them so strongly for Breck. "Yeah, he's pretty nice," she offered, watching him finish slipping on his dance shoes.

Kit grinned. "He's got a wicked face."

"How can you tell, there's so much hair hanging over it," Annie said. "I'd like to see it. His lips are awesome."

"The competition Saturday – if you'd gone, you'd have seen." Kit crossed to him then, stopping directly at his feet. Shocked, the girls stared in open-mouthed fascination.

Breck finished tying his shoes. His gaze moved slowly up all of Kit, finally settling on her face. She extended one pale hand and he looked at it before standing and shaking.

"She's shameless." Annie's whisper was tinged with jealousy.

As if they'd been friends for years instead of seconds, Kit put her hand on Breck's arm as she laughed and chatted. Her head fell back in a coy giggle, and her hair looked like a waterfall of cream. Nicole couldn't say why the sight bugged her, but it did.

Lola entered, briskly walking across the floor to the music system. She wore loose black slacks and a red tee shirt, tied in a knot at the side of her waist. As with most professional dancers, her brown hair was back in an efficient pony tail. She clapped everyone to attention and Kit sashayed back across the floor to the girls with a smile of secrets on her face.

"Let's begin," Lola spoke loudly. "I want to introduce Breck Noon." She put a friendly hand on his shoulder. "He and Nicole placed second over the weekend at the Invitational. Good job, you two." She paused while the group clapped. "And of course, congratulations go out to Trey and Kit who placed first." After another round of applause, she looked at Breck again. "Everyone, I've invited Breck to join the team. So, make him feel welcome."

One by one, the boys sauntered over and introduced themselves with a pat on Breck's back or a slap to Breck's palm. The girls followed, each shaking his hand until it was Nicole's turn. She pulled him in for a possessive hug.

"He's my partner," she said, her arm still twined in his. The comment sat on the air with pointed implication Nicole intended both the boys and the girls

Noon - Katherine Warwick

to understand. She and Breck were going to blow the dance shoes off of everyone in that room and anybody else that tried to beat them in competition.

The boys didn't say much. Nicole figured they wished one of them had been hand chosen by her mother to be her new partner. She expected Trey to sneer, and he did. She just squeezed Breck's arm, still woven tight in hers.

Tiffany and Annie were too taken with the novelty of Breck to be anything but in awe, but the soft sway of Kit's hips, the heavy blink of her eyes at Breck as she stood too near, had Nicole biting her lower lip.

"We will be rotating, Nicole." Lola smiled but lifted her brow at Nicole's obvious gesture of ownership. "Let's begin with our cha-cha routine. Breck, start out with Nicole and follow along."

They formed a staggered formation in the center of the floor.

It was during that awkward moment; standing face-to-face with him Nicole felt the sting of her hypocrisy. She could barely see his eyes but confusion and hurt was in the vulnerable set of his mouth, and the look left her unable to meet his gaze.

"Switch partners," Lola told them after they'd practiced for a while. "And we'll do it again."

Kit had positioned herself to be next in line for Breck and she bounced over.

"He's good," Chris whispered to Nicole. They readied for the next set. Nicole tried not to watch Breck and Kit, tried to focus on Chris, but every giggle coming from Kit had her head whipping around, her insides drawing into a tight fist ready to push Kit out of his arms.

"Arms higher when you come in, people," Lois called over the music. "Trey, eyes on your partner, same with you, Nicole."

As the hour moved and the other boys talked and joked with him, Breck felt more at ease. The shock of realizing that he was a better dancer than most of the guys, with the exception of Trey, left him with an added layer of confidence.

"You're pretty good, dude." Parker slapped an arm around Breck's shoulder after rehearsal.

Breck dipped his head. "Thanks."

"Glad you're on the team," Chris added. The boys all stood around Breck, who dropped to the bleachers and started removing his dance shoes.

Noon - Katherine Warwick

Trey strolled over.

Breck looked up into their faces, and gathered his dance shoes gently. He'd never been the center of attention, never had many friends, just guys that wanted to sell him the latest trip. To be surrounded by some of the school's most popular boys made him feel like he was in some bizarre dream. He looked at the shoes in his hands, their softness under his fingertips.

"So, you're one of us now. Cool" Chris playfully slugged his shoulder. It sent Breck's head jerking up.

Breck slid the shoes inside his backpack hoping the flush of heat on his face wouldn't be seen. He looked for Nicole. They were going to her house next, for more work with Reuben and he slung his backpack over his shoulder and stood. The other boys left after saying goodbye, but Trey stepped closer. For a moment the two boys just looked at each other.

More familiar with the look Trey held in his eyes than Breck liked, his stomach twisted. Trey could mean trouble. He'd dealt with that kind of mean all of his life, and where it was ripe and mature in his fathers' eyes, even in infancy, it was as plain as the smirk on Trey's face and plain was just as dangerous.

Trey blocked his exit. "You may be on this team." Trey's voice was low. "You may even compete. But you'll never be one of us."

Breck hated that his eyes went to the floor when he was affronted. Wished more than anything he had the courage to put a fist in the mouth of tormentors like Trey. But his heart simply pounded in a fear that froze him.

Trey's voice was snaky as he leaned in close. "Loser."

"Breck, let's go," Nicole called from across the auditorium. Her voice sparked him with courage. Breck shouldered Trey out of his way before dropping into a half-run to catch Nicole.

Two hours into rehearsal, Reuben sensed a storm brewing between his pair. "And together two cha-cha-cha, in tight three cha-cha-cha, back two cha-cha-cha." Reuben yelled over the music, occasionally clapping out the beat.

Breck was ripping Nicole in and out of the cha-cha routine with more punch than usual. Neither had said a word to each other since they'd walked through the door three hours earlier. It wasn't that their dancing was affected by the problem, whatever it was. In fact, their moves were riper with passion than he'd ever seen. They just weren't talking.

"Arms up! Come on, you know this. And two two three cha-cha-cha, better," Reuben demanded.

Breck's movements were sharp and rough and for the first time, Reuben sensed a deep well of something potentially savage lying hidden inside. It would come out, he thought, and when polished, it would make Breck a powerful, magnetic dancer.

"Good, again, again!" Reuben didn't stop for a break. He meant to push for the last few minutes to see where it got them.

Breck and Nicole went into the routine again with sweat beading their faces, drenching their arms and chests, their breath hard and heavy.

"I don't want to hear you breathing." Reuben circled them slowly, like a coach on the heels of a boxer. Breck's face was tight, his fingers gripping hard. Nicole's breath sped. "I said no breathing," he repeated.

Breck thrust Nicole out in a dip and with the sweat coating his hands and hers, she slipped, and took a drop sidelong on her butt and shoulder.

"You did that on purpose," she snapped.

"I did not."

"Okay, okay—" Reuben extended a hand to Nicole but she batted it away and pushed herself up.

"That was excellent." Reuben ran his palms over his naked crown. "But you were both breathing too loud. I heard it over the music."

"I have to breathe," Breck bit out.

With one smooth shake of his head, Reuben said, "Fine, but we don't want to hear it."

"Then how am I supposed to breathe?"

"Like a dead man," Nicole gasped.

"Dead men don't breathe."

Nodding, Reuben smiled. "Exactly."

"This is crazy," Breck muttered. He rolled his shoulders, wiped the sweat from his brow with the hem of his already-sopped tee shirt.

"Don't ever drop me again," Nicole warned.

"And you," Breck was in her face like a bullet, his finger poking at her raised chin, "you don't use me like you did today ever again."

They stood, nose to nose, breathing like racehorses that had gone too many times around the track. Reuben clicked the music off and stood back.

"I didn't use you!"

"You did, and it wasn't fair." Breck paced, hands shoved in his wet hair. Because he was sweaty, his hair stayed off of his face. Taken by the bare lines, the fierceness that colored his eyes a deeper blue, Nicole's heart fluttered and she stopped.

"I'm sorry," she said.

Reuben's head came up.

Nicole stayed put, not sure she should go anywhere near Breck, but a tremor of something she hadn't felt before wound tight inside. Something vulnerable, shadowed with fear and fury was on Breck's face that she couldn't tear her eyes away from, and so she had said the words – *I'm sorry.*

She watched his breathing slow; the bunched muscles in his shoulders relax. Guilt tugged at her conscience. She had used him during rehearsal at school, and it was wrong. But that was only part of what had driven him as they'd danced just now. It wasn't foreign to her because she recognized the force as something she carried inside of her as well – anger struggling with need. Their roots would be different, that much she knew. It drew her to him in a way she'd never been drawn to anyone before, feeling a kindred soul reaching out to her.

She stepped toward him then, and his eyes sharpened. She laid her hand over his arm. "I am sorry."

For a moment, he looked at her hand. Then his gaze traveled up her arm and locked on hers. "Okay," he said.

The sweet, boyish acceptance tugged her lips into the hint of a smile. She kept her hand on his arm and the moment stretched, broken only by Reuben's movements as he closed up for the evening.

"See you two Monday. Breck, you need a ride?"

Breck's gaze stayed fastened on Nicole, who still had her hand on his arm. "No thanks."

Neither of them saw the grin that spread across Reuben's face, nor the

Noon - Katherine Warwick

way he lifted into a gleeful tap dance as he got to the door, opened it, then let the door quietly shut behind him.

As lightly as she'd touched him, Nicole withdrew her hand. The studio was silent. His slow, steady breathing sung with hers. Beneath his wet tee shirt, the outline of lean muscle stretched over bone. She wondered what he looked like with his shirt off, and the thought sent a warm tickle through her.

"I can give you a ride," she offered. He shook his head. "Are you sure? It wouldn't be any trouble."

"I'm sure. Thanks." When he crossed to his things, she was pinched by disappointment. Following him, she swung her arms, searching for something to do that might make her appear casual.

He dropped to one of the seats to remove his dance shoes and she noted again the way he stroked them, his long fingers gently moving over the surface before he slipped them into his backpack. It was such a reverent gesture, her heart turned inside her chest. It stayed there, somewhere in limbo, as she watched him walk out the door.

Six

The walk home gave Breck plenty of time to think. It wasn't really that big of a deal being friendly and social with the kids on the team. He decided then he would work harder at being outgoing.

Truth was, he wasn't really petrified of people anymore, not since he'd started dancing. Dancing had helped him feel better about a lot of things. He'd seen that he could do something faster and better than a lot of other people, Trey Woods included. Funny how he used to think Trey was someone important: he had to be or why would everybody treat him like he was. *What an idiot,* Breck thought now. Trey was nothing but a tempermental peacock.

Confusion had his brows knitting when his thoughts shifted to Nicole. She'd apologized. Just recalling the warm touch of her fingers on his arm sent a fiery tremor through his system, as if she'd never touched him before, and yet that was a laugh. They'd shared sweat and breath, but nothing had shocked his body like the light feel of her hand after that apology. It didn't mean anything, he told himself, shaking off the warm swirl tearing through him. She'd only been making a point.

The faint scent of cigarette smoke pulled Breck from his thoughts. He was home. He looked up at his bedroom window and readied to hoist himself up. His heart dropped to his knees. There, instead of the ill-fitting plywood, was a piece of wood that had been nailed perfectly into place. He blinked at it in disbelief.

Panic clutched his chest. He turned to flee but saw the dark shadow lunge at him too late. Breathing, heavy and full of rage, filled the silent night air. He knew the grip that wrapped like a grizzly, one arm around his abdomen, the other around his neck, nearly choking him.

His father had been waiting.

Instinct kicked in. His fists pummeled as hard and fast as they could against the steel of his father's trunk and neck. His legs pounded and jabbed. He always fought back. With each bloody fight, he held onto hope that he would come out victorious, even if past odds whispered defeat was inevitable. But his father's sheer size was more powerful than his humiliation and need for survival could overcome and his best efforts began to wane there in the dark silence.

Before he could land another punch, he was twisted around, held by the hair, and hit in the stomach with what felt like a wrecking ball in full swing. Breath vanished. Breck looked up, saw black sky. Stars spinning. Then the blackness swallowed everything up.

*　*　*

The slap woke him. Sharp, like hot ice across his face. Breck opened his eyes. His father was just inches away, cigarette dripping from his mouth.

"Wake up, Breckie-boy."

Breck knew all ready; he felt the steel of the cuffs around his wrists, cuffs that had him locked prisoner just for this. He struggled to sit up but the muscles in his abdomen screamed, and he fell back on his manacled hands. His father was squatted next to him, cigarette dangling, ash sprinkling onto Breck's bare stomach.

"Thought you'd have some fun tonight?" Rob sucked in long on the cigarette. His other hand held a bottle of Coors. He tilted the amber liquid back into his mouth, lips glistening, twitching into a grin.

"Where'd you go?" Rob slapped him. Before Breck could answer, he slapped him again, until Breck was stunned into a daze. "I asked you something!"

It was easy to hate his father for what he was doing. Tonight, humiliation stung like the wounds. Still, Breck didn't say anything.

Rob sat back on snarling laugh, and Breck rolled to his side. Breathing heavily, he pinched his eyes tight. The reality of what his own flesh and blood would inflict was unbearable. Already his mind raced with images of escape he hoped would block out the heinous acts, even though escape was impossible.

"Wherever you went, you won't be goin' again."

Breck kept his face averted. "You can't stop me." A thread of pleasure tugged inside of him for defending himself, even if it would only cause more

Noon - Katherine Warwick

trouble.

"It's a good thing I fixed that window, isn't it?" When his father stood, Breck jerked reflexively. He held his breath until his father left the room.

Breck's breathing didn't slow. He rose to his knees, eyes darting for a way out. With his hands locked behind his back, balance was precarious, but he lifted to his feet stumbling over the corner of the mattress.

The trailer trembled with his father's steps and Breck looked toward the door. He froze. His heart tumbled to his feet. His father held his backpack in one hand, the shoes in the other.

"What are these?" Rob demanded.

Breck's eyes widened and he stumbled back, in vain hopes he could keep what he knew would follow from happening. He'd hidden the backpack after school like he always did; stuck it behind the file cabinets in the closet. And now, there stood his father, the dance shoes hanging from his hands like an animal ready to have its throat slit.

Rob took a step toward him. Dropping the backpack, he shoved the shoes in Breck's face. "What are these?"

Breck couldn't speak; dreams, freedom – future, all lay in the palm of his father's hands as he held the soft black shoes.

Rob slammed them across Breck's face, and Breck toppled over, back to his knees on the mattress. "What are they for?"

As bad as it was, as despicable as it would get, there were things Breck wanted now: a future, accomplishment, friends. He couldn't look at his father with the pearly image of Mrs. Dubois that now flashed before him and he turned away. He could see her smiling, could see the love and warmth her eyes held just for him.

"Not going to tell me?" Rob bellowed. "You'll tell me." He tossed the shoes aside and stormed from the room.

The vision of Mrs. Dubois vanished, survival taking its place. Breck forced himself to his feet, frantically facing the window in hopes he could somehow climb out. When he saw that would be impossible, he whirled; ready to dart into whatever awaited him beyond his door, for a chance to run.

Rob returned with something long and black stretched between both hands. "Tell me."

Breck backed away as his father inched closer. Tripping on boxes, books, and the junk scattered on the floor, he made a desperate lunge around Rob for the door even though he knew he'd never make it.

He was shoved to the floor, and landed on his back, his shoulders aching, stomach crushed when his body was pinned beneath his father's body weight. When his father lifted with the long, black belt, Breck grimaced, and tried to turn himself over. The stinging lashes layered, over and over, on his shoulder, his side, across his chest. The icy-cold cuffs dug into his wrists, smashed under his back.

Lifting his hips, he bucked, writhing against the endless slicing. When his father shifted, and stood above him, Breck brought a knee up and shoved his foot at his father's abdomen. Rob deflected the kick with a sharp swing of his arm before starting in again.

Breck turned himself over and scrambled to his knees only to get a gouging boot in the middle of his back that sent him back to the floor. He heard screaming but wasn't sure if it was his, or if someone else somewhere was screaming too. The sound was in his head, hollowing and horrid, as the prickly jags ripped into his skin. He tried to breathe, but with each cut, air stalled in his chest. The cold floor sent an icy chill through his body, challenging the lashings that fired deep. He couldn't open his eyes anymore. His muscles fisted then wept with each slash of skin. Then the screaming stopped. Breck fixed his heavy gaze on the open door and listened to the chugging breath of his father, until there was nothing but black.

By Wednesday, Lois was worried. Breck hadn't shown up for lessons and Nicole hadn't seen him at school. Lois called the school herself to check his attendance, thinking maybe Nicole had just missed him, but the attendance office confirmed her fears; he'd not been to school at all week.

In the studio, she stood with Reuben and Nicole as the first hour of another practice dragged by. Nicole was angry, but Lois knew it was merely her way of covering up disappointment.

"I knew this would happen." Frustrated, Nicole set her hands on her

Noon - Katherine Warwick

hips, and stared at her frown in the mirror.

Lois' brows met with a crease. "He's been here every day for six and a half months. This isn't like him."

"How do you know he's not just flaking off?"

Lois shook her head. "That doesn't sound right."

"Mom." Nicole kept watch on her reflection as she turned. "I know you think you know him, but he's just like every other every teenage boy – flaky. He's probably at the skate park or something."

"Yes." Lois looked up, hopeful. "That is a possibility."

Reuben grabbed his keys. "Let's go."

"Nicole." Lois started toward the door, after Reuben. "Do you know where he lives?"

Nicole shrugged a shoulder. She knew. Tiffany and Annie had driven her by once, in a night of girlish curiosity. "Maybe in that trailer park down by the post office. But I don't know for sure." Disappointment fingered its way to her heart even thinking that Breck might leave her someday. "You're going *now*?"

Her mother was already out the door. "Of course, he may be in trouble."

Nicole squelched the alarm that her mother's suggestion created inside of her. With the door open, the afternoon sun broke in like a beam of golden hope across the floor. Nicole turned back to her reflection and tried not to see the concern in her face. She wanted to think dance mattered to Breck, that their partnership mattered. Deep down, she hoped he cared about her. The studio door silently closed, and the light disappeared.

*   *   *

Lois' heart hung in that place where mothers' hearts often hang – on the guillotine of faith. She wanted to pull into the skate park and see Breck's mop of dark hair as he flew off the pipes. But the place was empty.

They drove to the trailer park in silence thick with worry. She looked over at Reuben. "Thank you."

Reuben's lip curved up just enough to comfort, his green eyes softened with understanding.

The tires of the black Jetta crackled over the rocks and gravel as they pulled into the trailer park. The sun had almost disappeared behind the low western mountains and now the sky looked like it was on fire, glassy blue with flames of orange reaching across the darkness toward the east.

Reuben and Lois got out of the car and knocked on a few doors, each time, Lois asked about Breck. A blonde woman with fat pink rollers in her hair lived in the last trailer. With a smoker's cackle she pointed in the direction of a mobile home that looked like it belonged in a junkyard. Lois' heart sunk. Plants had been abandoned, leaving behind crisp, brown skeletons. Windblown trash clung to anything and everything as if in a vain attempt to outrun the inevitable. The forsaken sight of the decaying home caused Lois' eyes to fill with tears. Even outside, she caught the stale scent of cigarette smoke.

Reuben's gaze fixed on the door. "Maybe you'd better let me find out what's going on."

Lois shook her head. Though her heart pounded, she was determined. Deeply in tune with that special sense only a mother was gifted with, she knew when something wasn't right, and that feeling was in the very air around them, cold and biting to the bone.

After knocking, they waited in silence. Leaves of the giant trees overhead danced and whispered in the wind. Reuben knocked again and the trailer trembled with the thud of footsteps. The door whipped open.

Rob Noon filled the doorframe, all muscle and tattoos – his head shaved to a military-length buzz. He wore a dull white tee shirt and well-worn jeans with cowboy boots. The muscles in his forearms tensed when he looked at Reuben.

"Excuse me," Lois began. "Are you Mr. Noon?"

Rob's dark eyes didn't leave Reuben even to glance at Lois politely. He opened the screen door as if he had to check for himself, the color of Reuben's skin. The stench of smoke followed him. "What do you want?"

"We're looking for Breck," Reuben said.

It was then Rob looked at Lois, who smiled. "I'm Lois Dubois." She extended her hand but Rob just glared at it. "Is Breck here?"

"No."

"Do you know where we can find him?" Reuben asked.

Rob took a step down from the trailer door. "If I did, I wouldn't tell you."

"We haven't seen him for a few days, I was worried about him." Lois lifted to her toes for a peek over the big man's shoulder, but saw nothing.

"He's fine."

Lois cleared her throat, the feeling of urgency pressing against her heart. "Mr. Noon, would you tell him to call me when you see him? Please."

He looked her up and down with a scathing glower. "Why? Who are you?"

"I'm Lois Dubois, and Breck works for me."

Rob's eyes widened for a moment before slitting. "Works?"

Again, Lois tried to catch a glimpse over Rob's shoulder into the darkness of the trailer. This time she caught dim yellow light, some nearly shredded curtains over a window along the far wall, and the back of a brown chair.

Rob sneered. "Just what is he doing for you, lady?"

Lois's eyes opened wide. Reuben stepped closer, forcing Rob to face him. "Don't talk like that to her, please."

"You work for her too?" Rob asked and Reuben nodded once. "You like 'em all colors, don't cha, lady? All colors and ages."

"If you would just have your son call me." Lois worked to keep her voice from trembling. Something dark and greasy filled her insides, and she couldn't dislodge the frightening way the feeling hovered near her heart. "I would appreciate it, Mr. Noon."

"What exactly does he do for you?"

"He dances with my daughter."

"Dances?" Rob boomed, flushing deep red, his fists opened and closed at his sides."What do you mean, dances?"

"He's my daughter's dance partner." A pit opened in Lois' stomach. The words tumbled out. "He's very, very good, Mr. Noon He'll be a champion some day, that's why we want him to dance with Nicole.'

Rob blinked hard and fast, breathed faster, choking on vicious laughter. "My son don't dance, lady."

"I'm so sorry, I thought you knew."

"Well I know now and I'm telling you, my son isn't no dancer."

"If you'll just tell him that I came by, please."

Without saying another word, Lois backed toward the car. Wherever Breck was, she hoped he was safe from the raw anger vibrating from this man. She looked at the darkened windows of the trailer, grief causing her heart to skip a beat. Reuben opened the car door for her.

Rob leapt off of the porch and strode toward them, gravel dust kicking up at his feet and Reuben nudged Lois inside the car.

"You hear me? My son don't dance."

Reuben blocked Rob from Lois. "We're leaving."

"Good," Rob shouted. "Forget it lady. Whatever he did for you, he sure isn't doin' it any more."

Lois shut her door and looked up through the glass into the furious face of a stalking bear. A shiver shook her.

Reuben started the car and she looked back at the trailer, watching Breck's father lumber back up the steps to slam the door. Her heart gaped, torn and empty. Where was Breck?

Seven

Breck heard the familiar pattern of his father's footsteps from the other side of the locked door. The trailer trembled whenever he'd go to the kitchen and grab a beer, then trembled again as he went back to his chair.

The TV was on constantly, so loud it drowned out his pleas.

Having his hands cuffed made movement difficult. The room was piled with so much stuff he'd fallen over boxes and garbage more than once trying to keep his balance while he moved around. That first day he'd screamed threats thinking a neighbor – somebody – would hear him. He'd only gotten another bloodied face.

No matter what he mustered inside to fight with, it was never enough. The days were long and cold with a neglect that threatened to dismantle what precious bricks he had carefully erected in his vital need for self-preservation.

Before, he would find himself easily sucked into the nothingness of being a Noon. Hadn't cared what anybody else thought, hadn't had anyone to account to that mattered. The Dubois' mattered now. Reuben, and the fragile friendships his heart clung to all mattered enough for him to spend the long days thinking of them, rather than the circumstance in which he was now a prisoner.

Fatigue drained him. He spent time trying to sleep, but his dreams were tormented, unreal. He saw his mother. Had glimpses of childhood – visions of a future he was desperate to avoid.

The Dubois' were in his last dream. He'd heard Lois' voice clearly, the loving tone reaching through the clouded vision like a hand from heaven.

But the voices had faded and he lay there, going in and out of sleep, body twitching from every sound, readying for the next assault. In his mind he heard music from rehearsal; saw Nicole and Reuben standing in front of the mirrors. Mrs. Dubois sitting in her chair, the same one she always sat in when she watched them rehearse. He'd fixated on the image of her smile that first day of seclusion so the splinters of pain in his wrists, the dull heat from the lashes on his chest and back, would fade.

Her smile was there again, twinkling, comforting, as Breck drifted in and out of sleep. So caught up in the hallucination, he didn't hear the door open.

"You got something to tell me?" Rob squatted down and pulled Breck's hair off his face, clutching it in his fist. "Those shoes," he hissed. Stale cigarette breath had Breck turning his head away. Rob yanked it back. That was when Breck caught sight of something shiny in his father's hand.

He couldn't see what it was; his eyes weren't focusing as fast as he wanted. He heard a loud buzzing sound, and then the buzz scraped at his head.

At first he jerked away but Rob pulled him back. "You're not enough like your old man." Rob pushed long, sheering strokes across Breck's head. Sable curls fell to the mattress in soft silence. "Dancing? You're messed up in the head, kid."

After all of Breck's hair was gone and only a close hedge of brown crowned his head, Rob turned off the shaver and sat back. Breck felt the cold air on his neck and scalp with his hair gone.

"A man's man doesn't dance," he said finally. "My boy don't dance."

"Mom danced!"

Rob sent a fist across his jaw. "Shut up!"

The blow cracked through Breck's head, and sent him back to the floor in a weak heap. It didn't matter now. Breck knew he was going to die there, so he wouldn't go with his mouth shut.

"You like to do it?" Rob's eyes glowed red with fury. "Do you?"

Breck half-nodded, emotion welling in his throat for something he'd come to love that he doubted he'd ever be able to do again. His friends, the music – the joy, all would be taken away from him, and the loss was like taking another lash, this one on his heart.

"What else do you do for the nice lady, huh?" Breck's eyes shot open and Rob smiled. "Yeah, she came here looking for you."

Struggling to sit up, Breck was overcome by waves of helplessness thinking of Mrs. Dubois being so close. He needed to get out, to warn her to stay away. But he could only lay there, limbs heavy, breath ragged.

"She says she's been paying you to dance, but I think she's paying you to do more than that."

Even with nothing in his stomach, nausea rolled in Breck's belly. The idea was so disrespectful and demeaning of Mrs. Dubois and who she was, he wanted to lunge at his father and strangle him. Again, he wrestled with the cuffs, but his father shoved him back, and again the fresh cuts around his wrists opened deep.

"You ever talk, I'll pay that nice, pretty lady a little visit."

Rob sat, and pulled out his pack of cigarettes, tapping one into his palm as if he were campside. He stuffed the box back in his pocket. "You're smarter than I thought." He eyed Breck, lit up and took his first puff. "Makin' money. Very smart. But I'm smart too. I figure, if she can make money off you, so can I." He sucked in long and held the smoke.

Another rush of fear slammed in to Breck. His father was capable of anything when it came to money. He wouldn't put it past the man to kill him so he could sell his organs and buy his next sixpack.

Smoke came out of Rob's mouth in a flat stream, like the tongue of a snake, Breck thought, wondering what his father had in mind.

Disappointment was a member of her family. It joined the Dubois' when she lost her first dance competition. She and her mother had vowed that would never happen again. That no matter what, Nicole Dubois would always place. They'd spent the last seven years ensuring that vow with endless hours of training and by finding and hiring the best.

They'd found Reuben and lost her father.

At first, Nicole thought it was just her father's demanding schedule that kept him from her performances and competitions. But with every audience he was never there. As her love for dance grew, her skill excelled along with it. She could only talk about this love with her mother, friends and other dancers. Her father never said a word. And if she and her mother were caught up in dance talk, he would quietly leave the room.

Her refusal to feel guilty was her way of protecting a tender heart. That her father decided her choices disappointed him was his problem, not hers.

As a new week approached and Nicole thought about starting over again, about breaking in a new partner, explaining Breck's flakiness to her friends, it was disappointment that was her real partner.

Forgetting Breck was harder than she thought it would be. She tried working out her frustration on the dance floor, sweating and pushing until she couldn't move another muscle. Reading only made her more miserable: her favorite books were romances. Not adept in the kitchen, she baked batch after batch of cookies, at first thinking she'd take them to Breck as some sort of peace offering – or an excuse to interrogate him. When batch after batch burned, she tossed them into the garbage and laughed at the irony of the situation.

Figuring she and Breck would run into each other at school, she couldn't wait to speak her mind. She spent the weekend mulling over various scenarios.

She'd see him at lunch, walk up to him in front of the entire student body. "You loser," she'd say, leaving him speechless and humiliated.

He'd be standing at his locker and she'd come up behind him, tap him on the shoulder and after he turned around, she'd go for the jugular. "My mother hates you and so do I."

Her favorite was seeing him on his rollerblades, going after him with her car, before pinning him against some wall until he squirmed like a bug and begged her to let him go.

In that deep, secret place in her heart, there was another scenario. The one she played over and over again.

"Nicole, I'm so sorry," he'd say. She'd have her back against the wall of the studio, her heart beating fast as she gazed up into his face.

"It's okay." Filled with forgiveness, she'd look deeply into his eyes.

"I was such a dweeb, a dork, an idiot." Then he'd lean in close. "A loser." She'd nod. "I know."

That wouldn't be the end of it, no, just the beginning. He'd look at her with those eyes like midnight until her insides were ready to burst. Then he'd say, "Forgive me?"

Nicole would nod and close her eyes. He'd kiss her and it would be the most wonderful thing in her life, even more – dare she even think – than winning a competition.

"Nic." Trey's whisper in her ear startled her back to reality. "Where were you, you looked like you were in la-la land."

"Don't do that." She slammed her locker shut.

Noon - Katherine Warwick

"We're going out for lunch," he said. They walked down the hall packed with seniors making a dash from the building.

Nicole looked for Breck, and heard Trey snicker. "Looking for loser?"

She shrugged. "He's missing a lot of school."

"Why do you care?""

"You're right," she said, shoving the hurt inside away. "Let's go."

Chris had the largest car, an older sky-blue Suburban, so Parker, Annie and Tiffany all piled in. Nicole was too distracted by her thoughts to notice that Trey was seated next to her, and that his arm was stretched out behind her, a move she would normally chastise him for.

The music was loud, the talking and laughing louder. They drove down Battle Creek Drive in the parade of other student-stuffed vehicles into downtown Pleasant Grove to see where the masses were hanging out for lunch.

A house under construction sat at the corner of Battle Creek and Sixth North, and since they were stopped in the traffic line up, Nicole glanced over. Her mouth dropped.

"Stop. Go back!" She leaned over the backseat, craning for another look at the construction site.

"Why?" Annie followed her gaze.

"Just do it."

Chris pulled a sharp U-turn so that the car sat right in front of the house under construction. It was being framed, and men hammered from rafters to floor, some perched like monkeys in a tree.

"Is that Breck?" Tiffany whispered.

Annie let out a gasp. "What happened to his hair?"

"He got sheered." Trey laughed.

Nicole jumped out of the car then stood for a moment. It took a moment for her knees not to shake, her pulse to stop skittering. Three weeks had passed since she'd seen him, and the pang of longing in her heart forced her to take a deep breath. He was lugging boxes from one spot to another, a tool belt strapped around his waist. Scruffy jeans and a ratty grey hoodie hung on his lean frame. His hair was gone.

Behind her, the windows of the car rolled down and everyone inside hung out, whispering. She strode across the dirt, kicking dust with every step as longing shifted to frustration.

"Noon," she yelled. He whipped a look at her over his shoulder and stopped before resting the box of tools against his bent knee.

"Where've you been?" she demanded, stopping so close she could smell the familiar musky scent of him. She had to lick her lips, steady her breath. Being this near him after the absence made her mouth go dry, and her lungs weren't taking in enough air.

The construction team didn't do anything more than slow. One worker stopped hammering so he could hear their conversation better. Another moved closer with his hammer and nails but kept his eyes averted.

Nicole heard the greetings her friends called to Breck from the car behind her, but she didn't turn around. Her attention was locked on his face. He looked over her shoulder at the car and jerked out a nod in hello before setting those blazing blue eyes back on her.

"I asked you a question," she repeated.

"I'm working." He started off across the site again.

"What did you do to your hair?" Though Nicole liked seeing his face, the round shape of his head, the sharp angles of his jaw, she couldn't dismiss how gaunt he looked.

He kept his gaze on the tools and set them down. Then he wiped at his forehead. Seeing the deep red-purple rings around his wrists, Nicole gasped and grabbed his hands, turning them. "What happened?" She thought maybe he'd tried to cut himself, but the rings went all around. "Let me see."

Snatching his hands free, Breck yanked down the sleeves of his hoodie, grabbed the tools, and started away from her, pulling his hammer out of his belt. "I have to get back to work."

"Work?" She grabbed hold of the hem of his hoodie, stopping him. "What about school?" When he didn't say anything, she tugged again. The hurt she'd carried inside and thought she'd bandaged, wept openly. "And what about my mom? I know you could care less about me, the team, Lola – but my mom loves you."

Suddenly he leaned close, his eyes pinning hers with fierce regret. "I'm sorry about your mom. But there's nothing I can do about it." They held the moment between them, locked in a silent battle Nicole was certain neither wanted to be engaged in. Then he pulled free and strode across the dirt.

"You're a jerk, Noon," she shouted so that everyone on the crew and everyone in the car heard. But no one saw the tears rushing in her eyes. She pulled her sunglasses out of her purse and pushed them on, then turned around with a determined swivel.

Back in the car, she slammed the door.

There was no point in turning around for one last look at Breck, though her shorn heart wanted for nothing more than that. When Trey's arm slid around her shoulders, she barely noticed. She strained for any sound of Breck. All she heard was the faint and lonely crack of hammers against wood.

Another rehearsal ended. Nicole could see that her mother was elsewhere, no doubt engrossed in thinking about their current debacle: that she was, once again, without a partner. She knew too well that her mother's mind was drifting to Breck. She'd been there without being there for days now, since Nicole had come home and told her she'd seen Breck working at the construction site.

Because they were finished, Reuben walked over and sat next to her mother, and the two started into a quiet conversation. On a heavy sigh, Nicole picked up her bag and left the studio. At least she'd not wallow in Breck's departure any longer. There were things that should be said, done.

It was only eight o'clock, but it was plenty dark outside. Dark enough not to be seen. Nicole threw her bag in the back of her car, started up the engine and drove. She was outside the trailer park in ten minutes, adrenaline pumping through her. She stared at the dull glow from behind the curtains of the trailer that Breck lived in.

So now what?

She turned off the engine and got out, determined to get to the bottom of his abandonment.

She plunged her hands into her pink hoodie so she'd be warmer, but it didn't help. She was still in her dance pants and sleeveless tee, and they weren't doing much to keep the nip of autumn away.

Noon - Katherine Warwick

A crackle somewhere in the distance had her turning around. Halloween streamers decorating the trailer across the drive were blowing in the wind. This place is creepy, she thought, shuddering. I wouldn't want to be down here tomorrow night. She was glad she was going to a Halloween party and felt bad for anybody who had to go trick-or-treating in a place as genuinely horrifying as this.

Tiptoeing around the perimeter of the trailer, she saw only one light on in the room where the TV blared. She jumped up, trying to see under the hem of the ratty curtain, but couldn't see anything.

When she heard another crackle behind her, she figured it was just the crepe paper streamers and continued on around to the other end of the building. When she came around the corner, she noticed a shadow standing in the dark entrance of the park. For a moment she froze, hoping she hadn't been seen. Then, the shadow was gone. Her heart sped in her chest. Figuring it was a good time to head back to her car, she quickly crept in that direction but two hands gripped her shoulders and spun her around.

"Nic?"

She looked up into Breck's face. Pale, his cheeks sunken and drawn, his midnight eyes flashed with pleasure at seeing her. He wore a heavy dark coat and had his backpack over one shoulder.

"You scared me." She sucked in a missed breath. "Where've you been?"

"Working. What are you doing out? You should get home."

Embarrassed now, she smoothed her hair into place, meeting his gaze with the determination she'd brought with her. "I came to talk to you."

He glanced at the trailer then back at her. "Go on. Get out of here."

"First tell me why you ditched us, Noon."

His expression was as hollow as his cheeks, and underneath the moonlight's lacy shadow of towering trees, she couldn't ignore the concern growing inside of her. He looked tired. It didn't help that his shorn hair made him look like he'd either been at boot camp or concentration camp.

"I told you, I have to work."

"Why aren't you going to school?"

He dipped his head. "It's none of your business. Now go on. Get home."

"Your dad doesn't care if you ditch?" She looked over at the lights in the window. Breck snickered. "But hasn't school called? Isn't it against the law?"

What happens in my house is against the law, Breck thought and looked at her hard. The sight of her was still like a dream, and he couldn't look away. The powdery perfume she wore softly snuck into his senses. She'd been dancing, that much he could tell from the way she was dressed. More than anything he wanted to drop his backpack and pull her against him, feel her body move in harmony with his. The absence of that from his life had created a deep craving for the music, the steps. For her.

But it was over, and he had to accept that. Her life was set up on a hillside, surrounded by orchards and protective fences. She drove a Mercedes, slept in a bed, in a room that hadn't been used as a bathroom or for other atrocities.

"You better go," he told her again.

"No." She lifted her chin. "I want you to tell me why you stopped. You owe me at least that."

When the door opened, Breck stared wide-eyed into the lamplight that fell like a carpet out onto the lawn and dirt. Nicole turned, saw that a giant of a man filled the doorway, blocking the stream of light.

Rob opened the screen door. "I thought I told you no visitors."

"I'm coming in." Breck started toward the trailer.

Rob's stare froze on Breck's face. "Then get inside. And you," he looked over Breck's shoulder at Nicole, "you better get on home. You never know what could befall a pretty little thing like you in a neighborhood like this."

"Go." Breck faced her, walking backwards toward the trailer.

Rob hacked out a high-pitched laugh. "Yeah, run along home or the big bad wolf will eatcha."

There was something bad in the air; it sunk deep to Nicole's bones. So creepy, she couldn't form the words to say goodbye, could hardly make her legs move and take her to the car. Fixed on the rundown trailer, on the way Breck kept his head lowered as he passed through the door and squeezed by the big man, Nicole stumbled over the dirt and rocks under her feet.

She felt safe once she was inside the car, and turned on the engine. But she couldn't take her eyes off Breck who disappeared inside the trailer followed by his father. The door slammed after them. Her body ached with something she didn't understand but knew – something was wrong.

◎ 67 ◎

The door shut and Breck kept a steady walk to the back of the trailer. He closed his eyes for a moment, hoping that nothing would slam into him, but his body was tight and ready.

He felt his backpack ripped from his shoulder and had but a second to swing around before his father's fist caught him across the jaw, sending him against the wall of the dark hallway.

The back of Rob's hand stung his cheek then, followed by a hard shove, and Breck stumbled. In his mind he saw Nicole, and something deep inside of him snapped. He lunged with both hands out. The advance was met with Rob's elbow, jabbed sharply into his throat, and he was thrust backward.

"You wanna fight me?" Rob punched at Breck's jaw again with a right fist. "Come on, kid. I wanna see what you got."

Breck swung, arms wound up like the blades of a helicopter. Flesh, bone, and the wet of mouth and eye caught on his fists. Then he heard the clinking of cuffs as Rob pulled the glittering manacles out of his pocket. A vibrating panic shot through him.

"You're a coward to cuff me," he shot out.

Rob's brows formed one mean line across his forehead. The left side of his lip curled.

"Let me fight," Breck panted.

His father let out what Breck thought was a growl of pleasure, but he didn't drop the cuffs. Breck lunged again. Words were spoken through angry hands and enraged fists. Rob laughed at Breck's attempts, egging him on by backing away and throwing out punches that merely grazed enough to enrage.

Then he dangled the cuffs.

The sight had Breck more incensed and determined, and he swung a shocking punch at his father's head, landing knuckles across his brow. Momentarily stunned, Rob froze. Then he grinned, and dangled the cuffs again, swinging them in Breck's face. "Time for lock up."

Breck turned to dart down the hall but his father snagged the collar of his heavy coat and pulled him back. Infuriated at the resistance, Rob jabbed his elbow into the side of Breck's neck and shoulder blade, driving him to his knees.

Pain speared from Breck's neck down his spine, and his knees gave. Blinking hard, in that moment of daze, Breck felt his right arm yanked in front, a single link snapped into place. Then his left arm was brought around. Rob pinned him against the wall with his weight, and snapped on the other cuff before ripping him up so they stood nose to nose. The two stared at each other.

"You think you can out run me, kid?" The rancid hiss of his father's breath in his face turned Breck's stomach.

He couldn't spend another night like this.

Breck took his cuffed hands and reached for his father's crotch, locking on with a grip that had Rob's eyes shooting wide open, his mouth dropping along with his hands. A groan squeaked from his throat as he took a necessary step back. Breck gave a hard thrust and it sent Rob back, doubled over in agony.

Breck shot off toward the living room.

Staggering to his feet, hands cupping his crotch, Rob took a flying leap and growled, tackling Breck's knees, sending them both flat on their stomachs. Breck flipped over and squared a powerful jab across his father's nose with his foot before crawling out of reach. He stood, gasping for breath. Fear shifted to steel when he saw the blood shooting out of his father's nose like a geyser.

Rob's eyes filled with rage. Seething, he came after Breck on all fours.

His heart thudding in his chest, Breck tried not to look at the madness on his father's face. He backed toward the front door, tripping on a rug and nearly falling.

"Get back here!" Rob pushed himself up, his hand on his nose where blood gushed.

But Breck was already at the door, working it with slippery, linked hands. Without looking back, he yanked it open. Tumbling down the stairs, he flew across the front yard and out toward the safety of the street.

Eight

He was out.

The thrill of freedom, the joy of victory pushed every footstep.

He had to stay in the darkness, the cover of night his only ally as he dipped in and out of yards and shadows, behind fences and trees so as to not be seen. His breath skipped as he leapt over the railroad tracks.

Breck looked back, fear driving the need to know if his father was behind him. Seeing nothing, he almost buckled with relief, nearly fell to a stop on the hard asphalt and kissed the ground, but he was still too close to home.

Crouching low, ducking nimbly, he stayed on side streets, dropping behind posts or hedges if he saw a car or a pedestrian.

After he crossed Main Street, he headed up Battle Creek Drive. Slowing, he gasped. Part of him wanted to scream with elation. Part of him wished he could take the cuffs still linking his hands and send them across his father's face in one last gesture of victory.

Panting, circling, he was alone on the long stretch of street with the exception of the occasional car that drove by. Fatigue devoured every muscle, fought with his lungs for air. The last few weeks of malnourishment caught up with him, and now his legs wobbled.

I can't stop.

One look at the cuffs and icy humiliation shot down his back. His tongue touched his lower lip – and tasted blood. The rest of him ached, a dull, familiar ache he knew would dissipate with time. Skin wounds healed, even if they left snowy scars.

He was across the street from the high school now and in desperate need of rest so he slowed. A house with a low, brick wall surrounding it looked inviting. Lights were on and all of the curtains were drawn, so Breck squatted low and crawled behind the wall, laying flat on his back on the cold, crisp grass.

Breath came in and out, fast and dry. He needed water. He closed his eyes for a moment. He'd only need a moment, he told himself. He felt sure his father wouldn't find him, even if he was chasing him.

He remembered the last time he'd run. He'd been younger then, more stupid. The consequences had never occurred to him – just the need to survive. His father had been faster, and had caught him on foot. He'd gotten a horrible beating that night, one that had left his back so shredded he'd been miserable for days while it healed.

When Breck opened his eyes again, he didn't know how much time he'd spent there, and he rolled onto his side. Grass crunched beneath his body weight. The lights that had been on in the house were now off.

Pulling himself up, he struggled for balance as well as strength. Lights were off at the high school, giving an eerily dark emptiness to something normally bustling with sound and energy. Things dark and eerie weren't foreign to Breck, and for a moment he thought about finding a corner somewhere at the school and staying there, but he couldn't take the risk of falling asleep and being discovered in the morning. Shivering, the way his breath crystallized when he exhaled warned him to keep going.

He trudged up Battle Creek Drive, wearily ducking under cover when a lone car passed. Finally, he found himself at the bottom of the long driveway with heavy black wrought-iron gates that were locked shut.

Grabbing the arrowed-spikes with both hands, he paused for a moment, like a prisoner with only cell bars between him and his freedom. He didn't know if he had the energy to climb, and for a moment, rested his head against the cold iron gate. After a deep breath, he followed the perimeter of the property for a while, hoping there was a break in the fencing. There wasn't.

Looking at the black gate now in front of him, he clutched the rods again. Trying to balance and lift himself without the freedom to use his hands independently forced him to use his neck, the curve of his chin, shoulder and elbows. Cold iron dug, pierced and bruised, but determination numbed the pain until he could twist his arms in such a way that he finally thrust his torso and legs over the top. He toppled onto the asphalt on the other side. His head hit the pavement with a thud, but the hood of his coat took the brunt of the fall. He blinked back stinging tears.

The stars were out. In the black silence, his breath clouded his view of the heavens. Too weak to move, he lay there and closed his eyes, feeling the first

Noon - Katherine Warwick

flickering of peace in a long time.

He was safe.

Garren Dubois checked his watch again. It was five-thirty, and he had to be at the hospital by six-fifteen for a surgery at eight. He was in the kitchen alone, toasting two English muffins, pouring some orange juice and trying to make a dent in the personal mail he'd not had a chance to look at all week.

Lois took care of the household things, but when something came addressed to Dr. Garren Dubois, she left it stacked neatly on the desk in his office. The stack had grown to a pile that needed his attention now.

"Morning, Dad." Nicole came in yawning. Still dressed in her pajamas, she rubbed her face and made her way to the refrigerator. She spotted the juice. "Can I?"

Garren didn't look up from the letter he was ripping open. "Sure."

Nicole poured herself a glass and looked out the kitchen window to the darkness of the backyard. "You know, it could be six at night, instead of six in the morning," she said. "It looks exactly the same out there."

Garren crushed the envelope and letter he'd just read and picked up the next letter waiting.

Nicole glanced at her father. He looked so serious. He always looked serious. It really could be nighttime, she thought now, because Dad looks tired already and the day hasn't even started.

She kept part of her attention on him as she moved to the pantry and scoured it for cereal. He was still opening and reading letters. Clearing her throat, she moved the box of cereal she'd chosen onto the counter and then went to get a bowl.

In the reflection of the glass cupboards, she watched him, his nose in the pile of mail. Again she cleared her throat, before taking her bowl to the counter where he stood. She poured her cereal.

"Oops, milk." She snuck behind him to retrieve the milk from the refrigerator, bumping into his back. "Sorry."

"Hmm," he said.

Pulling the bar stool closer, she sat and began to eat. The crunching seemed loud, but she could see it wasn't affecting her dad's concentration any. She cleared her throat again and he looked at her.

"You have allergies?" he asked.

For the moment that his eyes held hers, she actually felt butterflies. "No, why?"

He looked at the next letter in his fingers. "You're clearing your throat a lot, might be sinus drainage."

It wasn't. She looked into her bowl and chewed as quietly as she could.

"I hardly slept last night." Her mother shuffled in, still in her long quilted robe, hair smashed on one side, fluffy on the other from sleep.

"Why?" Nicole asked. She knew her father wouldn't.

Lois moseyed over to Nicole and kissed her on the head. "I was having mixed up, bizarre dreams."

Her dad was almost through the pile. "Dreams about what?" she asked.

Fully awake now, Lois glanced at Garren. "Oh nothing – the usual."

Nicole knew what that meant. Her mother had told her she'd been having dark dreams about Breck lately. She'd been more than willing to share the specifics, since they only had each other to talk the situation over with. Scary dreams. The kind mothers don't like to have about their children.

"But he's not your child," Nicole had told her.

Lois had only gazed quietly at her and sighed, and Nicole knew then that blood had very little to do with love.

Nicole looked at her father. "Your toast is up," she told him, noting the cold English Muffins had popped some time ago.

Garren took the leftover mail, tossed it in the trash and plucked the two halves of English muffin out of the toaster, then searched for the butter. "Where's the butter?" He was still looking for it when Lois handed it to him.

After buttering, he took a bite and headed for the counter next to the back door where he gathered his briefcase and coat. He tapped the alarm code in the keypad, waited for the beep, then paused by the door, juggling his briefcase with his muffins so he could open it. The door shut after him.

Nicole glanced at her mother. The look of emptiness and pure neglect was more than she could take. She knew the kind of day her mother would

Noon - Katherine Warwick

have in the house all by herself.

Nicole took a deep breath, rose, and carried her bowl to the sink. "I'm gonna go get ready," she said softly. Her mother didn't make a sound when she left the kitchen, but Nicole looked back anyway.

Lois sat at the counter, arms folded; chin resting on her linked hands, staring out the kitchen window into the dark backyard. Nicole wondered if she saw it too; that it could be six in the morning or six in the evening and you couldn't tell the difference.

The silver Mercedes rumbled slowly down the driveway. Garren knew deer often made their way to the lower benches of the mountains to forage. He pulled out the remote that would open the electric gates at the end of the drive and saw something lying just inside.

Somebody had dropped garbage bags inside the fence as a joke, he thought for a moment. Kids were always doing things like that; the two imposing gates seemed to beg for mischief. But as he pulled the car closer, he saw that it was body. Slamming on the brakes, he threw the car into park. It idled loudly as he got out and ran to the form.

Gently he turned the body to face him. The young man couldn't be much older than Nicole, Garren thought. Immediately Garren felt for a pulse at the boy's neck. Warm skin under the collar eased Garren's heart enough that he could think clearly. The faint pulse had him acting fast.

Pulling his cell phone out, he dialed nine-one-one, then he dialed the house. "Lois, there's a boy here. He's inside the gate."

"What?"

"I've called nine-one-one. I just didn't want you to be alarmed when you heard them pull up." Clicking the phone off, he stuck it back in his pocket.

The boy's face was ashen, blue around the eyes and lips. Garren wondered how long he had been outside. When his eyes fluttered open, Garren leaned over him.

"Can you tell me your name?"

"Breck." The name barely scraped from the boy's lips.

Garren's brows knit. "Do you know where you are?"

"At the Dubois'"

"How did you get here?"

"I climbed the fence."

"Does it hurt anywhere?"

Breck closed his eyes, swallowed, and shook his head.

"I've called nine-one-one," Garren said. "Can you sit up?"

When Breck's eyes opened wide, they were blood-shot, the whites creamy. "No. No nine-one-one," he begged.

"You may have hypothermia, internal injuries. You need to be seen."

Breck struggled to sit up, and that's when Garren realized why he couldn't. Pulling Breck to a seated position, Garren's eyes locked on the cuffs. Shock yanked his anger to attention.

"Please, no. You're a doctor, you can help me."

There was such fear and pleading in the boy's face, such desperation tearing his voice, Garren's anger shifted to fury. His stunned gaze darted from the shiny cuffs to Breck's trembling lips and heavy-lidded eyes. Sirens sliced through the cold morning air. "You need medical attention," he repeated. "Are you Breck Noon?"

Breck gave a nod. "Please. I'll be okay. I'm not hurt. Just – just cold."

Garren helped him stand. "Let's get you in my car and let me take you up to the house. Can you do that?"

Breck nodded, and with Garren's help, stood, weakly leaning on Garren's shoulder as he led him to the car. After he was inside, Garren shut the door and jogged around to the driver's side when a red and white search and rescue truck pulled up. Two paramedics jumped out. The sun was just peeking up over the eastern mountains, but the inside of the car was dark enough to hide.

Hiding the boy went against everything Garren knew to be the protocol of medicine, but the hollow, frightened look in Breck's eyes had him accommodating the plea.

"False alarm, fellas," he told the eager medics.

"You sure?"

"Thought I saw a body when I pulled up here by the gate, turned out to be a doe and her fawn resting." It could have happened; he rationalized. He had one leg in the car. The jittering that started to hum inside of him, that need to help, was a familiar feeling. The paramedics seemed satisfied but not too eager to move on. "Now if you'll excuse me, I'm late for surgery, and forgot something up at the house."

"You a doc?" Garren nodded. "You at A.F. Hospital?"

"No, Utah Valley."

"I got a brother-in-law that works in emergency, Kyle Markham. Know him?"

"Ah, no." Garren slid in and shut the door, then backed the car up the driveway. "You better not be pulling some prank, Breck—"

"I'm not, Mr. Dubois, I'm not." Breck's head rolled from side to side against the back of the seat. "I'm sorry, I…" His voice was worn to shreds from the cold and he decided he was too tired to speak. He closed his eyes. He wished he wasn't there, wished Lois and Nicole weren't going to see him like this.

"I'm sleep deprived to even consider this." Garren watched Breck through the rear view mirror, watched his eyes, his breathing.

Breck shivered convulsively, his teeth rattled like a jar of shaken beads. He wanted to die, to disappear so no one would see him.

"We have to get you inside and warm." Garren parked and turned off the engine.

Lois and Nicole were standing outside, their robes clutched tight around them, breath pluming out like steam. The sun crested the top of the mountain, and its blue-orange rays streamed down into the valley, coloring every surface to lavender.

Garren jumped out of the car and pulled the door open.

Lois gasped when she saw the dark, shaved head swing back. "It's Breck." She clutched her mouth with both hands, her face twisted into shock.

Nicole's stomach churned when her father pulled Breck out of the back seat and his cuffed hands fell forward. For a moment, she couldn't move.

"Get the door," Garren barked. Nicole darted for the door, and held it open, her eyes fixed on Breck.

Wrapping his arms around Breck in support, Garren eased him along. "Can you make it a little further?"

Breck nodded.

"Lois, warm some blankets in the dryer. Nicole, turn down the bed in your brother's bedroom."

Both Lois and Nicole disappeared. Garren helped Breck inside and through the kitchen to the back stairs. He thought he'd seen every kind of wound a body could have, but the sight of those raw, bloody wrists choked his throat. He'd bet his career there were deeper injuries wounding this body. His heart took a punch, like it always did, when he witnessed injustice.

"How are you doing? You doing okay, Breck?"

Breck barely nodded. "Yeah."

They took each step one at a time until they reached the landing.

With the bed turned down and ready, Garren sat Breck on the edge of the mattress. For the first time, his physician's eye scanned the boy from head to toe. "Get my extra bag, Nic. It's in the coat closet." Nicole left just as Lois came in, her face tight with worry.

"The blankets are in the dryer. They'll need some time to warm." She stood next to Garren.

"This coat saved your life, Breck," Garren said. He looked at Lois briefly and lowered his voice. "Go get the bolt cutters." Lois nodded, then slid silently out. "I have only one condition for helping you." Garren waited for Breck's eyes to meet his. The struggle going on behind the boy's face, in his hopeless eyes, forced Garren to take a deep breath. "I want you to tell me everything, and then trust me to make the best decision from there."

Their eyes locked. Finally, Breck nodded. "Can I lie down?"

"Of course." Garren helped ease him back on the bed and looked at his face. There was a lump the size of a golf ball on the side of it. The lower lip was swollen and cut. It looked like he'd been struck across the jaw where some blue was peaking. Garren couldn't get the coat off, and because he couldn't, he examined Breck's wrists. He swallowed the lump in his throat; it wasn't the first time those wrists had been cuffed.

Lois returned with the cutters and a pile of warm blankets. "Here." The word warbled with emotion.

"Let's take care of these." Garren reached for the bolt cutters and gently lifted Breck's hands.

Nicole's fingers wrapped tight around the black bag when she walked back in the room. The sight stunned her again, and she stood unable to move. Her father was gently lifting Breck's two cuffed wrists.

She was sure her heart stopped. Breathing was near to impossible; her throat was closed, choking on both bile and tears.

"I'm going to get these off now, all right?" Her father's soft voice would have comforted her, had her eyes not been glued to the limp wrists, crusted with blood. He held the cutters poised and ready, and waited for Breck to respond. Breck nodded but then closed his eyes. Garren snapped the cuffs in the center and they separated. Breck brought his hands out in front of him. After a long blink, he closed his eyes again. Cautiously Garren removed each cuff so Breck's wrists were bare.

Snatching his black bag from Nicole's frozen hands, Garren retrieved some clear antibiotic wash and cotton pads and carefully began cleaning each wrist. He slid a look to Lois, then to Nicole, continuing to work in silence.

"Now, let's get this coat off." Garren and Lois helped sit him up, and Garren removed the coat.

Nicole still hadn't moved, transfixed on the sight before her. Her mother crossed to her, took her arm gently, and led her from the room, closing the door behind them.

Her own fear and horror was reflected in her mother's eyes. "He's probably hungry, Nicky."

With a nod, Nicole headed downstairs.

*   *   *

She reached for the banister, needing to steady herself. It seemed to be a dream, a nightmare – something unbelievable and unreal. She'd never seen skin that gray, eyes that hollow, injuries colored fresh with the black ink of blood.

Without thinking, she wandered the halls on the main floor, looking at the elegant paintings that hung on the walls, feeling the soft carpet – like cotton under her feet. The halls were toasty, the house smelled like cinnamon and fresh bread. She was safe. She was home.

But she couldn't get warm.

Noon - Katherine Warwick

Not knowing what Breck liked or what would please her father, she grabbed two slices of bread and some milk and headed back up the stairs. She couldn't stop seeing Breck's grey skin, the blue around his eyes and mouth. He looked frighteningly close to death.

But he'd talked, she'd heard him. He'd opened his eyes. She'd seen the blue of them, though they looked washed white and hazy.

She stopped at the top of the stairs and pressed her eyes closed tight. Last night – it came back to her in dark, shadowy images. Her heart pulled recalling the conversation she'd had with Breck outside of his trailer. Breck had been so adamant about her leaving, and she'd been stubborn and stayed. Breck's father had been so awful; she'd felt the black evil, known there was trouble, that things were bad.

She should have done something.

Forcing herself back into the bedroom, it was hard to look at him and think she might have been the cause of the argument that brought on his injuries and suffering.

She found her mother sitting at the head of the bed in a chair, her father at the foot. Both were silent.

Her mother gently petted Breck's hand, her face alight with the joy of caring for someone. Nicole had seen that same look in her mother whenever she'd been sick or unhappy, crying over a broken heart or a disappointment.

Garren looked at her, then at what she'd brought. "Just set them over there. Thank you, Nicole." He so rarely spoke her name, she stopped. Blinking fast, she'd not allow her father to catch the tears springing into her eyes. Breck looked better, more color blushed his face and the bluing around his lips and eyes was gone. "How is he?"

"He's not shaking anymore," Lois whispered.

Her father's trained eyes were focused on Breck's face. "He needs to rest. But before I let him, I want to examine him." He looked at Lois. "What about his family?"

Lois glanced at Nicole, then back at Garren. "He has a father."

Breck opened his eyes. "No."

Garren sighed. Looking at his watch, he slid off the side of the bed and stood. "I'm canceling today." His heavy gaze still on Breck, he pulled out his cell phone and dialed. Then he left the room, his voice a whisper in the hallway.

Nicole moved closer to the bed. "Does Dad think he'll be all right?"

"Dad will do his best." Lois moved to where Garren had been, keeping her hand on Breck's. "And we'll make sure of it."

"Mrs. Dubois," Breck barely rasped a sound out and Lois leaned close. "Don't let—my dad can't know where I am."

She nodded, her lips pinched tight. "We'll take care of things. You just rest."

Breck looked at Nicole, eyes darkened with shame and fear. She knew he wanted to be anywhere but there. The pain that shifted across his face tore her heart open. She kept her gaze steadily on his, hoping he would know that he could trust her. She gave him a smile and then his lashes fluttered shut.

Even lying there, safe in her home, his face showed no sign of peace. His dark lashes pinched feirce and distraught against ashen cheeks. His mouth was a solid line of worry and a small crease ran between his brows.

Nicole looked at her mother, needing answers.

"Everything will be all right." Her mother's voice was the soft tone of unconditional love. She patted his arm, and left her hand there.

Nine

Growing up in Pleasant Grove, Breck had often pondered the name. The area nestled at the base of Utah's most majestic mountain, Timpanogos, was dense with trees, pioneer-era houses, and its own turn-of-the-century downtown. Life had been pleasant enough while his mother was alive, but after the accident and her death, there had been very little about life Breck thought was worth getting up for each day.

Now, sitting in the back of Garren Dubois' car, he looked out tinted windows. Things were different, or at least he hoped they would be. Mr. and Mrs. Dubois said they were going to make them different.

Just last night he'd run up this street, exhausted and afraid. Now, he was cruising down it in a heated, luxury car.

No one spoke as they pulled into the drive of the trailer park. Somebody had toilet papered one of the trailers, and the remnants hung like paper snakes in the trees. Always, his heart beat faster whenever he was within fifteen feet of home.

The Dubois' got out first, and Breck followed them to the trailer door, his eyes cast on the dirt beneath his feet. An icy chill prickled his skin. His heart pounded. Lois touched his arm, Garren patted his back. "Remember, no one will hurt to you again, one way or another." Garren's tone was steady.

But Breck knew his father did as he pleased, when he pleased, without concern for consequence.

Garren knocked. Waiting brought strangling fear from Breck's knees up his body. He wanted to run, just turn and run, to leave this place and his father's wrath forever behind him.

And He didn't want the Dubois' to get hurt. "We should go," he said.

Garren's hand wrapped around his arm. "It will be all right."

He might hurt you, Breck thought, *and I couldn't live with that.* "I think—"

The door swung open. Rob looked first at Lois, then at Garren before his cold stare fixed on Breck and he pushed through the screen door. "Looks like I got visitors."

"I'm Garren Dubois. I know you've met my wife, Lois. We'd like to talk to you about Breck."

"Pickin' up strays, are you Mr. Dubois?"

"Would you prefer we talk inside or out here?"

Rob didn't move except to cross his bulging arms over his chest. "Here, 'cept you, boy, can get your butt inside."

Garren's grip tightened on Breck's arm. "He needs to stay here for the moment."

Standing upright, Rob filled the doorway, making it clear he was bigger than Garren Dubois. "You telling me what to do with my boy?"

"Not yet." Garren's eyes narrowed. "This morning I drove down my driveway and found Breck nearly unconscious. He spent the night on the pavement, overcome with a myriad of injuries and consequences of neglect and abuse. I'm sure the police would find your home situation something that would require investigation to—"

"I don't know what you're talking about! Now get off my property and give me my boy!" Rob took a step that Garren met.

"I'm not finished, Mr. Noon." Garren's voice sharpened.

Like a shotgun had fired, there was no sound, only Rob's heavy breathing as he waited, forced into listening.

Rob's stony gaze danced between the three of them. "We don't got anything to say to each other. Now I thank you for bringing my kid back, but anything he may have told you comes from bitter insides. He's lazy. He hates that I make him work, that's all. He'd say anything to get out of it."

Garren ignored Rob's excuse. "As you know, Breck dances with our daughter Nicole. She's—"

"My boy don't dance." Rob advanced with red fury on his face, but Garren stayed firm and continued on as if the man hadn't said a word or moved an inch.

"We have spent a considerable amount of time training Breck and Nicole with the very best instructor. We'd like Breck to continue dancing as Nicole's partner, and we're willing to negotiate an arrangement that you find acceptable." Garren watched Rob's hard expression fade to greed. "Breck will work for us in our orchards, and do other odd jobs to earn room and board and the lessons. We'll take care of everything he needs to continue dancing. In exchange, we'll give you five hundred dollars a month."

"Five-hundred dollars for my boy to live at your house and dance with your daughter." Rob hacked out a laugh. "He ain't worth that much. You'll see. You won't get nothin'out of him."

"He's already agreed to it," Lois' voice cracked.

"Oh, sure he's agreed to it. He ain't stupid," Rob sneered then looked at Breck.

Breck lowered his head, unable to ignore the pull of disgrace drawing him back into the trailer, into hopelessness that beckoned with despair.

"It's a very common practice in the dance world," Lois said. "Many dancers board with their partners. Some come from all around the world to live and train here."

"So?"

"So," Lois went on, voice tattered, "Utah has some of the best ballroom competitors in the world."

"I don't give a—"

"One last thing," Garren's voice rode on a blade of steel, cutting him off. "We want legal guardianship. That will keep Breck where he can benefit and ensure that you benefit financially. And your parenting skills will not be made public, though that's something I might choose to do at some later date."

For the first time, Rob looked truly taken aback. He scraped a palm at his growing beard and glanced over the Dubois' shoulders at the sleek silver Mercedes parked in his dirt drive. "I need some time to think about it."

Garren gave one nod. "Take all the time you need, but Breck will wait at our home while you're deciding."

"Just wait a minute," Rob spat. "He's my kid."

A smile spread slowly across Garren's face. "Then we'll wait here while you decide."

Lois stepped forward, her hand protectively on Breck's arm. "Mr. Noon, Breck will have every opportunity to excel, we'll see to that. We're quite firm with our Nicole. She maintains a three-point-nine-five grade-point average along with her rigorous rehearsal schedule. We'll do all we can for Bre—"

"I don't give a hill of trash about grades and school. I don't want him dancing. He's got a good job on a construction team. He can work with men, like his old man."

"What don't you like about the arrangement?" Garren asked, for the first time, Breck heard something tighten the man's voice. "Is it just the dancing? Or that there will be no one to lock up at night, or withhold food from? Or, heaven forbid, take a belt to when you feel like it?"

Rob looked Garren up and down and then looked at Lois, eyeing the glittering rock on her ring finger and her tidy outfit. "For guardianship, I'll do it for seven hundred."

The muscles in Breck's body gripped and squeezed. He wished the ground would open up and swallow him, take away the shame of being bought and sold like a commodity.

"Very well," Garren said. Then he put his hand, comforting and gentle, on Breck's shoulder, and Breck looked at him. "Do you have things you'd like to get?"

Breck nodded, but hesitated.

Garren placed an easy pat on his back. "Will you need my help?"

"He doesn't have much." Rob took the stair up. "But you can go in, seein' that we're gonna be like – you know, family and all." A grin twisted across his face. He opened the door in a change of tune that was now friendly, and kicked aside hollow beer cans, empty cigarette and microwave food boxes. "You go get your things, Breckie-boy," he said. He cocked his head with a careless smile at Lois. "So, will he be comin' home for holidays?"

With a glance around the dismal, filthy trailer, it was clear to Lois that Breck wouldn't be setting foot back inside of there ever again, if she could help it. "Perhaps that's something we should talk about later."

Breck led Garren down the hall. He couldn't hide from it now. Garren would see how he'd lived, where the nightmares had come true, and his knees clipped as the two of them neared the room.

It still smelled like mold and filth, and the mattress showed freshly-stained reminders of blood. Breck didn't look long, and hoped Garren wouldn't either. It felt like being naked in a nightmare, waking up only to find that you

Noon - Katherine Warwick

were still without clothes.

Breck gathered two pairs of jeans, three shirts, his backpack and CD player. There was only enough to fill his arms but Garren held out his. "Let me."

Breck handed him the CD player and headphones, but kept the clothes to himself. There was a look in Garren's eyes as he took the CD player that left Breck feeling like, even with the clothes in his arms, he was still naked.

The song was distinctly cha-cha. Reuben chose the cut because of the spicy tang in the cymbals, the drums that encouraged the audience to clap along. Anytime you could get the audience on your side, you could lay a nice, fluffy carpet underneath the judges for the ride.

The tune boomed in the studio, rattling the walls. Reuben clapped, trying to pump just a little more energy from his pair. They were so close to perfection, he could hardly stand still. Music in motion, he called it.

Dance was his poetry.

Breck and Nicole had placed fourth in their last competition, and he'd not been surprised. Too close to the whole relocation incident for Breck. Even Nicole had shrugged the loss off with class. Reuben hoped she was finally internalizing real priorities.

Now, six months and thousands of hours of practice later, she was starting to get itchy for a win. Reuben could always tell. She'd get short, snap at everyone, and drive herself into the wood floor before she would settle for anything less than perfect.

Reuben didn't approve of her snapping at Breck for timing, like she was today. In his mind, Breck was coming along beautifully. Reuben had that fatherly pride that comes from time spent, effort given, and sweat shed for the good of someone else.

That Breck now held his own with Nicole was just one of the changes Reuben had seen take place over the last few months. His dancing had skyrocketed. He was truly gifted, and Reuben and Lois often whispered that old Rob must have dancing feet hidden somewhere because his son was a prodigy.

Breck wasn't afraid of hard work either. Reuben watched the boy wipe glistening sweat from his brow with a sopping wet tee shirt that now clung to his body. Breck's work ethic was giving Nicole a run for her money. She didn't think there was anybody alive with as much drive as she had.

Reuben clapped louder, pushed harder. "Once more," he told them. Both were panting. "Need a break?" he asked.

"I don't." Nicole shot her brow up along with her chin.

Breck took in some air. "Me either."

Reuben smiled.

As they went through the combinations again, Reuben noticed the studio door open. Garren popped his head in with a wave. He'd been doing that every now and again since Breck had come to live at the house. It pleased Breck – and infuriated Nicole.

Garren pointed toward the house, as if to signal that he was heading up for dinner and Reuben gave a nod. The door closed once again.

"Our hands aren't the same level when you come around from that second turn." Nicole shot out when she had her breath.

"Yes they are." Breck stopped, chest heaving, sweat dripping from hair gathered in black tips, around his face.

Sensing that the pot was beginning to boil, Reuben approached. "I think we've had enough for today."

"Well, I'm not tired, and I'm not satisfied." Nicole circled Breck, as if challenging him to take her on.

"It's seven-thirty," Reuben told her. "You've been at this since four. It's over."

"The competition is too close to rest," Nicole said. "And since we lost our last one…"

The comment froze Reuben and sent Breck's glare into an icy, hurt look.

"We're done." Reuben went about closing shop for the night even though his two dancers hadn't stopped sparring. It was time for him to call it a day. Gathering his bag, CDs and car keys, he headed to the door as silently as a draft.

"Don't kill each other," he called just before he shut the door.

"That wasn't fair," Breck's voice was hard. Though hurt tainted his tone,

Nicole couldn't deny her shocked pleasure that he'd told her off. "Don't do it again."

She might have said something snide then, something to keep her on top of the game, but she really didn't want to pierce that deep, hurt him that bad. It had been nasty enough just referring to his father and the beating the way she had by reminding him of their last competition. Still, she wanted to make sure he knew that she held the seniority in the partnership. And she wouldn't apologize.

She began going through the steps again, arms holding a phantom partner. He stood watching. A delightful tremor of revenge skittered through her. After a while he shook his head, strode across the floor and picked up his towel, wiping his face as he headed for the door.

"Quitting already?" she taunted, still dancing.

"I'm hungry, and I have tests tomorrow." He tossed the towel over his shoulder.

The muscles in his back were tight, and shifted, giving her a perfect view of strong male when he reached and yanked open the door. She wet her lips. Dance was filling him out nicely. All those lifts and spins had added beautiful contours and sleek lines to his body. She licked her lips again, her mouth uncomfortably dry.

Then she frowned. She didn't like that he felt comfortable enough to take that tone of voice with her, but then she'd seen him doing a lot she wasn't used to.

She looked at herself in the mirror. Still yearning for height and a more ample chest, she pushed the sweaty hair off of her face with a disgusted grunt. In her mind she saw a flash of Kit with her voluptuous body. Compared to Kit, she looked like a pre-teen, rather than a girl of nearly eighteen. Stepping closer to the mirror, she examined the blue thumbprints under her eyes.

Breck was the one behind her circles. She'd felt pressed between two closing walls since he'd moved in.

Strolling the length of the mirror, it was resentment she tried to walk off. The novelty of Breck living with them was wearing thin and reality was left: a bumpy, rocky chasm she was beginning to dislike.

There were myriads of irritants. Like the fact that she had been forced to allow him to see her first thing in the morning, something her vanity never allowed anyone. It was unavoidable. Four people living under the same roof were bound to see each other in every light.

Familiarity breeds contempt, she had heard her mother say it more than once. Her contempt was growing in a Petri dish the size of their pool.

When he'd had Chris and Parker over one night to hang out, she'd gotten more than her hair wet with frustration when the boys monopolized the pool and hot tub. It was her idea to have the girls over for a night of chick flicks and hot tubbing. But the boys showed up first and her mother just smiled and rolled out the red carpet.

The guys were already in the hot tub, laughing and talking when Tiffany and Annie showed up, bathingsuits in hand.

"Let's just make it a party," Annie suggested.

Nicole refused. "No way."

"Come on." Tiffany eyed Breck, who was sitting in the steam of the hot tub. She'd made it very clear that she liked him over the last few months. In fact, so had a lot of girls, and that was yet another thing that had crawled under Nicole's skin.

"Hey." Breck called when he saw them.

"Can I speak with you, please?" Nicole's tone was saccharine but she made sure her eyes squeezed lemons. Breck got out of the hot tub and dripped over. He always wore a tee shirt with his swim trunks. He smiled at Tiffany and Annie.

"Hey," they cooed.

Nicole tugged him by his sopping shirt to a remote corner of the deck. "I was planning to use the hot tub with my friends tonight."

"So let's share it."

"That's not the point. I wanted to have a girls' night."

"Sure, well," he looked her up and down. "We'll get out."

Stunned, she cocked her head back. "You will?"

"Yeah, just let me talk to the guys." Breck jogged back over to the hot tub. Nicole heard their voices shift to a low rumble. It pleased her that Breck understood that she got first dibs on Dubois recreational opportunities. Maybe he was learning something after all. Tiffany smiled and glanced over, then she

Noon - Katherine Warwick

and Annie stepped back as the dripping threesome got out of the tub.

Satisfied with herself, Nicole walked over, ready to tell the boys to get lost. But before she could open her mouth to utter a sound, the boys surrounded her and hoisted her up. She screamed, she kicked, but wasn't able to free herself.

"You are so dead, all of you!"

"And you are so wet." Breck laughed.

"Don't you—" the word *dare* was just on the tip of her tongue as she was swung out and over into the wintry cool water of the pool.

Anger propelled her from the bottom to the top, to see her friends gathered at the edge in hysterics. She didn't say a word, just slid up out of the pool, smiled and took off after Breck.

Soon, it was a mad house of chasing, screaming and tossing bodies into the pool. For Nicole, what started out as a hunger for revenge changed into something far more enticing when she chased Breck into the dark rows of the orchards.

"You're dead, Breck," she yelled. It was nearly black, and her shoes sloshed uneasily beneath her feet as she ran after him. The orchards always gave her the creeps, even in the daylight. But to be in their narrowed runs disappearing into nothingness had her stopping on a shiver. "I'm not chasing after you!"

She was angry now, angry because she was conceding. He was braver than her, running deep into those darkened hollows. "I'll get you when you come back to the house," she yelled, then turned around and began to walk back.

Her clothes clung like dripping paper-mâché against her skin; her teeth chattered. Every noise made her jump. A flock of fallen leaves scurried across the mounded ruts at her feet. All of it was scarier than she wanted to admit.

"Hey." Breck's voice popped in her ear. It frightened her so that she flailed her arms until she realized it was him, after which she continued to pound.

"You, you…" she blurted, furious that it was dark, she was wet and it was all because of him.

He grabbed her wrists. "Cool it." He started out laughing, but could see her anger was fresh and real, and that she wasn't going to stop. Swinging her around, he brought her back against him. "Hey," he said, tightening his grip.

Rage and fury melted when her body pressed into his. Nicole felt like she might fall to the ground if she'd not been against him. His body was warm against her back. The hard planes of his chest pressed shimmering heat through her. His legs, wet and cold as hers were unyielding behind her knees. She stood still, heart beating wildly.

"Let me go," she whispered.

"Not until we call a truce."

"Fine, fine, truce," she rasped out. The moon was overhead. The long rows of trees took on haunting forms as their branches sparred in the wind. Fear, need, and vulnerability swam through her, and she didn't like the combination heating in his arms.

"You okay?" He turned her around, his hands steadying her shoulders.

His hair, longer now, was wild, blown by the wind, lit by the moon. Nicole thought his eyes were black as they looked into hers, black holes she wanted to explore, yet that frightened her at the same time. She let her gaze drop to his lips, shadowed wide and full under the blue white cast of the moon's hue and felt his fingers tighten on her shoulders. Her eyes lifted, meeting his.

"It's cold out here." She began to shake. She was cold, but she was also fraught with something else.

His hands dropped to his sides, cooling her with disappointment. "Yeah," he said quietly. The moment stretched long, like a moonbeam shooting down just for them.

"Hey, where are you guys?" Parker was yelling from somewhere. His voice echoed down the start of the rows, only to be swallowed up as it reached them.

"Out here," Breck yelled back then took Nicole's hand. It was warm, dry, and she wrapped her fingers tight around his. "Come on." He led her through the row and out into the open grassy hill just below the house. When they were out in the clearing, he let go.

Nicole rubbed her hand against her shirt now as she looked at herself in the studio mirror. Then she looked at her hand. How different it could feel, a hand. Each time she touched Breck's hand was different.

How long had her stomach been rumbling? she wondered, sighed. It was

Noon - Katherine Warwick

time to go inside, to eat, shower and change. And if she could bring herself to, it was time to apologize to Breck.

Ten

For Breck, living at the Dubois' exceeded any expectations that might have had but a few moments to take root in his mind. Enamored with the beautiful surroundings, Lois' hospitality, and Garren's fatherly attention, he was more than willing to do whatever was asked of him.

He kept his room clean, not daring to ruin the overall order of the house. Following through on his share of household duties, he took special pride in vacuuming and dusting – the novelty of cleanliness.

He and Nicole rotated jobs like trash and dishes.

Summer meant work on the Dubois' property. There were acres of apple, cherry and pear trees that needed tending. Lois hired dozens of Latinos every year to help and Breck joined them.

He settled into the family as a member, feeling comfortable as a son to Lois and Garren. Where Breck wouldn't classify himself as Nicole's brother, the two of them shared a relationship more often like siblings than two teens that occasionally looked at each other with feelings that ran a different course.

Breck joined the ten-man crew that took care of the orchards during the day. The quiet of the trees allowed him time to think when he wasn't trying to understand the Spanish directions from the team leader.

His mind often pondered the opportunity the Dubois' had kindly laid in his lap. The oppertunity to explore deep, hidden parts of himself that would have never had the chance to flourish chained to the life he'd been dealt.

Everything was better now, and he had Lois to thank for that. It was Lois and her vision that kept him working hard, enjoying the pleasure on her face when he and Nicole danced, when he brought home good grades, or when he spoke of the latest girl he thought was hot.

There was nothing but awe in Breck's mind when he thought of Garren. Even now, propped against the trunk of a cherry tree, enjoying the lunch Lois had made for him, he was awash with emotion thinking of the man he secretly considered a father. He blinked back tears, glad no one was near enough to see them. Garren had opened his house and his heart to a soul struggling for things he'd never thought he would ever know: love, respect and dignity.

Often, Breck let his thoughts wander into the dream that if he were ever to become a father, it would be Garren's example he would follow. It was clear to him now that a man could be masculine in every sense of the word and not have to belittle or abuse others to call themselves one.

Working in the trees helped Breck overcome his initial disconcerting feelings he'd had for the orchards; they were just fruit trees after all, loaded with growing fruit. But in the beginning when he and Nicole had playfully found themselves hiding from each other when their friends would join them in night games, he'd had dark visions of something scary happening in the black, never-ending rows.

To overcome his angst he forced himself to become familiar with the orchards through the work. Because he thought it would be good for Nicole to get some dirt under her nails, he suggested to Garren that she join in the maintenance process. It would do her some good to come down from her window where he often caught her sitting, watching as they worked, and get her hands into the family fruit.

He was perched up on a ladder in the heat of the noon sun, listening to the Hispanic music one of the workers had on the radio when he looked over and saw her in her jeans and a white tee shirt coming down the row. She had a frown on her face, and her hair up in a sassy ponytail. His stomach lit with butterflies.

Pretending he didn't see her, Breck continued plucking cherries from the upper branches of the tree. Lois warned him every morning to be extra careful, that they couldn't afford to have an injury hold up the progress they were making in the studio. He was cautious in his climbing, reaching and picking. The most hazardous part of the job was the incessant wasps and bees foraging off the trees. He'd been stung more than once and had been surprised at how potent the sting was.

Nicole loitered at the bottom of the tree without saying a word for a few moments, so he decided to notice her. "Hey," he said, plucking a handful of cherries.

"Hi," she grumbled.

He looked up and squinted into the sun. It had been a while since he'd put on sunscreen so he slowly climbed out of the upper branches until his foot touched the top of the ladder and he continued down from there.

"Here to help?" He bent over and opened his work sack. Rifling through the water bottle, snack, and towel Lois had packed, he found the sunscreen.

She made a face. "This is your fault."

"Me? Why is it always my fault?" He squirted some white cream into his palms and began rubbing his arms.

Her eyes followed his palms as they rubbed. "I've lived here all of my life and never once had to work out here. Now, here you are, and Dad tells me he thinks it's a good idea that I join the troops."

Rubbing a thin layer of sunscreen on his face, Breck was able to conceal his grin. "Hey, summer's almost over. Most of the work's been done." He squirted some cream on his chest and began to rub.

She watched under her eyelashes. "Well," she shifted, "I guess it won't be too bad."

"It's not bad at all. We got fresh air, Latin music and tons of wasps and bees." He handed her the bottle with a playful grin. "Put some on my back, will ya?" Then he turned.

It was a mistake, he knew it, the moment she placed those delicate hands on his back. He tensed. The slow and easy way she rubbed was too pleasant. Every part of him became uncomfortably warm. "Uh, thanks," he said, turning. He took the sunscreen from her.

"But I missed a few spots." She held out her hands still laden with cream.

"Better put it on you, the sun gets awfully hot."

"Okay." She rubbed the cream into her arms. "What do I do?"

"You work the lower braches and I'll go up top." Sunscreen slathered, he once again climbed the ladder, glad to create some distance.

Not to be outdone, Nicole looked up at the top branches where the red cherries hung like tiny Christmas ornaments. "I can go up."

Breck shook his head. "No way." He pointed to a white bucket on the ground near her feet. "Put your cherries in there."

"Why can't I go up?"

"You stay low. It's too risky."

Noon - Katherine Warwick

Nicole frowned and picked up the white bucket.

Music wafted down the rows and caught on the branches. They could hear some of the men singing along with the strumming guitar.

It was pleasant, she thought, to be doing something like this with him. To be working together on something other than the dance floor. That she watched the clock each day, waiting for the time when she would see him emerge from the thickness of the orchards, bare chested in a pair of ratty jeans, and head toward the house made her realize her feelings for him were changing.

It had happened so slowly, indeed was still blossoming, she rarely had time to think about it. But now, alone with him, she was thinking about it. It was altogether exciting.

Nicole reached for branches a little higher up so she could keep a casual eye on him. His dark hair hadn't lightened at all from the sun he'd gotten lately, but his skin had browned nicely, making the blue of his eyes more brilliant when he smiled.

Seeing his scars was never easy. Still, they fascinated her, and she wondered if he'd trust her enough to talk about it. "Ever miss you father?" she asked. He froze for a moment.

"No way, are you kidding?" He only let a beat pass before he picked again.

"Just wondered," she added quickly. "Is it hard to talk about?" She stopped and looked right at him.

He pulled back his hand, depositing the cherries into his shoulder sack. Then he looked at her. "I've never talked about it with anyone."

For a moment they shared a silence and look that promised to connect them together. She moved deeper into the tree. "Want to?"

She didn't look up, but knew he still hadn't moved and she worried she might be overstepping boundaries. She opened her mouth to speak, but he spoke first.

"What do you want to know?"

Her mind raced with questions she'd asked him a million times in her daydreams. "Tell me about your mother."

She couldn't see his face, but his tone was soft. "She was great."

Nicole's heart dilated; there was such yearning in the quietness of his tone. She took her own mother for granted, but for the moment felt gratitude hearing the loss behind Breck's words. "What was she like?" she asked, prompting him to continue.

"She was fun. She liked to sing. My dad…" he paused a moment and Nicole looked up but only saw him stop briefly before he plucked another cherry. "My dad called her his little bird. And she was a good dancer."

"She was?"

He looked down at her then, and smiled. "Yeah."

She thought she heard him sigh, but it could have been the wind in the leaves. He was silent for a time, and she circled the bottom branches in search of more fruit. Positioning herself below him she continued to pick fruit where she knew they would be able to continue to talk.

"So, she worked?"

"Uh-huh, at Albertson's in American Fork. I would meet her at the store after work so we could ride home together. That's when we had the accident."

"All of you?"

"Just me and her," his voice was steady. "We were coming back." He stopped, and lowered his head to his chest before he continued. "A drunk hit us going eighty miles an hour on State Street."

"How terrible," she whispered. "How old were you?"

"Nine." Slowly he began his ascent down the ladder. The wind rustled the trees, cooling hot skin. "I'm done up top." That was when his life had changed, Breck thought as his feet hit the dirt, when grief had tormented his father into a monster seeking blame.

"So what happened then?" she asked.

He didn't answer right away. Nicole felt the pain she saw cross his face. His brows knit tight, his jaw spread hard. "My dad couldn't handle it. He told me, if I hadn't been there—" He kept picking, she noticed, so she did too.

She waited for him to elaborate, to have some of her questions answered with details, but he remained quiet and all that passed between them was the dying tunes from a radio that was further away now.

He stood right in front of her, and her eyes went to his light, white scars, striped across his chest.

"They're ugly, I know," he said. His fingers went to cover them.

Noon - Katherine Warwick

She looked up from the scars and into his eyes. Nothing about you could be ugly, she heard herself think, wanted to say. Instead she saw her fingers reaching out to touch his hand. Moving it gently aside, she placed her own fingers over the white markings.

"They're not," she murmured. He took a deep breath, and his chest rose under her fingers. She moved closer, her eyes shifting to his lips. Her heartbeat fast; underneath her fingers his ran faster.

She was closer now, and Breck didn't know what to do. She was looking at his lips. He felt ready to grab her and hold her, every fiber inside of him screaming to do something.

After a swallow, he took another deep breath. He couldn't touch her that way. She was Lois and Garren's daughter and he was supposed to watch out for her, be her brother – wasn't he? Then he heard laughter in the farthest corner of his mind. What a joke, he thought, looking at her just inches away, her lips lifting to his. They were dance partners that lived under the same roof. It was crazy. Still, he couldn't touch her and look Lois and Garren in the eye – that would be impossible. So he stepped back, reached down, and picked up his bag and his cherry sack.

Disappointment was in her eyes and his own face scrunched into a fret. "We should hit the next tree," he mumbled. He bent to carry her bucket, but she snatched it from him.

"I can carry it myself," she snapped and strode off.

He'd never kissed a girl. He'd never been kissed. The moment was so complicated; his mind ran with questions, with hesitation and doubt. Under the heat of the afternoon sun, his manly image of himself withered.

This year, Breck looked forward to Christmas. Instead of spending the night alone in that crowded, dank room he'd occupied in the trailer, he anticipated Brian and Tami and the girls coming for one of Lois' fancy dinners.

Lois had set up three trees, a twenty-foot tree in the entry, decorated with gold and cream bulbs and bows. Another was set up in the family room, this one in red and green, with popcorn and intricate ornaments Lois had collected from around the world. The third was much smaller, but sat in his bedroom. A special tree Lois had decorated just for him with miniature framed pictures of his life there. Every night he looked at it, heart so swollen with gratitude he couldn't believe his good fortune.

He loved the way Lois had decorated the outside of the house, with weeping evergreen boughs along the balcony and giant red bows, and enjoyed the sight now as he drove up the drive and parked. Most of the lights inside the house were off at this hour, but the Christmas lights were on, and the twinkling rainbow colors cheered Breck as he got out of the car and locked the door. Always, his eyes were drawn to Nicole's bedroom window. Her light was one of the only lights that burned. A buzz started in his chest. He wondered if he would always feel this hopeless thrill for her.

He had friends now – tons of them, and dates most every weekend. His grades had earned him a full-ride scholarship to UVSC in Psychology next year. He'd been elected Mr. Viking, a social honor that pretty much nailed the crown of most popular on his head. There was a certain joy of independence that being a senior in high school brings.

Early mornings didn't bother him. They usually meant he was at school practicing with the dance team. Late nights, like the one he'd enjoyed tonight, meant girls, friends, or both.

It happened so fast, the strong grip that wrapped around his arm and whirled him in a blur nearly choked him. His heart didn't have time to react, until he looked into the face of his father.

Rob Noon stood close, his breath pluming into the night like an angry bull. He wore a heavy coat and a knit cap. His cheeks and nose were red from exposure. "I've been waiting for you."

Months had passed since Breck had seen him. He thought he'd shed the old fear, dropping it somewhere where he'd left all of the other unpleasantries of his life. But standing face to face with his worst demon, he felt like he was back in that trailer.

Rob looked him up and down. "Pretty fancy. Where you been, boy?"

"Out." Breck tried to pass him but Rob shoved him back against the car.

"Out where?"

"On a date."

Rob smiled when he heard the shock that warbled Breck's voice. He stepped closer. "A date – a nobody like you?"

Cold bit through Breck's clothes – but the company chilled his bones. "What do you want?"

Delight vanished from Rob's face. "I'll get to that. You too good to talk to your old man now? Better not ever think so, 'cause I can rip you out of this fairy tale so fast those feet of yours will never walk again, much less dance." Rob breathed down on him. "Can't believe I let them rich people talk me into making you a dancer."

"They didn't make me into anything, I chose it." Breck shot out. Rob raised a hand to strike him then stopped, looking around. "Go ahead." Breck inched closer. "You won't hit me because you don't want Garren cutting off your money."

Rob's eyes darted from Breck, to the house. "Well, at least you got my brains, kid. I been watching you for weeks now. You got it good here. Way I figure it you're sitting up here on snob hill with all the fat, rich comforts of money. You owe me."

"You're getting enough."

"Well, I want more."

"I don't have any money."

Rob cackled then spit on the ground. "You're sitting on it."

Breck thought of Garren and Lois, of protecting them from this lunatic he was ashamed to call his father. "No. Now leave us alone." He started to move but was yanked back into place.

Rob snagged Breck's hair, snapping his head back. His other hand went to his throat and pinched until breathing stopped. "*Us? Us?* You think you're one of them?"

Breck tried to pry his father's hand from his throat but only felt nails digging into his flesh, saw diamond dust dance before his eyes as he fought to breathe. He could see the stars up in the heavens, moving and he sucked in for air that wouldn't come. Then he saw black.

Cold seeped through his clothes, startling him out of unconsciousness. When he opened his eyes he found himself lying beside the car. His head throbbed, the skin on his throat was sore. Looking up, he saw the clouds beginning to sprinkle snow. He heard nothing but the sound of soft cotton moving through air, as the light flakes fell around him. Easing up on his elbows, he rubbed his throat for a moment before he felt a sharp pull at his scalp and was wrenched upright. He stood, facing Rob again.

"You needed a little reminder," Rob snarled out a whisper. "Now, get in that house and get me more money."

Breck stood dazed a moment, pride kicking up its heels. "I won't ask them for more money."

"You do it, or there'll be consequences."

"I don't care what you do to me."

Rob snatched Breck's collar and pulled his face in. "You think you're all tough now. How tough are you gonna be when that pretty little thing you're dancing with gets tangled up with me one night?"

Breck's rage shifted to his fists. Rob laughed. He took the punches willingly, before he landed a few powerful ones in the middle of Breck's abdomen, sending him over in a heap, gasping for breath.

"Get me that money."

Breck forced himself to nod, even though he would rather take a thousand punches, die even, before he would give his father anything more of the Dubois'. Finally, able to unfold, he watched his father sneak down the drive into darkness.

Inside the house, the warmth did little to settle his shivering body and raw nerves. He touched the wet gouges at his throat. Breck ducked into the small bath on the main floor to see if he looked all right before heading upstairs. Redness bloomed just under his left eye and his clothes were dirty. After he brushed himself off, he ran his hands through his hair to calm it down, then headed up the stairs, his gaze focused on the light glowing under Nicole's closed door.

Leaning his forehead against the door for a moment, he closed his eyes, squeezing the doorframe in his hands. She was safe – for now. A fear he wanted so desperately to put behind him forever was grabbing hold again, beginning to spread. He had only to think of Nicole being hurt by his father and need drove him to knock.

"Yeah?"

He opened the door, keeping hold of the knob to steady himself. She was sitting on her bed, dressed in soft, pink pajamas. Her hair was on top of her head in a thrown-together ponytail. The innocent sight brought a weary smile to his lips. The *Ballroom Today* magazine she was thumbing through lay open on her thighs.

She tilted her head. "Hey."

"Hey." She looked childlike. He was relieved that she was safe. "Did you go with Tiff and Annie?"

Turning a page she shook her head. "They bailed. How was your date?"

He could barely find a memory of what he'd done that night, his mind still reeling from seeing his father, now tangling with fast-coming thoughts of how he would keep the man away. "Fine."

He stole one last look, the burden suddenly cast on his back weighing heavily on his soul. "'Night, Nic."

She turned another page. "Night."

She was okay; that was all he wanted to know. He closed the door and headed to bed.

His mind raced with options, and everything around him suddenly looked transparent, as if at any moment his father's words would come true and he would be ripped away from all he had come to love.

He fell onto his bed and grasped the pillow to his chest. This was his bed now, not Brian's. It had a frame and a headboard, a spread and pillows. There was a closet, and inside hung countless clothes that Lois had gifted him. On the desk he kept what few trinkets he had – the trophys he and Nicole had won, his yearbook, and a copy of a medical book Garren thought he might be interested in reading. He'd read it from cover to cover in two weeks.

He closed his eyes, chest tight with emotion. He'd have to figure something out. But what? He was a senior, danced from four until eight every week day afternoon with Nicole and Reuben, had finals to prepare for, college tests to take. The future looked like a maze, and he was blindfolded, just at the entrance.

Nicole sat by the Christmas tree with her nieces. She had a Christmas book open across her lap and was reading to the girls while Lois and Tami worked in the kitchen, readying dinner. Brian and Garren sat talking by the fireplace, oblivious to Lois and Tami prattling away over pots, pans, platters and crystal.

Reuben smiled, knowing well how easy it was to be distracted. His smile softened when his gaze settled on his wife. Gail was busy wiping cranberries from Jennica's hands after the toddler had reached into the crystal bowl filled with the red berries.

Taking a small cup of hot cider from Lois' table of food, Reuben handed it to his wife and then placed a kiss to his daughter's cheek. Then he headed over to Breck who sat near the hearth, staring blankly into the flames; a look laden with too much for a boy his age darkened his strong features.

Something was up; the kid hadn't been himself for days. It was Christmas Eve. He should be carefree, immersed in everything beautiful about the holiday.

"Hey." Reuben squatted down next to him.

"Hey."

Reuben readied himself for a digging session. "What's up, buddy?"

"Nothing."

"You've been a possessed white boy for days now."

Breck didn't laugh, just looked into the fire, his brows creasing. Reuben took a deep breath, catching the faint scent of cinnamon from Lois' simmering cider. Breck's eyes stayed on the dancing flames, and Reuben leaned back, looking at the festive tree done up in Lois' collection of traditional Christmas bulbs from around the world. He heard his wife's laughter, his daughter's squealing, and Nicole's voice as she read her nieces a Christmas story. But he didn't look over.

Reuben figured part of Breck was miles away, down in that trailer, trying to find the path that would lead him out for good. Dance, the Dubois: they'd all opened the door.

Because he had a feeling about Breck's inner demons, Reuben kept his voice low and made sure to send a reassuring nod at Nicole every now and then when he caught her curious glance on the two of them.

"Yeah, the holidays. They're something I had to learn to enjoy." Breck didn't say anything, so Reuben continued. "Hated 'em growing up. While everybody else was getting presents, I was getting whipped by my old man." It hadn't hurt in a long time because Reuben didn't let himself think about the past. The old pain echoed deep inside now.

"I'm sorry," Breck said, but still wouldn't meet his gaze.

"He was a mean sucker. Drunk himself to sleep every night but Christmas. He stayed sober one night a year so he could give us all our 'gifts.'" Reuben shook his head, hearing his sisters scream, seeing his mother cower in the corner while his father ran on a rampage. "Took me a long time to realize what a loser he was, and that I had to get out of there or I'd be one too."

Breck was checking him out warily; he could see that from the corner of his eye. "My sisters finally split. I was glad for them. But, being the youngest, I didn't have a lot of options. And I didn't want to leave my mama." An old pain trickled through his heart, remembering. "But she made me go. She gave me the money she'd been saving and told me to take the bus anywhere. And, being the obedient, loving son that I was," Reuben grinned at Breck, hoping to see a smile returned, but Breck's young face was stone-cold serious. "I headed out to L.A., but got stopped in Salt Lake City by a missionary couple. They saw my filthy clothes and asked me when I'd eaten last. They took me in for a few months. Fed me, bought me clothes, offered to send me to school. Said they had the sweetest granddaughter they wanted me to meet someday."

"Gail?" Breck asked.

Reuben gave a nod, pleased he'd gotten a word from him.

"You ever see your mom and sisters?" Breck asked.

"Sure I do. Took a lot of years, but, yeah, we finally all connected."

"What about your dad?"

It didn't surprise Reuben, the old, sharp feeling he felt then, pain, hate and sorrow all forged into one cutting blade that still pierced his heart. "Never."

Breck looked back at the fire, the corner of his jaw shifting to rock. Reuben figured he'd come this far, he wouldn't stop now. Not if there was something he could do, say, to help. "Seen your old man this holiday?"

Breck's face jerked towards his. "No."

"He tried to see you?"

When Breck looked away, Reuben had his answer, even though Breck shook his head.

"I need to get a job," Breck said.

"When would you have the time to work it?"

Breck rubbed his hands across his face. "Think I could teach dance? Think I'm good enough?"

Reuben's eyes narrowed seeing the head of the problem surface. "Sure you're good enough. I don't know if Lois is going to approve."

Breck looked at Lois, then at his hands. "I could fit it in. I won't take any time from Nicole and me."

"But you still have finals, the ACT and competitions. You're only a senior in high school, buddy."

"I can do it."

"Yeah, you can do it. You'd be great teaching. Weigh the commitment; see if it's worth it."

"It's worth it."Agitated, Breck stood, going to the French doors that opened out over the blackness of the back yard, the orchards stretching beyond. Reuben joined him.

"Then it sounds to me like you've made up your mind." Reuben laid a hand on Breck's stiff shoulder, hoping the kid knew what he was doing. Knowing very well the decision was Breck's alone to make, his alone to follow through on, or he wouldn't free himself.

Reuben took in a deep breath. Some things never change. It didn't matter the city, the year or the day. Some fathers live everywhere.

It was only the squeeze on his thigh from his child's arms that took his eyes away from Breck. Reuben scooped up his carefree child and gave her a deep hug. Some sons had to break the cycle.

Eleven

Breck paid his father off with the earnings he collected teaching private lessons every evening after he and Nicole finished practice. The extra three hundred dollars would come from his sweat and effort, not Garren's. He could see that he'd be able to continue to pay, continue to keep his father away and satisfied, which enabled him to put aside fears and concentrate on the next competition.

In March, the United States Dancesport National Championships were held at the Marriott Center, a facility that hosted everything from concerts to basketball games on the campus of Brigham Young University. The event was the grandest championship in the Intermountain West, recognized by the National Dance Council of America.

Breck was as determined as Nicole to take first place. Stories and rumors had spread through the dance community about Nicole and Breck, and they would be the most watched pair at the competition. The small talk made Breck a little edgy, though he could see Nicole and Lois didn't seem flustered by the whirling rumors.

"We're going to be late." He stood in the hallway, tapping his fingers on the wall outside Nicole's bedroom where he heard Lois and Nicole in whispers. His hands started to moisten anticipating the events of the weekend-long competition. The usual parade of butterflies he got before any performance was already lodged in his stomach. He knocked twice. "Hey."

"We're coming," Lois called. Seconds later the door opened. Lois emerged with Nicole's black garment bag slung over her arm. She smiled as she passed. He looked at Nicole whose face was taut with concentration.

Her hair was ready, pulled back tight with loops studded in rhinestones and glitter. He'd gotten used to her makeup when they performed; glitter and shadow enough to be seen by the farthest spectator at the event. But her face was unusually pale. No amount of makeup could cover the blue under her eyes.

He reached for her elbow. "You okay?"

"Fine." But she didn't look at him.

Openly he watched her as they drove to the competition. It scratched under his skin that she wouldn't tell him what was wrong.

Inside, the Marriot Center buzzed with the pitch of a busy hive of performers readying for the competition and spectators anxious to be wooed. Standing just off the massive floor, Breck moved in a circle, taking in the huge bowl shape of the facility filling with bodies crawling to seats. The sheer size of the building, the obvious differences in the production of this event versus other events he had participated in so far was mind-boggling. He'd felt confident before they had gotten out of the car, now he felt dwarfed with doubt.

"Wow. This place is massive."

"Come on." Nicole didn't bother looking around. Familiar with her pre-competition pattern, Breck figured her quiet demeanor meant that she was focusing on the comp. "Let's go warm up. Reuben will be waiting for us."

Nationals were underway, being a three day event, and so he and Nicole merged with the flow for Friday. They were competing in the Youth Latin category, and it was being held at the same time as the Standard Formation competition that their team from the high school was participating in, so Breck saw some familiar faces. None relieved his jumpy nerves like the sight of his coach.

Reuben created a crowd wherever he went, his years of coaching nurturing throngs of students as well as admirers, and a small group trailed him in awe even now. Once he was next to Breck and Nicole, the awe-struck dancers sloughed away.

"Guys." Reuben brought their heads in tight to his with a congenial group hug. "Are we up?" His green eyes met Breck's, then Nicole's. "Okay then, let's go over those crashes and dips to make sure they're smooth. And Breck, I want to see you do that final spin and turn out with Nicole one more time, the one at the end of the rumba routine."

Counting out the steps of rumba, Reuben circled them as they worked in a deserted corner of one of the center tunnels. Over and over they rolled, spun and dipped. Breck wiped his brow, the combination of practice and nerves sending him into a sweat.

Nicole's hand was clammy when Breck took it, so he gripped a little tighter than usual. They assumed their positions, counted out the final steps of the rumba routine and he jerked her in and out, then spun her. She stumbled, and both Reuben and Breck jumped over, grabbing her before she fell.

"You were holding me too tight!" With a weak push, Nicole was free of Breck's arms.

"I—" Confused, Breck stood alone.

Reuben quickly sat her down on the cold cement floor, taking her face between his hands. "You gonna be able to do this?" Nicole closed her eyes tight and nodded. "Breathe. Come on, breathe. Slow it down." Reuben's voice was like warm molasses. "That's better. Yeah, like that."

Breck hung over Reuben's shoulder. She looked paler than snow. That same kernel of concern he'd felt earlier at the house was making him take notice now. "Is she okay?"

Eyes still fixed on Nicole, Reuben nodded. "Sure she's okay, aren't you, sis?" His hands slid from her face down her neck and to her shoulders where he rubbed up and down. Breck felt like he was being left out of a loop he had yet to understand, was helpless to interpret, and he took a step back.

He kept his distance but with an eye on Nicole whose face was the color of sour milk as she sat with her eyes closed.

Reuben approached him after Nicole got up to get drink of water. "She gets like this at Nationals. Don't worry about it."

It was the biggest case of stage fright Breck had ever seen and didn't sound like Nicole, but coming from Reuben, he believed it.

When the competition began, eighty-five couples took to the floor in a colorful display of flowing brilliance. Most of the boys were in black with their partner's dress colors worn in the fabric of their shirts. The girl's costumes were tight and bright, revealing enough leg and shoulder to enhance the sensual movements of the Latin dances.

Breck decided to ignore the crowds and look only at Nicole and at Lois and Reuben, who were seated at one of the long tables on the hem of the floor.

"Dad's here." She barely whispered, but it seemed to Breck that Nicole's demeanor changed drastically. Color flourished in her cheeks. She stood more erect. It was a boost to both Breck and Nicole to see Garren at the table, smiling and chatting with Reuben and others that came around to say hello.

Nicole dismissed the weakness she felt in her bones earlier and readied herself for a win. With her father there, she wouldn't settle for anything less than first place. When the music began, she could only think of him seeing her, and all she wanted was for him to be proud of her. For him to fall in love with dance the way she had.

She didn't think about the hours of endless practice, the sweat shed, or the fights over technique. She smiled, listened to the music, and let it become a part of her. But halfway through the first round, during samba, she looked at Breck and felt the pure alignment of their bodies in a way she never had before. The thrill shot through her like electricity. As she danced, her body, her eyes, played off Breck in theatrical sparring. Heat met heat, flames reached and joined. Will demanded submission as desire and passion lit the floor with energy. She knew every eye in the building had locked on them.

Nicole never allowed herself to think anything personal during a performance. But today Breck was speaking to her, using his smile, his eyes, his face and body to speak words meant only for her. Something intoxicating exploded within her.

They were going to win.

As the day wore on and couples were eliminated, even until the final heat when only twelve couples remained on the dance floor, she rode a powerful current that eliminated any physical weakness.

"You okay?" Breck whispered through a smile. They took the floor for the semifinal round.

She nodded, afraid to look at him. He'd become a force she'd only felt in the arms of Reuben. It was a power she yearned to have, a power she was helpless to resist. That Breck had lassoed that power and swallowed it didn't make her jealous. They were partners, and if he looked good, so would she. But she needed to be just as enigmatic, and she felt the crush of pressure on her insides.

Unable to resist, her gaze finally wandered along his profile. Her heart stammered. He was watching the competitors, not aware that she was admiring the firm set of his jaw, his determined mouth. His skin was flushed, and his hair, slicked back for the Latin dances, exposed the perspiration beading down his face.

"Remember," she began. He leaned close, so he could hear better, and she took in the scent of his soap and skin. "They slow the music way down dur-

Noon - Katherine Warwick

ing semi-finals to weed out." She'd already warned him that this round was the hardest. He straightened and took a deep breath.

He took her in his arms, looking at her with a grin that was childishly sweet and innocent, not at all theatrical. They waited for the music to start. His expression reminded her of her own youthful pleasure for dance that she had come to take for granted. Swamped with admiration, she fought the tight push of emotion filling her chest.

Carefully, precisely, he led them through each of their five Latin dances one last time. They made no mistakes. When they danced, Nicole was sure the audience danced with them, feeling the drive, the passion, the bond they shared, induced by the drums, carried by the guitars and the violins.

When the music ended, the six finalists held their poses graciously while applause crackled off of the edifice. Not once had Nicole thought of Trey and Kit. She glanced casually to see if they were still on the floor. They were, but it didn't matter. She and Breck had performed like champions, and she wouldn't waste one glorious moment thinking about anything else.

Nicole had performed better than ever, with the best partner she'd ever had —would ever have, so she closed her eyes and heard the thundering applause all over again in her head. Together, she and Breck had made magic.

The crowd had been her witness.

Now, soaking in the fragrant bubbles of her bath, she smiled in spite of the aches she felt coming on — a sure sign of the flu or some other nasty bug.

The name of Noon and Dubois will be forever out there, she thought, her mind drifting over the day. There would be few moments that could compete with the satisfaction she got from receiving the first place trophy.

But the two-dozen red roses from her dad had been what brought tears to her eyes.

Breck had shared the moment with his usual ecstatic embrace. Feeling him wrapped tight around her, she'd been so dreadfully tired, she wanted to fall limp in his arms. She would have liked it even better if he'd kissed her, but that was never going to happen.

Noon - Katherine Warwick

No, Breck saw himself as her brother. That was painfully clear as he dated regularly, and the phone rang for him night and day. He seemed to dance further and further out of her reach.

Because she wasn't enjoying the hot bubble bath any more, Nicole pulled herself up and toweled off. Her head swam. Blackness threatened to cover her like a blanket thrown over her head. Reaching for the doorknob, she steadied herself, breathing deeply. Her heart pounded. The effort to push her arms through the pink terry-cloth robe was as if sand bags were wrapped around each one. Hair wet, body shivering, she pulled the robe tight, opened the door and made her way down the hall holding onto the walls with both hands.

She heard everybody down stairs, their voices echoing in and out of her brain as if it were being hollowed with each word. *Bed.* Inching down the hallway, it was the only thought she had. *Bed is only a few feet away.*

Breck's laughter took her jellied mind back to the competition, when she had looked up at him as they'd awaited the judges' scores. He'd taken her hand. His blue eyes had looked into hers and she'd thought they were saying something special only for her.

Falling onto the bed, she knew of nothing else except what her heart told her. Yes, he had been speaking to her. And in the grogginess of her mind, the crushing heaviness of her body, she reached out with her soul to know what it was he'd tried to say.

*   *   *

There was nothing like winning, Breck decided, but being a part of a family was the very best thing. Winning was definitely second. He didn't need to celebrate in some big way. Just being home with Garren, Lois, Brian, Tami and the girls was enough.

Garren surprised everyone by ordering Thai take out, and they enjoyed dinner on the floor of the family room, watching the little girls pretend to be dancers in a competition. Each begged Breck to be their dance partner, ending up in a squabble only diffused by candy Lois kept hidden for such occasions.

Breck kept glancing toward the stairs but Nicole never reemerged after their initial return home.

Noon - Katherine Warwick

"She's a little under the weather," Lois whispered to him when she saw him continually checking the empty back stair.

"Sick?" Something inside of him stirred. "She performed and she was sick?"

Lois gently took him aside, out of Garren's earshot. "She's done it before."

"We could have waited."

"She'd never have waited another year. She wanted this win. And," Lois smiled broadly, "she got it."

Lois went back to attending to dessert. Why had they both kept this from him? They were partners. He should have known.

He took the stairs two at a time.

He didn't bother knocking. When he found her face down on the bed asleep, he had to stop himself from storming over, flipping her onto her back and shaking some sense into her. Instead, he crept over slowly, looking at her face, half smashed as it lay twisted to the side. Those blue circles were still there; her skin was still ashen. Guilt gnawed at him. She looked wasted. He thought he should move her so that she was at least lying on the bed in the right direction.

Gently he lifted her legs, adjusting the robe so she would be covered and warm. She stirred then and he stopped, as if being caught would embarrass them both.

Turning her head, she merely sighed.

She looked peaceful and serene. Beautiful. He wanted to reach out and touch her forehead just once. The urge was more than he could resist, so he extended a shaking hand and softly laid it on her head. Her hair was damp, her skin cool. He allowed his palm to brush there before his skipping heart forced it back to his side.

When her eyes opened wide and looked at him, he froze.

"How are you feeling?" he asked, pushing his hands into the safety of his front pockets.

"Lousy," she grumbled. "Get Dad, will you?"

While Garren examined Nicole upstairs, the family waited in the kitchen over giant bowls of Lois' caramel corn. Breck ate to be hospitable. Lois made

Noon - Katherine Warwick

the best food he'd ever eaten, and she loved it when he devoured it. Tonight, however, his stomach was tied in knots, his eyes kept drifting to the back stairs.

"Dad tells me you're thinking about Psychology." Brian was next to him, sharing one of the colorful bowls of the sweet caramel corn. Over the months, Breck had come to enjoy Nicole's brother as his own.

"Yeah."

"A friend of mine's in family counseling," Brian went on. "He loves it."

Breck nodded. Helping to heal damaged souls and broken relationships would be like that. "Why'd you choose radiology?" he asked.

Brian reached for a handful of caramel corn, juggling it between his hands. "I saw how much time my dad put in and knew I didn't want that for me and mine." He popped the handful in his mouth and looked over his shoulder at his two daughters. "I wanted to be there for them, you know?"

The two blonde girls were fighting over who would hold the bowl of caramel corn. Breck nodded. If he had a family, that's what he'd want.

Again, he looked toward the back stairs.

"Uncle Breck. I wanna dance." He felt a tug on his pants and looked into the hopeful blue eyes of Rachel. He couldn't resist, and it would get his mind off Nicole.

"Teach her cha-cha," Lois called from the kitchen.

Breck took her little hands in his and began instructing. Rachel kept her eyes on her feet and a giggle in her throat.

"You're making me look bad." Brian popped another handful of caramel corn in his mouth. "Tami's been on my back for years to learn ballroom."

Breck shot him a smile and turned Rachel in a slow spin. "Then you'd better do it, bro... for you and yours."

Grinning, Brian rose, took Tami's hand and led her next to Breck and Rachel where he struggled with steps that Breck made look fluid. "It's harder than it looks."

"It's easier than you think," Breck corrected, watching Brian fumble over Tami's feet. He stopped when he saw Garren descending the back stairs. He was next to him in a flash. "Is she all right?"

The concern brought a smile to Garren. He patted Breck's shoulder. "She will be. I can't be positive without blood work, but I'm pretty sure she has

◎ 112 ◎

mononucleosis."

Lois gasped.

"Mono?" Breck repeated.

Garren nodded, looking at Lois. He knew what that would mean for their dancing and he crossed to Lois, ready to offer his shoulder for her tears.

Lois eased herself into the nearest chair, her face whitening. The room fell silent.

"Did you tell her?" Brian asked.

Garren nodded. "She's very upset, of course."

"Oh, no." Lois buried her face in her hands. "But how? She doesn't even have a boyfriend."

"Lois, it's a misnomer that mono comes strictly from kissing. The virus is spread much the same way a cold travels: by sneezing, contact with the un-washed hands of an infected person or touching something an infected person has touched recently. And, like a cold, it can be passed along when two people kiss."

A lump formed in Breck's throat seeing what this was doing to Lois. He could easily imagine where the news was taking Nicole. "Can I go up?"

Garren nodded. "She's dealing with the news…just warning you."

She wasn't crying when he knocked on the door that was slightly ajar and she didn't look over when she told him to come in. She was staring out her window, propped up in bed, clutching a floral pillow to her chest.

"Hey."

She kept her eyes out the window, into the darkness. Her blinks were heavy, and she held onto the pillow as if she were holding on for life.

He quietly crossed to her. "Why didn't you tell me you were sick?"

She shot him a look overflowing with frustration. "I didn't know I had mono."

"Not that. We didn't have to compete."

"Yes we did." Her voice cracked. She tightened her arms around the pil-low. "Dad said that wouldn't have made a difference. I already had it. Besides, it may be the last win I have for a while."

"*We*, Nicole." It irritated him that she could only be thinking about dance, that her drive was so intense she abandoned common sense along the way.

"Yeah right," she choked out. He saw tears pooling in her eyes, even though she kept her head turned. "You'll find another partner."

"What?" He tried to laugh but couldn't, the idea so shocking, it bruised him. "Now you're just being stupid."

Her head snapped around. "I could be sick for months. This could ruin my chances, my hopes for more Nationals."

"You just won a title, Nic." He didn't bother softening his voice. If she was going to be hard-headed about this, he'd need to break through her thick skull. "*We* just won a title. It's ours now, we own it."

"But that's not all there is."

"Yeah, there's more to life than dance competitions."

She sat up, tossing the pillow aside. "Maybe for you, but it's what I want."

"How can that be all you want?" Thrusting his hands up into his hair, he paced next to her bed. "What about after?"

"I'll figure that out when I'm there. For now, my goals are defined and now," she grabbed the pillow again, squeezed, "they're screwed."

Breck took in a deep breath. She looked so completely lost, like a child abandoned. His heart took a hit for her. "Maybe it won't be long."

She was focused on the darkness out the window but lifted a shoulder. "What will you do?"

He hadn't thought about himself. She looked over, braced for hurt. He had no doubts that he would stay her partner, if that's what Lois wanted, what Nicole wanted. Still, her suggestion caused the smallest twinge of disconcerting fear inside. "I'll be here," he said softly.

When she took a deep breath and brought the pillow to her chest, he sat down on the side of the bed next to her. She was calmed a bit by the news. In her eyes there was the faintest sparkling of pleasure that eased Breck a little.

He laid his hand on her knee, well hidden under mounds of blankets. Touching her now felt so different than touching her on the dance floor. He wanted to comfort her, to say all of the things in his heart that his voice could not yet say.

Nicole wondered if he was doing it again, speaking to her with those expressive eyes, so blue she could look into them and think there were messages pure and sweet there, just for her. That was what she wanted. She wanted him to be there for her. She knew that now. But life had a way of taking those most important and giving them distractions too irresistible to resist.

When his hand covered her knee, she looked at it, admiring the beauty of his long fingers. Feeling the need for reassurance, her weakened body gave way and she couldn't stop the tears that sprung into her eyes. Dropping her head to her chest, sobs wracked her as everything she'd dreamt about looked further out of reach.

It calmed her instantly when he drew her against him, wrapping his arms around her. His hand gently stroked her hair. It was shameful to respond so easily, like a child, quieting and relaxing against the familiar strength of him.

"Thanks," she murmured against his chest.

"Go to sleep," she heard him say. She fell asleep in the secure comfort of his arms.

Noon - Katherine Warwick

Twelve

Word spread like a communicable disease about Nicole's illness. It burned Breck when he saw those who professed to care, to be her friends, whispering and smiling behind her back because she was temporarily out of the dance game. Competition was such that the lack of one more party only made bad luck more pleasurable for those who could take advantage.

Kit showed up to the studio one afternoon while Breck was teaching a private lesson. In her jeans and pink baby tee, she had a smile that dared on her face. Primly, she sat in one of the seats alongside the dance floor and crossed her legs.

Her eyes fastened on him.

The committed teacher in him wouldn't allow Breck to send her anything more than a nod of greeting. He continued focusing on his student. "You're doing good," Breck told his young student, a girl eager to continue with instruction in the waltz. "Really great, Dionna." He slowed them to a stop, and stepped back. "You can practice more at home, okay?"

"We still have three minutes." Dionna held out her arms for more.

"Uh." Breck glanced at Kit who gave him a flirty wave then he took Dionna once again in the standard position. "One more time."

"What country did bear-hugging come from?" Dionna asked once they'd started swirling around the room again.

"That's not a form of ballroom," Breck said, whirling her effortlessly.

"Do you teach it?"

He fought a smile. "Everybody already knows it."

"I don't."

After they finished the rotation, he stopped and held her hands – and her – a safe distance out. "I'll see you next week."

She frowned before breaking into a sunny grin. "Okay. See ya, Breck."

Dionna shot Kit a girl's competitive sneer that only made Kit's smile bigger. She stood and sauntered over, waiting until the door closed with a soft thud. "Hey. Thought you might be rusty."

"Rusty?" She had a look in her eye he wasn't familiar with, but that teased him all the same.

"That you might need to refresh your memory," she said.

Breck crossed to the sound system. In the reflection of the mirror, he watched her follow, noticing how tight her jeans were, how snug her tee shirt fit. Heat shot to his cheeks and he decided it would be better to concentrate on putting away the CD.

"I thought with Nicole down you might need someone to run through steps with."

He slipped the waltz CD in its case without looking at her. "I'm okay, thanks."

"Oh, you're more than okay," she purred. "You're better than Nicole, you know that don't you?"

He shot her a warning look. "She's my partner."

Kit clasped her hands behind her back and moved closer. "Protective. I like that."

Jaw tight, hands uneasy, Breck wondered what was coming. His heart raced with the possibilities, with having to deflect them.

"So, wanna practice?" Kit tilted her head, and when she did, her hair shimmered like spun cream.

"I've just practiced."

She smelled as soft as she looked. Her rosey perfume floated around his head, strangling his throat with her scent. The room was too warm, and she was too close. "I need to get in for dinner," Breck's voice warbled, giving him away.

"Just one dance." Her lips curved.

He glanced at the large clock Lois had installed over the door. It was eight-thirty, dinner was already over. Naively, he thought one dance would satisfy her so he nodded. She placed her soft hand in his and led him to the middle of the floor.

"Wait here," she said.

Breck watched, he breathed, his heart danced as she swung over to the music and put on a slow song that would mean an even slower dance.

When she came back, her arms wound like liquid velvet around his neck.

She began to move.

"This isn't how that combination goes," he told her, trying to keep his voice even.

She laughed softly in his ear. "Are you afraid?"

She was looking at him so intensely; he couldn't look back. Before he knew it, she leaned up and pressed her lips on his. They were soft, just like the rest of her, moving across his like butterflies – butterflies that had invaded him and were now loose inside. Sweet heat tingled in his mouth, then spread. His arms were already around her so it was easy to pull her in tight. It was easy to kiss her so he did. Sweet heat melted, and poured through his system like a volcano had erupted. Every inch filled with a searing pressure that nearly burst through his skin. Breck heard his name when her lips left his for a breath and it sent a thrill through him he'd never felt, and he kept his mouth on hers.

Then he heard a cough. He knew the cough hadn't come from her, their lips were still locked. He heard another and jerked his head toward the door just in time to watch it shut.

With a firm push, he was free of Kit. The blood that had raced so euphorically through his system dropped to his knees. He was out into the darkness of the property and found Garren making his way back up to the house.

"Garren?" He met Garren's stride, glad it was dark so the man he had come to love like a father wouldn't see his red face.

Garren put an arm around his shoulder. "Sorry to interrupt."

"I – I'm sorry."

"What's to be sorry about? You're entitled to a life."

"It's just…I feel—"

Garren stopped and looked him in the eye. "Don't feel guilty. This is your home. You're free to do as you please."

Breck glanced up at the house, at Nicole's bedroom window, and Garren followed his gaze. "Commitment to your partnership does not mean celibacy from relationships." Garren patted his shoulder. "I just came out to tell you Lois put your dinner in the oven. Come up when you can."

Breck watched him walk away, and a pit grew in his stomach. There had been sincerity in Garren's eyes, truth in his words, but it didn't do much to change the reality deeply imbedded in Breck's heart – Nicole.

Noon - Katherine Warwick

Confusion kept his pace slow as he headed back to the studio. Kit had kissed him. His first kiss. His body had gone out of control like a stagecoach careening downhill without a driver. He was shocked.

Underlying that shock was a low hum that he couldn't tune out, one that had Kit's face flashing in competing images with Nicole's in his mind.

"Who was that?" Kit asked when he returned to the studio.

Breck brushed past her to retrieve his things. He didn't want to hear her soft voice. Most definitely, he shouldn't smell her flowery perfume again. "Garren."

"Mr. Dubois?" She followed him to where his jacket lay on a chair. "What, is he a voyeur or something?" She joked but Breck turned on her, and his chest nearly bumped into her breasts. He froze.

Her perfume snuck into his nose again, threatened to fill him if he took another breath. He had to get out of there. He snatched his jacket and headed for the door. Kit stayed alongside of him, as if they were in a race to the finish line.

But she got to the door first, and stood blocking it, her bright eyes dancing with delight. "Stay."

Heart thudding, he reached around her to open the door, but she slid over and his hand skimmed her waist. He drew back, eyes locked with hers.

"You'll think about that kiss," she whispered. "You'll dream about it. And you'll come back for more."

He couldn't move. When she stroked the side of his face just once, he forced himself to ignore the fire her fingers left behind. He opened the door and strode past. As if a hot iron had grazed his cheek, the burn of her touch lingered as he walked toward the house alone.

Nicole couldn't put a finger on it but something about Breck was different. He had an air about him that older boys carried, and it laid halfway between cocky and confident. He moved differently too. Awareness seeped from him like breath; as if everything around him lived with the sole hope of connecting with him somehow. Something raw and physical adorned his body with a masculinity she'd only seen in adult men.

It burned her withering pride into stubble.

Tonight, she could smell his cologne, dancing through the upstairs rooms like a phantom partner. It seared her senses, igniting jealousy. She couldn't take another weekend of his taking off.

Tossing back her blankets, she was feeling stronger so she stormed, albeit weakly, down the hall to his bathroom. She found him in front of the mirror, wearing only sweats, his bare chest glaring at her. He was running his fingers through his damp hair. He'd gotten bigger, and his added height stretched already beautiful, lean muscle underneath smooth skin, giving him the enviable physique of the accomplished, dedicated dancer that he was. She'd kept up, growing an inch or so herself, but she doubted she looked as perfect as he did.

She didn't like that she stared, hated that he caught her ravenous gaze slowly taking in every inch from the low riding waist band of his sweats, up and along every artfully cut line and groove of his abdomen to the gentle sculpted beauty of his shoulders.

He grinned.

She cleared her throat, leaning in the doorway for support. "What is that?"

"What?" He turned, checking himself out from every angle.

"That gasoline you use as cologne. It's gagging me."

Another cocky smile spread across his face. "It's Aquadesia. Every girl I know likes it."

The scent quickened her pulse, and made her angry. "Huh. Put something decent on."

Teasingly, he leaned close. "Can't take it?"

She tightened her grip on the doorjamb then turned and made her way back down the hall to her room. As she passed his bedroom more of his scent hit her, making her head swim, her knees weak. She paused in the door.

"Move," he said behind her.

Nicole let him brush by. "No need to be rude," she snapped, following him inside.

"I don't want to be late."

"Where are you going?" she asked.

Noon - Katherine Warwick

"Out."

"Again?"

"Yup." He went to his closet, looking. "How's this?" He pulled out a striped shirt, held it under his chin and looked at her. The blue stripes shocked his eyes into blazing sapphires.

"It looks okay."

He pulled out another, this one a deep raspberry color. She loved the way it lit his face. "This?"

That some other girl would be enjoying him instead of her, made her frown. And he smiled. "This be the one." He slipped it on, and she took in a deep breath watching what happened to his muscles when his body shifted.

"Why don't you get dressed?" he asked when her eyes met his. "You look like something puked out of the ground."

"Why? I'm not going anywhere. I never go anywhere," she muttered.

"Have some pride, some dignity, woman."

Woman? Was that how he really saw her? Nicole tried to stand on her own, even though she wobbled a bit. He was at her side in a flash.

"Careful." Real concern replaced the cocky show he'd been putting on, and it gave her a small wince of satisfaction.

She brushed his hands away. "You're going to be late."

The moment jagged between them when he didn't move. "Yeah," he finally said. "Put on something decent." He walked to the door, finished with the last button on the shirt.

"What, can't take it?" she asked, taunting him with her best smile.

Something curious crossed his face. It came from his eyes and she thought, if she could read them, they would be saying that, indeed he could not. She took a satisfied deep breath and slowly made her way to her closet.

It was so quiet downstairs, Nicole wondered if her parents had gone out, too. "Nobody tells me anything anymore," she mumbled, feeling sorry for herself. Breck had left, but his scent floated in the air, tormenting her. Figuring she had some pity coming, she decided to indulge in some woe-time. To her amazement, she was hungry. She decided to drown her loneliness in a bag of potato chips and not think about Breck and the fun he was having no doubt in lip lock with Kit.

"Mom?" When no reply came, Nicole swallowed utter abandonment. "Well, thanks," she muttered.

As she came around the corner into the family room, complete darkness stopped her. It wasn't like her parents to leave the lights off. Breck, in his hustle to get out, she thought bitterly, forgot to be decent and leave them on. "Twerp."

She ran her hand along the wall for the switch, but the feel of warm flesh under her fingers brought a curdling scream from her throat.

The lights flashed on. The room filled with laughter and shouts of 'surprise!' A rush of voices and bodies came at her; nearly knocking her over. All of her friends were squashed into the family room.

"Were you surprised?" Tiffany hooked an arm in hers.

Nicole's pulse had yet to slow. The sight of friendly faces lifted her sore heart. "You guys scared me."

"Take it easy there." Chris put an arm around her. "Let's get you to the couch."

Pulling her elbows free of them both, Nicole stood firmly on both feet. "I'm okay. Really, I am." Casually, she scanned the group for Breck. Commotion behind her had her turning around.

"We're here for a pooper party," Breck announced. Nicole found him standing on a chair, taking command of the room.

"Lois and Garren have left me in charge…" Whistling and cat calling followed. Breck put both palms up. "There's tons of food. The game room is down stairs, and we'll be featuring," he looked down at Nicole momentarily, "Nicole Dubois' on the big screen."

"Oh." Raising his hands again to quiet everyone, he added, "I know you all want to hug Nic because you haven't seen her for a while, but…" he paused for dramatic delivery, "no kissing. Doc's orders."

He jumped down and was right next to her, but talking to Parker. Nicole wasn't sure why, but she wanted him by her side and longed for his undivided attention. Maybe it was because she still wasn't feeling like herself. She tugged his sleeve. "Where are Mom and Dad?"

He leaned near so she could hear him over the noise, and caught another whiff of his bone-melting cologne. Her heart fluttered ridiculously. "They took off. Thought we'd want the place to ourselves. Nice, huh?"

"Breck." Kit called to him from the back of the room.

Breck shot his engaging smile Kit's direction and made his way through the jostling crowd without as much as a goodbye. Nicole's heart wilted. Watching him lean cozily into Kit's flirtatiousness wasn't easy. It was then Nicole realized where she stood with Breck; in front, with their arms in standard dance position. Blinking fast, she kept back the tears welling behind her eyes.

Annie grabbed her arm and soon she was greeting friends on her way to the TV. "You, sit down and rest." Annie settled her on the couch with the efficiency of a mother, fluffing pillows before sitting next to her.

Tiffany plopped down on the carpet at Nicole's feet. "So you'll be able to come back to school next week?"

Nicole nodded. "Just in time for finals. Hopefully I won't fall asleep."

"That'd be easy to do even without mono."

Since her videos were playing and half of the group had planted themselves in front of the big screen to watch, Nicole felt obligated to watch with them, but she kept a casual glance out the corner of her eye toward the kitchen where Breck was now playing host to Kit and some others, handing out cans of soda.

"Check out the costumes." Parker pointed to the homevideo, wobbing with age as the camera panned the dance floor for twirling dancers.

"The feathers in the hair were so tacky," Tiffany observed. "I for one am glad that style has gone out."

Annie reached for some of Lois'carmel corn overflowing in a big, round orange bowl. "We all looked like birds."

"Look, there's Trey. Dude, you look like a weasel," Chris announced.

"We were hot, weren't we?" Trey's breath slithered in Nicole's ear and she jerked back. She hadn't seen him before now, and wondered where he'd been. He slid down next to her, wedging himself between her and Annie, who was too distracted by the videos to notice.

Nicole couldn't believe Trey was considering them an item. "We were kids."

He slipped an arm around her shoulder. She didn't like him being this close, and a shudder of wariness rambled through her. His steamy scan of her from her head to her toes more than set her off, and she gave him a disparaging glare. He only grinned. "You look hot."

Nicole snorted out a laugh. He let out an angry whisper in her ear. "I'm sick of you treating me like this."

"How did you get an invite?"

His eyes danced around to see if anyone was watching and since everyone was engrossed in the video, he stayed close. "Of course I got an invite. We were partners."

"For about a minute."

"That's not the way I want it."

Because Nicole saw that Kit had her arms draped around Breck, she faced Trey with pleasure to be vindictive. "And how do you want it?"

"From you, I'd take it anyway I could get it."

"You'd let me kiss you, even with mono?"

Trey inched back, startled. But his face twisted with temptation. His lips curled, and he wet his mouth with a slow swipe of his tongue.

Nicole swallowed back disgust. When she was sure she was in Breck's view, she slid her arms around Trey's neck and stared into his ice-blue eyes. "You're not afraid?" Out the corner of her vision, she could see that Breck had broken free of Kit and was making his way over.

"Trey." Breck was behind the couch now, squatting down. "She's sick."

"Yeah, well, she wants me."

Nicole tossed Breck a smile meant to dig. When his brows knit tight, and his mouth formed a hard line, she had his full attention and meant to make the most of it. She turned to Trey. "Kiss me," she lulled, tugging gently at his neck.

Breck stood.

A chant began almost instantly and the group circled to watch the lip lock. The back of Nicole's neck tingled. Because she was only kissing Trey to hurt Breck, it was all she could do to kiss long enough to be convincing. Finally, she broke free, smiling as if she'd enjoyed every minute, even though her stomach churned.

Noon - Katherine Warwick

The room filled with cheers and sneers. Nicole couldn't help it; she looked up into Breck's face. The way his jaw set, the dark tension in his eyes, wiped the distaste of Trey from her lips with a swab of satisfaction.

"You're smokin' dude." Parker landed a hearty pat on Trey's back. "Now go home and take some Echinacea."

Trey laughed, glanced at Breck with a smirk and pulled Nicole into his side possessively. "It was worth it." Then he leaned into Nicole and kissed her again.

Breck turned and went back into the kitchen with a slug of fury in his gut. He grabbed a cup of ice, tossed some into his mouth and chewed. *Games*, he thought, wishing the ice would freeze the bitterness he felt. But it didn't. Every time he looked at Nicole cuddled next to Trey, his whole body drew into a ferocious fist.

Kit's hand on his arm did nothing to ease him. In fact he shrugged her off, angry he had to tear his eyes away from Nicole. He refilled the ice chest without saying anything to anyone. The laughter picked back up, talk flitted in the air, but the playful sounds didn't penetrate the wall of frustration surrounding him.

"Trey's brave," Kit said.

"He's stupid," Breck bit out. He turned, pulling out more soda from the refrigerator, and plunked two six packs on the counter.

"Actually, he's thirsty."

Breck looked up, saw Trey.

"You belong there, Noon." Trey leaned over the counter bar with a smug look. "Two Pepsis, bartender."

Breck slid a six-pack in front of him with a hot glare. Trey laughed. "Yeah. Behind the counter's where your kind belongs."

Breck's body twitched in restraint. "Take your drinks and get lost."

"I'm with the guest of honor." Trey pulled two cans from the plastic lace that held the sixpack together. "I'll be sticking around a while. Who knows, maybe it'll be you walking out that back door. You can go back to the trash can you crawled out of when she decides she wants me as her partner."

Kit covered a gasp.

Lunging over the counter, Breck caught the front of Trey's shirt in his fists, and the two boys tumbled backwards, with Breck landing squarely on top of Trey. The laughter, the chatting died. Parker and Chris jumped on Breck's back, pulling him off before he could do any real damage. It took both of them to restrain a heaving Breck, who jerked free of both boys' grip.

"You're an idiot." Fury burned like fire through Breck's viens.

"And you're still trailer trash, Noon." Trey's face was bright red. "Starting a fight at Nic's party? Only a low-life would do that."

Breck jumped on Trey again, their bodies like felled trees, toppling over the back of the couch before rolling across the floor, then ramming into an oak coffee table.

Chris, Parker and some of the other boys leapt on the mass of kicking legs and scratching arms like a football team in a tackle. When blood began to fly, the girls screamed.

Nicole's breath had stopped in her chest when Breck lunged over the counter. Afraid he'd hurt himself, she leapt to her feet. Now, she fought dizziness, stumbling over to stop the fight. Heavy grunts and the sound of fists against flesh made her stomach clutch. Breck and Trey were twisted into a burning pretzel of writhing anger she didn't dare touch.

She grabbed Annie and together they dragged the ice chest over, tossing its contents on the boys, bringing the brawl to an instant stop.

Breck sat back, breathing heavily, wiping the blood from his split lip. He looked at Nicole, and that was when Trey took the opportunity to slug him across the side of his face again.

Rage fueled Breck's final punch, and it landed right across Trey's nose. The quick snap sounded through the room like a cork popped off a bottle of celebratory champagne.

Stunned, Trey clasped his hands over his face. "You broke my nose!"

"Stop it," Nicole shouted. "Get out!" Trey looked up at her, eyes full of rage and disbelief. "Go."

Only the sound of heavy panting filled the air. The boys got up, brushed themselves off and assessed damage.

"You don't play fair, dude," Parker told Trey quietly.

Trey shot to his feet and Nicole pointed to the door again. "Get – out!"

Even with the disgracing silence, Trey sent one last glare at Breck. He had a hand over his nose but that didn't stop the blood from trickling down and into his tight-lipped mouth. Wading through the crowd, he shoved those in his way aside as he made his way to the door.

Still fuming and tense, Breck hardly noticed that both Nicole and Kit now stood beside him.

"He's such a loser." Kit scanned his face with a worried eye but Breck didn't see it.

He rolled his shoulders. His face, masked with a private message, was aimed at Nicole. She moved to the girls, now whispering about the fight, but she wasn't listening. Her eyes never left Breck.

He went into the kitchen to retrieve paper towels and Hydrogen peroxide. *This was my fault*, she thought. *The blood oozing from Chris's eye, the rip in Parker's shirt...Breck's bloodied lip...all my fault.*

The fight sucked the wind out of the party and where a few remained to help clean up, the rest left.

After Annie, Tiffany, Chris, and Parker had gone, Nicole straightened the floor rug that had gotten puckered in the tussle. She kept watch on Breck, now cleaning the kitchen, lip cut, his left cheek coloring to eggplant.

With caution she joined him. His tight movements warned her to keep her mouth shut, but she didn't—couldn't, knowing she'd caused the whole mess. "You're hurt."

He continued to wipe the counter as if she hadn't spoken. She reached out to touch him and he snapped around to ward her off, the blue in his eyes was like a fire at midnight. "Don't."

"Let me help."

"Forget it. What were doing tonight, anyway?"

"What do you—" He didn't even let her finish the sentence. He grabbed her by the arm, snagging her in front of him so they were uncomfortably close.

"Look," she shot back, frightened of him for the first time. "Where you come from people may use physical violence but in the rest of the civilized world it's not acceptable."

His grip tightened. "You think this is violence? This is kid stuff."

The danger behind his eyes sent an unwelcome shiver down her back. She couldn't move, aware that he was stronger, bigger, and that left her helpless to his whim.

"Let me go," her voice cracked.

After he released her, he leaned his back against the counter, his blue gaze hard and unforgiving. Her feet remained fixed to one spot, too afraid to move.

"Why did you do it?" His low tone warned her not to lie to him.

"I—"

"The truth, Nic."

If she told him that she'd behaved ridiculously to make him jealous, he'd know how she really felt about him and have the upper hand. She'd be giving too much of her heart away. He could hurt her then.

"Trey and I are getting back together." She lifted her chin. Even as the lie spilled from her mouth she felt the stab of regret. She opened her mouth, wanting to take it back but nothing came.

His eyes flickered with disbelief and hurt, and she reached out, drawing his wounded gaze to her outstretched hand. She wanted to see if it mattered. Did he care? Was he jealous, like she was? His gaze fell to his feet.

"Not as partners," she finally said.

"Whatever." He bent over and picked up an empty soda can, then placed it in the trash. With one last weary swipe he finished cleaning the counter. Without looking at her, he began turning off the lights, and left her standing alone in the dark as he trudged up the back stairs.

Thirteen

Spring four years later

Breck couldn't find a parking space and the itch of being late for rehearsal crawled under his skin. That he still had a good quarter of a mile to walk to reach the auditorium on the sprawling campus of Utah Valley State College only made the itch worse. He took his chances and pulled his black Jeep into the visitors' parking section. If there was a woman in the booth, he'd be charming. If there was a man, he'd take the risk of getting a ticket.

He was in luck.

She smiled big under her blue visor and leaned out of the parking booth. "Visiting the campus today?"

Breck nodded and flashed a smile. "Can you tell me where the Ragan Theater is?"

She pointed to a large building that he knew darned well was the Ragan Theater. But he looked at it with believable surprise. "Is that it?"

"You a performer?" She handed him a stamped card for his dashboard.

He took the card and made sure his fingers touched hers when he did. "I am."

"Actor?"

"Dancer."

"I love to dance."

"Yeah? Come see the show. My partner and I are doing a guest spot." Breck shifted the car into first so she'd hear that he needed to be on his way.

The arm on the gate slowly went up and she came out of the booth with a slip of paper.

"I'll be at your show." Then she pressed the paper into his hand and waved him in.

Her name and phone number. Brenda.

He pulled into the nearest empty spot, the grin still on his face, and stuffed her number in his pocket. He got out and swung his backpack over his shoulder then shut the door with care, admiring the playful toy with pride. He'd bought it himself.

Garren had wanted to give him a car of his choice for his twentieth birthday two years earlier, but Breck insisted that he pay for his own. He'd been given enough at the generous hands of Garren and Lois Dubois, he thought and as he walked across campus to the Ragan Theater it hit him in the chest, with a fist wrapped in gratitude whenever he thought about where he'd be if they hadn't found him – if they hadn't saved him.

Appreciation and love went straight to his bones, and whenever he was asked where he came from, he began his story when his life had started over: when Lois had approached an awkward kid who was wasting his life on a pair of rollerblades that would never take him where he ultimately needed to go.

Breck figured he fit in well now, blending with the other students all making their way to class. Sometimes he looked into the faces of those he passed and wondered where they'd come from, and what had brought them there.

Dance had taught him he could conquer any challenge, and which challenges were worth paying the price.

He rounded the corner of the theater. In a few moments he would meet up with Nicole and his body tensed just anticipating the inevitable. It had never been easy between them. It hadn't been hard either, just challenging.

"Breck."

He turned just in time to see Reuben jog up behind him. The sun's warm color only deepend Reuben's chocolate skin to a rich, espresso brown. Breck marveled that Reuben never aged, that his green eyes still pierced with that same brilliance as a neon light. The man could still outdance most of the top competitors, something Breck found silently amusing. Their palms slapped in a friendly greeting and they walked in through the stage door.

The low hum of pre-production buzzed around them. Props were set near the curtain, mikes tested and music blared. Dancers hung around the back, some going through steps, others visiting with each other. Every one of them turned and acknowledged Breck and Reuben with curious stares and whispers when the two stood on the fringe of the stage.

Nicole was right there in the middle of it all, talking to the production manager. Breck and Reuben remained unseen in the wings.

"Think she's seen the clock?" Reuben whispered.

It didn't matter, Breck knew by the snap in her voice they were in trouble. The years of disciplined existence had trimmed away any humor from her, leaving only a lean and very often tense woman.

"I don't want a spotlight, it's too hard on my eyes," she shouted toward the back.

The stage manager's head lowered. When it lifted and his eyes caught Breck's, his face lit with hope. Nicole turned around. For a second, her eyes slit and she paused. He saw the faintest smile before she stalked over.

"You were supposed to be here a half hour ago."

Breck threw his backpack across the stage floor and watched it slide until it hit the wall. "I'm here now." He would have placed his hands on her shoulders to calm her, but that didn't help anymore so he breezed past her to the center of the stage and looked around. "Remember our first performance in this theater?"

She was next to him in three long strides. "Let's not get nostalgic. Let's get to work."

He looked at her, sighed. "This isn't work, Nic. Tonight's about fun." That, too, was useless to say, but he said it anyway. It rolled off her professionally slick back.

"Are we going to practice before the teams get here or—"

"Relax." He placed his hands on her shoulders then, and felt her stiffen.

She smiled a brief, sweet smile meant to pacify, then rolled her shoulders free. He'd spent a lot of years trying to convince her that she needed less business and more pleasure, but it was a concept she avoided. He'd contemplated why, when she'd had plenty of guys chase after her. That was never easy to see. With every new man in her life, he was forced to stand at arms' length off the dance floor and watch.

None had taken her heart. Selfishly, he'd breathed a sigh of relief every time she'd move onto someone new. There was a place deep inside of him he held in reserve just for her. He couldn't help that he wanted her there. When he'd been lost, it was her hands that had reached out, taught him the steps, and led the way. Their partnership had been his first real relationship. Even through the ups and downs, respect had grown between them.

Commitment to dance kept them together.

He'd settled with himself that that would have to be enough, that the partnership was both the beginning and the end of whatever would happen between them.

She covered her eyes in the glare of the spotlight. Her long, shapely legs were bare, completely exposed under the short, sassy black skirt. Even now, his mouth watered at the sight. She watched her body with the precision of a runway model, an obsession most female dancers couldn't avoid but made him frustrated for her all the same. Her waist was tight, her arms lean. When she moved, there wasn't a soul alive that wasn't captivated. Including himself and in that thought, he followed behind her, the focused nature of her bringing out the teasing nature in him.

She looked to the control booth. "Kill that spot!"

Playfully, Breck mimicked her in pantomime. It would rile her, but he didn't care. What few dancers had gathered, along with stage personnel that had stopped to watch, laughed. At first, she didn't catch on. It only took a moment and she smirked at him, then smiled at her audience.

"Cue our music, Jeff," she yelled. Breck knew that gleam in her eye well, and readied for some fun.

Reuben clapped his hands and joined them on the stage. "We ready?"

She crossed her arms but the snap of disapproval was long gone from her tone. "I saw you walk in with him. You're both getting new watches for Christmas."

"Ready?" Reuben simply repeated.

Nicole turned and stood ready for Breck, mischief playing in her eyes. "I'm ready."

"Be nice." He took her hands.

With ease, they went through the two dances they would be performing in the program. Latin went perfectly smooth, reaffirming to anyone observing that Breck and Nicole had earned their name and world-class rank over the past four years in the world of ballroom dance for a reason. The rehearsal was a bittersweet reminder for Breck of how the years of being together had imprinted them with each other's thoughts. He knew, just like she knew, how she was going to move and react to the commands his body gave her.

Halfway through Jive, when Breck bent over, Nicole was supposed to run and jump over his back. Her eyes glittered from across the stage and he knew he was in trouble. She ran and playfully shoved, sending him flying forward on his belly in a slide that took him across the stage. The audience had grown, drawn into the theater by the open doors and inviting music. They cheered at the good-humored change of choreography.

Breck rolled onto his side and grinned, taking the joke in stride, enjoying that she was letting her hair down, even if it was at his expense.

Circling the opposite side of the stage, catching her racing breath, Nicole waited for Breck to stand. "Cue that playback when Mr. Noon is ready," she tossed, sending him a challenging look.

"You're crusin' for a bruisin.'" Breck was up on his feet and crossing to her, anxious to draw out the pleasant moment as long as he could. He held out his hand.

Nicole smiled, and didn't take it. "We're even now. Let's keep it that way."

He knew that would never be. They'd never been even, he thought, his hand sliding down to his side. That was precisely the problem.

"I said no spot!" she shouted toward the light, and stepped away from him.

*   *   *

Nicole was more nervous than she could ever remember being for any competition. Friends were in the audience, fellow students, teachers, old team-mates. Her father. *We might as well be performing for the Queen.* She peeked out the side curtain at the packed house. The house lights were up, and people were still finding their seats. This wait was far more nerve-wracking than she liked. *Get your wits, Nicole. You've performed for cutthroat judges and hard-nosed audiences. You had every one of them eating out of your hand, so what are you sweating about?*

Noon - Katherine Warwick

Her gaze followed bodies and faces; her parents were somewhere – she'd saved them front row seats. But those seats remained empty. Then her eyes lit on a mop of sandy blond hair. Her heart tripped for a moment until the head turned.

Trey.

The very sight of him sent a shudder through her system.

Nicole had no desire to be within five feet of Trey, let alone across a crowded auditorium. Her stubborn pride had pushed her into one of the worst times of her life, the weeks back in high school when she's played Russian roulette as Trey's girlfriend just to make Breck jealous. She didn't like to think about what it had cost her.

Everything had changed after that, and she had only herself to blame. Because she should have known better, been more responsible, she swept that distasteful period of her life in the corner of her soul where she stored things she couldn't face.

It was no secret that Breck and Trey couldn't stand the sight of each other. Things had gotten to the point where the two of them were barely cordial, though Nicole knew that was more Trey than Breck.

As a dance partnership, Kit and Trey always stayed just a step or two behind her and Breck. The pairs' hot breath at her and Breck's heels kept them moving faster to ensure they maintain their position in front.

Nicole only tolerated Kit, mostly because Kit still batted her lashes and turned a pretty shade of pink whenever Breck was within two miles of her.

She wanted to think time changed everything and in some ways, that was true. She was glad it had been years since she'd severed her relationship with Trey. But it saddened her to think no amount of time would give her what she really wanted.

"Full house?"

Whirling around, Nicole held the curtain closed behind her back not wanting Breck to see Trey.

Parting the curtain with his fingers, he peeked over her shoulder anyway. His smile flattened, his eyes went black. She put her hand on his chest. "Forget him."

He didn't look long; his eyes found hers again. She wished for a moment she was the reason behind the long-standing battle between him and Trey the way he looked at her; with regret veiled by resolve.

The resolve hurt the most.

Breck turned and she followed him back to their dressing room. She'd spent a better part of their partnership trying to read the messages he spoke with his face. He blamed her for not being able to communicate from the heart. But, she noticed that since he had started college and delved more deeply into the study of Psychology, he'd closed off part of himself. It pained her to think he was learning to conceal things, just like the rest of the world.

She shut the dressing room door behind her. "So?"

Already in the slick, black pants and sheer black shirt he would wear on stage, it was never easy to ignore the man that he had become. The garment outlined every sculpted plane on his abdomen, across his strong back. The slacks caressed the sleek, lean lines of his thighs. She looked away when he caught her admiring him.

"So," he answered. "I left Trey on the floor at your parents' house that night and haven't thought about him since."

"You make it sound like it's easy."

"It is. We have mutual disdain for each other. I'm sure he hasn't thought about me either."

"And the fact that you permanently altered his nose that night doesn't give you even a smidgen of satisfaction?"

"Let's just say his face matches his soul now."

She expected an answer like that. He was so far beyond of most of the men she knew, it was times like this she felt the pain of her past catch her in its noose, knowing he would never be hers.

They had both had other relationships, but one thing remained constant as the other loves fell away – their partnership. The hope she'd guarded so closely that it would grow into something more was still inside of her, though that hope had taken a beating from reality.

She picked up his sequined vest and fiddled with it. Seeing Trey and Kit opened old wounds she couldn't ignore, and she eyed him for his reaction. "What about Kit?"

"She's Trey's partner. If he's here then it wouldn't surprise me to see her."

"She'll want to see you."

His lips curved a little and she wondered if he was excited to reunite with her. Because the thought bruised her battered heart, she looked away.

He took the vest from her hands and set it aside for the jive number. "I'll say hi." Then he sat down and reached for his dance shoes, his gaze sharp, deciphering. "Are you worried?"

"I really don't care about your social life," she bit out. "As long as you perform as you're expected to." She bit her tongue, wishing she hadn't said the words.

His hands caressed the soft leather of his shoes. The act reminded her of how he used to touch them with such reverence when they had first started dancing together. He slipped them on, and she waited for a fight. When he lifted his head and their eyes met, she was ready.

"Perform as you're expected to?" Rising, he crossed to her, stopping close enough to start her heart thumping. "Get something going in your life besides dance, Nic."

"You don't know what I need."

"We couldn't have spent the hours, the years that we've spent close like this and not know each other inside and out."

"And that gives you the right to tell me how to conduct my life?"

"That gives me the experience to tell you that you need to make some changes. You've cut everything away. It's not balanced. You need other interests."

"Dance is my life. It's all I want to do, and I'm happy doing it."

"You think you're happy but Nic, nobody can be happy doing the same thing day in and day out."

"Why not? I thought that was the idea. Find something you love and stick with it."

"Sure, yeah. But it's all about you. Your days, your nights, they're all about you."

She was too stunned to speak. Only in the silent whisperings of her soul did she know the truth of his words. She'd drifted the last few years. When life hadn't given her what she'd ultimately wanted, she'd suffocated pain and disappointment by wrapping herself in the deceptive comfort of self indulgence. Only one other person had even had the nerve to point it out to her, and she'd denied the suggestion.

"You're just like him – like Dad, all self-righteous."

"Not self-righteous just honest. But I'll take the rest as a compliment." Breck turned and began patting on stage makeup because he was afraid he might try to choke some sense into her. She was still holding on to anger that had bored in so deeply now, he found it disrespectful and undeserving of Garren. "How long are you going to punish him?" he asked.

"As long as it takes."

"Until what? Until you feel justified? He's forgiven you."

"What does he have to forgive? I'm the one who's lost out. I'm the one he can't make peace with. You think I should just live with the fact that he still doesn't approve of my dancing? He accepts you, why can't he accept me?"

"He loves you, Nic. That's more than dance. Why isn't that good enough for you?"

He made it sound so simple. That pain flashing in his eyes just then reminded her that her father's love was more than he'd ever gotten from his own father. The emptiness she was trying to fill was a void so vast, so out of reach, another wave of disillusionment surged over her.

"So easily these things come from you now," she began. "Have you forgiven your father?"

His eyes went from hers to his own as he stood in front of the mirror. Calmly, he touched the makeup sponge to his hands, to the white rings – reminders that he would forever wear of his father's sins.

"I've taken care of my father the only way he would understand." Breck thought about the money he sent each month. He had severed Garren's ties to his father amicably, unbeknownst to one or the other. It was he that sent the money now, a cashier's check, just like Garren had – to keep Rob Noon out of their lives. To Breck, it was a small price to pay to keep the man where he belonged, and to protect the ones he loved.

She crossed her arms over her chest. "I didn't mean to bring it up. I'm—" His eyes met hers in the reflection of the mirror as he waited for the words. "I'm sorry," she finished. But there was so much more she wanted to say, wanted to know. *I love you.* The words were there in her head, had been forever. But she couldn't share them now when he didn't feel the same way. More than anything she wished he felt the same. *How can I change this? What do I do? Help me to find a way back to you.*

Her heart wouldn't take the truth from him – the truth would kill her. In his need to know, to understand all that life had dealt him, he'd settled himself with these things. But unanswered questions still besieged her; peace eluded her, another partner dancing just out of reach.

"I have to get ready," she said, her voice laced with emotion and loss. As she had done out of necessity throughout the years, she would lose herself in dancing. Turning, she went to the door. She didn't hear him move, only felt his hand wrap around her arm. Startled, she looked up into his face.

She hoped for something unspoken in his eyes. He held on as if he didn't want to let go. But he did, and she thought her heart might tear straight through if she looked at him any longer, so she opened the door and went out.

The room was black, the current in the air electric. The audience waited for music, for lights – for Noon and Dubois. Strumming guitars had the crowd cheering as lights – red, green and gold – lit on Nicole standing at the corner of the stage. Enrique Iglesias began to sing about *bailimos* – about belonging, leaving your life in the hands of someone you love. Nicole tried not to think of the words. She stood ready to dance.

The red-sequined dress kissed her every inch, flaring at her hips. She lifted the hem of the skirt, extending one long, fishnet covered leg.

Breck appeared on the opposite side of the stage. It amazed her even now as she gazed at him, a casual passerby taken in and seduced by the senorita there to tempt, how she never tired of looking at him.

They passed each other first, Breck's shoulders back, eyes locked on hers as he rounded her in a circle. He'd learned showmanship over the years. She wished that fiery look in his eyes was real. She flung her hem, fluttering her skirt in invitation. Linking arms, they wrapped around each other and the first steps of love teased. Then he took her in close, her body fusing to his as he swayed them back and forth. After countless dances, she marveled that her body still melted on contact with his. The fiery heat, the passion exchanged was with

Noon - Katherine Warwick

bodies, breath, and eyes, not words.

She played at wanting, needing, but then teased and pushed him away, and danced alone.

Stepping back, Breck circled, watching and waiting. The spotlight lit her, and he knew she would rip into whoever was behind the mistake later. She never broke, just spun around, then beckoned him to join her again with her hands and her hips – red liquid in motion.

Wrapping his arms around her, Breck looked into Nicole's eyes and saw submission, felt it in her body as he controlled her. But it was only for the dance, and they both knew it. Still, he would take the moment and make her completely his.

He held her, and thought their steps mirrored their lives. Together there was magic, beauty and harmony when they moved as one. Inevitably, she would spin out and dance on her own.

Because he was losing something he had yet to completely own, he took her hand with more fury when she came into him again. Surprise flickered in her eyes as they moved for the last, final moments of the song. He had her then, just for the dance, and he would want her long after the music stopped.

The final strains of melody sung around them, and Breck led them through their last steps. His mind flashed memories of when they had first danced together. Her face was close, their eyes locked, and he felt her heart beating hard against his. Her lips parted, poised and ready. It was more than he could resist. Years of waiting, wanting and dreaming filled him with desire that drove him to lower his head and cover her mouth with his.

Nicole couldn't hear anything, the roar of the applause, the calls and cheers all dissolved. The warmth of him enveloped her, and the world around her stopped. Her heart, body, and breath stilled at the command of his hands. All that she'd wanted from him, the countless times she had dreamt of him, now flooded with more life than the blood running through her veins.

Her eager arms slid around his neck. His lips were warm, salty with sweat. She forgot they had an audience and kissed him with necessity that held nothing back. Tears gathered in her eyes. Joy filled her heart. This was worth waiting for, more sweet than anything she could imagine.

Then his lips left hers. Gently, he tugged her arms free. It was then she stood back in a daze, finally hearing the thundering applause and whistles.

He turned her out for her curtsey. The squeeze from his hand brought her gaze to his. "What was that?" she asked through a smile. They bowed together.

"If you have to ask, I'll need to do it again." He brought her into his side, waving at the audience.

The curtain fell.

He held onto her hand, and Nicole looked at where they were joined, as one. Then her gaze found the endless blue of his eyes. Everything around them seemed to slow to a blur. Later, she wouldn't remember hearing any of the congratulations, feeling any hugs or pats of admiration. The moment was branded into her heart as theirs alone.

Only the sound of her father and mother's voices broke the magic winding around her and Breck.

"That was marvelous! Perfect!" Lois embraced Nicole and Nicole's hand slipped from Breck's, leaving her with an empty hollow in her chest.

Garren shook Breck's hand. "Impressive as usual."

Elated, Nicole waited for her father's approval. The twinkle in his eye kept the smile on her face. When he hugged her, she had to fight back sweet tears. "You were perfect."

"Thank you, Dad."

"I saw Tiffany and Annie in the audience," Lois bubbled. "I invited them along with Parker and Chris and a few other old friends to come over for a little reunion celebration. Of course Tami and Brian and the girls will be there. Oh, and Reuben and Gail. Is that all right with you two?"

Breck chuckled and kissed her cheek. "Whatever you want, Lois."

Nicole's lips still tingled from Breck's kiss. Something glittered in his eyes whenever he looked at her, and pleasure rippled right to her heart. He took her hand in his again, warm and reassuring.

"We'd better go change. Nic?"

In the dressing room, Nicole flushed from head to toe when the door shut. She could hardly bring herself to look at him. All the years they had shared spaces identical to this one, and suddenly she felt the uncomfortable need for some privacy. Hearing him behind her didn't help. Her heart pounded.

Noon - Katherine Warwick

She started to take off her dress. But she couldn't say anything. Conversation that normally blurted from both of their lips about performance or competition was nowhere to be found as they changed in quiet silence. Soon, her mind was floating in uncharted territory she knew could be dangerous. Down to her bra, panties and hose she stole a glance at him. He stood hanging the sheer shirt, but he looked at her over his shoulder. Their eyes locked. Nicole flushed from head to toe and turned back around, continuing to undress. Maybe this meant he saw her as more than just his dance partner. Maybe that kiss had not just been for show.

Fourteen

The reunion was like old times. Nicole stood in her parents' family room looking at the smiling faces of her friends and family with a full heart. No Dubois gathering could fully function without music in the background and she put on a favorite CD. Some of her dearest friends were there, and just looking at them bound her heart with emotion and happy memories.

With admiration she watched her mother take trays of food around, chatting with Tiffany and Annie, Parker and Chris. Her mother's friendship and love had never been exclusive; she loved them all as her own.

Always, Nicole searched for Breck, and when she found him, her body both relaxed and hummed. He'd kissed her. She pressed her fingers to her lips; her heart beat faster recalling. For a moment she pretended that it meant something.

Then Kit and Trey walked in.

Nicole froze only a moment before her performance smile slicked into place. Her quick glance at Breck told her he was just as surprised as she was to see the two competitors. She recognized the look in Trey's eyes, like a cat that had just cornered a mouse he led Kit to where Breck stood laughing and talking with Chris and Parker. The instinct Nicole felt to protect Breck was so much a part of her, she found herself striding over.

"Kit. Trey. It's been a long time."

"Nicole." Kit gave her an artificial hug. "Congratulations, the show was great."

"Thank you."

Trey was smoother than plastic. " Yes. Great performance. And that kiss." His brows shot up. "Well, that was showmanship like I've never seen."

"Pretty hot." Chris landed a hearty pat to Breck's shoulder. "I knew I should have stuck with dancing."

The joke didn't lighten the dark veil Trey's presence had cast over the conversation. Nicole flashed another smile. "It was a good act."

Noon - Katherine Warwick

"Was that what that was?" Trey's grin slid Breck's direction.

Parker jostled the ice in his empty glass as he grinned at Breck. "You always had the moves, man. And you always had the girls."

"Lined up, from what I remember," Chris elbowed Breck.

Trey's eyes slit with mischief. "If I didn't know better, Noon, that kiss would have convinced me that you and Nicole had finally hooked up."

Something protective flashed in Breck's eyes, and he looked at her just long enough that Nicole's heart skipped, before he tilted his head at Trey. Because she sensed the undeniable thickness in the air of a fight ripening, she slipped her arm in Trey's.

"Trey, have you said hello to my mother? She'll want to see you."

"Haven't yet baby doll. It was so nice of her to invite us."

"Yes. She's always been a thoughtful hostess," Nicole charmed. "I want to hear all about New York. Are you still out there training?"

"Not anymore."

Nicole steered Trey toward the food. "Oh? I thought you and Kit were happy back there."

"It's been fine, up until now. I'm making other plans."

Nicole wasn't listening. She glanced over her shoulder, hating that Parker and Chris had been lured to her mother's caramel corn and that left Breck and Kit alone.

Kit traced her fingers up Breck's arm, but the gesture didn't break Breck's tight jaw. He was too focused on Nicole, still trying to bind the angry energy that Trey had let loose inside of him.

"Hey." Kit's eyes were alight with curiosity, and pointed with the sharp arrow of desire. "It's so good to see you again. You look great."

Breck watched Nicole, watched how she had her arm linked in Trey's, and a knot hardened in his throat. "Thanks."

Placing herself in Breck's line of vision, Kit flipped a blonde curl over her shoulder. "It's been so long. I was hoping we could catch up."

"Sure." But Breck knew the catch up wouldn't take his mind off what was under his skin. Keeping Nicole and Trey in his line of vision, he dug deep down for a genuine smile. "How's New York?"

"I'd rather talk about you." Kit sidled up next to him with the slick move

◙ 143 ◙

of a woman on the hunt. "I want to hear everything, Breck. You can start with that kiss."

There was something to the low hum of laughter and voices that calmed and comforted. Garren figured he'd missed out on plenty of that for too many years because of scheduling demands and mistaken priorities. To hear the laughter and voices, vague echoes of a past he never knew, hurt now. Both mixed with regret inside of him.

He couldn't restore time and claim what he'd neglected along the way, but he could be better. He'd tried. He looked at Brian with pride and very few concerns. His boy had done well for himself, for his wife and two daughters. That they lived near enough for their father-son relationship to tighten helped ease whatever lingering guilt remained in Garren's heart where Brian and his youth were concerned.

Garren laughed along with the group, now gathered around a slow fire, catching the last bit of a story Breck was telling. He watched Breck rib Nicole after embarrassing her. Breck had been good for Nicole in ways he and Lois never could have been. *He knows her better than I know her*, Garren thought. The enduring weight of what he and Nicole lacked pressed him into sorrow.

Surrounded by her friends, family and admirers, Nicole was resplendent. Garren's heart felt isolated. One decision changed the course of our relationship, he lamented, not listening to the happy chatter, rather losing himself again in a loss that had occurred some seventeen years earlier.

He hadn't known that Lois' dream would become Nicole's dream, and one of them would forever be divided from him because of that. Finding Breck had helped, and he looked at the boy he considered a son. Lois had been right to take him in. Caring for Breck had changed their lives, brought their decaying marriage flesh and blood again.

Because of him, Garren knew what the five dances of Standard ballroom were---that Paso dobles wasn't a town in New Mexico, but a form of Latin Ballroom—Breck's least favorite. He knew that the quickstep could be done to modern music, that jive was exhausting, but a showstopper. He also knew people could, no matter what shackles weighed them down, rise up and make something of themselves. Change things.

When he'd seen Nicole dance today, the way she moved – it had been breathtaking. As a father, he had to swallow his pride and admit that she was perfect. Still, it was never easy for him to see her scantily clad, see the sensual movements that, when put to music were a sexual poetry of sorts.

Their battle of wills would never end. She'd been born with her mother's grace, beauty and talent. But from him she took stubbornness and drive.

Her eyes caught his and there, in that moment, he thought perhaps her heart had opened up to him the way she paused. Her smile, though brief, was just for him.

Guilt, fear, need, hope – all rushed through him and he rose and crossed to her. The same anticipation he'd seen in her eyes as a child was there now, when she'd needed him to tell her how well she'd done after a competition, and because he hadn't agreed with what she was doing, he'd never listened. The party would go on until the late night hours, Garren wasn't worried about stealing her for a few precious moments.

He leaned and whispered in her ear, "Let's take a walk."

When she wrapped her arm around his, that child-like need opened her blue eyes wide. Hope rushed through him, and he abandoned old pride and handicapping fear. Garren looked out the windows over the vast thickness of the orchards and led his daughter outside.

Long after midnight the voices that had just hours earlier filled the house with laughter slowly dissolved. Promises for another reunion were made, kisses and hugs exchanged, and then it was over. The emptiness inside of Nicole ached. She stood at the bottom of the grand, winding stairway of the entry and looked up.

Light streamed from the open door of Breck's old bedroom. He was there, retrieving something before he took off to his apartment. He had his own place now. After high school, he'd refused to stay on any longer, feeling like he'd taken enough from her parents' outstretched hands. She knew it was his way of

Noon - Katherine Warwick

finally being independent of things.

Her heart beat hard as she slowly took the steps. She heard him moving around inside. Anything she said would sound contrived. He hated it when she didn't just say what was in her heart. But her heart was ripe and vulnerable, the fear of rejection real. *I must be crazy, thinking he could feel anything but friendship for me after all these years.* The thought stopped her just outside his door. But her father's words in that orchard were there in her mind, lit by the glimmer of hope. *Change things.*

She couldn't remember the last time they'd had a father-daughter talk, but it didn't matter because he'd opened his heart to her and she'd been surprised and pleased beyond words. He'd done most of the talking, and when he'd apologized through tears, they'd embraced in a long moment of joined love she would never forget.

The last thing he'd told her was that she should have everything her heart desired. When she told him what she wanted was something she could never have, he almost looked like he knew what she was talking about, the glimmer in his eye so optimistic, she dug for courage.

Now, here she was outside Breck's door.

Everything she had tried in the past to lure him had backfired. She leaned her back against the wall and closed her eyes on a heavy sigh. *It's embarrassingly plain; can't you see he doesn't have feelings for you?*

But that kiss this afternoon had been more than showmanship. She would remember the burn of it on her lips now when she spoke to him.

He was standing over the desk, rifling through some yearbooks and scrapbooks when she entered. The lamplight was golden, the room quiet, and she looked at his broad shoulders, the way his hair curled at his collar, a tossle of dark curls and waves. She'd never touched it. Tonight she would.

Quietly, she came up behind him and stood as close as she could without alerting him. And waited.

He turned a page in the book – then another. Then his head came up and he stood still. For a moment he just breathed. She wanted to touch him, to spread her hands slowly across his shoulders, but she kept her hands at her sides feeling the energy in the room thicken.

Finally, he turned. He wasn't startled, wasn't even surprised. He just looked at her. She tried to let her eyes speak for her heart.

"I—" was all that came out. It had always been easier for her to communicate with movement, that's why she loved dance. She reached up to touch his hair. It was soft, and her fingers laced through it. So soft, she let her hand linger in the curls and stepped closer. The dark blue in his eyes looked black and alive. "Stop me if you don't want me."

"Nic." His dark lashes fluttered, his chest lifted and fell rapidly with breath.

"I'm going to tell you how I feel, what I want." It was easy to look into his eyes and think she saw invitation there. So many eyes had looked at her that way. But this was Breck; Breck whose eyes knew, whose face she could read, and at that very moment she would do something she'd never done – place her heart in the hands of another.

"That kiss," she whispered. Confusion fought with resolve on his face; playing like a picture, plain and pure. It challenged her. "You kissed me like you wanted me. Do you?" She couldn't believe she'd asked. She'd wondered so many times, wished it was truth so many more.

"I have." Boyish innocence made his voice crack, and she smiled with pleasure at all that she had come to love about him.

"Still?"

He seemed to ponder her question, his penetrating gaze cutting her straight to the heart for truth. In a flash his arms wrapped around her and he pulled her close. His mouth met hers.

Needs that had grown unattended inside of her now demanded notice. Hesitation that had kept her heart protected behind its iron gate swung open, freeing her pride. This was sweeter than the thrill of winning. She would give away every win, every first place – anything to stay locked in his arms forever.

It seemed as though he had always been hers. Hands she had held countless times, fingers long and gentle when they'd taken hers in dance, now wandered up to touch her face, framing it. His lips eased light and fluttering over hers.

"I love you," she heard herself say. Her heart froze in her chest. She waited for him to stop, laugh, to push her away as if the dream was a terrible joke.

"Nic." Covering his hands with hers, she closed her eyes. "I know what that cost you," his voice was gentle, accepting the tender token of her heart just as she hoped he would.

"Well, for a long time I didn't want to admit it to myself."

"I think we both felt that way."

"You too?"

He nodded, and brushed his lips across hers again. A sigh warbled contendly from her chest.

His blue eyes glittered. "As hard as that was for you to say, I want to hear it again."

"You would," she teased then bit her lower lip. Honesty freed so many deeply kept fears; faith set those fears in his caring hands. "I love you."

He laughed, low and warm, dropping his lips to her jaw before he kissed her there. "Finally."

Easing herself back, she searched his face. "Is it too late?"

He shook his head. "No way. Never."

She closed her eyes again, and pressed her head against his chest wanting so to hear his heartbeat, to get as close to him as she could. Trusting him was liberating in a way that lifted her soul, and started her dreams in a dance she had long ago thought she'd lost the steps to. "If you knew how long I've wanted this—"

"Not as long as me." He smiled, and held her so that he could look into her eyes, wanting her to see the depths of his feelings. "Not as much as I love you," he murmured.

The truth was too much to dream, let alone believe what was happening was real. As he looked into her face, he thought he could stay in this moment forever, just to ensure that nothing changed.

Years of living with her as a partner, friend, and rival had left him standing always at arms' length. Only in fantasy had he lived this moment, over and over. Hope had vanished long ago as he'd been forced to accept that her heart, her life, would never hold a place for him unless he was a part of her goals.

"What can I say," he kept her tight against him, feeling her body warm, soft, in a way he'd never felt her before. "I guess part of me can't believe it."

"I know," she laughed, sending a tremor of need through his chest. "I think I've always loved you. Even from the very start, when you wore those rollerblades everywhere, and I thought you were a dork. Something about you was different."

His arms tightened around her. "I was a dork," he half laughed. "I am a dork."

"I love you, Breck," she had to say the words again. That was risking everything, but she'd risk it. They had shared a kiss, yes, but she wanted his heart. "I want you in my life. Not just as my partner." The dark blue eyes that had eluded her for so long were hers now, as she read his face. "Stay here tonight," she whispered. "Please."

He looked ready to agree until something shadowed his expression. He looked off a moment, then back at her. "I can't."

"What?" She felt his arms loosen just enough to make her feel fragile. "Why?"

"I couldn't do that to your parents, Nic."

"Breck." She held his hands in hers, clinging to something she felt might slip away. "They love you."

"Yeah, like a son."

"And so that means that you and I can't allow ourselves to express what we've felt for each other for years now?"

Surprise and pleasure settled his face into a content smile. "Years."

He seemed to relish the idea. It was in the comforting way they fused together again, his arms pulling her in as if in the steps of dance but there was no music, no audience, and competition was gone.

There had never been anyone that, with one look, could penetrate her soul so deeply, as if he could, without any effort, navigate his way to that secret place she kept hidden just for him.

She had waited because of him, saved the most prized gift. She'd hoped, somehow they would be together. For years his had been the first face she'd seen in the morning, the one that she'd been just inches away from as their bodies pressed close in dance. They'd spent hours talking about school, friends and, of course, dance. There was no one else she dreamt of sharing her life with.

She traced his jaw with her finger, rose up on her toes, and pressed a kiss there. "You're the only one I've ever wanted, I want you to know that. There hasn't been anybody else, not ever, Breck."

The smile on his face stole her breath. "Nic." He wrapped around her, urgency keeping their bodies fused, and once again his lips pressed against her cheek, "I want you to marry me."

Lois' nerves fizzed. She'd been in the kitchen rattling pans and bakeware as loudly as she could for the last twenty minutes, hoping the noise would travel up the back stairway and awaken those still sleeping.

Earlier, she had looked out her bedroom window to see if Breck's car was still there. She'd grinned when she saw that it was.

Pancakes would be ready when everyone rolled, grumbling she hoped, down the stairs. She loved nothing more than to feed a grouchy mouth into a grin.

Fresh fruit was on the table, one of Nicole's favorites. She'd even made a pile of blueberry muffins just for Breck. The pancakes were for Garren, and she greeted him with a smile when he came down the stairs, his plaid robe hanging open, his striped pajamas underneath. The sight of him first thing in the morning still sent a sparkle to her heart.

He rubbed his hair, leaving it in a matted mess. "Smells like pancakes."

"It is." She poured batter onto the hot griddle and he sat at the table.

"Four place settings?" He seemed more alert at the sight of Lois' brightly decorated table.

"Breck stayed over."

"Good. I didn't get much time to talk to him last night."

Lois had heard Breck and Nicole talking late into the evening. Now, she was more than anxious to talk to her daughter. "They were up late." She flipped the pancakes.

"I imagine so." Garren opened his cloth napkin, set it on his lap. "She told me she wanted to talk to him."

Lois frowned. Men could be so vague. "Did she tell you why?"

"It's their business, Lois. I didn't want to pry." Sensing he might be in trouble, Garren looked to change the subject – fast. He rubbed his hands.

"Those pancakes ready?"

Lois slid them on a plate and came around the counter, plate in hand. "What do you know?" With a raised brow she held it just out of his reach.

"Lois."

"They're getting cold."

"Why don't you ask her?"

"I would if she was up, but—" Lois saw that he was looking behind her. She turned; Nicole stood at the bottom of the back stairs with a grin on her face.

"Honey." After Lois plopped Garren's pancakes in front of him, she hurried over and gave Nicole an embrace overflowing with girlish excitement. "Well?"

"Well, what?"

Lois slid her arm around Nicole's shoulders and led her toward the table. "Oh, come on."

"I'm starving." Drawing her flowered robe tight around her, Nicole plucked a strawberry out of the bowl of fruit. "Wow. Look at all of this."

Lois pressed out a sigh. "You were talking until all hours last night."

"Yes, we were." Nicole edged next to Garren and kissed his cheek.

"And did he say anything?"

He proposed, Nicole thought with another shiver of thrill. It had been the most wonderful night of her life. They'd spent the evening talking about plans, dates, what they wanted and didn't want for their special day. But they wanted to tell her parents together, so she filled her plate with fruit and looked at the muffins, Breck's favorite, and smiled. "He said a lot of things." Lois grinned, waiting for more. "Well, you wanted to know."

Hands thrown up in exasperation, Lois turned and went back behind the counter to pour more batter on the griddle.

"We talked, Mom." Nicole smoothed over the obvious impatience in her mother. "He's…" Her lungs fluttered out a breath. "He's Breck," she said wistfully.

A creak on the back stairs had all of them glancing that direction, but it was Nicole's heart that thumped like a rabbit's foot. There was nothing left of the teenage boy she'd seen descend those same stairs so many times before. The tall, masculine form of a man had taken his place.

He came in pulling the same soft gray teeshirt he'd worn the night before over his head. His jeans were well worn and baggy. "Hey. Morning." Breck crossed to Lois and kissed her cheek but his eyes went right to Nicole.

"Morning." Lois' warm smile bloomed. "Hungry?"

Breck chuckled at the obvious edge in the air. "Yeah. Smells great."

"There's fruit," Nicole piped, for lack of anything better to say. When their eyes met, she stopped chewing, the blueberries in her mouth sliding down her throat in a tasteless mass. He sat himself down directly across from her and her stomach bubbled.

"Morning, Nic."

"Morning"

"Muffins." Breck reached for one. "You outdid yourself, Lois." He reached for the butter, and Garren handed him the dish.

"We should hit Cascade Golf Course later."

"I haven't golfed in years."

Garren nodded. "I know."

But Nicole wanted Breck around, not off on some five-hour golf game. After last night, she wanted – no needed, to spend the day with him. There was too much, too new, to just go on about her day as usual. She was waiting for him to give her a sign so that they could tell her parents the news. Still, she recognized real joy on her father's face and wouldn't deny him. Breck's warm hand took hers. His eyes held hers across the table.

"Do you mind?"

That he'd ask made her love him even more. She linked fingers with his. "Of course not. Dad can have you for the day," she mused with a grin. "I'll take you tonight."

Cascade Golf Course spread up the base of Mount Timpanogos like a green, velvet blanket, dotted with men in white pants, pastel shirts and light sweaters. The May sun was warm coming down through soft, doughy clouds in a bright blue sky. A breeze drifted from the canyon, making the game more challenging for a rusty Breck who could only shoot twenty-five over par on a perfectly still day. Garren regularly let off steam with medical colleagues on the green, so he was relaxed as he stood next to Breck, eyeing just where the shot was supposed to fly.

The tension in Breck's arms had Garren breaking into a smile. "It has been a while, hasn't it?"

Breck squinted hard. "Is it that obvious?"

"It just looks like you've been spending more time on the dance floor than on the golf course."

Breck settled into the shot, looking at the ball. He'd spent more than a lot of time on the dance floor. *Nic,* he thought, and saw her bright grin in the glow of last night's lamplight as they'd discussed their future.

He took the shot and the ball flew haywire.

"Well, hmm." With a lift of his white baseball cap, he scratched at his head.

Garren patted him on the shoulder. "You hit any more balls like that and you'll be here after hours with a flashlight, son."

Breck could have been hit by one of those flying balls; the word *son* hit him just as hard – in the heart. He couldn't move for a moment, so taken with the emotion rolling through him. All he could do was stare as Garren started off.

Finally, Garren turned. "You coming?"

Breck swallowed gratitude and love and willed his feet to move. "Uh, yeah." He was glad he was wearing the white baseball hat, that it shaded his watery eyes.

They were quiet for a time as they walked to the next hole.

"It was like the old days having you stay the night," Garren said at last.

"Yeah, it was." *Except I proposed to your daughter.* Breck slowed to a stop, a pit growing wide and deep in his stomach. What would Garren think about his proposal to a woman he'd practically grown up with? Something about it kept him from asking Garren for her hand just then as a wave of discomfort suddenly made him antsy.

"Mind if I sit down?" Breck's knees nearly buckled.

Garren quickly backtracked. "Everything all right?"

Breck nodded. If he wasn't careful his face would give away the twist he felt inside. Garren kneeled down next to him, but Breck couldn't look him in the eye just yet, still sorting things out in his mind. "Give me a minute."

When he finally had the nerve to, he saw that same concern he'd seen on Garren's face any time he'd had a problem or been ill, and Garren had come to his aid. There was loyalty and love there, and it humbled Breck, taking the words out of his mouth.

"Wanna call it quits?"

Breck shook his head. "I need to redeem myself."

Garren laughed and extended his hand to pull Breck up. "You probably didn't get enough sleep last night."

"Yeah." The moment was the perfect chance to ask for Nicole's hand. But he couldn't bring himself to, not willing to disappoint or hurt the man he loved like a father. They walked a few steps further in another heavy silence.

"You're good for her."

"I love her."

"I know." Garren sent him an easy smile. "It was serendipitous."

"Yeah, well, we danced around it for a long time."

Putting an arm around him, Garren brought him into his side for a hug that lingered, even there on the golf course.

Noon - Katherine Warwick

Fifteen

"You've been smiling all day," Lois commented as they drove up Battle Creek Drive toward home. They hadn't talked about her and Breck while they'd shopped, but a mother knows things. Lois' heart hadn't stopped tapping since that morning when she'd witnessed the undeniable gleam of something special in her daughter's face.

Now, the sun was setting behind the western mountains, shooting purple fire into the sky, and over the craggy mountain peaks. Part of Lois didn't want to accept that her daughter had fallen in love. She still saw her as her little girl. The other part loved Breck like a son, and where she knew he was not her blood-child, to think that perhaps they had crossed a boundary, thrilled and terrified her at the same time.

"It's been a great day, hasn't it?" Nicole's tone held whimsy but she didn't care. She'd been running Mrs. Breck Noon through her mind all afternoon – like a lovely melody of sorts, one she couldn't shake from her head. One she could dance to endlessly.

"We did find some good deals." But Lois knew that wasn't what Nicole-was talking about.

"Do you think he'll like the shirt I got him?" Nicole asked.

"Very much. And the color will be wonderful."

Nicole could see Breck in it; the high periwinkle shade would make the blue in his eyes the color of the deepest part of the ocean.

She waited for the gates to swing open, and then drove up the long driveway with a tune on her tongue. "Think the boys are back?"

"Let's not hold our breath. You know your father and the golf course. And he probably took Breck out for something to eat."

When they didn't see the black Jeep, saw that the house was still dark, they both sighed with disappointment.

"You go on in, I'll bring the stuff," Nicole told her. She watched her mother take their purses and unlock the back door before going around to the back of her car and opening the trunk.

She looked at her watch. It was seven-thirty. She wondered what could be keeping her dad and Breck. She couldn't wait to see Breck, to finally spill the news together. Anxiety made her laugh. *It's just Breck*, she thought, but knew, in that instant, that she could never think of him without it thrilling her, ever again.

She had two bags in her arms when a hand wrapped fast and hard around her mouth, another around her waist. The faint scent of stale cigarette wafted into her nose. Dropping the bags, she kicked and opened her mouth to scream, but her screams were lost behind the calloused hand mashed across her face. The arm around her waist pulled her so tight, it pinched off air.

In seconds, she was carried out into the darkened mass of the orchards. Panic jagged through her body. She struggled with every angry and refusing fiber she had, back-butting her head into the assailant's face, writhing and clawing, kicking and jamming her heels wherever there was bone.

He squeezed tighter, growling in her ear. Again, she caught the stale breath of cigarette. When he had taken her deep into the orchards, far enough away from the house that any sound would be swallowed up in the endless, dark rows of trees; he threw her out in front of him and slugged her in the abdomen with one, hard punch that left her choking for air and toppling to the ground.

Clawing at the dirt, she tried to crawl away, but the heavy thrust of a boot slammed her into the back, sending her flat on her stomach. She choked for a breath, her heart pounding so feircly in her throat she wasn't sure she'd ever breathe again. Forcing herself over, Nicole sent both legs whirling up toward her attacker as if she was riding a speeding bike.

She couldn't see any details except that he was gigantic, and dressed head to toe in black. "Don't touch me again," she screamed, anger overriding fear.

She pushed herself to her feet, took in a deep breath and ran at him. Arms fueled with fury, she went at him like the blades of a helicopter. He grabbed for her hair and yanked her around, throwing her back on the ground.

There was no sound, only his heavy breathing coupled with her frantic gasps as she tried to crawl away. But his hand snapped around her ankle and dragged her back, sliding her right underneath him.

She stared up, frozen, and tried to stop her limbs from quaking.

"Nic?" In the distance, she heard Breck.

"Nicole?" Her father's voice was frantic, echoing off Breck's.

"Breck!"

In a flash, her assailant reached for her shoulder, took a handful of fabric, and tore it across her chest. Instinctively, her hands flew up to cover her exposed shoulder and breast but he backhanded her, sending her head thudding into the dirt, leaving her stunned.

"Nic? Where are you?" Breck was still calling; his voice getting louder even though her head throbbed and buzzed from the blow. "Nic?"

The dark figure looked over his shoulder toward the voices before he took off, disappearing in the blackness of the row. Still ready to fight, Nicole scrambled to her feet.

Then she felt it – like she'd been run over by a semi-truck; her body draining, her legs turning to noodles beneath her as she slid helplessly to the ground in a heap.

A light blinded her.

"Nic." It was Breck's voice. He was near. She tried to see him through eyes blurred with tears that wouldn't stop coming. She reached out with trembling arms, her body beginning to shake. Nothing came when she opened her mouth to speak. The earth rumbled beneath her, the pound of steps nearing, and at last he was there. He dropped to his knees next to her, wrapping his arms around her. His scent mixed with the moist dirt that covered her, his breath fused with hers. It was the last thing she remembered.

In the familiarity and security of the kitchen, Nicole sat with her mother on one side, Breck on the other. Her father paced a few feet away, his jaw in knots, body tight as a fist ready to strike. Her mother had warmed a blanket in the dryer and wrapped it around her shoulders but she was still shaking. She couldn't stop. Her head spun every time she closed her eyes and saw that figure looming tall and furious above her so she kept her eyes open, forcing the frightening image away.

She didn't know how she'd gotten into the house, she'd just opened her eyes and found herself looking into Breck's, so black with anger that any trace of blue had vanished.

He twitched next to her now, like a racehorse at the gate. She didn't dare look at him, afraid she'd see that black hate still in his eyes, a look that screamed of murder.

They waited for the police to arrive in a quiet so dense Breck could hear each of them breathe. He forced himself to stay in his seat, to control the urge to start throwing things every time he looked at Nicole's blackened cheek and swollen lip.

When he and Garren had pulled up behind her car and seen the open trunk, the fallen bags, his heart had dropped to his feet. But when he'd heard her scream, heard the shrill of it rising from the misty orchards like a waft of smoke, he'd never run so fast in his life.

She'd been out of it for the first few minutes; her body limp as he carried her to the house. He'd seen the tear in her clothing and pulled her close, desperate fingers digging into her skin until she'd winced. That anyone had intentions to hurt her left his blood boiling.

Now, he was scalding.

He jammed his hands through his hair, over and over. Emotion rose in his throat: fear, possession, the need to protect, all in a twisted knot that wouldn't leave his gut.

He didn't hear when Garren answered the doorbell. Didn't bother to look at the policemen that came in the room dressed in black uniforms with shiny silver buttons and brass tags, thick belts with even thicker guns hanging at their waists. He was wholly focused on Nicole.

Listening to their questions, he squeezed each finger on his hands until the flesh was white. He'd stopped feeling the ache in his jaw. As Nicole re-told what had happened, he felt responsible.

If he'd been there, she'd have been safe.

He looked at Lois, her face knit in concern, her hand clutching Nicole's. The victim might have been her. Because the thought hurt him so deeply, he scraped his fingers down his face and pounded the tabletop, bringing the questioning to a halt and all eyes to him. Pushing himself away from the table he

Noon - Katherine Warwick

stormed to the back door, where he stood in the shadows of the mud room.

Garren followed. "She's okay."

Breck twitched like a trapped animal. "It could have been worse. What if it had been Lois?"

"It wasn't. They're both okay."

"They'll never find who did it. Those damned orchards. You could die in there and not be found for days!" He looked at Garren. "I'm sorry, I just – they've always bothered me." A heavy feeling overcame him then, and he swallowed hard. Pushing past Garren, he went back into the kitchen and strode over to the table.

"Anything at all?" The taller officer asked Nicole.

She shook her head. "I told you, he smelled like cigarettes, but I don't think he was drunk."

The other officer scratched his balding head. "Well, we can file a report, but without anything more concrete for a physical description, finding a suspect won't be easy. You say you employ various ethnic groups to work the orchards, Mrs. Dubois? Do any of your men fit this description?"

Lois shook her head. "Most of my workers return to me year after year. I haven't had any problems." Her knuckles had whitened gripping Nicole's forearm.

Breck squeezed the back of the chair he stood behind until he lost feeling in his fingers, until everything inside of him screamed one name.

After the officers had finished, Lois took Nicole upstairs and ran her a hot bath.

Breck heard her wincing as she eased into the tub. "Take it slow," he told her through the door. "You sure you don't want to go to the ER?"

"Dad checked me out," she moaned. "He says I'm fine. I'm just sore."

Breck pressed his palms and forehead against the door and closed his eyes. He saw his father's face. "I'm sorry," he murmured.

"Did you say something?" she asked.

He shook his head, unable to repeat what was too horrible to think.

* * *

Breck tucked the blankets and quilt around her, then sat down on the side of the bed with his gaze locked on her face. It was still unfathomable that she'd been attacked. Though he secured the blankets with his own hands, it did nothing to bring him any comfort that she was safe.

Looking at her pained him, the swelling, the scratches turning from red to purple before his eyes. He ran a hand over her forehead, pushing her hair back. "I—" With too much to say from a heart swollen with the most important love he'd ever felt, he struggled with words.

Nicole reached up and stroked his tense jaw and her touch relaxed him for a moment. "I didn't think I would be capable of killing someone."

"Breck—"

"I'm serious."

"I can see that." Her hand slipped back down beside her. "Thankfully I can still dance," she said, as if trying to change the subject and the mood. "With world championships coming up, I wouldn't want—"

"Is that all you're thinking about? Dance? World?" He shot up, his hands diving into his hair. Fury burned through him again. "You could have been raped, Nic. This guy could have killed you, and you're worried about world?"

"I put up a fight, Breck. I wasn't going to let him do anything to me."

Something simmering inside of him finally let loose, Nicole saw it in his eyes. They changed, coloring with a horror she knew she would never fully understand. Slowly, he came toward the bed, then dropped to the side of it, his eyes fierce.

"You think you could have stopped him?" his voice ground out. "You're wrong. I spent years trying to stop a monster like that." His gaze lowered from her face to his wrists. He held them up and she stared at the white rings, her heart tearing. "If they want to hurt you, they will."

Her eyes blurred with tears. She longed to reach out and touch him, to take on this burden he'd held in two hands scarred with wounds still as fresh as if they had just been inflicted. "Breck."

His eyes were glazed with loathing so blatant she thought he could be capable of the same intense rage he'd been a victim of. She wasn't sure she should touch him; so she shifted in the bed, wanting to create space between them.

"Nothing happened," she repeated.

He didn't speak. Kneeling next to the bed, he lowered his head to his chest. It was a gesture she'd not seen him do for years. She reached out and ran her hand through his hair.

This was his fault; he knew it. He couldn't look at her anymore. Spindly guilt was there again, whispering, blaming. If he had never come into their lives, this wouldn't have happened. His father had screamed it over and over those first few years, "If you hadn't been there kid, she'd be alive."

Tears heated his eyes, and he buried his face in his arms. He hadn't been talking to his mother that day, they'd just been driving. It had been an innocent drive home from the grocery store.

Innocent, just like today.

A bitter laugh choked out of him. He lifted his head, rubbed his eyes. When he looked at Nicole, saw the love and concern on her face, felt it in his own heart for her, he knew what had to be done.

Taking her hand, he brought it to his lips. "I'm sorry."

"You keep talking like this was your fault. It wasn't. Don't blame yourself."

What she said didn't matter. All he could see was the way she looked under those trees, her shirt torn, body bruised, and the feeling was the same black feeling he used to get whenever his father would come after him.

His mind was already planning, and he pushed to his feet.

"You'll stay here tonight, won't you?" She still had a hold of his hand. He stared off into nothing until she tugged and he looked down. "Breck?"

"I'll be here." He leaned over and pressed a gentle kiss to her forehead. He wouldn't tell her he had something to do first. Pulling the blankets around her again, he sat on the bed and waited, watched as she fell asleep. Then he rose to leave.

Rob showered and cleaned himself up, then took long strides in the trailer. His body was still pumped, filled with the raw energy that always flushed through him during any violent contact. It had been so long, the twitching in his nerves made his arms jerk – his hands flex, readying for what was coming next.

This was what he needed, to sink his teeth into more flesh. Pulling back the curtain, he looked out the window. He tugged a cigarette out of his shirt-sleeve and lit up. Nothing had changed. His son sat up there on rich-row, living like a prince, and he was still in this low-life trailer park. The money hadn't done anything but buy him pleasures he couldn't pay for before.

He shoved a boot at his chair, watched it rock back and forth.

She'd deserved it, he thought, bringing the cigarette to his lips. But she deserved so much more. Little rich princess would have gotten it, too, if Breck hadn't come running through the trees like some knight in shining armor.

Looking at the smoldering gold tip of the cigarette, anger and resent-ment built, just like he wanted, for him to do what needed to be done.

Rob cursed, dropped the cigarette, and ground it into the carpet. In three long strides he was at the refrigerator, taking out a beer, opening it. Where did the kid get off thinking he could live like that?

The beer soothed his throat and he drank the entire can before crushing it and throwing it aside.

Breck had grown and filled out. That had been a surprise to Rob, but not a threat. He still outweighed him a good sixty pounds, was still a good four inches taller than the kid. Still, the boy had developed some, and he knew it would make their fight even more satisfying.

So when the offer came knocking at his door one day, it had been too tempting not to say yes.

"Are you Mr. Noon?" A tall man with sandy hair and a jagged nose stood outside.

He was prissy-looking. Rob hated prissy men, so he swung open the door, towered and scowled. "What do you want?"

"I'm looking for Rob Noon. I have a business opportunity for him."

It took Rob one second to forget the priss, his clothes, and the regal way the man walked into the trailer. He offered him a seat and waited.

"How do you feel about your son's dancing, Mr. Noon?"

Rob's jaw tensed, his hands flexed. "He knows how I feel about it. It stinks."

The blonde man nodded, a sliver of a smile on his lips. "How would you

Noon - Katherine Warwick

like it if he never danced again?" Rob sat forward, his nerves itching, as the man continued. "He has something of mine." The blond stranger calmly sat back and crossed one expensive pant leg over the other. The feminine gesture curdled Rob's muscles but if it meant destroying Breck's dance career, he'd ignore it. "And I want it back."

"What is it?" Rob asked.

With a slow shake of his head, the man continued. "No details. I believe your son has been paying you for quite some time now?"

"The old man's been paying me. Mr. Dubois," Rob corrected. "So Breck can dance with that cupcake of his."

The smile on the man's face spread to his light blue eyes. "Yes. Well, I'm prepared to give you what he's been paying you and more, if you can do one thing for me."

Rob had eagerly agreed. After they set terms, Rob rubbed his hands together and watched the man stand.

"Now understand me," there was warning in the man's voice as he made his way to the door. "I don't want her hurt."

Rob looked at the crooked nose, then at the light blue eyes that held something akin to his own. He crossed his heart before hacking out a laugh in the man's face. "I'll just scare her. When do I get my money?"

"I'll send you a money order it as soon as I know the job's been completed."

"Then in another six months?" Rob's greed rode his voice, had the man smiling as he shook off the stink of the trailer just outside the door.

He turned to look at him. "If things go as planned, you can start looking for a new place to live, Mr. Noon."

Rob heard the gravel crunching outside his window now, heard the engine of a car stop and his heart sent his blood on a race through his veins. It was time. Old passions never die, and the fire he felt whenever he hurt the boy still smoldered deep inside of him.

He faced the door, that smoldering heat ready to blaze.

Breck killed the engine and sat in the open Jeep, the cool night air chilling him to the bone. That and the sight in front of him – home. The thought shuddered out. The trailer really wasn't home, hadn't been for so long it seemed to be swallowed up in some sphere of his mind that had mercifully drawn away everything that had happened in this place, and hidden it.

Until now.

He only needed to think of Lois, Garren and Nicole and any doubt that he had to go inside and confirm what his gut was telling him vanished.

One light was on. The trailer trembled and the door swung open. His father's body filled the frame. For a moment, childish fear came alive from somewhere deep inside and Breck couldn't move. His knuckles whitened on the steering wheel and a flurry of bats broke loose in his stomach.

He couldn't see his father's face; it was too dark. But his voice snaked out, grabbed him by the throat, and tried to drag his soul back into that trailer as if no time had passed.

He reminded himself he was a man now. They were two adults. He wasn't going to have to take anything – without giving something right back if need be.

And then there was Nicole. He saw her face, and it was easy to get out of the car and stride over, every fiber filling with revenge.

Rob stood back so Breck could enter. After the door closed, the stale scent of cigarette, fermented trash and body odor hit Breck, a stench that made his head turn in disgust. He'd lived here, he thought with revulsion and a brief glance around. He'd grown up in this place pigs wouldn't set foot in. "See things haven't changed," he said.

Rob's hands flexed. "You come by to insult me?"

Breck kept his hands deep in his front pockets, as if that might help stave off what would eventually blast out, shredding the man in front of him. "It was you in that orchard tonight, wasn't it?"

Rob lit up another cigarette, watched as Breck looked at it. "I don't know what you're talking about. I been here all night."

"I recognized the style."

"What the hell are you talking about, kid?"

Noon - Katherine Warwick

"The way you hit. I knew it was you because it's the way you beat me. The only thing missing was the cuffs and belt."

Heat rose and swarmed around them as anger built. Rob took a step toward Breck, the cigarette dangling from his lips. "You're out of your mind."

The nerves in Breck's body danced like a storm ready to burst. "I'm not even going to ask why you did it. I'm just going to tell you this once, that if you ever come near her again, I'll kill you."

Rob snapped out a hand to grab Breck's throat, but Breck ducked back, out of reach. "Slippery little thing, aren't you?"

"Yeah, well, dancing's made me light on my feet."

Rob spit the cigarette out, not even watching where it landed. Breck looked at it, then at Rob. Because Rob had no intention of tamping it out, Breck looked again, and Rob lunged, sending them both crashing back onto the floor. Though Breck landed on his back, arms eager to deflect wrapped around Rob, rolling them both into furniture that toppled, sending glass and trinkets flying.

Rob lifted his right fist and hammered. A single punch landed on Breck's jaw and he jerked his head aside. Rob's fist then smashed into the hard linoleum of the kitchen floor, sending out a spray of blood.

In the split second Rob took to shake out his sore hand, Breck bucked him off and jumped up, readying for more. Fingers like claws, voice a raw growl, Rob shot up. Breck sprung out of reach. Facing each other, they circled, breathing heavily as each waited for the other to move.

"Think you're pretty fast, dontcha boy?"

"Another thing dancing has taught me," Breck panted out. He could feel it coming, the slow build of combustion that would enable him to put his hands around his father's neck and choke the life from him.

"You leave my family alone, and you'll still get your money."

"Your family? I'm gonna finish what I started. She's just too sweet to resist. I want a taste. " When the words stopped Breck in his tracks, Rob's grin twisted. "Oh, she may scream and fight at first. But she'll like it. They all do."

Breck leapt at him then, wrath eating through him. He went right for his father's throat, hands wrapping like a collar, and the two of them fell back to the floor, Rob taking a hit to his head when it slammed against the corner of the refrigerator.

Choking, sputtering, for a moment he stared into Breck's face as he struggled to pry Breck's fingers free. The kid had more in him than he'd planned. Pleasure mingled with pride, and now he would match him. If the kid wanted blood, he'd give him blood – his own.

Rob reached around, grabbed onto Breck's hair and yanked his head back. Releasing Rob's throat, Breck jerked his head into an angle that enabed him to jackhammer into his father's abdomen.

Rob released the hair. It became a fistfight then, with both landing punches to the abdomen, head and jaw. Over and over, fists flew, thudding against flesh. Bodies crumpled and then stood again as the pounds and grunts escalated.

But it was Rob who grabbed the brass lamp. It teetered on the table next to the couch and with one swing he brought it down on Breck's head in a crash that sent Breck flat on the floor, out cold.

* * *

When Breck finally opened his eyes, he could barely see. The room was dark. Pain splintered through his head, in almost every part of his body, but his foot felt like it was on fire. The stabbing flame shot up his leg. He hadn't screamed since he'd left this place. Now, Breck heard his voice ricochet off the walls in a howl released somewhere in the darkness of his mind.

He jerked his head up, looked. Blinking hard, he saw the glow of a cigarette tip across the room. Shapes – grey and black shadows, moved like vapors. His temple throbbed, and he lowered his head to the floor again, eyes pinched shut. Something was burning his foot.

He had to see, had to move his feet away from the pain. He opened his eyes, watched the glowing tip of the cigarette rise and come toward him.

"You did good boy – made me proud. You actually fought like you had balls. But then we both know dancers are fags and fags don't got no balls, do they?"

He heard rustling, watched as the smoldering light moved back down toward his bare feet. "I figure there's only one way to reconcile things," his father's voice slithered through his fogged mind. "You need to stop dancing." A sharp pause caused Breck to lift his head and look toward his father's voice. "For good. See you had a little accident," Rob told him.

Breck struggled up on his elbow, but couldn't see anything. Panic shot through him.

Rob flicked a switch and a lamp lit. At first blinded by the white glare, Breck covered his eyes with his hand. Slowly, his sight adjusted, and his gaze was fastened on his feet. Both had been stripped, but it was his right foot that almost had him retching. Flesh and bone covered in oozing crimson hung limp below the ankle. He tried to move it, but hot searing pain shuddered up his leg.

"You listen now." Rob blew out a plume. "I'm gonna tell you the rules. If you follow them, she'll stay a safe little Princess. If you don't, I'll tell ya what I'm gonna do to her."

There was silence, thick then hollowed out as Breck gasped through the pain, the shock and disbelief.

Nicole.

His mind dazed seeing pictures of her, of them together, of Lois – Garren. He couldn't move, all of the blood in his body thundered down below his ankle. He blew breath out, sucked it in. His fingers dug into his own flesh to try to redirect the pain.

"You won't be able to dance now," his father's voice cut through the incredulity like a knife. "But you still got one good foot. Use it." Rob inhaled and held the smoke before blowing out a thin stream, narrowing eyes dark with twisted pleasure. "I don't care what you do. Just stay off the dance floor. And stay away from the Dubois'."

Coming through a thick fog of agony, the words didn't register. Breck forced himself to move some so that he could see his father better. "What?"

"Forever."

Something started to grab hold of Breck in his bones, the graveness of the situation settled in like a poisonous snake winding around his soul.

"You can't dance, she won't want you," Rob hissed out. "She'll hate you in fact. That you were so careless and got your foot busted. Mr. and Mrs.'ll hate you too 'cause you abandoned their precious daughter, screwed up their investment. I don't have any use for you, though I may be able to get you your old job back on construction." He laughed, "I don't know if they'll hire a no-good hobble foot."

"I won't leave her."

Rising, Rob walked slowly around to Breck's feet, the cigarette dripping from pinched lips. "Those are the rules, or she gets another visit from me."

Breck squeezed his eyes shut. The pain, sharp as a spear in his right foot, shot up his leg in lightning hot jags.

"The way I see it, you and me had a father and son fight. You got hurt. It happens." Rob reached over and yanked at Breck's ankles, and the pain caused Breck to shudder, gasp, and scream. "Now, you gonna do as I tell ya, or am I gonna be paying that beauty a visit?"

Breck gasped again, fingers digging into carpet, sweat bursting from every pore. "Why did you do this?"

"You always did ask too many questions, kid."

"The money—"

"I got principles. I told you, my boy don't dance." Rob snarled, dropping his cigarette just next to Breck's head before tamping it out.

Disbelief weakened Breck, and he fell back, hands scrubbing his face. He was perilously close to being devoured by this place again. He wanted out, needed to get away from there. He tried to move, but couldn't. Then he smelled his father's rancid breath on his face and his eyes flew open. His father's face was inches from his. So close, the slight flare of his nostrils, the razor-sharp look in his eyes, shot an old echo of panic through him.

Rob snagged Breck's shirt and pulled him upright. "Now, better go get that foot taken care of before gangrene sets in."

Noon - Katherine Warwick

Sixteen

Nicole sat in the back seat of her parent's black Mercedes hiding ripe bruises behind dark glasses. She was still sore from the previous night. Even as she tried to think positively, her heart pounded in her chest.

Breck had called. He only said that he was in the hospital; that they needed to talk. Something inside warned her it was serious, even though she hadn't been able to get him to offer any details over the phone.

Now, both her mother and father were as pensive as she as they drove to the hospital.

Last night, she'd had a nightmare, dark and hot, with heavy breathing. Over and over she'd awakened in a sweat. Finding herself in her bedroom hadn't helped. She'd put on her robe and gone looking for Breck. When she'd searched the house and found he wasn't there, that his car wasn't parked in the back, she'd been curious, worried, and finally, angry.

Restlessness kept her up the rest of the night and into the early morning hours, waiting in the family room, thinking he'd walk in any moment. Then he called. It was the quiet, icy-sharp tone of his voice that had frightened her.

They found him on the fourth floor, in a pre-operative room. Pungent scents filled Nicole's head: cleaning fluid and the bland, empty scent of hospital linen. When Nicole saw Breck's battered face, she ran to his bedside.

"What happened?" Snatching his hand, she brought it against her thudding heart, and imagined the possibilities. "What? Breck, tell me."

"I had an accident."

"You should have called us right away." Busting with obvious frustration, Garren jagged back and forth at the foot of the bed. He'd rolled up the sleeves of his white shirt, tugged loose his tie, and looked ready to tear into someone.

"Where did you go?" Nicole's grip matched her need for an explanation. "I thought you were staying at the house."

"Who's your doctor?" Garren stopped at the side of the bed, and stared with a demand Breck had never seen.

"Dr. Lawrence."

Garren turned and disappeared, but his frustration hung in the room with unanswered questions.

"My foot," Breck barely whispered.

The blood drained from Nicole's head. Her gaze traveled the length of his body, covered in a white hospital blanket to a large mound where his right foot was.

Lois gasped and took a moment to collect her frazzled thoughts.

Breck hadn't thought out what he was going to tell them. He'd been dealing with the consuming pain. Now that he had some codeine in his system, he was too drowsy to put a story together that would make any sense. Unable to keep his eyes open, he closed them.

*　*　*

Lois and Nicole sat in the waiting room under fluorescent lights that caused Nicole's tender temples to throb. The antiseptic smell seemed to be in every room, down every hall, and the odor only made the throb worse. Her body was still feeling the effects of her own attack, but her mind wanted answers to what had happened to Breck.

When her father came in, the look of dread on his face had her up and at his side before she could take a deep breath and prepare herself. She gripped his arm, to steady herself for the news, as much as to comfort him.

"His foot." Because he labored so with the words, Nicole's heart numbed. "It was damaged so badly. Bones were shattered." He shook his head. His eyes met Lois' first, then settled on Nicole's. "He may never walk on it again."

Nicole didn't hear anything. She simply drifted away, dazedly heading toward the window. This moment was a dream; a muggy dream that was turning quickly into a nightmare. "Is he going to be all right?" It came out a frightened whisper. She didn't turn to see her father, the bearer of bad news. She was angry at him, that he could say such a thing. "Is he?"

"He was in a fight."

"A fight?" Then she whirled, facing him. "What was he doing fighting with somebody?"

Noon - Katherine Warwick

Lois lifted two red eyes, stained with fresh tears. "Nickie, you know Breck, he'd never hurt anyone."

"They caught him in a fight, mother. That doesn't just happen by accident." If revenge had been a color, she'd seen it last night as she lay in bed, as it colored Breck's face and arms a red that spoke of blood. That he might be capable of hurting someone, she had witnessed first hand.

"He'll need pins, therapy."

Blindly, Nicole reached for the only chair in the room, and sunk into it. Their career was over.

She couldn't cry – no tears came. She loved him, he was alive, and for that she was grateful. They had each other. They were going to be married.

They just wouldn't dance together anymore.

When she lifted her head, she found both of her parents' eyes on her and dug for courage she hoped would convince not only them, but herself, that everything would be all right. "It's going to be okay," she finally whispered.

Lois left Garren's arms and went to her. Kneeling down at her knees, she clasped Nicole's hands tight. "He'll need us."

Nicole nodded. Her heart was his; she had trusted it to him, placing her hopes and dreams in his gentle hands. Hands that would never hold her in dance again. The thought was so crushing, her insides peeled away, leaving her raw and hopeless. But there was more to life than dance; Breck had told her that over and over. She had to believe that.

She couldn't dance with somebody else, and she wouldn't. What they had together could never be duplicated. She was in love with him. She'd found a place where her heart could rest forever. That would never happen twice in a lifetime and she didn't want it to. At that moment, she decided to stop thinking about what they would never again do, and focus on the future they could build off the dance floor.

Breck was alone when the doctor came in to give him the prognosis. He'd insisted Dr. Lawrence come in when the Dubois' were out, that way he could decide what to tell them. Of course, Breck was sure Garren would have his own heart-to-heart with Dr. Lawrence, but his life was going to be solitary soon, and Breck figured taking the news alone was the beginning. It was better this way, he thought, looking at the doctor, his heart causing the monitor to beep more rapidly as he waited for the news.

Dr. Lawrence stood at the foot of the bed, a chart tucked under his arm. "How's the pain?"

Numb – Breck thought, like the rest of him, but he only said, "Okay." He'd spent the last hour alone and was finally feeling the weight of what had happened and what it was going to mean, slam him in the heart.

Nicole dominated his thoughts; her safety, her happiness. Just hours before, their lives had finally come together. He wanted her for his own – forever. Knowing that was never going to happen kept him miserably silent.

They'd never dance together again; he didn't need a doctor to tell him that. His eyes pinched tight, fighting tears. He'd miss what had changed his life. Because of dance, he had a family, friends, people who cared. And he would lose them all now – because of dance.

"You'll need to stay off that foot for two weeks. And I mean, completely off, with it elevated. When we x-ray it, if things look good enough, we'll start therapy." He took in a deep breath. "Therapy will be essential to your being able to regain even partial use again.

"I know you dance," the doctor went on. "But I have to tell you—"

"Don't,"Breck interrupted with a wave of his hand. A sigh that carried a heavy loss escaped him. "I already know."

"I'm sorry. Have you thought about pressing charges?"

Breck shook his head, knowing how foolish his answer must look. Dr. Lawrence raised a brow, but a doctor's wisdom kept him silent.

"How long before I can go home?" Breck shifted, groaned.

"I told Garren tomorrow. I think they're anxious to get you back where—"

"I'll be going to my own home," Breck said, and there was bitterness in it.

Again, Dr. Lawrence remained quiet – for a moment. "You know, you're going to need some help the first two weeks. You won't be able to do anything but keep it elevated. Understand?"

Breck knew that, and as he looked down at his foot, a voracious storm of anger flushed his body from head to toe.

"I'll see you tomorrow before you leave." Dr. Lawrence headed for the door. "If you need more pain medicine, the nurse will get it for you. "

Gripping the sheets in his fists did little to rid Breck of the need to tear into something. His father's sick, twisted mind had taken his life from him.

His head fell back into the soft pillow. Closing his eyes, tears streamed down his cheeks. Memories fused with pain. Injustice, cruelty – his father had delivered all of that and so much more. There was anger, but there was also a desperate need to know how a parent could do something so malicious to his own flesh and blood.

There was no way Garren and Lois were going to let him recuperate alone. It was both humiliating and humbling to Breck, who fought the offered love and help. Garren pushed him in the wheelchair to the car after being discharged from the hospital.

Nicole drove his black Jeep behind the Dubois' car, her hair blowing, eyes behind dark glasses. Had he not been in the throws of discomfort from weaning himself off pain medicine, he'd have shown her just how real and strong his feelings ran for her.

When they pulled up the Dubois' drive, panic had him scanning the orchards for his father. Nothing but trees budding with spring flowers stretched out in a colorful blanket before him.

Garren helped him out of the car, while Lois brought around the wheelchair they'd rented.

Nicole hopped out of the Jeep with a smile on her face, hair windblown, cheeks pink. "Great car." In a victorious gesture, she tossed the keys up and caught them again –her grin huge, and aimed right at him. "At last, I drive the jeep."

Breck labored to get into the wheelchair. "Forget it. Nobody drives my Jeep."

"I just did. And will again, Noon." She shot him a teasing smile as she walked in front of him toward the house, her hips swinging just enough to parch his throat.

While Garren and Nicole helped him get situated on the couch, Lois fussed with pillows and blankets like a mother bird making a nest. Breck bit back a smile. It was painfully clear that in spite of his intentions, he'd not be able to be on his own until he was on crutches. Every moment of his healing meant that Nicole was in danger.

The last thing he wanted to do was beg for more time. But inside he was thinking of only one thing. He needed to get to a phone, and in the Dubois house, having a private phone conversation was nearly impossible. Until the opportunity arose, he'd not let Nicole out of his sight.

"Hey, Nic," he called for her. She'd been in and out doing things most of the day since they'd brought him home. Neglecting him, he thought with a pinch of self-pity, and he'd had enough. Time was not on his side and he meant to have as much of her as he could. Lois' kindness had taught him that being cared for when you were sick or hurt was something loving families did for each other.

"Be right there," Nicole yelled from somewhere in the house.

Lois was behind the cook-top island in the kitchen, standing over a sizzling pan of something scenting the air with garlic. "What can I get for you, honey?"

There would be a great deal he would miss about Lois, Breck decided. He swallowed, his mouth uncomfortably dry. "Nothing, thanks." The smells were tantalizing to Breck, who'd had hospital fare for two days and could swear he'd lost ten pounds. "How come you never taught that daughter of yours how to cook?"

"I can cook just fine, thank you." Nicole was not too far away now and his stomach fluttered anticipating laying his eyes on her.

"If toast and eggs is on the menu," he teased. "Where are you? I need a back rub."

Lois smiled over the boiling pot. "She knows some things."

She knows a lot of things, and Breck would have laughed if his foot wasn't starting to come out from behind the pain medication. His whole body was in a knot, thinking about what he had to do.

Noon - Katherine Warwick

Lois looked up from the steaming pan and smiled when Nicole appeared, freshly dressed in jeans and a soft pink shirt. Rose buds and trouble, Breck thought, unable to take his eyes away.

She batted dark lashes. "All you had to do was ask."

He'd ask for so much more if he could. He would be her lover, her husband. He wanted her, and the pain coursing through him knowing she would slip through his open arms pierced deep. Would she see, as she'd always seen so clearly on his face, that it was all a lie?

"What's wrong?" She dropped to the couch next to him. "Where's that pain stuff the doctor sent?" Scavenging around where he sat did not turn up the white pharmacy bag chock full of medications he'd been sent home with.

"I'm okay." He reached out and ran a hand along the smoothness of her cheek. Before he lost himself in the feel of her, the blue depths of her eyes, he set his teeth.

Then he pointed to his shoulders.

Positioning herself behind him, she began kneading. Her sweet perfume filled his head. "When you feel up to it we'll break the news," she whispered, and he had to wet his lips, close his eyes and try not to think about kissing her.

The news…Breck's heart plunged. A future that had looked so promising was vanishing with every hour that ticked by. They would never break the news. He knew then he would have to be brutal to ensure that she never think of him, never come looking for him. The idea of hurting her so deeply thrust a shudder through his system that nearly broke his body in two. Pulling back, he snatched her upper arm, bringing her face close. Shock opened her eyes wide, replaced by thickening desire that caused her lids to blink heavily over those ocean-blue eyes he'd be unable to explore the rest of his life.

"Nicole—" he wouldn't say he loved her, that he wanted only her. It would only hurt her more when he left. What had been would be in her memory, just as the words he couldn't utter would remain locked in his heart.

He did his best to conceal with a face that could easily give him away. When she smiled, he knew he'd succeeded.

It was the beginning of the end.

Garren came in, rubbing his hands together. "Smells great. Nicole, why don't you and I help him over to the table?"

Noon - Katherine Warwick

"No," Breck protested. "I'll sit here."

"We'll come to you," Lois cheerily carried over the soup. "Nicole, bring our place settings."

Uncomfortable with the ends they were taking to care for him, Breck shifted. "It's no big deal, guys."

"You're right, it's not. Because we're your family." Lois set the steaming soup in front of him on the coffee table, then ladled the creamy mixture into bowls and handed them out. It made him weak it smelled so heavenly. Giving into the gravitational pull of love, Breck ate.

Stomach full, heart fuller, Breck watched Lois and Nicole clean the kitchen after the hearty chicken noodle soup. The sight of the two women he loved most in the world laughing and talking was all the after dinner entertainment he needed.

"We're lucky men." Garren was stretched out next to him on the couch, contentment obvious. Breck nodded, looked over and wondered: if he'd been honest years ago when his father had first demanded more money, would he be sitting there with a busted foot and an unstable future.

When night finally came, Breck refused to sleep anywhere but on the couch. He figured it would be better that way. He'd not have Garren helping him like the cripple he was, up to his old bedroom. If he stayed in the family room, he'd be a floor away from Nicole; from the temptation to hobble down the hall and just look at her while she slept. And he'd be closer to a phone.

He lay in the darkness buried under a pile of blankets Lois had insisted upon, and he'd let her indulge in tucking around him, and waited until the house was still. He could still smell her perfume, and it took him back to the darkness of the skate park, when he was sixteen, and he'd first seen her – a smiling angel with hope on her wings.

Departure from the Dubois' lives would mean leaving all of his friends behind as well. They'd hate him for what he'd done to the hand that had fed him. He'd come to know everything and everyone that was good because of them, and he would leave in an ungrateful silence that would be heard by all.

He shifted, taking care not to move his right foot. A dull throb ached deep inside the bones, and he tried to ignore it

The phone was on the table next to the couch, and Breck rose on his arms, maneuvering himself without moving his foot, so he could reach over. Becoming tangled in the blankets, he finally whipped them back and tossed them off, panting and sweating at the minute effort.

Dialing, it struck him that he'd not called the number in so many years he was surprised to see he still remembered it. The phone rang and rang while Breck's heart buzzed in his chest.

"Who is it?" Rob demanded. Breck checked his watch; one-thirty. From what he remembered his father's night was just warming up.

"Me."

"Why are you calling?"

"We need to talk."

"I was in the middle of something. Call me tomorrow."

"There are things you need to know." Breck's voice rose to a loud whisper and he cupped the phone.

"I can know them just as good tomorrow," Rob shouted.

"No." The snap of pleading jumped into his voice out of desperation. "Just give me a minute. My foot—it's—I can't walk on it for two weeks. The Dubois' are helping me out – I can't do anything until then."

"That's not what the terms were."

"I know, I know. But I can't move the foot for two weeks."

"That's not my problem."

It is your problem Breck's anger screamed. "Look, as soon as I'm on crutches, I'll be out of here. Until then, I'm here and I'm breaking them into it slowly."

"I don't care if you puke in their pot pies. You're not keeping your end of it and that means—"

"That means you give me some time!" Breck heard silence on the other end and for a moment wondered if his father had hung up. He hated saying the word, but he closed his eyes and did anyway, "Please."

Rob's laugh slapped Breck in the face with enforced humility. "You got two weeks." The phone clicked.

It took Breck some more maneuvering before he could hang up the phone. When he did, he felt a chill he hadn't in a long time. He couldn't reach the blankets. In his haste, he'd tossed them too far out of reach and now they lay discarded on the floor. He fell back against the couch and looked at the ceiling. It was going to be a very long, cold night.

Seventeen

Breck found it easy to be crabby and mean. He growled hearing the stirring of fabric, the tinkling of glass. The aromatic scent of bacon frying, eggs sizzling tickled his nose. He was trying to stay asleep. It had been a fitful night of being cold, uncomfortable, in pain, and worse, in bone-deep agony with guilt nagging at his conscience.

He was finally warm. Blankets were once again up around his neck and he snuggled down into them. He thought he felt the light flutter of a kiss on his face, smelled something sweet and familiar, but couldn't be sure. He was having what looked to be a promising dream, and didn't want to wake up.

Nicole was on the dance floor moving, alluring, beckoning to him. He'd never seen her in the sheer white dress, but he liked it. Taking her into his arms, he felt her movements, soft and swaying, against him. They danced together. Dance. He could do it. His foot moved effortlessly beneath him. He led them into a turn and heard the familiar chants and thundering applause that always accompanied their performances.

Wanting to see the pleasure on her face, he looked but couldn't find her. White, misty fog billowed around him. Blindly, he reached out, yelling her name, but heard nothing.

When he awoke, he was thrashing in the blankets. Pain shot up his leg. Garren was on the couch, restraining him. Nicole and Lois stood by with panic on their faces.

The pain in his foot was agonizing. "My foot."

"You moved it." Garren's hands were on Breck's shoulders, steadying him. "Lay still. Let me take a look."

Breck bit down. "No. I'm all right." He waved Garren back and forced himself to sit up, dragging his hands down his face. When he could, he opened two sleepy eyes to find three faces watching him. "What?"

"You were screaming," Nicole said quietly.

Lois moved in close. "Are you in pain?"

The night had been arduous but it was over and Breck blew out air. "No pain, I promise." The dull ache was starting to ebb and he was grateful.

Lois returned to the kitchen and Garren stood, chin in his fingers. Breck averted his gaze from the studying look he knew so well; Garren was bothered by something, and he prayed it wasn't that he could read the deception.

Nicole squeezed next to him on the couch. Somewhere between her fresh scent and sparkling eyes, his lungs took an involuntary breath.

"You were calling my name." Bringing his hand to her chest, she pressed it against her heart.

"Was I?"

With a finger she brushed the hair from his face and nodded. She'd come downstairs and seen him, tied up in a knot of sheets – like he was in a war. She'd untangled the sheets, tucked them in, then looked at him until she thought her soul couldn't take any more of the joyful pressure inside. She'd never known she could love anyone so much. No one had eased into her heart with so much familiarity that he'd become a part of her long before she'd even recognized it.

When her father stepped away she leaned close, needing to kiss him. Her lips brushed his ear. "When should we tell them? Today?"

The way he lowered his head and didn't look at her froze the blood in her veins. She refused to believe his reaction was anything more than discomfort.

"Give me a little more time to feel better," he said, still not meeting her gaze.

He struggled to his feet and she was up in a flash, helping him. "I need to bathe," he snapped, causing her to draw back. Breck hobbled up the back stairs with her father's help. A thread of doubt ran through her, and she let out a breath, wondering why she couldn't dismiss it.

Later, after Breck had sat in a tub, leg hanging over the side, then dressed with Garren's help, he conceded to sit on the family room couch in the hub of the house to watch movies and surf channels.

Garren left for the hospital, Lois went about her errands. Nicole insisted she stay and play nurse. The idea percolated Breck's blood more than he cared to admit.

He couldn't let it.

She took over where Lois left off, bringing fresh linens and pillows, scented with her perfume, he was sure. She took her time fluffing and tucking and wrapping him up until he forced a sigh. It wasn't going to be easy to deflect her attempts at Florence Nightingale. "There," she stood back. "Comfortable?"

"Yes."

"Warm?"

"Very."

"Your foot – does it need propping?" He shook his head. "Food. Do you want dessert? A drink? Mom made some caramel corn."

"No, thanks." He'd try not to look at her – try not to feel like ripping off the blankets she'd carefully placed around him so he could pull her over for a kiss. "You don't need to stay here."

"You can't move, of course I need to stay. Don't be such a loner, Breck. I know it's easy for you to fall back into that when you're sick."

Because what she said was true, he shifted grumpily. It had taken him a long time to allow himself to be cared for with kindness. Sucked in by guilt, he figured he deserved to stay at heel.

"Hey." She stroked his hair and he finally looked at her.

She'd never know the ugliness of a life like his, and it was good that they would part ways for no other reason than that. His past was a part of him, whether he liked it or not. It would always be there, and if she was a part of his life, it would be a part of her as well.

"Something's up." She sat next to him, cuddled. "You never could hide things from me."

That will change, he thought dismally.

"You're biting," she began. "You always do that whenever you're mad or—" her eyes lit with mischief, "—when you're jealous."

"Do not."

"Yes you do." Satisfied, she wrapped her arms more tightly around him. "So which is it?"

Both. *I'm mad because you can see all of this and I'm trying so hard to protect you. I'm jealous that you can stay in your life, do everything you deserve to do, have worked hard to do – have earned, and you can continue doing it because you don't have monsters at your back.*

He longed to tell her that he wouldn't let any monsters into her life, no matter the cost.

"Since you're not going to tell me, I'll talk. When should we tell everybody? I'm dying to tell Mom. She'll be so excited for us. I know she'll want to start planning right away."

He closed his eyes long and hard. "Yeah."

"So, when?"

"Let me get better first."

She leaned back and looked up at his face. "Something's wrong."

"No." The very burden of everything weighed into him like lead. "I just need some time."

The look in her eyes told him she didn't want to wait. He knew how hard this was for her, holding her dreams back. "All right," she finally said. "There's something else." Once again she laid her head against his chest. "I've been thinking about teaching."

"Yeah?"

Nodding, she snuggled deeper. "You were right about me." The thoughtful pause left him with a barb deep in his heart knowing how open hers was, how vulnerable. "You know, when you told me I needed to get something else in my life. I just didn't want to listen. I'm sorry," she eased back and looked into his eyes.

He could barely breathe for the love he felt inside. "It's okay." He swallowed.

"Teaching'd be great." In fact, he knew it was just what she would need to lose herself in so that she could forget him. And start over.

"Kids, you know, just starting out."

"Like we were."

"Mm-hmm."

Comfortably, she lay against him, with no idea how his heart was tearing inside.

Noon - Katherine Warwick

Something was different about him and because Nicole couldn't put her finger on it, she fought fear nipping dangerously close to her tender heart. It was nearing two weeks since his accident and still they had not told her parents about the engagement. He kept saying he wasn't up to sharing the news, but she was beginning to feel the doubt that had taken root inside, burrow deeper.

She was antsy for him. He hadn't touched her since just after the surgery, not even made an attempt. But she was a fighter. She had too much vinegar in her veins to sit back and throw her hands in the air. Sure, he was recuperating. But it was his foot, not his heart, savagely hit that night.

She'd seen darkness brewing behind his eyes. No one had been able to reach inside of him and pull out whatever was causing him discomfort beyond the physical, and the days seemed to drag the two of them further and further apart.

He was finally able to sleep in his old bedroom, his limited healing having given him the freedom to hop or move with crutches. She found him there, propped up in bed with a ballroom magazine. She'd put on some jeans and a powder blue tee shirt she knew made his eyes light up.

Standing in his doorway, she waited for him to look over. He was leaving tomorrow, going back to his place, to his life, balancing the world on that pair of crutches. They hadn't discussed their future once in the two-week interim and the air between them was unsteady enough for her to wonder where she stood.

He glanced over, but there was indifference on his brow and her heart trembled at the sight. She gripped the door jamb without thinking. "Hey."

Slowly, she crossed to him. He'd been the one to tell her to drop worldly images of seduction in exchange for what came naturally in her heart. Now, her heart was begging to understand him.

Kneeling next to the bed, she crossed her arms, leaned and studied his face. How many times had she stared in awe, unable to stop her tripping pulse when she looked at him? Not only was he the most beautiful man she had ever known, but his kindness, his patience with her through the years, only made that beauty more remarkable.

When he said nothing, when he didn't lift his eyes to look at her, she leaned close, wanting to kiss him.

He blew out a sigh and turned another page. He didn't speak, didn't do anything but look at her as if she was out of her mind for wanting it. "What?"

A slap would have stung, but this cold refusal bruised her heart. Nicole sat back, almost made an excuse for her behavior, but thought better of it, accounting what he had been through. "I've missed you – us," she said carefully. "Haven't you?"

"We both know partner relationships never work." Breck shot her a steely glance. It would only be a glance because he couldn't bear to see her face wither from hope to hurt.

When he stared back into the magazine, thick silence engulfed them both with awkwardness they hadn't felt since they were kids. Waiting was tortuous; he could see her floundering just out the corner of his eye.

She was unable to think – to find any words. The first layer of her heart had been stripped off and she was in shock. When he put the magazine down and looked at her, she might as well have been looking into the cold, marble eyes of a shark.

"Come on, Nic. You know I'm right."

"I – I thought we were different."

He let out a whip of a laugh, the tail of it catching her soul. "Guess not."

"You don't believe that. I know you don't." Humiliation bled red up her face, and Breck felt like his chest was being crushed from the anguish of it.

"We got caught up. It was a mistake to think about marriage."

"No." Nicole stood. She blinked the tears cresting in her eyes so he couldn't see them. This was not Breck. This was someone else. Breck was deeply kind and tender. Breck would never open a woman up, give her the sweet promises of love and then dump her with a laugh. "What's wrong? This – something's wrong."

Breck dropped his legs over the side of the bed, gesturing to his foot. "I can't dance anymore. It's over."

"But it will heal, you'll get better."

"I don't know that. You don't know that."

She had to step back, the slap of words hitting her like a gust of wind. "Are you telling me that you don't want me as your partner any more?" She could barely say the words, and she certainly wouldn't let them stay in her brain long enough to really think about what they meant.

"I can't dance," he snapped, struggled to stand. "I can barely walk. Who knows what will become of my foot."

"So you're giving up?"

"What else can I do?" Relief was rushing at him, fast and hard. Soon it would all be out. She would know, everyone would know, and he could leave them all in safety – and take this nightmare away with him. "I'm useless on the dance floor."

"Therapy, we can—"

"There will be no *we*, Nic."

"But I love you. We don't have to be dance partners."

"You love partners," he bit out. "Partners who win. Find somebody else," he shouted and it sent her back. "And find another man. It's over. I can't believe you're making me say it. But then I shouldn't be surprised, you never could admit the truth." They stood in the thickness of the room, disbelief and disappointment, anger and finality swirling around them like a whirlwind, sheering the fragile skin of loyalty to shreds.

Nicole wouldn't believe it. Two weeks ago, he'd whispered that he loved her. She'd felt it in his kiss, in the undeniable and irreplaceable comfort of possession.

"I…I'll wait for you while you go through therapy."

Again he laughed, and the sting lingered. "Like you'd wait; you're itching for World and any other title you can get your greedy hands on. Find yourself another boy. I'm tired of being your puppet."

Her mouth opened but she couldn't speak. He'd never spoken to her with such raw cruelty before. As if she was facing a demon, not the man she'd seen grow and change into someone she had dreamt about spending the rest of her life with, she stared at him.

Her head, her eyes, swam in a blur. She wasn't sure, but she thought his hand reached out to comfort her. When the tears filling her eyes were blinked away, his hand hung still at his side. Searching his face for sorrow, for that smile that weakened her knees, a hint that this was some very cruel joke – she saw nothing. Without being able to speak or move or feel, she stood in his presence like a boxer, beaten dull yet waiting for the next blow.

He'd more than stunned her, he'd annihilated her, and his own heart had broken in the process. To keep himself from comforting her, he gripped the crutches. He couldn't look at her. But he could say more.

"It's better this way," he bit out. She didn't respond. "You can't tell me that your first thought when you saw this," he gestured to the cast on his foot, "wasn't about dance – about your future," he added sharply. "It's your life."

"My first thought was your safety. I never once thought about dancing with anybody else."

"You said it yourself; you're in this for the long haul. I never was. Even from the beginning. Let's face it; a hobbling dance partner doesn't fit your picture of perfection does it? Could you swallow the losses? Could you walk away from it all?"

Nicole stepped away from him now that she knew the man she loved was lost somewhere inside of this stranger she was sharing the most horrifying moment of her life with.

He reached out and snagged her, his hand like a cuff around her wrist. "What, can't we part with a kiss?" Saying the words curdled his stomach, but the utter fear in her eyes stopped his heart.

Because his lips were curled with meanness, she pulled free and shook her head, backing toward the door.

He shrugged casually, as if she didn't mean anything to him, then turned and eased himself back onto the bed, unable to look at what he'd left behind in her. With an angry shove, the crutches toppled to the floor. He snatched the magazine, and hoped she wouldn't see that the pages were shaking in his hands. Or hear his heart thudding in resistance in his chest.

Her heart had fallen somewhere inside of her, she wasn't sure where, but it wasn't beating anymore. It had been crushed, and now, she stood without feeling. She couldn't look at him. Nicole Dubois didn't beg, and she'd not back out the door. Mustering dignity, lost in confusion, she reached for the knob and turned her back to him as she opened the door. If she left, she'd be leaving behind more than Breck sitting in his bed. The fact that her soul had crumbled into blackness told her that she was already dead.

Her head was high when she went out the door.

As if he'd broken open a poisonous vial, everything was infected. Garren and Lois practically tip toed as they packed up his Jeep before he was ready to take off to his place. Nicole was set to drive him home, something he wasn't looking forward to but couldn't do without. Worry hung in the air like a deepening fog. Breck forced himself to ignore their benevolent attempts to make peace with indifferent conversation. He would say goodbye without even a thank you. A thank you would encourage. Ingratitude would discourage and disgust.

"You'll call?" Lois asked, helping him into the Jeep. Her perfume sung sweetly into his senses, dragging his memory to a fragile place he didn't dare go. It was bright and sunny out, and his eyes were swollen and ready to tear anyway. The sun was making it worse. He hid behind a pair of reflective sun glasses he kept in his glove compartment.

"If I can."

Out the corner of his eye he saw her hand go to her mouth, her smile fade.

Garren patted the Jeep. "Let us know if we can help."

Breck kept his eyes straight ahead but gave a swift nod. Nicole started the car and the engine roared. But it wasn't until they were down the driveway that she let it out.

"You're a jerk, Noon."

"Shut up and drive." His voice sliced through the engine's roar. She shifted gears roughly, jolting him. "And be careful with my car!"

They drove without speaking for a time. Stops were noisy, the open Jeep sucking in every sound they passed. The high school was breaking for lunch and they both watched students pile into cars, laughing.

Breck closed his eyes, unwilling to let the familiar scene worm its way inside of him. He waited for Nicole to make a comment, to try to salvage the discomfort by reminiscing, but she only shifted at the stop sign and drove on.

She helped him into the doctor's office, waited while he had his x-ray, sat through the doctor's news. Though the bones had begun to heal, there was still no guarantee he'd have much mobility in his foot. Therapy would take a full year or more. Dancing or anything else requiring extensive pressure or movement was out of the question.

When they pulled up to his apartment hours later, he looked up at the second floor and blew out a breath. He had the crutches, but those stairs would be treacherous every time he had to go somewhere.

Ignoring him, Nicole hopped out and unloaded his bags on the curb like a cabbie. Then she looked at her watch and stood near the corner.

She was being cold and indifferent on purpose, Breck didn't blame her, but he didn't like being forced to beg either. "Take my bags up for me, will you?"

"Take them yourself. Tiffany's picking me up."

"It won't take you that long to take up two bags."

"I know," she said, looking down the street for her ride, "because I'm not doing it."

With effort, he was finally able to get out of the car. He felt like he was ready to topple forward but got the rhythm and crossed to her like a bat walking on broken wings. "C'mon, Nic, I need your help."

She never looked at him. "Here's Tiff now." She waved, and started in the direction of Tiffany's oncoming car, leaving him to stand alone on the sidewalk. He lowered his head to his chest.

Tiffany waved and smiled as she pulled up and parked. She was out and at Breck's side in a flash. "I'm so sorry about what happened." Her arms were around him in a hug of familiarity that he stole momentary comfort from. "What did the doctor say?"

The memories just seeing her brought to him made it hard to keep the icy tone he'd held with Nicole. "I'm going to be fine."

"Nic said you can't dance anymore. Breck, I'm so sorry."

He shrugged and lost his balance. Tiffany and Nicole both jumped to steady him, though Nicole quickly stepped away. She still cared too much, he thought with the razors edge of both pleasure and pain.

"Yeah, well, I had to get serious about a career sooner or later. Dance wasn't going to do anything but distract me, right?" He took another swipe at Nicole with that razor then. "Hey, Tiff, could you carry my bags up for me?"

Noon - Katherine Warwick

"Sure, of course."

As Tiffany headed toward the building, Nicole slid up next to him. "You're lucky she came along," she hissed. "I wouldn't have helped you if you'd been limbless." She joined Tiffany further up the stairs.

Breck hopped up the flight, his crutches in one hand as he steadied himself with the banister. Since Nicole had driven his car and had his keys, the girls let themselves in and were opening blinds and windows.

Tiffany turned when he'd finally made it – panting and frustrated – to the doorway. "You sure you're going to be able to do this alone?" The concern on her face would vanish once Nicole unloaded how awful he'd been, that much Breck was certain of.

Nicole's blue eyes were filled with disappointment. "Tell her."

Breck hobbled into the kitchen for some water – and a distraction. He struggled just to reach a glass and Tiffany rushed over and took the glass down, then filled it for him.

"Thanks." He drank, then set the glass on the sink with a clank. Still, he didn't look at Nicole. "I won't be dancing anymore. Ever."

Taken aback by the news and the cold tone, Tiffany looked from Nicole to Breck. "You're dropping out? Permanently?"

It was still hard to accept reality, even having had two weeks to digest it. Breck took himself to the couch and fell onto it, exhausted at the effort just to get in and around his apartment. "I can't hold up Nicole's progress while I recuperate."

Tiffany lowered next to him on the couch, her disbelief shifting from Nicole to Breck. "But you'll be back; you're going to keep competing after—"

"I'm done with it." Breck closed his eyes.

He was wallowing in self pity now, Nicole thought bitterly looking at him. He wasn't even going think of the possibility of a full recovery, of dancing again. He'd given up. It was more disappointing to her than any loss of theirs. But then, she'd lost more than her dance partner. The love of her life had abandoned her.

Still numb from the words he'd so easily tossed her way, she forced herself not to look at the troubling shadows hovering over his face, or the fact that she knew leaving him there was like abandoning a five-week old kitten on the street.

Oh, he'd manage. He was a grown man. Her family was willing to see him through this and he'd shrugged them off with the ease of an annoyance. He deserved the discomfort, the loneliness, the tribulation of enduring alone. At least she would take comfort in knowing she wasn't alone in hell.

"Come on, Tiff, let's go." Nicole swung her purse over her shoulder and headed toward the door.

Tiffany rose with reluctance.

Breck looked at Nicole, knowing it was the last time he would see her. Bone tired from the lies, the anger, the loss and thoughts of a future he had yet to navigate, he wanted to close off the pain now wracking every part of him. She looked fierce, indignant, unforgiving, and he was the reason.

"Nic," he said. She turned, and a flicker of hope colored her eyes. It was worse than if he'd tormented her with one last kiss. "My keys."

The hope in her eyes slit to black and she flung his keys across the room at him.

Eighteen

Nicole stood on the beach and took in the thick, night air. The sea sparkled, shimmering black and silver under a glossy moon. Waves reached, then shrunk back into the never-ending body of ocean, then reached again, breaking white against pearly sand. She walked, her bare feet digging into gravelly sand, still warm from that day's hot Miami sun.

A fine mist from the sea kissed the perspiration on her skin and her gauze blouse clung. The heavy air carried the scent of nearby restaurants and salty sea.

She should be running. But joy, the euphoric drug she knew so well after winning another title, was nowhere to be found.

Wins were hollow glories.

They hadn't been at first. She'd relished every title and place with gritty vengeance, searching every crowd, every audience for Breck just so she could see him while she shoved her trophy, her money, her flowers right in his face.

But Breck was never there.

She sat down and brought her knees to her chest, feeling the sand give underneath her. When she realized he would never be there, she stopped caring if she won. Winning hadn't done much to rebuild the damage having Breck come and go from her life had left behind. Winning became an extension of the competition; it was all she knew.

Because she often felt the need for restoration as much retribution, when it came to her personal life, Nicole could never dismiss Breck completely. His image would haunt her whether she thought of him or not. Dreams would have him playing either a minor or major part. A crowd of strangers would have men with his hair color leaving her to strain and look twice before knowing that still, he was not there. A familiar laugh, carried on a breeze, would have her turning to find nothing, as if he was hiding just behind her shoulder, taunting her.

It made her more determined to forget him, more difficult not to.

Years have a way of changing people whether they liked it or not, she

Noon - Katherine Warwick

knew now. Time wore you down or made you stronger, and she'd never been a quitter. Someday, their paths would cross. That she hoped for, as she would want for no greater win than to shatter his heart the way he'd shattered hers.

But he'd vanished.

She'd rebuilt her life, focusing on other dreams: on young students needing her help, and on another partner. Wouldn't Breck be surprised if he could see things now, she often mused.

"There you are."

Nicole turned. The familiar silhouette crossing the sand didn't startle her. He had his coat slung over his shoulder, shoes in his hand. "You disappeared."

She looked back out to sea – where the ocean and the black sky became one, and made herself forget the most important night she'd had in her life, the night she and Breck had joined souls when he had proposed to her. "I wanted to be alone."

"Still?"

She shook her head and stood, brushing off sand. He slipped his hand into hers. She was accustomed to his hand now, though it had taken her so very long to forget the firm yet gentle feel that had been branded there by Breck.

They began to walk back toward the hotel, the moonlight casting just enough light to make the crook in his nose look like something on a horrid mask. For a moment, it frightened her and she shivered.

"Cold?" Trey offered her his light blue linen coat. When he turned and smiled, the spooky image faded.

"No." Old fears that had once tagged like a clip of irritating fabric at her neck had been put to rest by the years they had spent as partners.

"We were great tonight." He held her hand and they crossed the busy esplanade back to the hotel, dodging people. "Happy?"

She presented her best smile – her performer's smile. "Of course."

They wove through the busy hotel lobby without speaking, both waving to friends and fellow competitors who happened by.

"So." Trey leaned against the elevator wall once they were inside. There were others in the car with them. "How does it feel to be one of the best dancers in the world?"

She'd dropped bragging long ago, the empty victory lost in who wasn't there to hear it. Lifting her shoulders she watched the floor numbers light as the elevator sped upward.

"Were you in the competition?" A woman with red hair piled on top of her head asked.

"It was excellent," her male companion piped, eyeing Nicole with that glint of male admiration she easily recognized.

"She and I were the Standard Viennese Waltz winners." Trey crossed to Nicole and stood near enough to send a message of ownership. He knew not to put his arm around her, and she stiffened when he did.

"Congratulations." The woman smiled. Nicole didn't like the appearance that they were a couple off the dance floor as well as on. In spite of the fact that Trey had been her partner since Breck's departure, he was also a man she still couldn't bring herself to have as more than a partner.

At her room door, he hovered too near, and she went in without speaking to him. When she went to shut the door, his arm shot out and blocked it. "Wanna continue our celebrating?"

"Goodnight, Trey."

"Just a drink before bed?"

"Trey." She sighed. "Thank you. You're a great partner and you know I love you." She leaned up and kissed his cheek. She did care for him, in a Platonic way. He had been there for her, after Breck had taken everything there was to take. "See you tomorrow, okay? Goodnight." Then she shut the door with a thud.

Trey took a deep breath. She'd kissed him on the cheek and he reached up to touch the moisture her mouth had left there. Then his hands shot to the door jamb as if he might tear it off before storming into her room.

It was just what he felt like doing.

But he couldn't. There was still enough pride, enough reason in him, that he didn't want to risk the future with an act that would only land him in jail.

Turning away from the door, he paced. The win had been exquisite, their performance perfect. After years of hard work, of going to every competition on the face of the planet, they finally had the reputation and the name to blot out the untarnished name of Dubois and Noon with Dubois and Woods.

He'd wondered if it would ever be possible.

Noon - Katherine Warwick

Convincing Nicole and her mother that he could step in as Nicole's new partner had been harder than any win he'd stuck under his belt. But she was what he wanted, and he'd done what it took to finally get her.

Lois had held onto some in-the-clouds fairy tale that Breck would show up, foot healed, and sweep Nicole back to the dance floor with only a minor glitch in their career. Trey had had to charm until he thought the smile he'd plastered on his face would become permanent. He finally broke Lois' dream, in part by persistence, in part because of Nicole's itch to get back into the game and win again.

Trey looked at Nicole's hotel door with pure, physical yearning. She was the only woman who remained elusive to him; a tortuous dream he held in his arms, always teasing with endless possibilities that disappeared the minute the music ended and the two of them left the dance floor. He was tired of it.

It wasn't a matter of wanting her because she was so highly desirable. It had nothing to do with the fact that she was one of the best female dancers in the United States. It had everything to do with the fact that he wanted to re-place every win she'd earned with Breck Noon with wins by the team of Woods and Dubois. He wanted to make her his: to own her, knowing that Breck never had and never would.

But he wouldn't convince her tonight. That door was locked tight, and Trey wanted her to come to him willingly. But if that looked impossible, he'd take what he wanted.

Trey went out into the night. The dark streets and even darker bars of Miami weren't unfamiliar to him. He'd charm, he'd dance, he'd whisper prom-ises in eager ears – and get exactly what he asked for, while he waited for what he really wanted.

Reuben clapped the beat, shouted the counts and still, Trey wasn't get-ting it. The frustration in the studio ripened thick with a battle.

"Try watching me," Reuben's voice had the obvious edge of impatience. He stood in front of Trey and demonstrated the rumba move. Trey quickly fol-lowed, but the sigh from Nicole told him he lacked the stylizing they were all

Noon - Katherine Warwick

reaching for.

"You're still too stiff. Practice rotating your hips and nothing else," Reuben said.

"I need a break." Trey stopped, even though he knew they both expected him to continue.

One glance at Nicole and Reuben in their huddle left Trey feeling like an outcast. It was always this way when he couldn't get a step or combination. He had the most difficulty with the Latin dances and they had yet to replace the Dubois – Noon wins in Latin because of it.

The door to the studio opened and Lois entered, dressed in light tan slacks and a lavender blouse. Her motherly smile sparkled across the room to each of them. Reuben killed the music so she could speak. "Trey, you're welcome to come up to the house for dinner afterwards."

Trey didn't glance at Nicole for approval. "Why thank you, Lois." It wasn't the first time she'd invited him for dinner, and it wouldn't be the last. He was dancing where Breck had danced, sharing meals across a table where Breck had eaten. He meant to take Breck's place in every way.

Trey headed to where Reuben and Nicole danced through the rumba routine. Time. It would take more time, but he had all the time and money in the world. As he looked at Nicole in the reflection of the mirror, he decided he would take whatever time necessary to convince her that he was the last partner she would ever have, and the only lover she would ever need.

Conversation over dinner centered on dance and the next competition. Often, Trey tried to introduce new subjects in an effort to burrow deeper into the lives of the Dubois' and ingratiate himself. Inevitably, Garren read the newspaper while Lois chatted. Trey found Garren's neglect annoying. He tried to bring him into the conversation, only to be granted a mere glance or patronizing nod. He felt sure Breck had gotten further with the old man. He knew it for a fact.

"What do you hear from Breck?" Trey shot each one of them an innocent, questioning look, taking a forkful of Lois' steaming mashed potatos. It was the first time, he noted, that Garren put down his paper. Nicole actually looked at him.

"Delicious potatoes, by the way, Lois."

Noon - Katherine Warwick

"Thank you." Lois' eyes saddened remarkably, and her picture-perfect smile withered.

"We don't hear from him," Nicole's voice was icy.

Trey opened his eyes wide for emphasis and took another bite. "Never?"

Like opening a shaken bottle of soda, Lois carried on. "We don't even know where he is. I don't understand. He—"

"Mom, don't." Nicole looked like she'd lost her appetite, the skin on her face suddenly white, her expression stiff.

Having struck a nerve that brought him pleasure to rip open, Trey pressed for more. "You know, I never really heard the whole story. I heard plenty of rumors, of course. What happened exactly?"

"Nothing," Nicole snapped.

"Honey, Trey's your partner," Lois said. "He's like family."

"Yes, I know that. But it's over. We don't need to discuss Breck – ever." Nicole pushed away from the table and took her plate, with half-eaten food, to the sink.

Trey looked purposefully at Garren, and waited for an explanation.

"Breck left," Garren said flatly.

"But it was so unlike him," Lois' voice still held hope. She shook her head. "I think something happened."

"Something did happen," Nicole's tone was hard and unforgiving as she flicked on the hot water. "His foot, remember?"

"Not that." Lois rose, taking her nearly-full plate with her. "He was different after the accident."

"Of course he was different." Nicole took her mother's plate, rinsed off uneaten dinner, and set it in the soapy water filling the sink. No one knew better than she how different one night had made him. "He gave up his future."

"Dance was not his future. He didn't have much choice, did he?" Garren's voice was firm, his face tight. Even after the years, disappointment was still there.

"He could have tried. He didn't have to give up. All the years we invested in him, the money, the—"

"Let's not have this discussion again."

"Whatever." It still hurt that her father defended Breck, when she'd been

Noon - Katherine Warwick

the one Breck had promised his future to. Something her parents still didn't know. "He couldn't take that his career was over, so he left. It was cowardly."

Trey fought the grin of pure satisfaction yearning to spread his lips wide. Each of the Dubois' had dealt with Breck in their own, pathetic way. Lois with her fairy tale endings had been hit with an emotional boulder. He couldn't believe she was still trying to carry it on her back. Garren's displeasure of Nicole and her career was legendary, made more acute by Breck's abandonment. Nicole simply hated Breck. That was the most gratifying.

Enjoying the fiery conversation, Trey sat forward. "Even if he couldn't dance anymore, he could write, email, call. You treated him like a son, after all, taking him in off the street the way you did."

"That's what hurts the most." Lois' eyes glistened. "To not know if he's all right."

"You know." Nicole dropped the dishrag into the sudsy water. "I don't care if he's a cripple or a millionaire. He left. I always knew he would."

Garren stood, paper in one hand, plate in the other. Displeasure was obvious in his heavy-footed walk to the kitchen.

"I still think he's going to walk through that door one day," Lois sniffled.

Nicole put an arm around her mother's shoulders. "I wouldn't open the door if he did."

"Well, I would." Lois wiped her cheek. "I love that boy."

"He's a man, Lois. He has a life of his own." Garren set his plate in the sink with a clank.

Lois looked into Trey's eyes, mustering a brightness that might have pinched his guilt if he'd not been rubbing his hands together under the table.

"Well," Trey said. "Now you have me."

Garren glanced over but didn't respond before excusing himself. Lois nodded once then she turned and dipped her hands into the soapy water.

Seeing that her mother was settled, Nicole motioned for Trey to follow her into the quiet of the living room. It was dark, and she tore into him without even switching on a lamp. "What are you doing?"

Casually, he lifted his shoulders. "Just asking questions."

"You know that subject is closed."

With his best grin of charm and innocence, Trey wrapped a hand around her bicep to comfort her. "Hey," he pulled her close. "I'm sorry, really." She looked flustered and vulnerable and so in need of a kiss. The temptation reached deep. Slowly, he drew her toward him until she was so close, the blue flecks in her eyes flickered.

"No, Trey."

"I want you."

"We tried this once before, and it didn't work, remember?"

"We were kids then." His eyes fastened on her mouth, ripe and ready to taste. He dipped his head, and she pushed against him.

In a flash that stole her breath, he snagged her wrists, his gaze like hot lava. "Don't tease me. I was never good at taking it."

"I'm not." She'd been in and out of a lot of relationships, had learned from experience to keep the control in her hands. But no one had ever gotten rough with her. "Now let go."

Because she was still alarmed, she took the opportunity to step away from him when he freed her. She walked to the large window overlooking the sloping front yard and orchards that faced west. "I think we should understand that we will always be just dance partners, Trey." She turned, looked at him. "Nothing else."

Watching him, she waited for signs of acceptance. The blank look on his face confused her. He'd been so insistent only moments ago. When he stood there as if he'd not heard her, she found it curious. "Trey?"

"What?" He lifted a shoulder. "Sure. For whatever reason, you don't find me attractive that way."

He crossed to her. She'd left him no options but to take now. And he would, when the moment was right.

It took all of the strength he had to simply put his hands on her shoulders. If he wasn't careful, his mind would careen off into that place he went when the craving became too intense for his body to stand. He gave her a friendly smile and only briefly let his fingertips linger on her collarbone, near her throat. "Let's go watch a movie, relax a little." His arm slid around her. Like a snake, he thought with twisted amusement, and he let it curl around her neck.

Noon - Katherine Warwick

* * *

He'd had too much to drink tonight, and he knew it.

Barely able to move limbs thick from intoxication, he figured he was better off staying in the chair. The TV was on, something was droning: soft voices in deep conversation. His mind searched for what the program was.

He'd not sat down drunk. No, he'd been fully sober when he'd fallen into the chair and started flipping channels. But nothing had appealed to him. The empty hole living inside of him wasn't going to be filled with television. He'd filled that cavern the only way he knew how. The dozens of empty bottles littering the floor at his feet seemed to stare up at him.

He lit up, focused his gaze on the black and white images on the screen. It was one of his favorite movies – Casablanca – when he'd believed that love lasts forever, that life was good, and that he would make it no matter what because he cared.

No part of that man remained in him now; he knew that. But he ignored the sorrow that death had left behind.

He had his place, his beer, his smokes and enough money to replenish them when he felt like it. Things he couldn't replenish or replace were far from him, and he liked it better that way. When he couldn't replace her, he'd learned that he could live better pushing the memory of her far, far away.

Like he'd pushed Breck.

Drawing in a miserable breath, Rob held the waft of elixir in his lungs. It was the kid that had always come between them. Even in his memories of her, the boy's face was on hers, in her eyes, in the way she looked at him – with disappointment, like he should have been better to the kid.

It wasn't his fault Breck had become a dancer, turned into a priss. *I needed the money, baby. Old man Dubois paid me good.*

Until Mr. Woods came around.

We took care of Breck and his dancing, we did. Rob let out the smoke, coughed a little and closed his eyes, tired. *We took care of that for good, me and Mr. Woods.*

Rob's mind wandered for the date. *I should be getting more money soon.*

Noon - Katherine Warwick

Money. He thought of his wife again and smiled. *You'd be proud of me, baby. I'm makin' even more money now, have been for a while. And I'll bleed priss-boy Woods for more pretty soon. I need a raise,* he thought. If Mr. Woods didn't agree with that, well, it was a good thing he'd been keeping copies of all the money orders over the years…a good thing. Might come in handy if he had to squeeze the man a little.

I just wish you were here with me, babe.

He was too tired, too dulled to open his eyes again and look at his watch. His limbs felt weighted to the worn Lazy Boy. He made it rock once, thinking it might comfort him. When it didn't, he reached out a hand and laid it on the arm of hers, still untouched, but soiled with a faint dusting of grime anyway.

Money would be coming soon.

It was his only comforting thought, and as Rob's head rolled to the side, his body relaxed and the cigarette at his fingertips fell to the floor.

Nineteen

Warm spring air settled into the valley, and Nicole opened the windows of the studio so the breeze would take the chill out of the room while she waited for her first set of pupils to arrive. She'd taught all ages for some time now, but teenagers were her favorite. They were there because they were following their own dreams, not the dreams of their parents. No one understood that drive or appreciated that obsession better than she did.

The scent of something burning leaked in. No doubt a farmer was blazing his prunings before the growing season began.

Dismissing the sharp scent, she crossed the floor to the mirror and wiped away a smudge with the hem of her blue shirt, thinking about the students she had acquired. They were all different, and while they all had potential, only a few possessed the will that would make them champions.

Jamie and Courtney would be champions. They never ceased to amuse her, the two of them. Neither knew what they had – yet. Each lesson was a trial of her patience as she first had to warm up the awkward teens with conversation and then work to keep them together.

It had been that way with her and Breck, and the similarities often had her heart turning within her.

Jamie arrived first. It was easy to like him, adorable as he was with a magnetic grin that flashed under sparkling brown eyes, whenever she could get a smile out of him. He kept his full head of unruly waves neatly tossled with some sort of hair gel. She never saw him in anything but a white teeshirt and his black dance pants, the budding physique of what would be an enviable dancer's body underneath. He was eager to learn and knew he was good. She liked that about him.

"She late again?" Tossing down his duffle, he crossed to the center of the room and casually glanced at his reflection in the mirror.

"Yes." Nicole watched while he broke into some rumba steps without coersion. "You've been practicing. Looks good." She countered his pleased grin

Noon - Katherine Warwick

with one of her own.

"It has to be just right, you know?" he managed through a set of fast spins.

"Yes. I know."

Courtney jogged in, her brown hair in a ponytail, face flushed. She peeled off her sweater, dropped her bag and slipped on her shoes before she said a word.

"Can you try to get here on time?" Jamie shot, hands on his hips. "Nic's a busy woman."

The comment made Nicole grin. She clapped her hands to signal it was time to begin, then waited for her pupils to take the floor near her. "Let's start with samba."

Jamie sighed, flicking out nervous hands as he glanced at Courtney with that natural reticence of a young boy wary of a young girl. It always brought Nicole a hidden laugh.

"Samba is one of your favorites, isn't it, Nicole?" Courtney asked, batting a flirtatious gaze Jamie's direction as she smoothed back her hair.

Nicole smiled. "It is, as a matter of fact."

*   *   *

Her career was successful; her life pleasant with enough socializing to keep her feeling admired and wanted. Nicole was nearly satisfied. Some of her friends were settling down, having families. Only part of her was envious of this. She wasn't willing to take that step until she found someone she wanted to spend the rest of her life with.

Annie had married, had a baby, and, like most new mothers, was anxious to share that new baby with everyone she knew. To Nicole's pleasure, it was her turn. Today, she was treating them both to lunch and shopping to celebrate.

Because she was so near to the heart of Pleasant Grove and the old downtown area, Nicole was tempted to drive by the trailer park. She had to go that way, she rationalized, it was the most direct route to State Street, to Sonic, where she and Annie were meeting for a fattening lunch of burgers and fries, laughter and loud music.

Noon - Katherine Warwick

Crossing the railroad tracks, bubbling curiosity started in her stomach. She wondered if Breck's father knew where Breck was. For a moment she played with the possibility of knocking on his door.

Her car screeched to a stop when she found charred black rubbish where the Noon trailer once stood. Bright yellow police tape was everywhere, like celebratory streamers, keeping a small crowd away from the ruin.

She pulled over and got out, wondering why her heart was thumping so. But she knew. Now, she'd never know where Breck was. She would never be able to grill him about why he'd gone, slap his smug face, scar his heart like he'd scarred hers. She would never lay eyes on him again, and a lump of finality rose in her throat that she couldn't swallow down.

Two officers stood guard while two men with rubber gloves and transparent bags sorted through the rubble. Neighbors and gawkers loitered, whispering. Burned wood and the stink of charred steel filled her nose, and she blinked back the moisture in her eyes from the chemicals floating invisibly in the air. She stepped through the outlying debris and joined a small blonde woman, dressed in a ragged pink and turquoise housedress that stood alone, weeping.

"What happened?" Nicole asked her.

The woman rubbed the back of her hand under a runny nose. "Thought we was all going down. It was horrible."

Nicole scanned the burnt piles and couldn't see anything recognizable. Breck, she thought, this horrifying place is gone now. She wished he could see it with his own eyes, and wondered if he knew.

"Did he get out?" Nicole asked.

The blonde shook her head. "They say he was asleep and the cigarette lit it up."

"Did you know him?" Nicole asked. The woman never looked away from the blackened piles, her eyes fixed on the streams of smoke still rising into the air. "I'm a friend of Rob's son, and I wondered if he's been notified yet."

"I called him."

"You did?"

"Yeah, Rob give me his number some time ago, in case of an emergency." Her voice broke off and Nicole saw more tears in her eyes. She waved her hand in front of her face. "Me and Rob, we was close, you know?"

◎ 203 ◎

Noon - Katherine Warwick

Nodding, the discomfort of the woman's mourning mixed with Nicole's revulsion of the man. "So," curiosity forced her a different direction, "you spoke with Breck. Is he coming here?"

The woman shrugged, whipping out a ragged tissue she'd had hidden the sleeve of her flowered housecoat. "I dunno, he didn't say. They was never close them two." She blew her nose. "Still, blood's blood and he needs to come pay his respects, you know?"

All Nicole could think of was the price Breck had already paid. She wouldn't have been surprised if he decided not to come. "Do you have his number? I'd like to call him and tell him how sorry I am."

The woman nodded and dipped her hand into her housecoat pocket, then gave her a piece of paper. "I don't know for sure, but I think he's in Miami."

Nicole held the paper as if it were a fragile slip of glass. For a moment, all she could do was look at the number. She would hear his voice if she called. She would hear him breathe.

"I told Rob not to light up when he was tired. I told him that over and over and now look what he done." The woman's demeanor was crashing fast. "A horrid thing—burning."

"Yes," Nicole said, her mind seeing scars on the smooth flesh of a youthful chest and back. She couldn't help but think Rob had gotten what was coming to him. She tucked the paper in her hand and said goodbye to the woman. Without another glance at what had once been the Noon trailer, she walked back to her car.

Nicole made herself go through the rest of the day, even though she only thought of one thing – Breck's phone number buried deep in her purse. She enjoyed her visit with Annie, cooed and played with Annie's baby, and did just as she'd planned and took them shopping.

Now, driving herself home, her mind drifted to Breck. So what if he's coming back into town. That doesn't mean anything. She'd not tell her parents. They were bound to find out about the fire, about Rob's death, but they

Noon - Katherine Warwick

wouldn't know Nicole had Breck's phone number and that he was seconds away with the press of some buttons.

But the chances of them crossing paths…her insides fluttered at the thought. The years of fantasizing, of scheming – plotting…the possibility was exciting to her, and she enjoyed it for a moment.

She toyed with canceling her plans of going dancing that night, her nerves too unsettled. But staying home wouldn't accomplish anything. She certainly wasn't going to call him.

'Sorry about your father, Breck'— he'd never buy it because they both knew that few people would be sorry to see Rob Noon gone.

If he wanted to see her, to see her family, he'd do it. She'd not go begging to him. A call would put her dangerously close to her knees. No, she needed to forget Breck, forget these fantasies of revenge and continue on with her life.

At home, she scanned her closet for dresses to wear out dancing, and suddenly felt the need to pick red. Pulling the glittery dress from the hanger, she put it under her chin and watched the blonde highlights in her hair electrify, reflecting off the crimson fabric. Tonight she'd prove to herself that she could have any man she wanted. It would be a little game, she mused, like the old Nicole.

Twenty

Nicole hadn't counted on seeing Breck at Bruisers.

But she had – flesh and bone – breath and heat. She'd looked into his eyes, both familiar and different now. Her hands had held fast to his and found the same determined drive there, but more – more take than give.

His body, to have felt the strength of it against her again and to be led by a man who knew precisely where to take her – these were things other men, other partnerships, could never duplicate.

Still shivering from the cold air as much as the shock of seeing him, Nicole clutched her bare arms and pinched herself. She had only to turn around and go back inside to find him. But this was not a dream. He'd laid his mouth on hers, and she'd been taken back, dizzyingly taken back and knew that kiss.

The door swooshed open. Music blasted on the waft of air, carrying along with it the muddled scents of the club, perfume, cologne, sweat and breath. She was too afraid to look. Too afraid she'd be heartbroken if she turned and found Breck not there.

"Nic." His voice melted her insides, and she closed her eyes, as if that would keep tears from falling. She didn't need to turn. Her body leeched the heat of him, his scent, that magnetic aura as he stood behind her.

"Don't touch me."

"Okay." His voice was soft, so familiar, so comforting. It took everything in her not to turn around and look at him.

"I heard about your father." She kept her voice void of emotion. "Is that why you're back?"

"Part of why."

Her heart skipped but she ignored it. She wouldn't ask what the other part was. She couldn't be that near him and not feel that dull ache in her heart spread through her. "Did you ever patch things up with him?"

"No."

But he was doing the honorable thing by being there, after everything.

She wasn't surprised. "I'm sorry about that." Her own relationship with her father had improved some and she knew the peace that came with that.

"I've missed you," he said.

Her throat closed for a moment, her heart ached. So many times she'd played this moment in her head, but she wasn't about to be sucked into forgiveness by old memories. Resolve erected protective walls around her heart and she turned and faced him. "So you're here to make arrangements for your father." She got a better look at him, standing there in the darkness lit only by a smattering of stars in the sky. He was dressed in dark clothes that made him look somewhere between mysterious and dramatic; she felt the familiar pull from the aura that always hovered over him even with years that had distanced them.

Her gaze fell to his feet, casually crossed as he leaned against the railing. She remembered how easily he'd moved them both just moments earlier. "Your foot!" She couldn't hide the thrill in her voice.

"Yes." He smiled.

Too excited not to respond, she neared him. "Oh, Breck. That's such wonderful news! I – the doctors said you'd never be able to dance again and," she pointed to the door, "you were doing it so beautifully." After a moment, she realized where she was, that she was a mere foot away from him, and drew back. "I'm happy for you," control forced her voice to flat calm. "I am." But she'd not ask how he did it, what he went through or how he'd learned to dance again, or who he'd held in his arms on the dance floor in her absence.

"I need to get back inside." She started for the door, but he reached for her.

"Nicole." She glanced at where his fingers wrapped gently but with a squeeze of purpose around her arm. "I want to come see you – see your parents."

Without looking into his eyes, she put her hand on the door to open it. "I don't know that they'll want to see you." She lied just to hurt him. Out of the corner of her eye she saw that his head tipped forward – but only briefly.

"I have things I need to say to them."

Her eyes locked on his. "You think they'll care after all this time?"

"That sounds like you talking."

"I can't speak for anyone but myself."

"You don't have to listen."

"And I won't."

"Fair enough."

"You know where they are." She reached for the door again but his hand held firm on her arm. "I'd like to get back to my evening, if you don't mind."

"You looked great out there. Better than when—" he paused. "Better than ever."

He'd always been able to one-up her by being more humble than she and it still took her down a rung. But she'd learned to control her reaction enough to look convincing. Other men had taught her that.

"Thank you." She pulled on the handle again and felt the cool air whisper on her skin where his hand had been. This time, she opened the door and strode in without looking behind. Her legs began to weaken, her body felt ready to give. She didn't want him to think he could mop her up with a grin of victory on his face.

She reached the bar and clung. One quick glance up and down the stuffed area told her she was out of luck with a seat, unless she batted her eyes, wooing one out from under some admirer. Feeling the need to breathe, to settle, she found the most eager-looking male and squeezed in.

"I'm all danced out." Beyond the man she saw Breck working his way through the crowd – his eyes locked on her. Her knees were ready to buckle. "May I have your seat please?"

The man was off the stool in a second. "Sure."

"Thanks." Her body didn't relax when she took his warm stool. "Let's dance later."

"Excuse me." Breck wedged in, and the look in his eye was hot and determined.

It lit the flame of her fury. "Excuse you," she snapped at him. "This man and I were having a conversation." She looked at the eager stranger. "Weren't we?"

He nodded.

"That's what you and I were having before you left right in the middle of it."

"We were through."

Noon - Katherine Warwick

Breck leaned close, the sweetness of his breath nearly stealing hers from her lungs. "We're far from through." He turned to the stranger who was watching with fascination. "Pardon us."

"Wait a minute." Nicole stood to object, but Breck's hand took hers and he tugged her in the direction of the front door.

"I've waited long enough," he said.

* * *

Neither of them spoke as he led her out to the parking lot. When she was sure they weren't going to be seen or heard by any of the patrons, she stopped and pulled her hand free. "I agreed to follow you outside, that's it. If you think for one second that I'm going anywhere with you, you have a serious case of jetlag."

She heard the beep of a key remote and turned around to find her back against a dark Toyota.

"Get in."

"I'm not going anywhere with you." She pushed past him but he blocked her. Reaching around, he opened the passenger door. "Get in."

"Forget it, Noon."

"How did you know I've been on a plane, Nic?" His blue eyes sparkled, narrowed. "Been checking up on me?"

"In your dreams." She planted her hands on the hard, lean muscle of his chest to shove, and the feel of him sent rippling fire from her fingers to her toes. Before she could, he stepped even closer, his body pressing hers tight to the car so she couldn't move.

Seeing fierce determination draw his jaw tight, only served to strangle her resolve and send it withering to her feet. The moonlight cast soft white over the taut planes and carved angles of a face she'd tried so hard to forget and never could. To find her gaze magnetically fastened infuriated her.

"We need to talk. Get in. Please."

"Who do you think you are, coming back here expecting me to just drop everything so you can talk? I don't owe you that. I don't owe you anything."

Time and all that it had taken from them stretched delicately between them. Nicole tried her best not to stare; to fixate on the way his face had changed, thinned, become even stronger and more striking. He'd grown, filled out: muscles that had only begun to blossom in their youth had fully bloomed and pressed enticingly against his shirt and slacks, the full length of her. A long dead feeling both familiar and sweet came to life and wound deep inside near her heart.

"You don't, that's true. I thought you'd want to know why I left, where I went."

"I have no interest in what you have to say." She held her head erect, her body stiff. Making her disinterest clear, she slid out from the box he'd put her in, surprised, cold, and mortifyingly disappointed when she found herself striding to her car alone. Yes, she wanted to know, but it would be an empty day on the dance floor before she would ask.

Rather than stop her, Breck watched her walk to the car, unable to take his eyes away for even a moment. Of all of the things he'd missed, it was Nicole that had never left his thoughts. More than anything he could restore in his life, he wanted her. He'd not expected open arms. A slap or two, a slug even, was what he had prepared for, followed by a lot of words and even more hard work to convince her he'd not meant what he had said all those years ago. Opening her heart would take time. But he had time now. He owned it free and clear.

He welcomed the whispering to follow her – to go home. Seeing Lois and Garren was the next thing he felt desperate to do. As faded pictures of his life with the Dubois' flashed through his mind, he opened the rental car and got in.

He'd only spent a few weeks wallowing in darkened hotel rooms after he'd left town to know that self-pity was not going to get him anywhere. He'd had a deep need to rise above what Rob had shackled him with in the way of limitations and prove to himself that he could – to see what his life with the Dubois', with dance—and Nicole—had taught him.

He'd learned that if he was going to make anything out of his life, he would have to take every opportunity and make it his. He had. And he would, still.

The wrought-iron gates had closed by the time Breck pulled up to the

Noon - Katherine Warwick

estate, so he parked his car on the street and strode to the gate. There were no breaks in the surrounding fence, that he knew. Looking at black iron spikes in front of him, he placed both hands around the cold metal and started to climb.

Breck stood at the door feeling like the prodigal son. He owed the Dubois everything yet had given them nothing in return. Though no Dubois blood ran through his veins, he owed it to them to make things right again. It was the second thing he needed to do after he'd gotten off that airplane. The first hadn't gone well. But he was determined to make that work and would take whatever steps necessary to do it.

This was a necessary step.

Often he'd thought of seeing Lois' face again, calming and lovely as it had always been to him. But nothing prepared him for the swamp of emotions that threatened to overtake him after the door swung open. His knees buckled, his hands shook and he couldn't find words, they sat in a jumbled mess, wrapped around his thudding heart.

Eyes that had once comforted him with just one look were still warm and friendly, drawing his heart out into the open. The years blinked by as she pressed her hands together at her heart, her eyes glistening over a trembling smile.

"Breck." Her arms came out next. Nothing promised to ease away the lost time and bring them back together like her embrace surely would. Holding onto her as long as she would allow, he smelled the familiar scent of home coupled with the delicate scent of perfume she'd always worn.

Garren came down the stairs with a grin the size of which Breck had never seen and no hesitation in his step. The eager greeting humbled Breck more than having the door slammed in his face.

"Look, Garren. Look at him." Lois stepped back so that Garren could embrace him. "You look taller."

"Come in, come in." With a welcoming hand on Breck's arm, Garren led him to the back of the house. "Breck. Can you stay a while?"

"Of course. I know it's late, but I didn't want to wait to see you both."

"Nonsense, this is your home." Lois fluttered around him like a mother bird, and he soaked up the attention like a starving chick. They sat comfortably on couches he didn't recognize in the family room.

Breck looked around, unable to see enough, fast enough, to satisfy the need to reconnect with what had once been his.

"The place looks great." Walls that had once been taupe were now deep brick in color. The plaid couches he remembered from his youth had been replaced with a set in soft leather.

"You guys look great." He didn't see the new grey hairs threaded through Garren's hair, nor the deeper wrinkles around Lois' eyes when she smiled, like she was now. In his swollen heart, the two people he'd loved most in the world looked the same. He pressed anxious hands together wishing a blink would restore everything the way it had once been. It would take more than a blink. He was prepared to beg on his knees for their forgiveness, if that's what it took for them to understand what had happened. Nicole wouldn't come down, and so he focused on the faces in front of him waiting with open hearts.

"I –" He broke into a laugh born of momentary awkwardness. "I thought maybe you wouldn't see me."

"Oh, Breck." Lois leaned close, all but ready to jump to his side to soothe rattled nerves, but Breck put up a hand to stop her.

"Let me." His face grew serious, his eyes shadowed with so many emotions, both Lois and Garren sat like stone. "You need to know what happened when I left. Up until yesterday, I wasn't able to tell you. But, my father's death has," he paused and took a breath, looking at them like he had so many times before, with admiration, respect, and pure love. "It's opened a door I thought I'd never open again."

Lois gripped Garren's hand.

"The night Nicole was attacked in the orchards…when she described the attack," Breck had to stand, to move, responsibility still rifling through him. He paced next to the couches. "I knew it was him. I knew the way he hit. It was the same way he'd beat me." He looked at them both with remorse scorching his soul.

A tiny gasp escaped Lois' lips and she put her fingers over her mouth to stop it.

Noon - Katherine Warwick

"It was no secret my father hated my dancing. He hated it enough to hurt Nicole and all of you, if I didn't stop.

"Anyway, I went to see him that night after the attack. We had a fight, and it got nasty. He knocked me out and when I woke up…my foot." Breck dropped back to the couch, dragging his hands down his face. The look of astonishment and horror on their faces had him afraid to continue.

"He threatened to hurt her, really hurt her – if I didn't give up dancing for good. When I refused, he threatened the rest of you and it was something I couldn't ignore. I mean, part of me wanted to stay and fight back. But I…" Emotion swelled in his throat. How could he say something he'd only said to one other person – that he loved them? "I couldn't take the risk of anything happening to any of you."

Lois reached out her hand but Breck couldn't take it. Yet. "It sounds like a cop out, and I'm sorry. Infinitely sorry. I can't imagine what you must have thought of me leaving like that. Abandoning everything and everybody without any word, no thanks whatsoever."

"It was one of the hardest things I've ever had to take." The raw honesty on Breck's face salved Garren's scarred heart with truth. A truth that he knew for certain would only help in the end, even if it was uncomfortable for the moment.

"I'm so sorry," Breck's gaze never wavered. "It was the only way I could see to take care of things."

"You should have told us," Garren's tone held the sorrow of an old wound. "You could have. We would have helped you."

"I understand that now. But part of me was still afraid of him. He'd show up, demand things. I couldn't keep him pacified. I—"

"You mean he'd threatened you before?" Fury snapped into Garren's voice, sharpened his eyes. "When?"

"It doesn't matter now, he's gone. It's over," Breck put in, amazed that after all these years, fatherly love still ran through Garren's veins, just for him.

Garren looked away for a moment. "You should have told me."

"I'd taken so much from you—"

"Taken?" Lois's eyes widened with tears. "We gave because we loved you."

◙ 213 ◙

Garren's countenance held heavy regret. "When you started teaching… that was it, wasn't it? I should have seen it. I should have pulled it out of you."

"It wasn't your problem."

There was something in Garren's eyes that told Breck to tread carefully. "We were your family."

"It's over now." The last thing Breck wanted was for either of them to carry any guilt. "I took care of it. And it wasn't a bad thing for me. I mean, hard work never hurt anybody." He could barely look into their faces. Forgiveness was already there, just as he knew it would be.

Garren let out a heavy sigh. "Have you told Nicole this?"

"She isn't ready to hear me."

Garren reached out and placed a hand on Breck's shoulder. "Do you have a place to stay?"

"I don't."

"Would it fit into your plans to stay here?" Lois nearly jumped to her feet, looking ready, Breck thought, to burst. Since it fit so perfectly into his plans, he wouldn't deny her.

He took her face in his hands and gave her a quick kiss on the cheek. "I never could say no to you."

Like heavenly fingers reaching down to awaken her, the sun oozed through splintered cracks in her shutters, lighting her bedroom to the soft, pale yellow of morning. Nicole stretched, yawned. And groaned. Last night was turning into a dream-like blur. She sat up in bed.

Breck was back.

Anger had subsided, and now she was feeling plain old grouchy. She debated going back to sleep.

Grumbling, she pulled on the flannel pajama bottoms she wore with her light pink cami tee. She'd heard the low murmur of voices late into last night as she'd gotten ready for bed. Pride had kept her from eavesdropping. She'd done the respectable thing and taken her nightly bath and then settled into bed with a good book.

Noon - Katherine Warwick

Pleased that she'd held her ground, she padded down the hallway with another yawn and a smile. *I bet he thinks he can just walk back into our lives and begin where he left off.* "Ha, think again," she chuckled, taking the stairs down.

She knew better than to think her parents had given Breck anything but an open-armed reception. But he'd not get that from her. With relish, she would ignore his attempts to ingratiate himself back into her family circle.

She'd be the only one.

Brian, Tami, and the girls would be thrilled that Breck was back, and she wondered if they knew yet. Given her mother's enthusiasm, her unconditional love for anyone and everyone, she figured they'd all be over later. *Fine, I'll head down to the studio while Breck pulls the wool down.*

The tidy kitchen told her that she was the first one up and enjoyed the fact that she could please her father by brewing some coffee for him. It was a little something she'd been doing ever since they'd connected that night, talked things out in the orchards. Enthused, she opted to make herself something celebratory. But everything took too long or required too much work, so she reached for some toast, dropping two pieces in the toaster.

"Drop me in a piece, will ya?"

Nicole whirled around and her eyes flashed. Breck stood across the room in a well-worn black tee shirt and even more raggedy black sweats, a cocky grin on his face.

"You're not—"

"Staying here, yeah. I am." One hand rubbed at his hair, the other slid under his shirt and rubbed at his chest, exposing a flash of smooth, chisled lower belly. He yawned.

How could her heart flutter and drop at the same time? When he came toward her, she backed away as if he was an apparition. Outrage began at her toes and snarled its way up. "You are not staying here."

"Yes I am." He reached around her, his arm brushing her shoulder, and plucked one of the pieces of toast that had popped. It danced between his two hands from the heat.

Like he'd never left, she watched him open the plate cabinet, reach into the refrigerator for butter, swipe the toast and then sit casually at the counter. "Yours is getting cold." He nodded toward the toaster.

◎ 215 ◎

Noon - Katherine Warwick

She couldn't eat, couldn't think, not with him sitting there like that – like he had so many times before. "I lost my appetite."

"Give me your piece. And get me some orange juice."

"I will not." She crossed her arms and deliberately stayed put. She could see him much better now. The soft glow of colored lights at Bruisers had made him look too mysterious, too untouchable and unreal. With the morning sun casting its rays into the room, he was completely real. The shadow of beard on his face, the faint lines around his eyes that had not been there years before, and that smile: it was even more stunning as time and age had only made his face more dramatic.

His hair was longer, like it had been when she'd first laid eyes on him: waves and soft curls that hung in an alluring frame around his face. She'd never seen him with a tan. The rich deep color shocked his blue eyes to an electric brilliance that both glittered and pierced from across the room. It was clear that whatever he'd been doing, wherever he'd been, he'd not suffered the worse for wear.

He caught her eyes appraising him and smiled as he chewed. A flash of heat shot to her face and she looked away, grabbing the cold toast.

"Butter it and stick it back down. Makes it crispier," he said.

She ignored him. She would continue to ignore him. If her mother's Samaritan efforts were going to mean that he was sharing the same roof with her, so be it. Either that or she would seriously consider moving out, something her common sense had kept her from doing up until now, economically minded as she'd become. She would not let him get under her skin.

She sat at the table rather than the counter. He started to laugh.

"Something funny?" she demanded.

"I always did like you first thing in the morning." He got up and moved to her, sitting directly across.

Warmth flushed her cheeks. She stuffed her hair behind her ears and tried to eat without looking at him. She'd forgotten how it felt to be under his penetrating gaze – like being under the sun at mid day.

Pushing away from the counter, she removed herself from his warm heat threatening her. "I have things to do."

"Yeah, I need to talk to you about that."

Noon - Katherine Warwick

Stopping, she put her hand on her hip more than eager to be mean and nasty. "I can't see where we have anything at all to say to each other, Breck."

"You rehearsing with Trey today?"

"Of course." She hemmed a moment but had to ask. "How did you know?"

He stood with his empty plate and went to her. Near enough to make her eyes widen as he looked down into them. "I've been following your career." He set the plate on the counter without his gaze varying from hers, the intensity grabbing hold of her deep inside.

She found herself falling into old habits – trying to read him like she used to. But things had changed. His brilliant blue eyes, his expressive face, no longer spoke to her.

She didn't like the idea that other women had no doubt learned to read his thoughts and emotions. It was a dream of hers to think that he'd allowed only her that sacred vision. "Then you know that we've taken—"

"I know what you've taken." His voice was sharp and he moved even closer. "I know what you've won, where you've placed. I know that Trey sprained his ankle two years ago and it kept you out of comps for three months. I read that you two had a falling out, but you patched things up again and you've been together ever since. I saw tapes of you in Blackpool. I sat in the audience at world three years in a row and watched you. I know it all, Nic."

"You – you do?"

Nodding, he kept her pinned with a look that sent a dangerous skittering throughout her body. "And since you won't listen to me, won't let me explain, this will sound obsessive. Maybe it was, maybe it is. But there wasn't a day or a night that I didn't think about you. Not one."

Her heart was loose in her chest, flying out of control. Old flames ignited memories, reminding her of how she'd wanted him. Instinct had her backing away and creating distance. If she was any nearer to him, she would find her arms around his neck, her lips chasing his.

And that could never happen again.

She'd hurt him back. That was her plan and she'd stick to it. "Well." She mustered all the cold energy she could. "I never once thought about you."

She expected the comment to hurt him, but his jaw just tightened, his

Noon - Katherine Warwick

eyes darkened with determination. "I expect you wouldn't," he began, voice flat. "I hurt you – devastated you. I didn't deserve one thought."

"You're blowing this out of proportion. You did not devastate me." Her voice shook in spite of her efforts to control it. "We didn't have anything, you said so yourself. And you were right. We never meant anything to each other."

He clamped a hand around her arm. "That's a lie and you know it."

"If it was more to you than that, well, I'm sorry but—"

"Don't."

"Don't what? You didn't see things the way they really were. It really was just a fling, something fun. But then you always were naive that way." Then she did see it, hurt silently welling behind his eyes. And the revenge was more bitter than sweet.

"You were always good at games, Nic," his voice stayed low, "so good." His fingers dug deep for a moment before he released her. "Let me explain."

"There's nothing that you could tell me that would change anything,"she lied, her heart taking a beating.

"Then you'll have to live with the way it's going to be." He turned, and headed toward the back stairs. She gasped, aghast.

"I don't have to live with anything you cocky, toast-stealing, smug-faced—"

"See you in the studio." He didn't bother to turn around, or stop. She wanted to hurl something at him. She wanted to run and jump on his back and scream in his ear. Instead, she watched him head up the stairs like she had so many times before, unable to look at anything else.

Twenty-one

She was alone in the studio – she'd escaped there. Playing music that would draw a cobra from its basket, she danced in a mix of moves that popped with hip-hop and freestyle, hoping to bleed Breck from her soul.

He'd both angered and stirred her that morning at breakfast and she was fighting it. Her body was still drawn to him as if no time had passed. Her soul yearned to know what was inside of him in spite of all she was doing to distance herself. So she was moving, allowing herself a voice in the safety of the only place she was completely protected, where no one could watch and no one could touch her.

Pride drove the angry punches and jerky movements of hip hop. She would like nothing more than to land her fist in Breck's beautiful, smug face. She could do more than that, and as she pounded her feet, twisted her shoulders and jerked her body, slowly she worked out the frustration and found nothing left but the liquid, soft, sensual moves that they had once done so well together.

Except now, she danced alone.

By the time the song ended, she was breathless and still harbored unsettling feelings about him. Pushing moist hair from her face, she walked in circles, waiting for Reuben and Trey to show up.

Breck spoke with such confidence about the future, she felt cornered. Whatever he thought was going to happen, he would be disappointed. He'd not get one thing from her though she doubted he would come to her for anything. He had a life she was millions of miles and years removed from, what he did in that life held no interest to her.

When the door swung open, her heart gave away her innermost thoughts wishing Breck would walk through that door. Trey was there instead.

He seemed happier than usual. He nearly skipped across the floor, wrapped his arms around her and swung her in a circle.

"Trey—"

"I like you all sweaty and hot." When he tried to kiss her, she pushed at his chest.

"Stop it—"

"We need to celebrate."

She went still in his arms. He'd hated Breck, surely he hadn't heard. "Why?"

He'd read the paper, seen the obituary and the story on the fire, and fallen to his knees with glee. The old maniac was dead, and Trey's money and peace of mind were once again his own. In the years since they'd met, Rob Noon's greed snowballed, rolling and gathering until it threatened to fall apart, exposing Trey along with it.

"Let's just say I've finally gotten rid of an albatross."

"Trey, no."

Her resistance caused the bubbles in his blood to pop and explode as he pulled her against him, as he began to imagine them at last together. "I just want a congratulatory kiss. Come on, baby."

The struggle escalated into a battle that stirred him deep down—until she slapped him. The sting had him stepping aside until rage and pride forced him forward. Snagging her wrist, he pulled with the speed of a whip and had her against him again. "I'm sick of this."

"So am I. Quit coming on to me."

"You know what I think?"

"I don't care what you think unless it has to do with our partnership." She struggled to free her wrist but only felt his nails claw until she winced – then he smiled.

"That's right." His voice had an eerie calm that drove a shudder through her system. "That's right."

She glanced at the red half-moons blooming beneath his nails. "There's no excuse for violence."

He leaned close. "Violence and passion are cousins, baby."

"I see some things never change."

Both Trey and Nicole jerked around to find Breck just a few feet away. His hands were in his pockets but his body was tense and ready to spring. Trey dropped Nicole's wrist instantly and she rubbed it.

Trey's eyes widened, then slit. "Noon. It's been a while." He'd been elated at Rob's death; and forgotten that might it bring Breck back. Fury swirled in his viens though he crossed to his enemy, hand extended.

Breck glanced at the extended hand with enough disgust to cause Trey to withdraw. "Still taking where you're not wanted?" Breck's dark eyes shot to Nicole's for a moment.

"Partners have disagreements over style. You know how it is."

"Is that what that was?" Trey nodded. "Obviously she still doesn't care for yours," Breck said.

"She's dancing with me, isn't she?"

A sly grin spread across Breck's face. "For now." Then he strode over to the seats and sat.

"What are you doing?" Nicole felt the heat building inside the sudio and decided to change the subject to one that she had more control over: her anger at Breck. Trey could wait.

Breck settled himself in the seat. "I came to watch."

Trey snorted.

In six long strides, Nicole stood in front of Breck, hands on her hips. The deep purple silk shirt he wore turned his blue eyes into exotic gems, fringed with dark lashes. Money had bought the black slacks he wore with it, in an expensive fabric just as soft and flowing as his shirt, and for a moment she wondered how he'd earned it.

A smile of amusement lifted his lips. He leaned toward her, his voice low, "You can thank me later for coming in when I did." Stretching out his legs, he settled his back against the chair.

The door flung open and Reuben was there, looking around with a giant smile. "Where is he?" When his eyes lit on Breck, he danced over with delight that spilled without compunction. "Buddy, I can't believe it's you!"

Reuben yanked Breck up for a hug. "Man, it's good to see you. Lois told me you were back and I couldn't believe it. I had to see you with my own eyes. Where the heck have you been?"

"All over." It did Breck good to look into the familiar face of someone he'd idolized. "You haven't changed a bit."

"Well you look fine man, fine." Reuben wore joy in his smile as he looked him over. "Man, I'm glad you're back." Startled, Reuben stared at Breck's foot. "Your foot...."

Easily moving his foot in a circle, Breck grinned. "Good as new."

"I'd say it is." It was then Reuben first acknowledged Trey and Nicole standing quietly back, watching. "Hey." He faced Breck again, enthusiasm overflowing like shaken soda from a bottle. "You're going to stay and watch, right?"

Breck looked at Nicole. "That's why I'm here."

* * *

Maybe it was because Trey had frightened her that Nicole was jittery, unable to perform to her usual standard of excellence. She'd tripped over his feet once, missed a turn, and was off-center during their BotoFogos. She didn't want to think her mistakes had anything to do with the mystifying figure sitting alongside the dance floor, watching.

Breck was like an inky spot in her vision that wouldn't go away. And he was mystifying – she didn't know where he'd been, what he'd done, and she had no idea why he was back, other than to take care of his father's remains and reinstate himself in her family's life.

It was her good fortune he had walked in on her and Trey when he did and she was glad for that. Pride kept her from thanking him.

With Breck as her audience, she had more to prove. She wanted him to see how far she'd come, and just where she intended to go – without him. So she made sure she and Trey pounded out their dances until she was satisfied.

"You need to get that last part down," she snapped at Trey. They had been over and over their Latin routine intended for the annual world competition in Miami. Trey's stylization could keep them from placing, and it was more than she could swallow.

"We've been over this, man." Reuben stood in front of Trey. "Your hips are too jagged, not fluid enough. Think honey pouring from a jar."

Trey didn't say anything, just lifted an impervious brow and circled, silently seething. His light blue eyes glittered at Nicole. "How about we work on that move later, baby – in private."

Nicole rolled her eyes, moving away so Breck couldn't see the flush of

Noon - Katherine Warwick

fear and anger on her face.

"Let's go over the set again," Reuben told them.

Breck didn't leave his seat once during the three-and-a-half hour practice, not even when Lois tiptoed in with a snack, for which he kissed her on the cheek. An army couldn't drag him away. Rifling jealousy had been a resident in his heart since the day he'd left. But every time he saw Trey and Nicole perform, saw them in pictures or on tape, it became a force stronger than hunger, the consuming factor that drove his ambition. Jealousy had healed his foot, forced him in dire pain, back onto the dance floor. Jealousy had kept the women in his life to a skeletal minimum.

He only wanted one.

To see her in the flesh, in the arms of a man he'd grown to hate and mistrust like Satan himself, was more than he could take. It was torture to be an observer, to see the way Trey looked at her, eyes ready to devour, hands inching beyond boundaries they were all taught to respect.

Trey would never have her. Breck had crossed his fingers across the miles, spent nights twisted in dreams that speared his heart and wrenched his soul, dreaming of her dancing in the arms of faceless men. He'd survived the nightmares by telling himself that someday, she would be his.

She still had it. Every part of her responded to the song and the steps as if she were desperate to understand them – internalize them, make them hers, and then thrust them out into the open for the world to embrace.

He wanted more than breath itself for their bodies to live and dance together, and sustain each other. The night at Bruisers had been a teasing act of self-inflicted cruelty. He'd felt her, smelled her, kissed her. They'd hushed the crowd with a unity so beguiling and perfect, even time hadn't tarnished the beauty only they could make together. He wanted all of that again and more.

"I've had enough." Nicole broke free of Trey in obvious disgust, their practice fraught with glitches.

"One more time," Reuben insisted.

She turned, shoulders slumped. "I said I've had enough. You," she looked at Trey and her posture turned steely, "don't walk through that door again until you're smooth. Your stylization is embarrassing."

A fog of silence rolled through the studio. Trey snatched his coat and

Noon - Katherine Warwick

duffle and stormed out without a word.

"I'm sorry." Weariness caused her head to bow. "I just—" she looked over at Breck and straightened. "I don't know what's wrong with me today."

Reuben let out a sigh that said he, too, was tired of a battle he wasn't sure they'd ever win. He sat on the chair next to the sound system, and lowered his head into his hands.

"I don't know, sis." He rubbed his naked head. "He's just not getting it. I mean, we've worked on this for so long now and—" His head came up, his eyes shot to Breck. "He ain't no Breck Noon, you know what I'm saying?"

He slapped the palm of his hand on his thigh before rising. "Man, I just can't tell you how good it is to see you."

Nicole looked at their refeflections in the mirror and ignored the thrill she felt when Breck rose and casually walked over. He stopped directly behind her. "I think Nicole's forgotten what it feels like to dance with a champion."

Reuben's eyes glittered with mischief. "Indulge the master, will you kids? For old time's sake."

"I said I was done for today." Nicole stooped to take off her shoes but Breck's arm slid around her so fast she'd have lost her balance had it not been that his body was there, strong and unwavering. She clung to him.

"Whew." Reuben's teeth gleamed. "It's gonna get hot in here."

"Put on some music, Reuben." Breck grinned, Nicole captured in his arms.

The slow strum of the guitar began, fingers teasing strings until the bass and drums kicked in the driving thud that pushed the beat. The Spanish singer's smooth voice whispered Spanish words of *te quiero amor mio...I want you my love.*

It seemed impossible, but he was there on the dance floor with her. Pain that had refused to leave dulled, dissolving in the melody, leeched out of her soul under the powerful commands his body demanded from hers. She couldn't find breath, was searching for her heart – it was lost somewhere inside. Her eyes met his and refused to look away, even for a blink. His hands slipped into place, taking ownership. Enticing will. As the guitar strummed, as the drums beat, she abandoned that will to the dance.

The dance was their old samba routine, where one demand led to another. Where their bodies joined, spun, twined. Mirrored. Where give and take met need and want, compelled by the impulsive taunt of instruments harmonizing for them alone.

As if something inside of him was reaching out and luring her, her body and soul yeilded to his. It didn't frighten her. These were feelings too strong to ignore and they lived inside. Like a genie to its master, they had lain dormant, and as she looked into his eyes and moved with him, were awakening again.

Complete, her soul sighed in his arms – home. And when his hands drove her, it wasn't with the arrogance of showmanship, but with a beauty and intimacy she'd known no where else.

Bailamos...let's dance...

Effortlessly, their bodies spoke to each other, responding to each move with the fluidity of two streams joining. Years washed away were forgotten as feet stepped to a memory no longer a ghost, but alive with flesh and blood and breath.

She couldn't hide the thrill her body rode on; it was as if she was strapped to a rocket, and she was glad to be soaring into bliss with him. She couldn't stop, responding to him as if two halves had finally been joined. She couldn't keep her eyes from gazing into his. They were fastened like snaps – held tight as the music played, as his heart beat in unison with hers.

The song ebbed softly out. He smiled, taking them down, gently slowing their movements like a tender lover. Every part of her remembered him then, recalling that night so long ago, and longed for reunion.

Reuben clapped heartily and it seemed he appeared out of nowhere.

Breck had taken her to another place with the dance, and because of that, she made sure she kept distance between them as soon as he let go of her.

"You haven't lost a thing, man." Reuben broke the thick silence. "It's unbelievable. Seriously. How'd you do it?"

Breck's gaze shifted from Nicole to Reuben. "Vladimir Korishkova."

"No kidding?" Reuben was rightfully impressed. The Russian coach was a highly sought after transplant. Because Nicole had sworn she would never ask

Noon - Katherine Warwick

for information, she gathered her things with a turned ear.

"So you weren't just sunnin' on the beach in Miami?" Reuben teased.

Far from it, Breck thought. But he'd let Nicole think whatever her imaginative mind wanted to, since she didn't care to ask. "I met Vlad through Kit. We hit it off, and he helped me back."

"Cool," Reuben said. "And your plans now?"

Breck noticed Nicole slowly donning her sweats, packing her bag. "I'm looking for a partner."

She paused for a moment before striding toward the door and going out. Breck looked at Reuben who lifted his shoulders. "Can't tell you it's been easy on her."

"Trey?"

Sitting on down on the bench, Reuben changed his shoes. "He's good. But he's not you."

"I've been watching them," Breck told him.

Reuben replaced his dance shoes with slip-on sandals. "She needs you, man. She wants wins, and she's not gonna get them with Trey. Not in Latin anyway. Talk to her."

"She won't listen to me." Breck looked at the door. "I doubt she'll dance with me."

There was excitement in Reuben's eyes when he stood. "But you two are like nobody else out there. She's gonna have to give in – on principle of integrity alone. I know that girl, and she'll do whatever it takes for a win. She's been dancing with Trey, hasn't she?"

"If he can't get there, why has she stuck it out with him?"

Reuben shrugged. "He's got it two thirds of the time. When he's got it, he's good. But when he's tuned out, man, he might as well be doing country line dancing, you know?"

"Is their relationship strictly professional?"

Reuben's eyes softened and he nodded. The gesture brought a sigh from Breck. "He's been on her back for years. The guy can't separate his ego from professionalism. You know she hates that."

Breck had seen more than that earlier. Trey was wound up like a coiled snake and that meant at some point, he'd spring.

◎ 226 ◎

Noon - Katherine Warwick

"You talk to her and I'll bet she'd see the light. Trey can dance with anybody, he'll mend eventually."

"Trey's career isn't of interest to me."

"Imagine not. It's just so great that you're back." He slugged Breck's arm playfully. "You gonna tell me why you up and left us?"

"You want to know?"

"Do I want to know? Was I born with tap shoes on?"

Breck took another look around as Reuben pushed the door open. "I've missed this place."

"What did you do to her, man?"

"I did what I thought was best for her at the time."

Reuben put his arm around Breck's shoulder for the long walk to the house. "You may be the second greatest dancer I've ever seen."

"You being the first of course," Breck laughed.

"Of course. You white boys just never can get the woman-thing right. Now, where've you been?"

He'd get it right, Breck told himself. As he approached the things he wanted most from the rest of his life, he'd see to it that he got every last one. And all of them had Nicole—love, family and dance.

If it took Nicole time to understand there was only one man that could evenly handle the scale on which she chose to drop her dreams, that was fine. No one knew how to master Nicole Dubois better than he.

Because he'd anticipated her refusal to be his partner, he'd made other arrangements.

Heading to the rental car, he enjoyed the familiar scent of aspen mixing with evergreen on the property. How many nights had he enjoyed a view of the stars overhead, just like tonight, or the sight of the fluffy grey spread of orchards under moonlight. Ignoring the flash of memory of that night he'd found Nicole, bruised and torn, he looked back at the house and thought he saw movement in Nicole's lit, bedroom window. He smiled to himself. "You're fighting a battle you're not going to win, Nic."

Noon - Katherine Warwick

And the pleasure would be his to convince her.

In fifteen minutes he was walking into TGIF's. Even on a Monday night, the place buzzed with the trendy hype he remembered from his youth. He scanned the restaurant until he saw her, all blonde and smiles, waving him over.

"Kit." He took her in for a hug. "You look great."

"Thanks." They admired each other, eyes catching up what time had distanced between them. Her trademark had always been pink, Breck remembered, and she wore it now, in a tight tee shirt and white jeans. Her sunny hair was to her shoulders, lightly curled.

Though they'd dated in high school for a short time, the lock on his heart had always belonged to Nicole and even now, he looked at Kit as nothing more than the good friend that she was.

She sat down first and he followed.

"How long has it been?" she asked.

"Three years maybe? When you were last in Miami."

"That's right – you and Vlad." She leaned and peaked under the table at his foot. "Wow. You walked in here like nothing had ever happened. I had my doubts about his mystical creams and oils and stuff, but, wow."

He nodded. "He was great."

The waitress brought water and menus. Kit set her menu aside and looked at him. He'd only gotten better looking and she was flattered to be sitting in the booth with him. When he'd called, she had allowed herself the brief fantasy of something she had never been able to let go of – that he wanted her. "You look hot, Breck." The compliment lifted one corner of his lip. "So, what you've been up to? I want to hear everything."

He put down the menu, sat back and folded his hands. "Healing, dancing and getting my bachelor's."

"All this on crutches?"

"The crutches only lasted three months. Vlad's ancient Russian healing oils and exercises he made me do were the answer. I swear they're what put my foot back together."

"When did you start dancing again?"

"As soon as I could put pressure on it."

"Impressive." Her scan was deep, and lingered on his succulent lips a

Noon - Katherine Warwick

moment. "But then you were always impressive." She leaned forward hoping the light was doing for her what it was doing for him. He looked determined and wonderfully masculine. She was feeling old feelings again.

"What about you?"

"Not so fast," she flirted. "Tell me about school."

"I graduated in family relations and counseling."

Her brows shot up. "Seriously?"

"Not off base for a guy like me."

"I guess not."

"I wanted to study people and relationships," he began. "To know why communication could be so easy for some and so hard for others, and how the dynamics of it figured into making relationships successful."

It was the first time his eyes left hers when he looked out over the restaurant and she studied the changes in his face. He was troubled by something; his eyes darkened a shade.

"How is she?"

His sigh spoke volumes words never would. "Fine from what I can tell. Seems to have taken on life without any glitches. But then I've only been here, what, two days now."

"Your father died in that fire. I'm sorry."

"Don't be. You're still dancing." Breck reached for his water, sipped.

It disappointed Kit that he was going directly to the reason for the meeting. She was glad when the waitress came and she took her time ordering something she didn't want to eat.

After the waitress left, she leaned on her elbows, hoping the low cut of her teeshirt would draw his gaze to her breasts. It didn't. "Trey and I broke our partnership right after your accident. Did you know that?"

"You didn't mention it in Miami."

"It was ugly. But then that wouldn't surprise any of us that know Trey." She didn't bother covering up the loathing she felt. In retrospect, she was glad the partnership was over and she was safe from Trey's temper. "I can say it now, but I was too hurt then. He's always just wanted one thing – Nicole." The way Breck's jaw tightened, she knew he felt the same, and her heart took a hit. "I can see you still share that in common."

◎ 229 ◎

"I won't lie to you—"

"You never did, that's why it was so easy to love you."

He couldn't respond for a moment, taken aback by the admittance. She read it in his face. "You didn't know?" He shook his head. "I've been in and out of love with you since high school."

"Kit—"

"You're a one of a kind. Trey's kind are a dime a dozen."

"I'm sorry he hurt you."

She reached across the table and took his hand in hers. "Lots of people thought I deserved it."

"Nobody deserves that."

"Your parting with Nicole wasn't picture-perfect either."

His hand went stiff and he drew back. "I did what I had to, to protect her."

The response was so honorable, she knew then she'd fight for a chance with him. "I believe you."

"But it was unfair to her." His fingers absently ran up and down his water glass. "Now, she won't listen to me. So I'm going on with my life."

"I'm guessing that's where I come in."

He nodded. "I'm looking for a partner. Interested?"

She'd dreamt it in her youth, fantasized about it forever after, but to have the offer, she almost couldn't believe it. "Very."

"I've followed your career; I know you're up for it. I want world." When his eyes leveled with hers with that pin-sharp blue that dove in deep and wrapped around her tongue, she was left without words and could only nod.

"But I have to be upfront, Kit." He put his water down. "Ours will be a temporary arrangement."

"Until you can convince Nicole."

He waited for her to react and when she didn't, he nodded. A fever budded and scrambled inside of her, ready to spread.

"I can live with that." She lifted her water glass to her lips, noted that he watched. If there was even the tiniest sliver of chance for her, she would take him any way she could get him.

Noon - Katherine Warwick

Twenty-Two

The call from Sheriff Brande wasn't urgent. They had recovered some items from the fire; he could come by the Pleasant Grove Police Department any time and pick them up. Curiosity and child-like hope was the force behind Breck's drive to the police station now. He couldn't believe his stomach was filled with butterflies. He couldn't believe he still cared, still wished for something.

The police station was quiet and smelled of institution; stale, old coffee, dust and paper. Tall, spindly, Sheriff Brande's face was kind when his eyes smiled. He came out from behind a bullet-proof glass office holding a plastic bag in his hand. "Again, I'm sorry about your father."

Breck looked at the bag. "Thanks."

"We didn't find much. The key belongs to the Dodge. It's in the lot out back. Miraculous that it wasn't touched by the flames."

Breck nodded, his father had always loved his trucks.

After he shook the Sheriff's hand, he walked out to the parking lot to where they had impounded the truck. One peek in the bag and hope dashed. Nothing but scraps of an old frame, a lighter and his father's watch, well charred, glass cracked, the hour hand forever frozen at the two.

When he opened the door of the truck, he was sickened by the waft of stale cigarette smoke that came after him. For a moment, he just looked at the worn upholstery where his father once sat. A pack of Marlboros had been flung on the dashboard. Other than that, the inside was spotless. Just the way Breck remembered his father kept his trucks. Rather than get inside, he closed the door and went around to the passenger side. He opened the glove compartment on a compulsory gesture and found it stuffed with papers.

Slowly, he leafed through insurance records, receipts from gas purchases and a paper-clipped stack of tissue paper thin receipts from bank money orders. He studied the copies, all written to Robert Noon in the same, scrolling handwriting. Each check was for one thousand dollars, and signed by Trey Woods.

Breck looked up at the clouds, his thoughts lost for a moment in a haze of disbelief. A patrol car pulled up alongside him and parked. The officer nodded at him before vanishing into the station.

Breck didn't look again at the checks, just stuffed them into his back pocket before slamming the door of the truck closed.

When Nicole pulled up the driveway and saw Reuben's car, she looked at her watch, sure she'd done the unthinkable and forgotten a private lesson. Then she saw the Easter egg pink convertible VW next to Breck's rental car.

The thump of Latin music vibrated from the studio and she strode directly over.

After flinging open the door, she stood inside with her mouth open. Reuben was following Breck and Kit around the floor as they danced through a cha-cha routine.

Two can play at this game, she thought. *Two can play very well*. Calmly, she walked over to the chairs and sat. She forced a pearly smile, a casual yet confident pose, and watched Breck move Kit with the ease of a champion dancing with an amateur.

Kit, she thought, *will never be me*.

She had improved, Nicole couldn't deny that. In fact, the more she watched, the more she squirmed in her seat. This was a very different Kit than the one she had seen even nine months ago at competition.

"That went better." Reuben crossed to the music and switched it off. "But we'll need to take the last three sets and go over them until they're up to snuff with the front end."

"Excuse me." Nicole stood then, her back erect as a ruler. Walking toward the threesome, she kept her smile engaged. "Kit, I didn't know you were in town."

"Yes." Kit pressed a fallen strand of hair off her face with a glittering smile. "I'm living here now."

"Really." Nicole's smile shifted to Breck. "We need to talk." Hooking her arm in his, the sweat coating his arms slicked and heated her skin. He'd showered in his old bathroom, used the zesty soap that had sent her blood in to a skip when she'd smelled it on him years ago. Ignoring her body's response, she began to lead him away but he eased his arm free.

"I'm in the middle of a private." He turned and was back with Kit and Reuben before she could counter.

Kit tilted her head at Nicole.

It only took Nicole a moment to regain her composure and lift her chin. She backed in the direction of the chairs, still unable to believe that Breck was using her studio to dance with another woman.

Reuben gave his customary single clap. "Let's start from the top." When the music began again, Nicole mustered enough grace to walk calmly out the door.

Kicking up dust behind her, she nearly jogged up the drive and into the house.

"Who's responsible?" she demanded. She tore through the house, looking for someone to cream. The scent of Breck's soap was still on her skin, perfumed by his sweat.

Her mother was in the kitchen, over the stove. The house smelled like Thanksgiving but being thankful was the furthest thing from Nicole's mind. "Who said he could use the studio?"

Lois checked the pot of boiling potatoes. "We did, of course."

"He's staying here and he's using the studio. Mom, he's a grown man capable of living life on his own. You guys are doing too much for him."

"We'd do the same for you and Brian."

This she knew, and her heart caved thinking about it. Still flushed from Breck's touch, the fact was that Breck was not her brother, or she wouldn't be getting hot and flustered about him.

"He can take care of himself. And he needs to."

"I'm aware of that. But it's only been a few days, Nicole. He's got plenty of time to do all of that. For now, I'm enjoying having him here, and he can stay as long as he likes."

Nicole opened the oven. "A turkey? It's May."

"I know." Lois gleamed as she diced celery for the stuffing. "But we have so much to be thankful for."

"You're making a turkey dinner?"

"Mm-hmm."

Lois' sincerity broke through Nicole's anger, for about a minute. She kissed her mother's cheek. "You're too much." Plucking a celery stalk, she bit down. "But does he have to use the studio?"

"He's family."

She knew where Breck was concerned she'd have to tip toe. Her mother just didn't want to see him as anything other than the prodigal returned. "Kit's dancing with him."

Lois slid the celery from her knife into the stuffing bowl. "Yes. I watched them earlier. Isn't he absolutely perfect? You'd never know he'd had an injury."

It hadn't escaped Nicole, Breck's perfect form. She'd felt it first hand, yesterday, and the memory flushed her from heart to toes. "How long have they been at it?"

"Most of the day."

Nicole frowned.

"I've invited everyone for dinner."

"Everyone, who?"

"Reuben and Gail, Kit, Brian and Tami, you know. Everyone's anxious to see Breck. Oh." She wiped her hands on her apron and reached in a cupboard for cornstarch. "You think Trey would like to come?"

"We'll be with Reuben from five to eight."

"Reuben will be dining with us at six."

Nicole couldn't deny Reuben anything, and he deserved everything, so she thought of alternatives. "We'll practice without him."

"Can't you cut in for a dinner break?"

Nicole watched her mother drain the hot water from the potatoes. "This from the woman who keeps a whip on the wall of her daughter's studio?"

The joke didn't ruffle Lois, she only gleamed with more sparkle. "Now, now."

"Kit and Trey don't get along very well." Nicole was not about to spend any more time than she had to in Breck's presence.

"He'll drive up and see the cars," Lois informed her. "You'll have to at least extend the invitation."

Noon - Katherine Warwick

That was what she was afraid of. And as much as she felt the pull of old habits to use him for her own advantage, Nicole was certain that doing so would be tantamount to sticking her hand in the fire and expecting it not to burn her.

*   *   *

Lois insisted they do the traditional turkey dinner casually by gathering in the family room, buffet style. She'd smartly made a children's table for her granddaughters and Reuben and Gail's daughter, Jennica, knowing full well that the little girls could be chatty and distracting when they got together.

A day to be thankful, Lois thought, enjoying the way Breck immersed himself. Like no time had passed, her boys were teasing each other, talking about past, present and future. The mood was Christmas morning, and she couldn't help but feel as though she'd been given the most wonderful gift. Her eyes glazed with tears and she stole another look at Breck, her parched mother's heart still eagerly soaking up as much of him as it could.

"Breck, you're going to have to come and go more often because turkey's my favorite meal and I only get it at Thanksgiving." Brian dipped a spoon into the fluffy stuffing.

"Mom always did like me better."

Lois paused only a moment as she went from the counter to the couch, her full plate in hand. She heard the name – Mom – come from Breck's lips, and her heart skipped. Tears quickly followed. Unaware the utterance had touched her, Breck continued serving himself. How wonderful it was to have him back. Lois settled herself on the couch next to Garren with a sigh of contentment.

"When are we going to get you down in the studio, man?" Reuben looked at Brian who'd just sat down next to him around the coffee table.

"You been talking to my wife?"

Tami's eyes flashed. "Shh – It's supposed to be our little secret."

"You still haven't learned how to dance?" Breck made his way over, his plate piled high and steaming.

Brian took a forkful of potatoes to his mouth and shook his head, avoid-

◎ 235 ◎

ing his wife's elbow, now in his ribs. "He's eating so he doesn't have to answer to that," Tami laughed.

Trey watched with envy and disgust. The easy camaraderie the family shared excluded him and he didn't like it. Like no time had passed, no sin had been committed; Breck was received with open arms. He couldn't take it. "Do you dance, Garren?"

As if everyone in the room suddenly remembered he was there, they granted him a cordial glance that stung his raw ego. Garren shook his head.

"Dad, I'll do it if you'll do it." Brian tore into a buttery roll.

With little space available, Breck decided to sit on the floor, crosslegged. "I'll teach you." Both Garren and Brian looked over, eyes wide with obvious trepidation.

Lois lit up. "That's a wonderful idea."

Garren hadn't started to eat yet, too uncomfortable with the direction of the conversation. Now, the knife and fork in his hand shook too much for his liking. "I guess I could try."

"Might as well learn from the best." Kit squeezed herself right next to Breck. "Have you seen Breck dance since he got back?"

Garren wiped the white napkin across his mouth and shook his head. "But I've wanted to."

"He's wonderful." Kit didn't let a pause go by. "The best I've seen."

Trey couldn't keep quiet, "Or certainly one of the best. I hear you're training to compete again."

Breck's look steadied at Trey. "I am."

"Well," Trey continued, meeting his steady gaze with steel. "I guess we'll look forward to seeing you in a year or two."

Reuben let out a cough, tapping his chest with his fist in a gesture of mock disbelief. "It's not going to take that long. He's been training with Vladimir. He's ready."

Trey's thin smile shifted from Reuben to Breck again. "Is that right? Vladimir's excellent. Did you find his techniques exhausting? I've heard the Russians are merciless."

"It's what I needed. It kept me focused on what I wanted."

"And what would that be?"

Noon - Katherine Warwick

Nicole was sure her banging heart would be heard in the deadly silen. of the room. Still, she wasn't sure what to say.

"The food's great, Lois," Kit finally said.

"Thank you, Kit."

"Yes," Gail spoke up. "These orangey yams are something else. Will you share the recipe?"

"Of course."

Breck and Trey still stared at each other. The vibe with its nasty tentacles was reaching out to Nicole who finally found her voice. "Will Vladimir be your coach then?"

Her question had Breck shifting his hard gaze to her. "Reuben is working with Kit and me."

"Working with two competing pairs?" Trey asked levelly. "Maybe you should have consulted with your star couple first."

"If I'd thought my star couple couldn't handle it, I would have. Besides, I've done it before." Reuben's green eyes flashed. "You're both excellent partnerships, different, but excellent. I don't see a problem."

"Very democratic," Brian let out a laugh and blushed. "And then there will be Dad and me, floundering like fish out of water."

Nicole stood with her half-eaten plate, her appetite gone. She had just seen her father commit to something she'd never had the nerve to ask him to do. To see Breck breeze in after a three year absence, offer to teach her father and brother to dance, and then hear them accept, left her choking on pride.

Trey took her hand and tugged, so she looked down at him. "Grab me another roll, will you, baby?"

"Sure." Conversation had broken up into groups, and she was glad they were no longer talking about dance. If anyone was going to teach her father, it would be her.

"Your mother is an angel." Kit was next to her at the buffet, dishing up seconds of cranberry Jello.

"Yes," Nicole said. "Congratulations."

"For?"

"Dancing with Breck."

Kit's shoulders lifted easily. "You turned him down." On a well-turned

◎ 237 ◎

Noon - Katherine Warwick

swivel, Kit went back to the family room.

"Baby, my roll," Trey called before pinning Breck with a tilted look of concern. "Breck, was that your father who died in the fire a few days back?"

Although other conversations continued, voices hushed considerably. Breck's jaw twitched. "It was."

After Nicole took her seat next to him, Trey extended his arm around her. "Sorry to hear that. It must have been devastating."

"We weren't close."

"Gosh," Trey's tone was innocent. "I can't imagine not being close to my father. He taught me everything I know. In my book, that's what a good father does. "

Breck's eyes slit, hinting that Trey was getting uncomfortably close to an explosive topic.

"How about some pie, Trey?" It was Nicole's first response – an old reaction – to defend Breck.

Trey slid a hand along her thigh. "Sure any kind. You pick, baby."

Nicole didn't like being used, and she sent Trey a furtive glare of disapproval before rising and crossing to the kitchen.

"So you're, what, all alone now?" Trey continued.

"He has us," Lois piped.

"You've always been so charitable, Lois." Trey took the pie from Nicole when she came back. "Taking strays in off the street like you have."

Garren cleared his throat but Trey missed it, too caught up in the pleasure of watching Breck's face pull tight. He took a bite of the pie. "Wow, this is perfect, Lois. Best pie I've ever eaten."

"Breck." Garren stood, fingers anxious as they hung at his sides. "How's your golf swing?"

"Rustier than rusty."

Garren jerked his head toward the back yard. "Let's go sharpen it up."

* * *

It seemed as though Garren was swinging a baseball bat and not the delicate steel of a golf club. He hadn't said anything since he'd walked, a few paces ahead of Breck, into the darkness of the back yard, club in one hand, a bucket of balls in the other. Now, he was slamming white balls aimlessly into the abyss of the orchards.

Breck watched, scratching his head. "You okay?"

"Fine." Garren swung with a grunt. Every muscle in his forearms twitched. "He annoys me."

"He's good at that."

With a nod, Garren let out a sigh and turned to face Breck. Darkness shadowed his face with concern and anger. "Why Nicole is dancing with him, I can't fathom. The man is – well – I don't trust him." He leaned lightly on the club. "And I don't like what he does to you."

Breck shifted. "He doesn't do anything to me." For a long moment, he felt that familiar look of Garren's penetrate deep, like a surgeon's tool, making him feel he like a kid again.

Garren turned slightly, looking out over the orchards. "But you two are beyond needing my help to make your decisions. And Nicole never involved me in hers – ever."

"Trey's good, that's why she's dancing with him."

"But why won't she dance with you now that you're back? You two were perfect together. Not that I don't love Kit, she's a doll. But I hate to see Nicole in a situation because of pride."

Breck laughed. "It wouldn't be the first time."

A smile spread on Garren's lips. "You're right about that." Then his smile faded, mixing with a father's need to protect his own. "I just don't like him. There's something more there, what, I'm not entirely clear on, but it's not honest. I question his motivation."

It was the first time Breck had ever heard anything critical from Garren's mouth, and the caring look on his face humbled him.

"Nic can handle anybody. I wouldn't worry about her handling Trey." Though Breck had his own worries about Trey and Nicole's relationship, he wouldn't share them with Garren. He'd take care of things himself.

Breck took a wood out of Garren's bag, stood back and looked into the darkness of the orchards. Then he got into position to drive. "Pretend this ball is Trey." It took him three seconds to send the ball flying into nothingness.

Noon - Katherine Warwick

Garren chuckled and reached for another ball.

Nicole leaned her elbows against the deck railing and looked out into the blackness of night. Breck was still practicing his golf swing, now at the hem of the orchards with her father and Brian, who had wandered out to join them. The three of them would swing, laugh, and then the low murmur of their voices, twined in conversation whispered on the cooling night air.

Like no time had passed, Breck was there again. As she watched him, she was bothered by where he'd been and what he'd done with those years. It was because she cared that the questions still haunted her. She could admit that to herself.

She turned and looked through the French doors into the house. Trey was laughing alongside mother, doing dishes. The picture couldn't have been more perfect, or more plastic. She knew Trey as well as she knew herself and he was playing her family tonight. She'd have a talk with him about it later.

And then there was Kit.

She'd heard about Trey and Kit's involvement. Word had spread through the dance world gossip like spilled ink and when they'd called it off, the breakup had left a nasty stain. She wouldn't ask Kit about details.

"He's something."

Nicole looked up briefly at Breck, tried to calm her fluttering heart before shifting her gaze back to Trey, still at the sink with her mother. "He's trying. That's more than I can say for you."

Breck leaned back against the railing on his elbows. "He was baiting me."

"Wouldn't be the first time. Ignore him."

"I thought you didn't care anymore."

"I don't – that way. You're like a brother to me."

"A brother?" His laugh was low and calculating, sending delicious and dangerous tremors through her system. He leaned close. "Yeah right…" his voice trailed off. She had three seconds before she knew she was in trouble. He hoisted her over his shoulder and began to carry her.

"Don't even think about the pool."

Noon - Katherine Warwick

"I'm just doing what any brother would do to a spoiled sister."

She screamed. She sent her fists into the small of his back. No amount of wriggling would free her from the vise grip he had around her buttocks and hips. Because everyone began to gather on the deck to watch, she fought harder.

Trey strolled out, his hands in his pockets, a contemplative grin across his face.

"Don't do it, Noon," she warned.

"You choose – the pool or the orchards. And when I hunt you down, it will not be a pretty sight when I find you, that I can promise."

She bucked. "Neither one, now put me down before I pass out. I can't breathe."

It should have been a simple toss. He was ready to stand back and watch her get wet, but she wrapped her arms around his waist and they both toppled into the water with a crashing splash.

They came up at the same time, to laughter. All three young girls were at the pool's edge, overcome with giggles. Nicole was euphoric having gotten him by surprise. She shoved water in his face, then tried to dart away but the heavy water slowed her down. With one warm, slippery arm, Breck had her around the waist and dragged her back through the water, bringing her flush against him. For a moment, her heart fluttered, reckless, thrilling. Their faces were so close she had the ridiculous fantasy that he would kiss her with those generous, glistening lips. The site pulled a hot chord down in her belly that grew tighter as his hard, slick body held hers.

His smile spread fast, not enough warning for her to take a deep breath. Then he dunked her – and held.

She needed to get wet, he thought, palm clamped on her head. He could see she'd not had enough humbling while he'd been gone. He meant to hold her underneath the water just long enough to infuriate her. When he felt the undeniable panic in her body struggling beneath his, he brought her up. She clung to him, just as he knew she would, gasping and gulping.

Selfishly, he held her, pushing the wet hair off of her face so he could look at her, wet and helpless as a kitten. "You okay?"

"You – you—" she coughed and sputtered. "I couldn't breathe."

He tucked his arm around her waist and swam for them both to the shallow end. He needed to get out of the water fast – the cold liquid was so charged with electricity, he'd get fried if he didn't put her somewhere safe, if he didn't take his hands off her.

Setting her gently on the shallow steps, he was afraid to look at her trembling lip as she drunk in air. More than anything he wanted—needed to still that trembling with the gentle demand of his mouth.

"Rachel, go get Aunt Nickie a warm towel, okay?"

The three girls ran back toward the house and everybody else went inside, now that the raucous play was over.

Only Trey sauntered over.

"That was low." Nicole's eyes were round with fiery anger that didn't do anything but make Breck want her more. His body craved her, and being in the cold water wasn't helping to cool him down. He wanted to kiss her, lean her back against the hard edge of the pool and take her mouth until it was dry from the heat of it.

"That was brotherly. Thanks for pulling me in."

"You deserved it," she stuttered.

"Well, well." Trey hovered at the edge, hands still tucked in his pockets. "You have such class, Noon. Really know how to make a – splash – at a party."

Breck slicked his hair back. "We were just having fun, weren't we, sis?"

"Sis?" Trey's brow cocked. "Glad to know your feelings are platonic."

Breck saw Rachel running back with towels so he stood on the lowest step and took them from her. "Thanks, Rache." He handed the first to Nicole, then took one for himself.

When Trey saw that the young girl was out of earshot he squatted down. "You're classless, Noon."

Nicole got out, wrapping the towel around her in hopes of stopping the shudders wracking her body. "Take your dog fight out back, will you please?"

Breck wiped water out of an ear. "Just thinking the same thing about you, Trey."

"At least I have the decency not to mar a perfectly good social engagement with childish behavior."

"But not enough decency to treat a woman with respect."

"Kit always did have a big mouth."

"Yeah, full of enlightening things to say about you."

A knot surfaced in Trey's jaw. "Don't believe everything you hear from the lips of a rejected woman. It's bound to be unbelievably one-sided. Unless of course that woman is Nicole Dubois."

Breck heard Nicole's whispered gasp and wanted to fly at Trey, but he held back, wringing his towel between two tight fists as he came out of the water.

"This conversation is over," Nicole told Trey, crossing between the two of them.

"It just goes to prove one thing," Breck's face was inches from Trey's now. "Trash doesn't just come from a trailer."

Trey's hands flew out and wrapped around Breck's throat sending them both stumbling back. Dropping her towel, Nicole dove into the snarl of arms and teeth, screaming. She yanked at Trey's arms.

"Trey stop!"

Trey dropped his hands from Breck's throat, and that was when Nicole saw the fury bubbling just below the surface finally break free in Breck. Face chillingly hard, he lunged at Trey, taking them both across the cement in a flesh-searing thud.

"Stop it!" Nicole volleyed back and forth between the two men, locked in a writhing twist as punches hammered from Breck's fist into Trey's face.

She heard the thundering of feet and glanced up – her father, Brian and Reuben were racing down the slope while the rest of her family flocked on the deck. Garren yanked Trey back, and Brian and Reuben held Breck. Testosterone simmered, spiking the air while the men heaved for breath, strove for control. Twitchy as a doberman, Breck leveled Trey with a black stare.

"Anybody going to tell me what that was all about?" Garren looked from Trey to Breck.

Eerily composed, Trey brushed off his clothes, straightening upright. The fingers at his mouth touched wet, his tongue tasted tinny blood. "Is this what your daddy taught you, Noon?"

Breck started again, but Brian and Reuben clamped him back.

"Easy, man, easy."

Brian blew out air. "Anybody hurt?"

Noon - Katherine Warwick

"Not at all," Trey's tone was ice.

"Trey, you should go." Nicole went to him, winced at the bloodied, broken skin on his face.

When he saw her disgust, his ego took a boulder. His steely glare slid back to Breck. "Perhaps I should." What he really wanted was a mirror. If his face had been compromised, he'd do more than see that Breck's foot was busted. "I apologize, Garren. It was juvenile – inexcusable to take a family gathering as nice as this and turn it into a three-ring circus."

Without saying a word, Breck tore free of Reuben and Brian and headed toward the darkness of orchards.

It hurt Trey to smile but a small one slit his face when Breck stormed away. "Obviously he's upset about his father."

"You were egging him," Nicole shot, looking after Breck. She handed her father the wet towel and wrapped her arms around herself. "Dad, I'll be back in a minute."

Trey swallowed the jealousy creeping up his middle. It wasn't easy to stand there, bleeding and hurt, and watch her run off to Breck. His eyes slanted for a moment, then opened wide and pleasant. He looked at Garren, Brian and Reuben with the mask of exoneration.

"Again, my sincerest apologies. I'll need to beg Lois for her forgiveness. Excuse me."

Garren clamped a firm hand on Trey's shoulder, stopping him. "Mind what comes out of your mouth when you're a guest in my home, young man."

Trey worked to steady himself. To have Garren Dubois reprimand him was the final cut in the ribbon of his pride. But he swallowed arrogance for the sake of what he wanted – a future with Nicole. Humbly, he bowed his head before bringing up a sorrowful expression the devil himself would have been proud of. "If I said anything to offend you, Garren—"

Garren jerked his head toward the house. "Goodnight, Trey." Then his gaze drifted out over the orchards.

Nicole shivered stepping into the thick shadows shrouding the orchards. It had been years since she'd set foot in the dark rows, even in daylight, having found herself dragged there unwillingly the last time. Calling Breck's name, she crept anxiously, hoping to find him quickly and get out of there.

"Breck?" There was little light, with the moon hidden behind cottony clouds stretched thin. What breeze there was seemed to tickle the leaves of every tree, making them whisper in hissing conversation, chilling her bones. The scent of chlorine from her clothes mixed with the earthy smell of stirring leaves and damp earth beneath her feet.

"Where are you?" She ventured deeper. "Please, Breck. Let's talk." Each twig that snapped made her jump. Because she was wet, she began to shiver convulsively. "Breck. Please."

When she heard a crackling that was not caused by her own steps, she whirled. Breck stood in the middle of the row, hands deep in his pockets, head bowed. Her body wracked with shuddering, but she went to him. He wouldn't look at her.

"Are you hurt? Breck?"

"I wanted to kill him." His voice was a soft whisper, carrying fear and grief.

She shook so badly, she didn't know if her hand would steady or startle him. But she touched him anyway.

"Something inside of me popped." Moving from her, he jagged back and forth in the aisle in spite of scratchy, naked branches. He looked possessed, she thought, possessed by guilt.

"I shouldn't let him get to me. I know how he is. I even know why he does it." He let out a hollowing groan that lie on the edge of misery.

Her heart wept watching him fight ghosts with flesh and blood. She wished there was a way to take the pain. She would take it – and she would keep it as far away from him as she could.

"He deserved it," she said.

"Nobody deserves it."

Unbearable torment twisted his face when it finally lifted to hers. She thought for a moment that was the face that must have looked with pleading at Rob Noon too many times.

She didn't even feel her feet move – she was just there, her body pressing into his, everything inside of her yearning to take his suffering, and she wrapped her arms around him.

His arms enveloped her, but there was no warmth as their two wet, chilled bodies cleaved to each other. He stroked her hair, gently and she closed her eyes, her cheek burrowing into his chest in search of his heart.

"You're freezing," he murmured.

She stopped feeling everything except his hands brushing over her. Numb with wet cold, the shuddering finally left her as his heat began to warm them both.

"I'm so sorry," he whispered.

Her heart was stuck in her throat. She marveled at how easy it was for a man that hurt so inside to be so easily sorry. *If only I could be that quick to forgive*. She wrapped more tightly around him, as if by so doing she could borrow some of that effortless mercy.

He wanted to tell her everything, his past, his flight, and his future. He wanted to love her, dance with her, make her his right there in the frightening shadows of the orchards. Eyes willing and ready looked up at him, pulling need inside of him open and desperate to share.

All he could do was hold her close, and he kissed her brow, allowed himself at least that. His struggles had taught him many things, not the least of which was that restraint usually brought more satisfaction than indulgence. And it would be indulgent of him to push Nicole to step a direction she was not ready.

He held her under the curve of his arm, enjoying the easy feel of her by his side, and they walked back to the house together.

"Promise me you'll ignore Trey."

He couldn't make that promise, not until he knew she was his and his alone. She looked up at him.

"I want that promise, Breck."

"I can't give it to you."

"I don't like you getting hurt."

He managed a grin. "I don't like it either."

"Don't fight him anymore."

Noon - Katherine Warwick

"I'll do my best, sis."

The name was a sharp reminder of where they stood with each other. But old feelings were budding rapidly inside of her, and she wondered at the logic of letting them bloom and carry her away. Knowing how easy it would be, she slid out from under his warm arm and walked on her own.

"You're a great friend."

He shot her a smile that she caught and held. "Then we agree that I'm not your brother?"

She couldn't agree more. She thought his arm moved to swing out and capture her again, but his hands just hid in his front pockets.

Twenty-three

"Again, again." Reuben snatched his water bottle and drank. "Come on, no time between."

"Shove it," Trey shouted. He refused to do one more set. Panting, drenched with sweat, he circled Reuben and Nicole like a shark ready to kill.

Nicole was more than impatient. They were days away from flying out to Florida for their next try at another world title, and Trey was dancing like his feet were on backwards. "Trey, we need—"

"You have no idea what I need." He shot over to her in a flash, his sweat sprinkling her. "No idea."

Sensing there was more to his message than dance, Nicole stared him down, unwilling to take anymore of the innuendo he had been pushing at her over the last few months. Since Breck had arrived on the scene, Trey had done nothing but amplify his intentions to shift their partnership from professional to personal.

Impatience shown in Reuben's crossed arms. "You're far from ready. Let's get back to work."

"Yeah, well, maybe I won't be going."

Nicole's shock and irritation were obvious. "What?"

"You heard me." Trey simmered.

When Reuben didn't do anything more than hang a disparaging glare on him, he exploded. "What are you staring at? You're here to coach, nothing more." Nicole strode to Reuben in a protective gesture that only fired Trey up more. "He's forgetting his place."

"My place?" Reuben's green eyes turned to stone before he gracefully went to his things and gathered them up. "I'll be ready to coach when you're ready to apologize."

After the door had shut behind him, Nicole spun around. "What's wrong with you? That was completely out of line. I wouldn't blame him if he refused to come back. We can't afford to alienate him now, the competition's in—"

"I know when it is!"

"Then get your act together. We have a lot riding on this."

Catching her wrist, he wrenched her around in a snap that shocked her eyes wide. "I know what we have riding on it. Let's talk about what *I* have riding on it." He tossed her out in front of him, his veins skittering with excitement, and slowly walked toward her.

"I thought you and I were on the same page." Nicole rubbed her wrist. "I've worked my butt off here. I'm the one who's given my all and more, carrying the two of us because of your inability to be consistent with your stylization."

"Hold it! Just hold it!" The muscles in Trey's arms strained against tight flesh. His eyes, sharper that spears, tore through Nicole's anger, leaving a thin line of fear at what he might be capable of.

"Just what would you be willing to do for World, Nic?" He was near enough to see the fury she'd had in her eyes moments ago changing into fear. It pleased him. "What would you do if your partner wouldn't go?" She was stunned at the suggestion, looking deliciously like a trapped doe. "What if I said I'd only go if you… well, you're a smart woman, you figure it out."

The slap stung, crushed an ego so badly beaten that when his hand struck her back he didn't even care. She stumbled, and he lunged for her, backhanding her to her knees. Falling on her side to the floor, she scrambled like a bug in imminent danger.

Her cry finally broke through to him, clearing the rage and arousal from his head and body. When he saw her cowering in shock, tears streaming, he dropped down beside her and brought her against him. If she discarded him, his life would be over. "I'm sorry, baby." Rocking her, he refused to let go, even as she squirmed for release. "No, no. I didn't mean it. I didn't. I was angry, I'm sorry. It will never happen again."

"Let me go." But the more she fought, the tighter he squeezed until his grip became more than a gesture of comfort, but another show of wills.

"When I know you've forgiven me. I couldn't live without knowing that you've forgiven me, baby. Please."

This was more real, more dangerous than that night in the orchards.

Noon - Katherine Warwick

Nicole knew he was going to hurt her badly if she didn't pacify him. Forcing herself to relax in his arms, she nodded. She tried to hide the panic and fear chasing after her heart by keeping her face averted. "I forgive you. Now please let me go."

As if he was deciding, he paused. Heavy breathing wracked his chest, just under her head. His heart fought angrily beneath her ear. She waited in shocked horror for his arms to slowly uncoil.

"I'm sorry." His hands freed her body but wrapped her cheeks, bringing her face directly in front of his. "Nic, I'm sorry."

Because she saw real penitence, jumbled tears of contrition, she tried to forget what had just happened. When he stroked her cheek, she felt the ache from the blow.

"You hit me," she muttered in disbelief.

He nodded and closed teary eyes. "I know. I'm sorry, baby. I just – I'm under so much pressure."

His hands pressed on her cheeks, and another wave of panic raced through her when she felt the strength between his palms. So easily he could crush her. Tears flushed from his eyes. He shook his head in regret, but all she could see was a face so enraged it was more horrifying than the dark, faceless stranger who had threatened her years ago.

"I swear it will never happen again." He reached for her hands but she moved back. "If it does, you can beat me with a baseball bat, call the police, shoot me – whatever. I swear, I'll lie down on the ground and let you kill me."

"Stop it."

"So you will? You'll kill me if I ever hit you again?"

Because he was frighteningly serious, she wasn't sure how to respond. Slowly, she stood, until she was looking down at him, crouched and pleading at her feet. "I would never hurt you, Trey. I – I couldn't do that."

An odd, empty look passed over his face and she thought he might break out into laughter. His just tilted his head, sighed. "Then we're okay?"

She wasn't sure they were okay, or partners, or anything. She only knew she needed to get away from him to clear her thoughts. "Let's talk tomorrow at rehearsal." Guardedly, she gathered her things.

"No." He was up before she could take a step, and had her by the arms.

"Nic, I have to know now. I can't wait until then. I won't eat, I won't sleep, I won't breathe until I know you've forgiven me and forgotten this whole thing."

She'd never forget. How he could think she would? "Fine." She was impatient to be alone and away from him. "We're fine, Trey." She patted his arm and hoped that he wouldn't see her hand trembling. "See you tomorrow."

She kept her focus on the door, and made her way over on legs still shaky beneath her. It wasn't until she was safely inside the house that her body buckled. With her back against the back door, she locked it, and didn't move for a long time.

*   *   *

I've been hit.

As if the incident had just happened, it slammed into her very being with a force ten times stronger than the blows themselves.

A man that I know, that I thought I could trust, struck me.

Nicole stood in front of the bathroom mirror. It was quite clear that she'd had some kind of encounter. The left side of her face was rash-red.

She couldn't light on one thought; too many were streaming at once in her head. Statistics she'd read, stories she'd heard, women she'd seen all battered and bruised in distorted news photos came at her like a fast wind.

Now she was one of them.

I should have seen it coming, I should have stopped him. I could have. I could have stopped being afraid and run from the room. I tried. I just couldn't get my feet to move. And I shouldn't have slapped him. That's what started it. This was my fault. I shouldn't have hit him.

She lowered her head into her hands and tears welled in her eyes; a sob reached up and choked out of her throat.

She forced herself to wet a washcloth, to lay it over her face and take deep breaths. She forced herself to think of pleasant things – her nieces, her friends, her parents – Breck.

Dragging the washcloth down her face, she gazed into her eyes, red and swelling, and could barely look at herself. She could never tell them. It was too humiliating, too embarrassing. She'd look like a fool, a weak, whimpering baby.

Noon - Katherine Warwick

They'd never understand why she'd hit him in the first place. Her mother with her rosy glasses would never see Trey in the black light in which he really lived. Her father wouldn't say a word, but his look would say it all. "*I warned you. Dance is not the place to invest your dreams.*" And Breck – Breck would understand. It was impossible to think of what he had endured. She looked at the redness on her cheek and touched it with her fingers. Closing her eyes, she saw Breck's scars.

If she discussed it with anyone, it would be the end of their partnership and World would be out of reach until she could link up with another partner and train again. She'd worked too hard to drop everything, find another partner and start over. She wasn't willing to wait.

The discoloration would go away within a few minutes. And then no one would know—ever. She couldn't give up years of work just for this little misunderstanding. Too much was at risk.

Do you know how desperate you sound?

She stared with empty shock at her reflection and couldn't look herself in the eye any longer. As despicable as it sounded, it was the truth. And she wouldn't lie. If she was willing to follow through, she had to be willing to take the consequences.

She kept her eyes focused in the mirror. She could finish this competition with Trey. She'd be firm and distant – only in his company during rehearsing and at the competition. They'd work hard and with luck they'd place. Then she would dissolve the partnership and start over.

Noon - Katherine Warwick

Twenty-four

Even in September, the breathy air of Miami was warm and thick, like a lover's blown kiss. Palms lining the beach bowed and beckoned as if saluting and welcoming the hundreds of dancers coming from around the globe to compete for one of the most coveted titles in the world of ballroom dance: World Champion.

They had traveled together: Lois, Reuben, Trey and Nicole, Breck and Kit, being inextricably intertwined by ties both loyal and tight within the community of dance. Cordial on the flight, the air between them remained transparent and counterfeit. Sharing a limo to the Fountainbleu Hotel, they enjoyed the lush scenery, the complimentary drinks, and the CDs Trey brought and played.

Lois, Kit and Nicole were sharing a suite, as were Reuben and Breck. Trey had arranged for his own suite on the same floor.

With panoramic views of the sea and a birds-eye view of the bustling esplanade below, the balcony off the suite was the first place Nicole went to breathe in the salty air and take in the bustling scene of Miami.

"It's like being on a never-ending vacation," she sighed. Though she had been to Florida for competitions in the past, all she could do as her eyes searched the horizon was wonder what Breck's life here had been like.

Lois placed her bag on the foot of the queen-sized bed she and Nicole were going to share, and started to unpack. "Except that my hair looks like it's having a never-ending bad hair year."

Nicole didn't need to look, she just smiled. The moisture made her mother's fine hair like a clown's wig. "Good thing you look beautiful with it pulled back."

Lois smiled and slipped a blouse on a hanger. "Thank you."

The door opened and Kit blustered into the room, all pink and smiling. "This place is packed. You should see the vendors. There's tons of new stuff downstairs." She leaned into the large mirror hanging on one of the walls

◎ 253 ◎

and wiped away a flake of mascara. "The guys are ready. I say we go down and explore."

Nicole came in from the balcony. She'd decided weeks ago when her mother made the arrangements for the trip that she would start fresh with Kit, and she'd found her surprisingly pleasant. It turned out they had more in common than she had supposed though Breck was still the unspoken denominator.

"Good," she said. "Then we can all go downstairs together."

"I just love the vendor displays, don't you?" Kit's enthusiasm was contagious. It was Nicole's nature to bypass all of the fringe accoutrements accompanying competitions. Decidedly, she would spend more time less wound up this trip.

"You girls go on down." Lois was still unpacking. "I'll meet you later. You have your cell, Nicole?"

"I do." She dialed Breck as they went out the door. It seemed strange to be calling Kit's dance partner, but Breck was family. When he didn't answer, they knocked on the door, heard music blaring on the other side. Knocking turned to pounding and good-natured shouting. And laughing.

"Hey." It roused Trey from his room a few doors down.

"They can't hear us." Kit bubbled, gesturing toward the door with a flip of blonde curls.

Nicole had noticed that Kit and Trey were making an effort to get along. She didn't doubt Kit's motives, but knowing Trey like she did, she found herself juggling the ball of suspicion.

Things between the two of them had improved as well. He'd been meek as a kitten and obliging as a gentleman. If she didn't look at him and see that flash of fury in her mind's eye every time she saw his face, she would almost believe his penitence was real.

"We're going down to the vendor displays. Want to come?" Kit asked him.

"Yeah, just let me get my wallet."

"Get a bomb while you're in there," Nicole continued to pound on Breck and Reuben's door. "We'll need it to get these two to out."

Trey smiled, and disappeared into his room.

Shutting the door behind his back, his smile dissolved. He was ready to explode. How much longer would he have to play at this ridiculously humiliating game of being friends?

Though he was alone in the spacious suite, he felt trapped. He hadn't been invited to share a room with Reuben and Breck. No, the exclusionary twosome had made their point quite clear when they'd booked a suite without him: he was an outsider.

One glance in the mirror and Trey bristled. Not only had his nose been damaged irreparably by Breck those years ago, but he still had a nice little scar from their last entanglement along his eyebrow that had him looking more like a gang thief than a desirable dancer.

Breck's face was perfect. So was his foot.

He'd have to look at that face all weekend during the competition. See those perfect feet perform over and over again. They'd practice side by side, eat meals and laugh together, and he'd have to pretend to enjoy all of it.

But he could.

There was only one option, really – to destroy Breck and Kit with the win he and Nicole deserved.

A knock came at the door and Trey blinked rapidly, banishing the blackness that had overrun his thoughts. Opening the door, he looked into the cordial faces of Nicole and Kit. Reuben and Breck stood just behind them, in a humorous, but private conversation.

Trey put on his smile. "Hey."

Tables filled the spacious outer halls of the hotel – booths bursting at the seams with everything from fabric, to costume designs, to shoes shiny and matte, heeled and flat. A rainbow of rhinestone options, every shade of glitter and eye shadow a female performer could want. Hair accessories, yards of feathers, strips of rhinestones. And all of it was stuffed with rows of stagnant people.

"Uh-oh." Reuben sighed, stopped. They stood at the opening of the maze meant to draw in dancers and suck money out of their pockets.

Nicole linked her arm in his and tugged, but he wouldn't budge. "Come on, it will be fun."

Noon - Katherine Warwick

"Fun?" Reuben's brows went up. "That's what Gail keeps telling me, that shopping is fun."

"Shopping?" Breck stopped short, bumping into Reuben. His face carried the same horrified look that had frozen onto Reuben's.

"Come on guys, where's your competitive spirit?" Kit scanned the tables and displays from her tiptoes. "We have to think offensively about the next competitions. Start trends, be aggressive and exciting with our costuming."

"I'd rather be out by the pool." Trey wiggled anxious hands deep in his front pockets, searching the lobby for an exit.

"Much better idea," Reuben agreed. "Breck?"

"Hmm." Moving at a snail's pace through tiny rows with hundreds of people didn't sound at all appealing. But then being poolside with Trey sounded just as unappealing.

Breck made the conscious choice not to let Trey get to him, but he knew well enough that to place the two of them together purposefully would create a natural combustion.

"Why don't you guys do your shopping or whatever and then meet us at the pool," Trey suggested. "We can do lunch poolside, relax." His arm slipped around Nicole's waist with the purpose to entice her and infuriate Breck. It did one of those.

Nicole slithered out of Trey's arm, looking at Reuben. "When will we rehearse?"

"We have a day, sis. Let's unwind."

The need to practice, to be ready, was itching under Nicole's skin, but she forced herself to nod and agree. Any time she could spend away from Trey, she'd take, without it being obvious to everyone else. "We'll meet you when we've cleaned out the place."

Trey slipped Nicole his credit card and whispered loud enough that everyone could hear, "Do some serious damage. On me, baby." Then he kissed her lightly on the cheek. "Onward." With an open arm, Trey grinned at Reuben, Breck, and gestured toward the pool.

* * *

Noon - Katherine Warwick

Golden, smooth skin was everywhere; some of it barely covered by swatches of fabric – mere excuses for swimsuits. The hot afternoon sun only made the silken planes and rounded crests look more desirable under its heated glow.

Trey scanned the massive deck with moving bodies like a lion searching the horizon for a possible meal. The pool was turquoise and sparkling. The scent of tanning lotion and perfume aroused his senses. Bikini-clad babes dipped painted toes in the crystal water. He'd told Breck and Reuben to save him a chair and hoped they'd had the sense to pick a spot fraught with beauties.

Reuben was easy to spot, his dark skin glistening like a chocolate sculpture of *David*. Trey had always been envious of Reuben's perfect physique. He'd heard plenty of female dancers whisper about the hardcore, masculine definition that made Reuben a specimen to be admired and awed.

Breck sat on a lounge chair in black swim trunks and a white tee shirt. Something about it didn't set well with Trey, and as he spread out his towel on the chair next to him, his mind flashed possibilities. He smiled. "Good spot."

"I'm a married man," Reuben said on a laugh, shifting in his chair. "This is going to be—whew, I need some sunglasses. It's bright out here."

"Uh-huh," Trey agreed. "I know the trick."

Breck leaned back and closed his eyes.

"Don't want to get a tan?" Trey slipped off his own shirt and eyed Breck's. "Then you won't have to use the fake stuff before comp."

"I burn easily."

"I seem to remember that about you."

"Drinks from the bar gentlemen?"

All three swung their eyes up to a leggy red-head shaped like a cello, holding a platter and a pen.

"Honey, just one look at you and I'm thirsty." Trey licked his lips. She smiled, but her eyes lit on Breck. "Sir?"

"I'll take a Pepsi."

"Make that two," Reuben piped then leaned back and settled in for a long day of well-needed relaxation under the sun.

That the buxom beauty was ignoring him, made Trey simmer. "Give me a Coke."

Noon - Katherine Warwick

The woman's admiration was just another reason to hate Breck, that and the ever present fact that women gawked at him. Here he was with a twisted nose and a frigging scar – all carved by the hand of the man sitting next to him. There had to be some skeleton somewhere, some imperfection he could tweeze out and expose to the ballroom community that would have them treating their beloved prodigal son like the plague.

"Want to hit the water?" he suggested.

"Na," Reuben's voice told him he was already half asleep.

Breck put a lazy arm up to shade his eyes as he swept the deck for Nicole and Kit. "I'm going to wait for the girls."

"Speaking of girls," Trey's curiosity bank needed a deposit. "Tell me you had tanned goddesses at your fingertips when you lived here. It must have been a fat paradise."

Breck's shading hand dropped to his side, his eyes closed again.

"Silence means yes, I take it."

"Silence means I'm not going to tell you, Trey."

Trey's smile flattened. He'd been cordial, friendly, and Breck wasn't buying any of it. "No problem, I respect that. I wish I'd been more like that with women. Then I wouldn't have lies jumping up out of nowhere, biting me."

When Breck didn't say anything, Trey felt pressed to go on. "I mean, Kit and I – well, no matter what she told you, you're man enough to recognize when a woman is manipulating things to save face."

Breck stretched out both legs, silently soaked the sun without responding.

Because the silence was causing sweat to bead on his forehead, Trey swiped at it, his mind searching for a subject. "Why don't you just use sunscreen and go on in?"

"Why do you care?'

Trey let out a laugh meant to cover a moment that was making him look foolish. He filled with rage. He would allow Breck this petty little conversation, but that would be all. When they hit the dance floor, that's where his leniency would come to a stop and he would make sure everything went the way he wanted it.

Noon - Katherine Warwick

Twenty-five

Kit made her way through the crowd on Nicole's heels. They'd seen some familiar faces, seen more that were not. The hugeness of the world competition scared Kit. She'd been relieved in the past to have been an observer. Now, she looked forward with frightened anticipation to the competition, knowing the chance at placing was real.

Still, she knew Breck would rather be taking the competition with Nicole in his arms. Even though reality hurt, she cared enough about him that she wanted him to be happy, first. "Why didn't you want to dance with Breck?"

Nicole strummed through fabric and stopped. "I have Trey." She pulled out a sleek fuchsia shade and examined it. "I didn't think it was fair to just drop him, even if I had been Breck's partner."

Nodding, Kit felt the fabric Nicole held in her hand. "This is nice."

Kit let the filmy fabric drop from her fingers and moved onto another booth. "I always wanted to dance with him, but I guess that's no big secret to anyone, right?" She looked Nicole in the eye. "I was in love with him."

Again Nicole stopped, but only briefly, as if to show Kit she didn't care much about the surprising admission. Kit saw questions in Nicole's eyes, but the pride hazing over kept her from asking.

"I still love him." Kit answered the unasked question then moved, her back facing Nicole so any traces of regret wouldn't be visible. "But he doesn't feel the same for me. I don't think he ever has. That's no big surprise, either."

Kit stopped at a jewelry display and fingered some garish earrings that looked like gold birthday cakes. "His heart, like mine, has always been in one place."

Nicole was browsing the earrings, but the tense lines in her face told her she was listening. As a woman, Kit wanted to share what she knew: that Breck was simply waiting for her, that he still loved her. But she also knew that sometimes not knowing would drive a woman to discover for herself.

"How's it going with Trey?"

Nicole's demeanor shifted from interest to ice instantly. "Fine. He's a hard worker."

"He's never lost his temper with you? Gotten pushy, aggressive?" Kit watched Nicole's face carefully.

"No more than any other partner I've had. Certainly Breck and I had our share of disagreements."

"Consider yourself lucky then."

"Why?"

"Let's just say that Trey's got some anger management issues."

"Huh." Nicole kept her eyes ahead as they moved to the next booth, and Kit figured she'd had enough of the topic.

Lois found Kit and Nicole oogeling over purple and black false eyelashes in a flashy booth specializing in show lashes. She smiled at the two of them, looking more like young girls than championship dancers as they held various brightly colored lashes, the length of butterfly wings, up to their eyes.

"Do you think these are wild enough?" Nicole held up a pair of black lashes edged with gold glitter.

Lois made a face. "They just get more and more outlandish every year, don't they?"

"But the judges eat them up." Kit plucked up a pair in purple and gold.

Bored, Nicole passed to another booth. This partnership would be over after the competition, and her interest in investing anything more in it was already dead. Her thoughts were magnetically drawn to Breck, to where he was, what he was doing. " I've had enough. You?"

Kit nodded. Seeing that her mother was near to salivating, Nicole tilted her head at Kit with a smile. "The guys are at the pool, mom. We're heading out." She kissed her mother's cheek.

"I'll meet you all for dinner later." Lois' eye caught fabric in one of the booths further down the aisle and she meandered on with the ease of female distraction.

Nicole hooked her arm in Kit's. "Let's go."

*   *   *

Noon - Katherine Warwick

"Now there's the best looking body I've seen all afternoon," Trey announced.

Breck slid up on his elbows. Nicole and Kit, graceful as two runway models, strolled across the deck toward their chairs. His stomach tightened. The lavender one-piece suit without straps Nicole had on was sleek, classic and, he decided, too revealing. The angled bones of her shoulders looked delicately carved out of ivory, her breasts pressed in soft glory against the taut fabric, and her legs seemed to be everywhere. In two seconds he was at her side.

"What's this?"

She didn't stop walking. "What?"

"Hi, Breck." Kit was right at his side in a tiny pink bikini but he barely glanced at her, his eyes on Nicole's face, trying to fight the gravitational pull of her luscious shape, dripping in lavender

"This thing you're wearing,"Breck gestured to the suit with an anxious hand. "It's practically not there."

"You think?" She took the chair next to his and flicked her hotel towel out, spreading it flat.

"Baby, you look hot," Trey told her, shifting in his chair.

"Thanks." Nicole shot Breck a teasing glare before sitting primly.

"Hello, everybody." Kit wiggled and waved, finally getting a hello from everyone except Reuben, who was snoring like a chainsaw at full roar.

Breck stood over Nicole, unable to sit and relax. In a frustrated snap, he leaned close, his voice a searing whisper. "Go change."

"Change?" Nicole wiggled herself into comfort, noting the way his fists curled and uncurled. "It's a bathing suit. Relax, Noon."

"It's a colored piece of fabric, barely wrapped around you. I can't believe – did your mother approve of this?"

"My mother?" She enjoyed a laugh. "I'm all grown up now, in case you haven't noticed." Slipping on some dark glasses, she enjoyed watching him fuss. It was extremely satisfying to see that her bathing suit had done precisely what she'd hoped it would do.

The part of Breck that was like her brother wanted to protect her from the hungry eyes everywhere. The part of him helplessly and hopelessly drawn to her wanted to enjoy the sight of her, a budding flower all ripe and ready to

Noon - Katherine Warwick

pluck. Neither wanted to share her with anybody else. He sat back, tense as a drum.

"Anybody want to get wet?" Trey stood.

"Sure." Kit was up in a flash, snapping her bikini bottoms into place.

As if Kit wasn't there, Trey looked at Nicole and extended his hand. "Nic, what say you and I make a splash all these folks will never forget? The first of many at this competition."

It was a direct challenge, and Breck had to bite back to keep himself from saying anything. Trey led the girls over to the pool like a sea-god with two dancing mermaids at his side. Easing them in one by one, they splashed and played at each other like children.

"Noon, the water's great." Trey hung on the pool edge with a serpent's grin.

Sweat beaded on Breck's face, pearled down the center of his back, but he ignored it. "I'm gonna sit this one out."

Every part of him was coiling up, watching the trio enjoy themselves in the crisp, aqua-colored water. It wasn't easy ignoring the things he chose to keep hidden.

After a while, Nicole came up out of the pool like the goddess of water, dripping from every curve, slick with a sheen that made his blood slip. He felt pressed against his chair, the sight of her coming at him like the heated blow of an open inferno. She cruised by, water from her body, her hair, sprinkling him with tantalizing droplets that sizzled on his hot skin.

"Whew." She reached for her towel, dabbed it on her face first, then her chest, imprisoning him as he watched her dry herself slow and easy. "That felt great."

Nicole sat, lying out again. Shading her eyes with her hand, she looked at the pool, at Trey hanging on the edge, watching legs walk by. The sight was disgusting, so she thought of another topic that had been nagging her.

"I can't believe you left this place to come back to Utah." Skillfully, she got comfortable, glistening under the rays of the sun – and Breck's focused gaze. "It's so beautiful here."

He'd squeezed his towel in both fists, and now his knuckles were white. "Yeah, well, day after day of beach, heat, and bodies can wear on a guy."

◎ 262 ◎

Noon - Katherine Warwick

"Where did you live?" she finally asked.

He was pleased that she was attempting to cross a bridge he'd left open. "I had a place near the university."

She was quiet again. They both heard Kit and Trey laughing and looked over. Kit sat up on the edge of the pool and Trey hung on her thighs with his arms crossed.

"So you went to school. You get a degree?"

"Family Relations."

"Really?"

"Come on, that can't come as too much of a surprise." Because Nicole didn't say anything for a time, he shot her a sidelong glance. She was observing and considering behind those dark glasses, and something around his heart finally relaxed. Maybe she would listen. Understand. Believe.

"And with this degree you intend to…"

"Help people understand how to better communicate with each other. Save relationships." *Heal*, he thought, *just like Garren had helped him heal.*

"There's a science to this?"

"Where there's understanding, there's hope. Hope can heal."

Nicole didn't need a text book to know that. She had a better understanding of her father and that had given her glorious hope. Her better understanding of Trey had been a frightening hole she wanted to stay away from. She had yet to understand all of the questions and reasons behind Breck's actions years before. Would there be hope in the wake of discovering those answers?

The redheaded waitress was coming toward them, her bathing suit skirt wagging over shapely hips. She set her smile on Breck and flipped a handful of fire-red hair over her pale shoulder. "How about another Pepsi, Mr. Noon?"

"That'd be great. Nic?"

Nicole sized up the redhead with one sweep, and shook her head.

"Oh, I've picked up tickets for tomorrow. I'll be there for your competition."

Breck grinned. "Yeah?"

She nodded flirtatiously. "Not enough men in this world dance. I'll be right back with that Pepsi."

He thought he heard Nicole snicker so he turned his head her direction.

◎ 263 ◎

"If I didn't know better—"

"Don't even go there, Noon."

"And after all this time."

"Drop it."

"I'm flattered."

"I said, drop it."

"You're jealous."

"Am not."

He leaned over and in one swift pull she was next to him, chair and all. The look of shock on her face sent a grin on his. "Newsflash, Nic. I can read you now."

"Well, I am not jealous."

Putting both hands behind his head, Breck laid back and smiled.

Even with the heat and sweat, costumes were elaborate: makeup was heavy, bordering on macabre. No one noticed when beads formed at a dancer's hairline, or perspiration dampened a man's shirt like he'd just been dipped head first into a pool of water. They were dancers, competing. Looking the part of a standard or Latin dancer came with the theatrics as well as the drawbacks of the territory.

It was the middle of the junior Latin competition. Children from the tiniest tots barely in shoes to young pre-teens were swinging their partners to the jive. For Nicole, it was a trip down memory lane as she recalled her early years and thought about her own students. She particularly enjoyed watching the smallest couples whose tiny bodies danced nearly as well as the adults, giving a strange illusion of miniaturized perfection.

Lois always spent the extra money and bought a table right on the edge of the dance floor so they had a dancer's eye view as they watched the on-going competition.

Reuben dropped his puffy face into his hands. "Why did you guys let me sleep out there?"

"You were wasted," Breck laid a careful pat on Reuben's back. "And snor-

Noon - Katherine Warwick

ing."

"Man, oh, man. I feel like a cooked tomato."

"Think you'll be all right by tomorrow?" Nicole's concern was genuine.

Reuben nodded, shifting carefully in the chair on a half groan. "I've arranged for both couples to have privates with Vladimir."

Trey crossed his arms over his chest. A look of defiance set in his brow, his jaw drew tight with the announcement.

"That's great." Nicole was thrilled. She couldn't wait to meet and be coached by another one of the world's best. The fact that Vladimir had been three years working with Breck only sweetened the opportunity.

"He's agreed to fit you in. He's doing it as a favor, because he's a friend of Breck's."

"We don't need him." Trey snatched his water glass and chomped on an ice cube.

"Yes we do." Nicole didn't even spare Trey a glance. "When?"

"At seven tomorrow. Breck, you and Kit will follow, at eight."

"They can take both appointments," Trey's voice was sharp. "We're not going to train with him."

"Trey, it's a fantastic opportunity." Nicole did look at him then, and worked hard to suppress the frustration building inside. "We have to take it."

His eyes flashed with warning. "No, we don't."

"We'll be there," Breck finally said, breaking the tension. But his gaze he kept on the competing couples, junior amateurs in Latin, now taking the floor.

Nicole sat back with worry creasing her brow. She couldn't understand why Trey wasn't jumping on the opportunity. It was a godsend, and not taking it made them look incredibly ungrateful, not to mention foolish.

Nobody spoke during the first few rounds of the heat, too interested to see the younger set dance for placement and to critique. When Lois finally joined them, the way she glowed, Nicole knew something was up. Her mother sat down, eyes sparkling with pleasure Nicole only saw when she won a title.

"I have some wonderful news, Nicole."

"What?"

"Dad's here."

Nicole's eyes flashed. "Dad?" Thrill tumbled with disbelief and both

◎ 265 ◎

stopped her heart. Every trace of frustration dissolved, and she forgot about her troubles with Trey.

"Garren...here?" Reuben searched the room.

Lois nodded enthusiastically. "He and I are getting a room just down the hall from you kids."

Trey shifted, and slid an arm around Nicole's shoulder. "He's here to see our win." His confident grin flicked from face to face until it stayed on Breck's with hard victory. But Breck was looking at Nicole with nothing but joy.

"That's great, Nic." Her eyes met his and held.

"Is he coming down?" Trey asked.

Lois looked at the dancers on the floor, now in their semi-final round. "No. He's going to get some rest. But he'd like you to go up and say hi," and she looked at Breck. "You too, Breck."

Nicole pushed away from the table. "I'll go up now."

"Room four-eighty-four." The gleam in Lois' eyes was permanent.

"Mind if I go with you?" Breck was already standing, and touched Nicole's elbow lightly. She looked briefly at where his fingers met her skin, then up into the afternoon blue of his eyes.

"Of course not."

Trey was half way out of his chair in protest. "What about tonight?"

"We'll meet up later," Nicole tossed over her shoulder as Breck escorted her away.

* * *

Electricity crackled in the elevator as they rode up. Nicole kept watch on the floor numbers that flashed overhead.

Breck reached out and put his hand over hers.

"Can you believe it?" she asked. The deep pleasure in his eyes comforted her with the unspoken joy she knew he was feeling for her. "I don't know if I should be elated or terrified."

He squeezed her hand. "He came to see you win."

"Yes." She tried to laugh. "No pressure or anything."

"You'll do your best."

Noon - Katherine Warwick

"And so will you."

"Of course." But he wanted her happiness more than the win. She read it on his face, the way he looked at her. "What if I don't?" Her hand turned in his, palm met palm, and fingers twined.

"It won't matter to him." Breck's voice pitched lower. His hand gripped hers tight. "He loves you."

"I know."

Twenty-six

Because Trey refused the private lesson with Vladimir, Nicole was left to watch Breck and Kit's lesson. She could no more ignore the pit growing in her stomach than deny the pleasure she'd had knowing that her father had come just to see her compete.

She watched Breck and Kit, over and over, effortlessly perform to perfection. Breck looked magnificent – every move like liquid glass blown by fire – without blemish and so magical, she couldn't tear her eyes away. The knot forming in her throat was not jealousy, but bone-deep awe.

He moved the two of them with a command she'd only seen in infancy in their partnership, but that had blossomed into a masculine force that now demanded notice.

Desire slipped hot and fast inside of her; she wanted to dance with him.

It was as she watched them, observing the kind way he included Kit in his discussions with the hard-to-understand Russian teacher that her dreams shifted. She thought of the first time their hands had joined, of how he'd learned to keep his shoulders erect, head high, because he'd not known how to do so on his own. He'd given all of himself to her over the years; hours and hours repeating step after step, enduring all of the aches and pains that, to her, had become extensions of her body in movement. He'd taken whatever she'd dealt, whenever her mood dictated, with the kind of grace she had only known in one other man – her father. They'd been friends and enemies, and firsts. They'd won competitions together and lost them.

He'd come back from a crippling injury and, she thought now, watching him glide, had worked until there was no trace of the wound left anywhere in his life. But more than that, Nicole knew what other crippling handicaps he'd left behind, and that was what she admired most. He was a champion in every sense of the word, and he deserved to be recognized.

It amazed her still that he'd vanished. He danced as if he'd not missed a day of training. Why had he gone?

Noon - Katherine Warwick

The question had needled her heart for so long and was still there, peircing, needing to be answered so that she could understand and pull out the mote once and for all. Understanding and hope, he'd told her – that's what she needed.

Tears threatened to expose her, and she blinked them back and rose to leave. There was more to life than dance. Breck was right.

She looked at him again when she reached the door. He was watching her, even now, waiting for her to come to him. From across the room, as the music blasted, as Kit worked out steps with Vladimir, their eyes connected in that way only shared by them. She sent him a smile, hoping in her heart, he would win.

The light tapping awakened both Reuben and Breck, but it was Breck who bolted to the door with his heart pounding. At four o'clock in the morning a knock, a call in the night, meant something was wrong.

Nicole.

Red rimmed her eyes; faint trembling puffed her lower lip. His heart didn't bother to slow. He tugged her inside. "Nic. You okay?"

Yawning, Reuben came up behind Breck in his white boxers and teeshirt. "Everything all right?"

"Can we talk?" Urgency drew Nicole's delicate features tight.

"It's early, Nic." Reuben ran his hands down his face, winced at the left-over burn that still stung his skin. "And it's our day today."

She nodded but her eyes stayed earnestly with Breck's. "I know. I couldn't stop thinking about what you said. I – we need to talk. Please."

"Yeah, sure." Breck grabbed a tee-shirt and slipped it on. Then he tugged on a pair of cargo shorts. "We'll go out in the hall."

They walked to where an open balcony allowed a cool breeze through billowy sheers. Sliding out into the night, they stood looking out over the pool area below.

Sun umbrellas were synched tight, creating shadowing spears across the expanse of the deck. A forgotten white towel lay in a heap near the pool's edge.

The sea, just yards away, perfumed the air with salt with every crash of waves against the sand.

Breck leaned against the railing, looking at the moon with clouds drizzled across its buttermilk belly. His heart had finally slowed, beating now with apprehension, with hope that she was finally ready to hear him out. He looked at her. She hadn't slept, that much he could tell from the pressed look of her white shorts and flowered blouse. "What's up, sis?"

"Please don't call me that."

"I'm sorry." He turned to face her, reaching out but then drawing back before he touched her.

She took a deep breath that quavered out. "Tell me."

Gone was anger, contempt – jealousy even. There was nothing but pure need, open and sparkling in her eyes, need to finally put something cankering and troublesome to rest. Part of his need to release himself of this chain had waited for this moment, and he rejoiced inside, seeing sincerity at last in her face.

"That night you were taken into the orchards." It was still hard to fathom, and he felt an old echo of shame all over again. "It was my father." He waited for her response to the truth and saw disbelief color her eyes.

"How did you know?"

"The way you described it…He beat me the same way. Later that night, I went to see him…He's the one that destroyed my foot." She gasped, as if working to hold back shock. The tone of his voice was oddly unemotional now; he'd rehearsed what he would say to her many times over the years. "He told me that if I didn't stop dancing, he'd hurt you again. Badly." He had to touch her, and he reached out and ran a finger down the side of her face.

"He threatened your family, Nic – the only people I cared about in the world. I had to leave. I didn't want to take any chances." He didn't want anything to be left misunderstood so he went on, even though reliving the details would be painful for them both. "Those things I said to you that night, those ugly things…I didn't mean any of them. I had to make sure you'd hate me that you'd never try to come find me, for your own safety."

She put her hand up to stop him, pressing her fingers to his lips. "Don't." A look of complete understanding settled over her. Her fingers moved from his mouth to his face. "Don't say anything else. Please."

Her light trace softly fluttered over his cheek and jaw until her fingers were once again at his mouth and her eyes filled with tears. "I'm sorry. I should have known." She closed her eyes, thinking of how easily she had read things in his gaze. "I should have seen that something was wrong and helped you."

Placing her lips on his then, she was urgent but gentle, the need to comfort and restore had her arms sliding up around his neck. "I'm so sorry." Her mouth barely left his when she said it again, "I'm unbelievably stubborn. You should have made me listen, you should have told me."

His arms snapped around her, pulling her in with such force and need that she winced, and was pleased to have had her breath stolen at the hands of his desire.

"Nic. The moment I was able, I came back. I wanted you."

"I'm sorry I didn't listen, that I made more pain for you."

"You're right. You are stubborn." He pressed his forehead to hers.

She drew away, holding the railing with one hand, his hand in her other. The pain had been so agonizing when he'd vanished, she wondered if she could go there again. But he deserved to know where her heart had gone in his absence.

"I lied when I told you that you leaving didn't matter to me— that I never once thought about you. I thought I would die at first. I couldn't understand. I felt...I knew you loved me, and to have you be so..." She shuddered remembering, and his hand tightened around hers. She took a deep breath. "To have you be so cruel...

"You were right. It devastated me." Then she stared out into the night as moments of thought dripped between them. "I didn't deal with it. I ignored it, hoping it would go away somehow. I should have known better. Nothing goes away on its own, especially when love is attached. All I wanted to do was lash out at you, but you weren't there." She felt guilty for that now, knowing what he'd done for her.

"I immersed myself in dance. And men." His eyes filled with a fear she'd known so well – the unknown – helpless, vast, more consuming than a raging brushfire. "It was stupid, and it only deadened the hurt temporarily because with every morning, I'd look for you. I love you. Still. I always have. It never stopped, not one day."

Child-like, forgiving, his gaze was open with a need, deep down only she could fill. A chord in her heart plucked tight, and she wrapped herself around him again.

"All this time," she murmured through tears. "If only I'd known. Breck, I still can't believe he hurt you like that." She would be there for him now. The utter loneliness he must have endured those years broke her heart, and she vowed he would never be alone again.

He stroked her hair and spoke against her head, after another kiss. "It's over now."

"I'm so sorry." What he had been through for her humbled her. She wished that she could erase the years of loss between them, but that was impossible. She was only able to go forward with hopes for a future they could share. Her heart was beating that same possessive way it had all those years ago when she had first known she loved him. Time and distance hadn't changed that, and she supposed that was why her heart kept gravitating back to his.

She felt his body succumb to hers, his head burrowing deep in her shoulder. His silent tears seeped through the soft fabric of her blouse, wetting her shoulder. The moon finally slid away and the sounds of a city awakening began to dance in the air.

It seemed to Nicole that a daze had been carelessly thrown around her shoulders; suddenly she and Kit were at the ballroom. She barely noticed things that usually snagged her attention; admiring stares, familiar faces, flashy dance steps. As if she were in some sort of perpetual dream that began last night and was deliciously lingering, she went through the motions of set up.

Reuben met with Breck and Kit. She watched them fine tuning parts of their samba routine in a stolen corner of a hall. Again she found herself with a smile of marvel. Her body yearned to be next to Breck, but Kit had worked hard and it showed. She deserved to be in his arms.

She waited for Trey, her stomach fisting in that familiar slug of revulsion. Soon it would all be over. It was the first time she was anxious to be done with a competition, but no one would know that. She was a performer, and she could do this one last performance with the devil himself, even if her body and mind wanted to dance with an angel.

"We've got to rape this competition," Trey said in her ear.

"That's disgusting." Since her heart was neutral about the win, she tilted her head impartially.

"What?" He eyed her. "You don't care if we win?"

"I care." Trey followed her gaze to where Breck rehearsed with Kit. "But dance isn't everything."

Trey let out a sneer. "You're telling me this now?" He pulled her tight against him, eyes flashing. "You'd better perform as you're expected, babe, or it will be your last performance with this champion."

She would have laughed with the irony of the situation, but recognized the look of razor-edged dementia too well. "I'll do my best. That's what I always do."

"Then quit looking at your ex-partner and pay some attention to me."

After I go wish them luck, she thought but wouldn't say. She pulled free and headed toward Reuben, Breck and Kit.

Feeling the desperate need to shift the odds in his favor, Trey ran scenarios through his brain. If he could place he and Nicole close enough during competition, he could use an old stunt everybody in the dance world was guilty of at least once in their career – tripping. But even as the thought lingered he knew that wouldn't be enough to satisfy his insatiable appetite to destroy Breck. He wanted to make Nicole his, make sure that Breck knew he'd had her, and send Breck away with his head forever bowed – the way it belonged.

The lights were bright as he stood off-deck with the other competitors, ready for the first heat. The audience was applauding, and Nicole had made her way back to him, readying for their number to be called.

Trey put on a smile.

They were surrounded by foreign couples all perfect as plastic. He knew the competition would be brutal. The Russians were legendary dancing machines that never made a mistake. It was the same with the South Africans and Germans. The bitterness of regret for not having taken that private with Vladimir ran a hard course through his phsyche.

◎ 273 ◎

He'd not taken it on principle – the principle that Breck had been coached by the man and that Trey Woods didn't take leftovers of any kind. Of course, Nicole and the Dubois' did not fit into that category, not when he was destined to be one of them.

Before the music started, Trey took Nicole in his arms in stance. Anger and desperation that had been there just moments ago froze with the ice of fear. Not fear of the competition – the marrow deep fear of losing her. Her nearness, her perfume, skin smooth beneath his hands, all taunted deprivation rampant inside of him.

The simple movements of cha-cha were easy and by the time they'd finished and gone into Jive, the pulse of the lively dance reached in and fed him. She was responding beautifully, willingly. They danced like two butterflies in mid-air. Hope sprung from their oneness, but when he gave her his deepest smile and saw only the artificial glittering of showmanship returned, the deep roots of passion and revenge that had been growing unattended extended their greedy fingers even deeper, and claimed his soul.

When the beat of the dances of love thudded, everything he'd held back began to squeeze to the surface. He hadn't been able to maneuver Nicole near Breck and Kit during any of the heats. By the time the semi-finals came, Trey's mind was in another world. One where the only thing he could see, the only thing driving his body to move, was the distorted visions he let flash in his mind of Breck utterly humiliated and ruined, and images of Nicole, as he forced her into submission.

"It's like you're not even here," Nicole whispered through a smile when they walked off the dance floor before the last set of semi–finals was to begin. Only six couples, including Breck and Kit, remained in the heat. It was a feat in and of itself to be alongside them, but Trey was too distracted to enjoy it.

Trey followed Breck as the men went to the dressing area to change into fresh costumes for the final cut. Only a slight sheen was on Breck's face and chest, while Trey dripped with sweat.

Breck shook hands and exchanged friendly chat with the other male competitors. Shirts stripped and pants were changed for brighter colors, different styles. With a twisted need to scrape for anything he could use to bring Breck down, Trey sauntered over.

Noon - Katherine Warwick

Breck's chest was bare for only a millisecond when he wiped sweat with his used shirt before reaching for the fresh one. Slivers of white caught Trey's attention.

"What're those?" The very picture of Breck being beaten into submission sent a pleasant black riffle through Trey who knew a juicy piece of gossip when he saw it. Wouldn't the dance world just love to know about Breck's sick past?

Breck continued to dress as if Trey hadn't said anything.

"I asked you a question, Noon."

"Scars," Breck answered flatly.

"Wow," Trey feigned disgust. "Your old man do that?" Breck just shot him a look that meant he had his answer. "What, you never fought back?"

The knot that surfaced in Brecks' jaw pleased Trey. Still, Breck didn't defend himself. Without a story, Trey had nothing but secret scars that would always remain hidden.

"What do you say you and I put our pasts behind us?" Scrounging for anything, Trey sat next to him and tied his shoelaces.

When Breck didn't even bother to look over, Trey held back the urge to grab him by the shirt and shove his fist into his face.

Breck stood.

"We could get a drink later," Trey joined him.

Breck slid him an amused snicker before going through the door to where the women waited for the call to go on stage.

*   *   *

Drama sizzled in the air. Heads leaned in whispers. Fingers pointed when the six remaining couples took their positions on the floor. Drums rolled, and the audience's collective gaze latched onto Breck, his secretive absence causing him to be a standout during the competition.

Nicole knew a lot of the whispers hummed with wonder why Kit was dancing with him and not her. Breck's spectacular appearance was as unreal as a religious apparition. Strangely, the undercurrent of gossip didn't bother her. She'd come to perform with the partner she'd chosen and she would accept the result of their work.

Noon - Katherine Warwick

What she really wanted was to be at the family table, cheering for Breck and Kit.

She could see them out the corner of her eye as she stood waiting on deck. Breck was in head to toe black, his aura oozing from where he stood on the floor and out into the audience, a magnetic force even she couldn't keep her attention away from. The room electrified with him in it.

When he'd disappeared years ago, speculation ran wild like nasty tabloid fodder. It had hurt then, to hear that he'd been seen here and there, with whomever. Lies, she thought, now that she knew the truth. She'd learned for herself the hard way that no matter how painful the truth was, it left you with real peace inside.

Her eyes met and locked with her father's across the room. She smiled more broadly for him. The competition would be hard for him and her mother, pulling them in two directions. But it didn't matter if she didn't place here, that was a truth she'd accepted days ago when she'd witnessed sheer perfection in Breck and Kit.

She barely noticed when Trey began to move her in the dance of paso dobles. The music of the matador pounded in the room, inciting visions of a regal matador and a tapping, readying bull.

Nicole sensed heated tension in Trey's hands. His eyes were menacing hooked like claws with hers. Each push was rough, each drop more frightening as he let her head fall nearer to the floor than was allowed.

Trey dragged Nicole in, tossed her out, the nails in his hands digging into her palms. They separated, like the matador and bull, and she circled him, flaring her skirt, teasing with legs that dared to tempt.

He stood erect, waiting, watching. Temptation became too real and too much to ignore. Lost in the passion of the dance, his body couldn't stop the determination storming within him and he reached for her too soon, throwing off their timing.

The error wasn't anything the audience in general would catch—a split second's mistake – but he knew the judges who were roaming the floor hadn't missed it. He snatched Nicole in tight. "We're screwed," he said between teeth.

She didn't respond, rather continued to smile and dance as if nothing had gone wrong, even though she'd felt the mistake the moment it happened.

Strangely, she wasn't disappointed. Her eyes yearned to wander to where Breck and Kit danced, just at their right. When Trey began to move her spins their direction, panic crept in. She strove to keep them in place, but there was too much strength in his arms, in his hands, and he changed the choreography, covertly dragging her in their direction.

It would take only seconds for him to be close enough to trip them, and only moments were left of the music. She began counting down the final beats in her head, straining in another direction as much as she could with out compromising style, taking liberties with the steps that forced him to remain brushing against her without being obvious.

As she fought his pull, his eyes met hers. There was only one way to keep him from taking her too close. Missing a step, she caused him to miss two, and soon he was glaring at her from behind a performer's mask. His rough grip tightened.

"You did that on purpose," he hissed.

Finally the music ended. Breck and Kit remained a safe distance away. Trey held her hand in a vise grip as all of the competing couples bowed and then moved off the floor.

"What was that all about?" he whispered.

"I could ask you the same."

Nicole risked a glance at Breck. Like the gentleman he had become, his arm was poised around Kit's waist as they awaited the scores off deck with the other finalists.

"Mine was a mistake, yours was deliberate," Trey whispered through a smile.

The audience was still standing. Chants were belting out of – "Breck and Kit, Breck and Kit." Nicole joined the thundering applause. Etiquette required the popular partnership remain on the sidelines with the other couples, but when the current of applause refused to stop, Breck turned a full circle and waved, sending another rocket of cheers echoing off the walls of the room.

Twenty-seven

As the first-place winners, Breck and Kit returned to the center of the floor where the judges shook their hands and laid golden trophies in their arms. From the sidelines, Nicole kept herself from dashing over; she was so pleased for them it was what she wanted to do.

Her mother and father stood with the rest of those congregated in applauding ovation. Joy surged inside of her in such a way that she would only find release if she placed herself in Breck's arms.

She saw him searching the crowd and fought the urge to jump up and down like love-struck groupie. When his eyes finally connected with hers, every sound and movement around her seemed to disappear into a vortex of slowing silence.

He smiled, and her body went toward his of its own volition. Crowds came onto the floor and mashed in between them. Fingers wrapped around her arm, and she jolted, finding Trey at her side.

"Where are you going?"

Her relief would be complete now that the competition was done. "It's over."

"What?" White shock covered his face. She went to pull her arm free, but he held on. "You sure you want this?"

"I think we both know it would be for the best." It didn't matter what had happened on the dance floor. All of it was over, and she could begin again. When his fingers fell away, she left him without saying anything more, both relieved and surprised he didn't demand an explanation.

"Nicole," one of the female judges took her aside. "I can't believe Breck is back."

"It's wonderful, I know."

"But why weren't you dancing with him?"

Again, Nicole scanned the crowd for him, afraid she might lose him, lose her chance to share in his joy. She'd always been able to pick him out in a crowd, that shock of dark hair gleaming. When she saw it, her heart fluttered with impatience.

"I made some errors in judgment," she smiled graciously at the curious judge. "If you'll excuse me, I have yet to congratulate him."

There'd never been so many bodies, so many obstacles. She did her share of congratulating and taking hugs from fellow competitors. When she was finally next to him, when her body finally brushed against his, the magnetic force that had always pulled them together had his head turning, his eyes looking right into hers.

Breck's win was as if she'd won the title. Tremors of disbelief and awe sang through Nicole, fresh and sweet. Months of aching work spun through her head without details. No regrets. No sorrow. She couldn't wait to join her parents and Breck downstairs for the celebratory dinner. Her father had made reservations knowing that one of his loved ones would take first place. She smiled, glad he'd been there to witness Breck's return performance. There hadn't been a moment of the competition she'd wanted it any other way.

She brushed the final sweeps of blush over her cheeks and smiled at her reflection in the mirror. Nothing would compare with what she'd ultimately gained from this competition. She felt as though finally, all of her dreams were coming into place.

She locked the door of her hotel room and heard rustling in the hall. Trey stood in the open door of his suite, just two doors down, in jeans and a black short-sleeved shirt, unbuttoned. Steadying himself with a warbling clutch at the door knob, his free hand held a brown bottle. "Hey, baby doll."

Because he looked so lost, she pitied him. "You could have joined us for dinner."

"Me? Why would I want to celebrate with the man who took the rest of my life away from me?"

"Breck's not responsible for what's happened between us."

Trey staggered toward her like a passenger on a ship at sea. "Besides, you could care less if I join your exclusive family."

Noon - Katherine Warwick

Though it was undeniably true, Nicole had been raised with manners and the compassion she felt for him was real. "If you think you can make it, we'll wait for you."

Trey raised the brown bottle to his lips. "Do I look like I care?"

"Then I guess I'll say goodnight." She turned to go but he reached for her.

"I have something of yours."

"What?"

"Your warm-up suit. You left it down on deck. In your rush to congratulate your ex-partner, you dropped it."

She didn't remember leaving it. "Oh." Wanting to be free of anything that tied her to Trey as soon as possible, she suggested, "Can you get it? I can put it away before I go down."

"What do I look like?"

"Then I'll swing by and pick it up tomorrow—"

"I'm taking a stand-by flight tonight. You come and get it now. You'll have to look for it, my vision's a wee bit *fluzzy*."

Glancing at her watch, the decision would make her a few minutes later than she already was, but it would be worth it not to have to see him again. She quickly passed him, striding into his room. The bed was unmade, costumes were strewn about and empty bottles littered the floor but she saw no sign of her warm-up suit. She turned. "Where is it?"

He shut the door and she heard the click of the lock. His eyes roved her from head to toe in a languid look that sent chills down her spine. "You look good."

"If you'll just find the warm up, I'll let you get back to your evening of inebriation."

He let out a laugh before swinging the brown bottle to his lips and tilting his head back. After a belch, he wiped his mouth with the back of his hand. "We went out with a bang, didn't we...killed our reps royally."

"It's over now—"

When he flung the bottle at her, it whizzed by her ear and she ducked. The sound of shattering glass behind her sent her heart racing.

"Maybe I can go into the circus since my dancing career is over!" he shouted. "I could throw knives instead of bottles!"

It took her a moment to settle her nerves and breathe again. "You'll find another partner."

Just as suddenly as he'd exploded, emotion washed his face and he began to sob, shaking his head. The sobs wracked his body until he dropped to his knees in a crumbling heap.

"Trey—"

He didn't stop, completely ensnared in his loss. Hesitantly, she crossed to him, thinking long and hard before putting her hand on his shoulder as the sobs drained out. He looked up, face swollen like a ripe tomato.

"Here. You need a cool cloth." She went to the bathroom and wet a washcloth. Seeing herself in the mirror, memories of the day he'd struck her flashed through her mind in vibrant red. When she came back out, he was gone. "Trey?"

She felt taken in by something dark and foreboding that had suddenly filled the room, and she tossed the wet rag back into the bathroom before heading straight for the door. But he was suddenly there, blocking it, and she couldn't reach for the knob.

"They're waiting for me," she said, working to keep her voice from betraying fear.

He'd take her away, steal her, he decided. Have the satisfaction of taking that prize at the very least. Trey's mind raced with the fantasy of having her all to himself at last, of Breck in utter anguish knowing he'd had her first. "The princess always gets what she wants." He snagged her arm, bringing her face within inches of his. "But not tonight."

"Let go or I'll find that baseball bat."

"Ah, but I haven't hit you…yet."

She couldn't stop the panic that shot through her then and kept her from being able to pull free. His eyes went dark with harmful intent. Releasing her, he tossed the bottle back into the room and it landed on the carpet in a thud. "None of this would be happening if his old man had done what I told him. None of it."

"What?"

His eyes leveled with hers and he didn't move for a moment. It was a despicable thought, made even more abominable by the fact that it had really happened.

"You disgust me." She went to pass him toward the safety of the door but he blocked her with surprising agility, in spite of his drunken state. "You and Rob hurt him deliberately."

"Very imaginative."

"It's the truth, you just said so."

He lifted a shoulder. "So what if it is. Like you, I had my goals. I wanted you."

"So you made an arrangement with his father to disable him? You're sick." She took another step around him but he dropped his bottle, grabbed her arms and threw her against the nearest wall. Her head banged, shooting splinters of pain through her skull, down her neck. Breath seared in and out as he held her pinned.

"I still want you," he growled. "And I'm taking you with me tonight."

"You're out of your mind," she snapped. "I wouldn't go to the lobby with you. Now let me go."

Pounding on the door startled them both. For a moment, they stared at each other.

"Go away," Trey shouted. "Probably room service," he mumbled, holding her firmly in place.

"Trey?" The voice was Breck's. The pounding resumed. "Have you seen Nicole?"

"Breck!" Nicole shouted. Trey's eyes widened with desperation. Trying to command a body that would not respond as quickly as he wanted it to, he wasn't prepared for her to lift her knee between his legs. He doubled over in a grunt.

"Nic?" Breck's voice came through the door again, the knob and hinges rattled.

Having temporarily disabled Trey, Nicole scrambled to the door and opened it, flinging herself into Breck's arms.

Trey let out a defeated laugh as he pulled himself upright with a groan, his hand rubbed unabashedly at his crotch. "Noon...of course."

"Are you all right?" Breck's gaze swept Nicole.

◎ 282 ◎

Noon - Katherine Warwick

She nodded, shuddering with relief and stayed locked around him.

"Of course she's all right. I wouldn't hurt her. D'you think I'd hurt her Noon?" Calmly, Trey glanced at the couple, jealousy and hatred mixing on his reddening face. He crossed to the wet bar, popped open another bottle, and put it to his lips.

"Breck, let's get out of here." She'd never tell him the truth – that his father had entered into a pact with the devil to destroy him. She pulled him toward the open door. Breck didn't move. His eyes were fastened on Trey in a fervor that spoke of revenge.

Trey took another deep drink before sneering, "What?"

The man was so lost he couldn't see out of his head straight much less know where his life was headed. It was pathetic. Even knowing what had transpired between him and his father, Breck couldn't add to Trey's misery.

Keeping Nicole against him he turned, and headed toward the door.

"Your old man should have killed you that night, 'stead of just busting your foot. He'd have done it. Your old man woulda done it, 'cause he hated you. He hated you even more than I hate you. Howzit feel, Noon, knowing your old man couldn't stand the sight of you?"

Nicole felt Breck's limbs harden to steel. They stopped in the door frame.

"He was greedier than you counted on though, wasn't he?" With steady calm, Breck faced Trey one last time.

Trey let out a harsh laugh. "Albatross. Stupid trash was what he was."

"Not too stupid to keep copies of your checks in the glove compartment of his car. My guess is he was tightening the noose you hung around your neck the day you made your deal."

Nicole let out a little gasp, and covered her mouth with her hand. The heat in the room was rising, and she held Breck in place, sure he would jump on Trey and kill him.

Trey took another drink. "Whatever. He got what he deserved."

Breck's jaw turned to stone. It would be so easy to lay into Trey, the rage he felt inside demanded it. Part of him wanted someone else to hurt as much as he had. But that pain, those scars though deep, were at last beginning to heal. He couldn't change where he'd come from, but he'd changed who he was and where he was going and because of that, he didn't feel shame.

◎ 283 ◎

Noon - Katherine Warwick

"So did you." With his arm protectively around Nicole he escorted her through the door without looking back.

The celebration dinner lingered late into the evening and rather than take a cab, it was decided by all to enjoy the balmy night by walking from the restaurant back to the hotel.

Along the beach they strolled, nearly in the same spot Nicole had stood months earlier, alone. Even though she and Trey had gone home with a title that night, things had looked dismal and dark. *How things can change*, she thought, looking out over the impossibly black sea to where it met the moonlit sky.

Her father was right.

He walked some feet ahead of her in the sand, his ivory linen slacks and the sleeves of his white shirt rolled up, his hand clutching her mother's. They looked like second honeymooners enjoying a private stroll. He'd changed things himself, and their family had been blessed because of it.

Nicole heard Reuben's deep, warm laugh behind her. It mixed with the crashing waves in a musical way that was inherently natural. She could never find words enough to fill the canyon of gratitude and love she had for Reuben. Kit was harmlessly charming him, and she was glad to have Kit as a friend. Glad the competition had been the right time for Kit to meet new, prospective partners and new coaches so she could continue to compete.

Clouds filtered across the moon, darkening the sky for a moment before they spread open, sending milky-white beams across the sand.

Breck's hand slid into hers.

His hair was mussed and wild. His eyes reflected brilliantly white sand, and twinkled into hers when he brushed a kiss across her knuckles. Her gaze dropped to his lips, warm and full under the white-blue cast of the moon's hue.

Music blasted from a portable CD player not far down the beach. A group of playful teenagers from the competition danced around a bonfire on the shore. The jazzy Latin beat fit Nicole's mood. She could dance right there on the sand. The most important people in her life were with her, and that was all

◎ 284 ◎

Noon - Katherine Warwick

she needed.

Breck smiled and waved at the partying teens as they passed. Music had the power to change things – he'd seen that in his own life. He would be forever grateful that he'd learned to dance to whatever melody life brought.

There were so many things to be grateful for, emotion filled his chest to nearly bursting. Everything he'd wanted, he now had within reach. Every opportunity was theirs, now and forever. He held Nicole's hand tight. Nothing would come between them again.

Knowing that Trey had packed his bags and headed home Breck took as an unexpected bonus. They'd see each other on the dance floor again, that was a given. But he doubted there would be anymore trouble between them.

"Breck." One of the teens in the group recognized him. "You rock man. You were awesome today."

With a nod and another wave, Breck acknowledged the youth. He thought it amusing so many were in awe of the win. None of it mattered nearly as much as the woman by his side.

He was pleased with the win, of course. Part of his heart had pulled for Nicole to take it. The nasty taste of competing against someone you love was something he never wanted to experience again. He'd compete with her from here on out, or he'd not compete at all. But he was glad the win had opened doors for Kit and finally closed doors for he and Nicole.

"Come on." He started at a half-jog, tugging Nicole along with him.

The spontaneity sent her into a laugh. "Where are we going?"

"Hey, guys, over here," Breck called to Lois and Garren, Kit and Reuben. With a quick jerk of his head, he gestured back toward the young dancers and their music. His grin was huge when he stood in front of the partying group. "Can we crash?"

They lit up at the opportunity to rub shoulders with two of the dance worlds shining stars.

"What do you wanna hear?" one of the kids asked.

Breck slipped his arms around Nicole's waist, drew her close and smiled down into her eyes. "Whatever." He leaned near her temple and pressed a kiss there, then found her mouth. As her arms wound around his neck and her body fused to his, he closed his eyes and let the slow beat of the music relax a body that had revved at competitive speed for months.

"I love you," she whispered, the softness of her lips forming the words against his. His breath sighed out.

The song lulled, and rather than do any steps requiring either of them to draw on skill, they moved in a slow, tight rock. For Breck, this place was just where he wanted to be.

She was as nervous as a young girl waiting for her first date. Nicole fidgeted in front of the mirror of the studio. She made herself go through some dance steps while the minute hand ticked by on the clock. Practicing made her heart steady, her pulse slow.

She needed just the right song.

Watching herself cross to the music system, she was happy with what she saw in the reflection. She looked beyond the light pink dance pants, the white shirt she was wearing for the rehearsal, beyond the stylish hair and smiling face. The inner radiance shimmering back at her was what put the gleam in her smile.

Ah, just the right CD. She smiled. Slipping the CD into place, she pushed the repeat button so the song would play over and over. Then she waited for the piano chords that for years had been too painful for her to listen to. Their song. Filling the empty studio, echoing with the hauntingly familiar tune, nothing but that beautiful yearning she had felt back when Breck first came into her life flowed through her now.

The lyrics no longer tortured her, she'd made them come true.

Closing her eyes, she thought of memories and danced, holding a phantom partner. But she no longer had to dream of phantoms. He was real. He was hers. And he was coming to dance with her.

She didn't hear when he came in. She simply melted into him when his arms slid around her and he held her close. He took her hands, and she knew what dance would be first. She knew by the way his pinkie lifted on his right hand. The way his shoulders erected, tilting just enough to stir excitement. The way his hand pressed firmly into the small of her back, ready to command. And

Noon - Katherine Warwick

when his eyes latched with hers and he smiled, her heart joined his in that oneness her body had learned could come from no one else.

His face was brilliant – at last at peace, and she leaned up and pressed a kiss on the side of his cheek, taking in a deep breath and his unique scent, intoxicating and thrilling.

They slid as one, swaying into a turn, and his fingers closed over her left hand. He slipped a band on her finger and the sudden pressure drew her gaze there.

"What's this?" The diamond's reflection glimmered in her eye.

His lips tickled her ear, shooting heat to her belly, joy to her heart. "This means I'm the senior partner now."

about the author

Katherine Warwick specializes in writing women's romance with ballroom dance as an integral part of the story. She is the mother of six children, one of whom has autism. She lives in Utah.

For more information on Katherine and her other novels, visit her websites: www.katherinewarwick.com & www.ballroomdancenovels.com

Read an excerpt from WILDE,
the next book in the ballroom series

His hips moved in a rhythmic calculated grind that made Anna's heart stammer. From the first row, she watched intently. Two dancers engaged in the samba – the Latin dance of love. She didn't look at the woman he danced with – her eyes were locked on him.

One lone guitar strummed. At first slow, tempting, like rain softly stroking a window. Gradually, the trickle became a lilting stream as drums began a savage beat. Crossing to center stage, he moved like a tiger, predatory, focused, intent. Heat filled the room. A puissant energy hovered in the air with the promise to electrify and ignite. Muddled voices twisted in whispers of awe. White lights flickered, then dimmed to red-hot pink in time with the music. Somewhere, a glass ball twirled, shooting millions of sparkling stars into circular orbit around the Capitol Theater. Around him.

Anna was taken by his face, finely sculpted with classic lines that both sharpened and eased with the theatrics of performance. His hair was slicked straight back, making it look darker than in the myriad photos and videos she had studied of him.

He was well-formed inside those black pants. Hard legs lunged and slid to the beat. Muscles pressed taut against the sheer fabric of his shirt, melding with the demands of movement. The tapes she had watched did not do justice to the masculine presence pouring from him like streaming lava over the attentive audience.

Anna leaned forward, straining to be closer.

As he danced, he owned both the floor and the woman. Anna's breath stilled. She glanced to see if others were as captivated as she. Every head, all eyes, were focused on the stage.

As the music grew, so did the thrumming in her veins. The woman in his arms, the woman he shared the floor with, was his toy—his plaything, as he turned and tossed her at whim.

Anna's feet itched to be on the floor, her body yearned to know what it would feel like to dance with him. The past few years of study and waiting were coming to an end, and she could hardly stay in her seat. Easing out a slow, controlled breath, she knew this intense reaction would not do. No one must see her like this – so taken by something she did not possess.

In an effort to slow her racing pulse, she looked at his partner. The woman was tall, languid, lovely, and because she was, Anna's brow lifted in displeasure. Yes, the woman was lovely, but certainly not his equal.

But Anna, would be his equal – at least on the dance floor.

She longed to catch his eye but knew the impossibility of it. He was focused, professional. Perfect. Everything she knew he would be as a dancer. The way his eyes stayed fastened on his partner with a look that spoke of dominance sent a thrilling rush down her spine. Though never given to submission, Anna wanted those eyes to look into hers that way.

She watched the way his hands directed the woman in the steps of the dance, gently yet with enough force to lead and demand complete cohesion.

Guitars threaded the melody. The dancers, now pressed together, slowed to it in sliding dips and lunges. He held the woman's waist and pinned her hips to his before she arched back like water streaming from his hands. Then he brought her up and their bodies fused, faces so close Anna's heart stopped. Would they kiss?

Were they more than dance partners?

The audience applauded, standing in ovation while she continued to sit. The shirt he wore clung to him as though he had stepped through a mist. The deep V-cut in the front bared glistening taut ripples underneath. The very sight sent heat through her system.

He raised his partner's hand before they took their bows and the applause thundered. As he waved, his eyes scanned the audience, found hers and held. Anna knew she had piqued his interest.

She merely tilted her head at him.

His partner tugged his hand, and the tight line holding their gazes broke. Something deep inside of Anna, something woven with both need and admiration, plucked hard.

Within moments, they would meet face to face.

He gave one last wave to the audience before escorting his partner backstage.

Because those around her were staring, wondering why she alone was not standing in appreciative applause, Anna rose – then clapped.

A light flashed in her eyes, then another. The photographers smiled, nodding in gratitude before quickly disappearing. All eyes were on her now. It was a feeling she was used to, one she had learned to ignore.

She had but one thing on her mind—to make her way backstage.

Printed in the United Kingdom
by Lightning Source UK Ltd.
120757UK00002B/146